CROSSFIRE

Dick Francis was one of the most successful post-war National Hunt jockeys. The winner of over 350 races, he was champion jockey in 1953/1954 and rode for HM Queen Elizabeth, the Queen Mother, most famously on Devon Loch in the 1956 Grand National. On his retirement from the saddle, he published his autobiography, *The Sport of Queens*, before going on to write forty-three bestselling novels, a volume of short stories (*Field of 13*), and the biography of Lester Piggott.

During his lifetime Dick Francis received many awards, amongst them the prestigious Crime Writers' Association's Cartier Diamond Dagger for his outstanding contribution to the genre, and three 'Best Novel' Edgar Allen Poe awards from The Mystery Writers of America. In 1996 he was named by them as Grand Master for a lifetime's achievement. In 1998, he was elected a fellow of the Royal Society of Literature, and was awarded a CBE in the Queen's Birthday Honours List of 2000.

Dick Francis died in February 2010, at the age of eighty-nine, but he remains one of the greatest thriller writers of all time.

Felix Francis is the younger of Dick's two sons. Over the last forty years Felix has assisted with the research of many of the Dick Francis novels, not least *Twice Shy*, *Shattered* and *Under Orders*. But since 2006, Felix has taken a more significant role in the writing, first with *Dead Heat* and then increasingly with the bestsellers, *Silks* and *Even Money*. *Crossfire* is the fourth novel of this father-and-son collaboration.

Books by Dick Francis and Felix Francis

DEAD HEAT
SILKS
EVEN MONEY

Books by Dick Francis

THE SPORT OF QUEENS (autobiography)
DEAD CERT
NERVE
FOR KICKS
ODDS AGAINST
FLYING FINISH
BLOOD SPORT
FORFEIT
ENQUIRY
RAT RACE
BONECRACK
SMOKESCREEN
SLAY-RIDE
KNOCK DOWN
HIGH STAKES
IN THE FRAME
RISK
TRIAL RUN
WHIP HAND
REFLEX
TWICE SHY
BANKER
THE DANGER
PROOF
BREAK IN
LESTER: The Official Biography
BOLT
HOT MONEY
THE EDGE
STRAIGHT
LONGSHOT
COMEBACK
DRIVING FORCE
DECIDER
WILD HORSES
COME TO GRIEF
TO THE HILT
10-lb PENALTY
FIELD OF 13
SECOND WIND
SHATTERED
UNDER ORDERS

CROSSFIRE

DICK FRANCIS

and

FELIX FRANCIS

MICHAEL JOSEPH

an imprint of

PENGUIN BOOKS

MICHAEL JOSEPH

Published by the Penguin Group
Penguin Books Ltd, 80 Strand, London WC2R 0RL, England
Penguin Group (USA) Inc., 375 Hudson Street, New York, New York 10014, USA
Penguin Group (Canada), 90 Eglinton Avenue East, Suite 700, Toronto, Ontario, Canada M4P 2Y3
(a division of Pearson Penguin Canada Inc.)
Penguin Ireland, 25 St Stephen's Green, Dublin 2, Ireland (a division of Penguin Books Ltd)
Penguin Group (Australia), 250 Camberwell Road, Camberwell, Victoria 3124, Australia
(a division of Pearson Australia Group Pty Ltd)
Penguin Books India Pvt Ltd, 11 Community Centre, Panchsheel Park, New Delhi – 110 017, India
Penguin Group (NZ), 67 Apollo Drive, Rosedale, North Shore 0632, New Zealand
(a division of Pearson New Zealand Ltd)
Penguin Books (South Africa) (Pty) Ltd, 24 Sturdee Avenue, Rosebank Johannesburg 2196, South Africa

Penguin Books Ltd, Registered Offices: 80 Strand, London WC2R 0RL, England

www.penguin.com

First published 2010
001

Set in 11.5/16 pt Sabon LT Std
Typeset by TexTech International Pvt Ltd
Printed in Great Britain by Clays Ltd, St Ives plc

A CIP catalogue record for this book is available from the British Library

ISBN: 978-0-718-17831-4

www.greenpenguin.co.uk

MIX
Paper from
responsible sources
FSC www.fsc.org FSC™ C018179

Penguin Books is committed to a sustainable
future for our business, our readers and our planet.
This book is made from Forest Stewardship
Council™ certified paper.

ALWAYS LEARNING PEARSON

Dedicated to the men and women of the
British forces who have lost
limbs in Afghanistan

For them the battle is never over

and to the memory of
Dick Francis
1920–2010
the greatest friend and father a man could ever have

With loving thanks to grandson and son
William Francis
Lieutenant in the Army Air Corps,
graduated from
The Royal Military Academy, Sandhurst
August 2009,
seconded to the Grenadier Guards
at Nad-e-Ali, Helmand Province, Afghanistan
September–December 2009

Prologue

Helmand Province, Afghanistan,
October 2009

'Medic! Medic!'

I could see that my platoon sergeant was shouting but, strangely, the sound of his voice seemed muffled, as if I was in a neighbouring room rather than out here in the open.

I was lying on the dusty ground with my back up against a low bank so that I was actually half sitting. Sergeant O'Leary was kneeling beside me on my left.

'Medic!' he shouted again urgently, over his shoulder.

He turned his head and looked me in the eye.

'Are you all right, sir?' he asked.

'What happened?' I said, my own voice sounding loud in my head.

'A bloody IED,' he said. He turned away, looked behind him, and shouted again. 'Where's that fucking medic?'

An IED. I knew that I should have known what IED meant but my brain seemed to be working in slow motion. I finally remembered. IED – Improvised Explosive Device – a roadside bomb.

The sergeant was talking loudly into his personal radio.

'Alpha four,' he said in a rush. 'This is Charlie six three. IED, IED. One CAT A, several CAT C. Request IRT immediate backup and casevac. Over.'

I couldn't hear any response, if there was one. I seemed to have lost my radio headset, along with my helmet.

CAT A, he'd said. CAT A was army speak for a seriously injured soldier requiring immediate medical help to prevent loss of life. CAT Cs were walking wounded.

The sergeant turned back to me.

'You still all right, sir?' he asked, the stress apparent in his face.

'Yes,' I said, but, in truth, I didn't really feel that great. I was cold, yet sweaty. 'How are the men?' I asked him.

'Don't worry about the men, sir,' he said. 'I'll look after the men.'

'How many are injured?' I asked.

'A few. Minor, mostly,' he said. 'Just some cuts and a touch of deafness from the blast.' I knew what he meant. The sergeant turned away and shouted at the desert-camouflaged figure nearest to him. 'Johnson, go and fetch the bloody medic kit from Cummings. The little rat's too shit-scared to move.'

He turned back to me once more.

'Won't be long now, sir.'

'You said on the radio there's a CAT A. Who is it?'

He looked into my face.

'You, sir,' he said.

'Me?'

'The CAT A is you, sir,' he said again. 'Your fucking foot's been blown off.'

I

Four Months Later

I realized as soon as I walked out of the hospital that I had nowhere to go.

I stood holding my bag at the side of the road, watching a line of passengers board a red London bus.

Should I join them, I wondered. But where were they going?

Simply being discharged from National Health Service care had been my overriding aim for weeks without any thought or reason as to what was to come next. I was like a man released from prison who stands outside the gates gulping down great breaths of fresh, free air without a care for the future. Freedom was what mattered, not the nature of it.

And I had been incarcerated in my own prison, a hospital prison.

I suppose, looking back, I had to admit that it had passed quite quickly. But, at the time, every hour, even every minute, had dragged interminably. Progress, seen day-by-day, had been painfully slow, with painful being the appropriate word. However, I was now able to walk reasonably well on an artificial foot and, whereas I wouldn't be playing football again for a while, if ever, I could climb up and down stairs unaided and was mostly self-sufficient. I might even have been able to run a few strides to catch that bus, if only I had wanted to go wherever it was bound.

I looked around me. No one had turned up to collect me, nor had I expected them to. None of my family actually knew I was being discharged on that particular Saturday morning and, quite likely, they would not have turned up even if they had.

I had always preferred to do things for myself, and they knew it.

As far as my family was concerned, I was a loner, and happier for it, perhaps the more so after having to rely for months on others for help with my personal, and private, bodily functions.

I wasn't sure who had been the more shocked, my mother or me, when a nurse had asked, during one of her rare visits, if she could help me get dressed. My mother had last seen me naked when I was about seven and she was more than a little flustered at the prospect of doing so again twenty-five years later. She'd suddenly remembered that she was late for an appointment elsewhere, and had rushed away. The memory of her discomfort had kept me smiling for most of the rest of that day, and I hadn't smiled much recently.

In truth, 25198241 Captain Thomas Vincent Forsyth had not been the most patient of patients.

The army had been my life since the night I had left home after another particularly unpleasant, but not uncommon, argument with my stepfather. I had slept uncomfortably on the steps of the army recruiting office in Oxford and, when the office opened at 9 a.m. the following morning, I had walked in and signed on for Queen and Country as a private soldier in the Grenadier Guards.

Guardsman Forsyth had taken to service life like the proverbial duck to water and had risen through the ranks, first to corporal, then to officer cadet at the Royal Military Academy, Sandhurst followed by a commission back in my old regiment. The army had been much more to me than just a job; it had been my wife, my friend, and my family; it had been all I had known for fifteen years, and I loved it. But now it appeared that my army career might be over, blown apart for ever by an Afghan IED.

Consequently, I had not been a happy bunny during the previous four months, and it had showed.

In fact, I was an angry young man.

I turned left out of the hospital gates and began walking. Perhaps, I thought, I would see where I had got to by the time I became too tired to continue.

'Tom,' shouted a female voice. 'Tom.'

I stopped and turned round.

Vicki, one of the physiotherapists from the rehabilitation centre, was in her car turning out of the hospital car park. She had the passenger window down.

'Do you need a lift?' she asked.

'Where are you going?' I said.

'I was going to Hammersmith,' she said. 'But I can take you somewhere else if you like.'

'Hammersmith would be fine.'

I threw my bag onto the back seat and climbed in beside her.

'So they've let you out, then?' she said while turning into the line of traffic on Roehampton Lane.

'Glad to see the back of me, I expect,' I said.

Vicki tactfully didn't say anything. So it was true.

'It's been a very difficult time for you,' she said eventually. 'It can't have been easy.'

I sat in silence. What was she after? An apology?

Of course, it hadn't been easy.

Losing my foot had, in retrospect, been the most straightforward part. The doctors, first at Camp Bastion in Afghanistan and then at Selly Oak Hospital in Birmingham, had managed to save the rest of my right leg so that it now finished some seven inches below my knee.

My stump, as all the medical staff insisted on calling it, had healed well and I had quickly become proficient at putting on and taking off my new prosthetic leg, a wonder of steel, leather, and plastic that had turned me from a cripple into a normal-looking human being, at least on the outside.

But there had been other physical injuries too. The roadside bomb had burst my eardrums and had driven Afghan desert dust deep into my torn and bruised lungs, to say nothing of the blast damage and lacerations to the rest of my body. Pulmonary infection and then double pneumonia had then almost finished off what the explosion had failed to do.

The numbing shock that had initially suppressed any feeling of hurt had soon been replaced by a creeping agony in which every part of me seemed to be on fire. It was just as well that I remembered only a smattering of the full casualty evacuation procedure. Heavy doses of morphine did more than inhibit the pain receptors in the brain, they slowed its very activity down to bare essentials such as maintaining breathing and the pumping of the heart.

The human body, however, is a wondrous creation and has an amazing ability to mend itself. My ears recovered, the lacerations healed, and my white blood cells slowly won the war against my chest infection, with a little help and reinforcement from some high-powered intravenous antibiotics.

If only the body could grow a new foot.

The mental injuries, however, were proving less easy to spot and far more difficult to repair.

'Where in Hammersmith do you want?' Vicki asked, bringing me back to reality from my daydreaming.

'Anywhere will do,' I said.

'But do you live in Hammersmith?'

'No,' I said.

'So where do you live?'

Now that was a good question. I suppose that I was technically, and manifestly, homeless.

For the past fifteen years I had lived in army accommodation of one form or another: barracks, Sandhurst, officers' messes, tents and bivouacs, even in the backs of trucks or the cramped insides of Warrior armoured cars. I had slept in, under, and on top of Land Rovers and, more often than I cared to remember, I had slept where I sat or lay on the ground, half an ear open for the call of a sentry or the sound of an approaching enemy.

However, the army had now sent me 'home' for six months.

The major from the Ministry of Defence, the Wounded Personnel Liaison Officer, had been fair but firm during his recent visit. 'Six months' leave on full pay,' he'd said. 'To recover. To sort yourself out. Then we'll see.'

'I don't need six months,' I'd insisted. 'I'll be ready to go back in half that time.'

'Back?' he'd asked.

'To my regiment.'

'We'll see,' he had repeated.

'What do you mean, we'll see?' I had demanded.

'I'm not sure that going back to your regiment will be possible,' he'd said.

'Where, then?' I'd asked, but I'd read the answer in his face before he'd said it.

'You might be more suited to a civilian job. You wouldn't be passed fit for combat. Not without a foot.'

The major and I had been sitting in the reception area of the Douglas Bader Rehabilitation Centre in Queen Mary's Hospital in Roehampton, London.

Part of Headley Court, the military's own state-of-the-art

rehab centre in Surrey, had been temporarily closed for refurbishment, and the remaining wards had been overwhelmed by the numbers of wounded with missing limbs. Hence I had been sent to Queen Mary's and the National Health.

It was testament to the remarkable abilities of the military Incident Response Teams, and to their amazingly well-equipped casevac helicopters, that so many soldiers with battlefield injuries, which would in the past have invariably proved fatal, were now routinely dealt with and survived. Double and even triple traumatic amputees often lived when, only recently, they would have surely bled to death before medical help could arrive.

But not for the first time I'd wondered if it would have been better if I had died. Losing a foot had sometimes seemed to me a worse outcome than losing my life. But I had looked up at the painting on the wall of Douglas Bader, the Second World War pilot after whom the rehabilitation centre was named, and it had given me strength.

'Douglas Bader was passed fit for combat,' I'd said.

The major had looked up at me. 'Eh?'

'Douglas Bader was passed fit to fight and he'd lost *both* his feet.'

'Things were different then,' the major had replied, somewhat flippantly.

Were they? I wondered.

Bader had been declared fit and had taken to the air in his Spitfire to fight the enemy simply due to his own perseverance. True, the country had been in desperate need of pilots but he could have easily sat out the war in relative safety if he had wanted to. It was his huge personal determination to fly that had overcome the official reluctance to allow it.

I would now take my lead from him.

We'll see, indeed.

I'd show them.

'Will the Tube station do?' Vicki said.

'Sorry?' I said.

'The Tube station,' she repeated. 'Is that OK?'

'Fine,' I said. 'Anywhere.'

'Where are you going?' she asked.

'Home, I suppose,' I said.

'And where is home?'

'My mother lives in Lambourn,' I said.

'Where's that?' she asked.

'Near Newbury, in Berkshire.'

'Is that where you're going now?'

Was it? I didn't particularly want to. But where else? I could hardly sleep on the streets of London. Others did, but had I gone down that far?

'Probably,' I said. 'I'll get the train.'

My mind was working on automatic pilot as I negotiated the escalator up from the Underground into Paddington mainline railway station. Only near the top did I realize that I couldn't remember when I had last used an escalator. Stairs had always been my choice and they had to be taken at the run, never at a walk. And yet here I was, gliding serenely up without moving a muscle.

Fitness had always been a major obsession in a life that was full of obsessions.

Even as a teenager I had been mad about being fit. I had run every morning on the hills above Lambourn, trying to beat the horses as they chased me along the lush grass training gallops.

Army life, especially that of the infantry officer at war, was a strange mix of lengthy, boring interludes punctuated by brief but intensely high-adrenalin episodes where the separation between living and dying could be rice-paper thin. With the episode over, if one was still alive and intact, the boredom would recommence until the next 'contact' broke the spell once more.

I had always used the boring times to work on my fitness, constantly trying to break my own record for the number of sit-ups, or push-ups, or pull-ups, or anythingelse-ups I could think of, all within a five-minute period. What the Taliban had thought of their enemy chinning it up and down in full body armour, plus rifle and helmet, on an improvised bar welded across the back of a Snatch Land Rover is anyone's guess, but I had been shot at twice while trying to break the battalion record, once when I was on track to succeed. The Taliban obviously had no sense of sport, or of timing.

But now look at me: taking the escalator, and placing my bag on the moving stairway while doing so. Months of sedentary hospital life had left my muscles weak, flabby, and lacking any sort of condition. I clearly had much to do before I had any hope of convincing the major from the MOD that I could be 'combat-ready' once more.

I stood at the bottom of the steep driveway to my mother's home and experienced the same reluctance to go up that I had so often felt in the past.

I had taken a taxi from Newbury station to Lambourn, purposely asking the driver to drop me some way along the road from my mother's gate so that I could walk the last hundred yards.

It was force of habit, I suppose. I felt happier approaching anywhere on foot. It must have been something to do with being in the infantry. On foot, I could hear the sounds that vehicle engines would drown out, and smell the scents that exhaust fumes would smother. And I could get a proper feel of the lie of the land, essential to anticipate an ambush.

I shook my head and smiled at my folly.

There was unlikely to be a Taliban ambush in a Berkshire village, but I could recall the words of my platoon colour sergeant at Sandhurst: 'You can never be too careful,' he would say. 'Never assume anything, always check.'

No shots rang out, no IEDs went bang, and no turban-headed Afghan tribesmen sprang out with raised Kalashnikovs as I safely negotiated the climb up from the road to the house, a red-brick and flint affair built sometime back between the world wars.

As usual, in the middle of the day, all was quiet as I wandered round the side of the house towards the back door. A few equine residents put their heads out of their boxes in the nearest stable yard as I crunched across the gravel, inquisitive as ever to see a new arrival.

My mother was out.

I knew she would be. That was why I hadn't phoned ahead to say I was coming. Perhaps I needed to be here alone first, to get used to the idea of being back; to have a moment of recollection and renewal before the whirlwind of energy that was my mother swept through and took away any chance I might have of changing my mind.

My mother was a racehorse trainer. But she was much more than just that. She was a phenomenon. In a sport where there were plenty of big egos, my mother had the biggest ego of them all. She did, however, have some justification for her high sense of worth. In just her fifth year in the sport, she had been the first lady to be crowned Champion Jump Trainer, a feat she had repeated for each of the next six seasons.

Her horses had won three Cheltenham Gold Cups and two Grand Nationals and she was rightly recognized as the 'first lady of British racing'.

She was also a highly opinionated anti-feminist, a workaholic and no sufferer of fools or knaves. If she had been Prime Minister she would have probably brought back both hanging and the birch, and she was not averse to saying so loudly, and at length, whenever she had the opportunity. Her politics made Genghis Khan seem like an indecisive liberal, but everybody loved her nevertheless. She was a 'character'.

Everyone, that is, except her ex-husbands and her children.

For about the twentieth time that morning, I asked myself why I had come here. There had to be somewhere else I could go. But I knew there wasn't.

My only friends were in the army, mostly in my regiment, and they were still out in Afghanistan for another five weeks. And, anyway, I wasn't ready to see them. Not yet. They would remind me too much of what I was no longer – and I wouldn't be able to stand their pity.

I suppose I could have booked myself into an army officers' mess. No doubt I would have been made welcome at Wellington Barracks, the Grenadiers' home base in London. But what would I have done there?

What could I do anywhere?

Once again I thought it might have been better if the IED explosion, or the pneumonia, had completed the task: Union Flag-draped coffin, firing of volleys in salute, and I'd be six feet under by now and be done with it all. Instead, I was outside my mother's back door struggling with a damned artificial foot to get down low enough to find the key that she habitually left under a stone in the flower bed.

And for what?

To get into a house I hated; to stay with a parent I despised. To say nothing of my stepfather, to whom I had hardly spoken a civil word since I had walked out of here, aged seventeen.

I couldn't find the damn key. Perhaps my mother had become more security minded over the years. There had been a time when she would have left the house unlocked completely. I tried the handle. Not any more.

I sat down on the doorstep and leaned back against the locked door.

My mother would be home later.

I knew where she was. She was at the races; Cheltenham races, to be precise. I had looked up the runners in the morning paper, as I always did. She had four horses declared, including the favourite in the big race, and my mother would never miss a day at her beloved Cheltenham, the scene of her greatest triumphs. And, while today's might be a smaller meeting than the steeplechase Festival in March, I could visualize her holding court in the parade ring before the races, and welcoming the winner back after them. I had seen it so often. It had been my childhood.

The sun had long before given up trying to break through the veil of cloud, and it was beginning to get cold. I sighed. At least the toes on my right foot wouldn't get chilblains. I put my head back against the wood and rested my eyes.

'Can I help you?' said a voice.

I reopened my eyes. A short man in his mid-thirties wearing faded jeans and a puffy anorak stood on the gravel in front of me. I silently remonstrated with myself. I must have briefly drifted off to sleep because I hadn't heard him coming. What would my sergeant have said?

'I'm waiting for Mrs Kauri,' I said.

Mrs Kauri was my mother, Mrs Josephine Kauri, although Josephine had not been the name with which she had been christened. It was her name of choice. Sometime back, long before I was born, she had obviously decided that Jane, her real name, was not classy enough for her. Kauri was not her proper name either. It had been the surname of her first husband, and she was now on her third.

'Mrs Kauri is at the races,' replied the man.

'I know,' I said. 'I'll just wait for her here.'

'She won't be back for hours, not until after dark.'

'I'll wait,' I said. 'I'm her son.'

'The soldier?' he asked.

'Yes,' I said, somewhat surprised that he would know.

But he did know. It was only fleeting but I didn't miss his glance down at my right foot. He knew only too well.

'I'm Mrs Kauri's head lad,' he said. 'Ian Norland.'

He held out a hand and I used it to help me up.

'Tom,' I said. 'Tom Forsyth. What happened to old Basil?'

'He retired. I've been here three years now.'

'It's been a while longer than that since I've been here,' I said.

He nodded. 'I saw you from the window of my flat,' Ian said pointing to a row of windows above the stable boxes. 'Would you like to come in and watch the racing on the telly? It's too bloody cold to wait out here.'

'I'd love to.'

We climbed the stairs to what I remembered had once been a storage loft over the stables.

'The horses provide great central heating,' Ian said over his shoulder as he led the way. 'I never have to turn the boiler on until it actually freezes outside.'

The narrow stairway opened out into a long open-plan living area with a kitchen at the near end and doors at the far that presumably led to bedroom and bathroom beyond. There was no sign of any Mrs Norland, and the place had a 'man look' about it, with stacked-up dishes in the sink and newspapers spread over much of the floor.

'Take a pew,' Ian said waving a hand at a brown corduroy-covered sofa placed in front of a huge plasma television. 'Fancy a beer?'

'Sure,' I said. I'd not had a beer in more than five months.

Ian went to a fridge which appeared to contain nothing but beers. He tossed me a can.

We sat in easy companionship on the brown sofa watching the racing from Cheltenham on the box. My mother's horse won the second race and Ian punched the air in delight.

'Good young novice, that,' Ian said. 'Strong quarters. He'll make a good chaser in time.'

He took pleasure in the success of his charges as I had done in the progress of a guardsman from raw recruit into battle-hardened warrior, a man who could then be trusted with one's life.

'Now for the big one,' Ian said. 'Pharmacist should win. He's frightened off most of the opposition.'

'Pharmacist?' I asked.

'Our Gold Cup hope,' he said in a tone that implied I should have known. 'This is his last warm-up for the Festival. He loves Cheltenham.'

'What do you mean, he's frightened off the opposition?' I asked.

'Mrs Kauri's been saying all along that old Pharm will run in this race and so the other Gold Cup big guns have gone elsewhere. Not good for them to be beaten today with only a few weeks left to the Festival.'

Ian became more and more nervous, continually getting up and walking round the room for some unnecessary reason or other.

'Fancy another beer?' he asked, standing by the fridge.

'No thanks,' I said. He'd only given me one two minutes before.

'God, I hope he wins,' he said, sitting down and opening a fresh can with another still half full on the table.

'I thought you said he would,' I said.

'He should do, he's streaks better than the rest, but . . .'

'But what?' I asked.

'Nothing.' He paused. 'I just hope nothing strange happens, that's all.'

'Do you think something strange might happen?'

'Maybe,' he said. 'Something bloody strange has been happening to our horses recently.'

'What sort of things?'

'Bloody strange things,' he repeated.

'Like what?'

'Like not winning when they should,' he said. 'Especially in the big races. Then they come home unwell. You can see it in their eyes. Some have even had diarrhoea, and I've never seen racehorses with that before.'

We watched as my mother was shown on the screen tossing the jockey up onto Pharmacist's back, the black-and-white check silks appearing bright against the dull green of the February grass. My stepfather stood nearby observing events, as he always did.

'God, I hope he's OK,' said Ian with a nervous rattle.

The horse looked fine to me, but how would I know? The last horse I'd been close to had been an Afghan tribesman's nag with half of one ear shot away, reportedly by its owner as he was trying to shoot and charge at the same time. I tactfully hadn't asked him which side he'd been shooting at. Afghani allegiance was variable. It depended on who was paying, and how much.

Ian became more and more nervous as the race time approached.

'Calm down,' I said. 'You'll give yourself a heart attack.'

'I should have gone,' he said. 'I knew I should have gone.'

'Gone where?'

'To Cheltenham,' he said.

'What for?'

'To keep an eye on the bloody horse, of course,' he said angrily. 'To make sure no bugger got close enough to nobble him.'

'Do you really think the horses are being nobbled?' I asked.

'I don't know,' he said. 'The bloody dope tests are all negative.'

We watched as the horses walked round in circles at the start. Then the starter called them into line, and they were off.

'Come on Pharm, my old boy,' Ian said, his eyes glued to the television image. He was unable to sit down but stood behind the sofa like a little boy watching some scary science-fiction film, ready to dive down at the first approach of the aliens.

Pharmacist appeared to be galloping along with relative ease in about third place of the eight runners as they passed the grandstand on the first circuit. But only when they started down the hill towards the finishing straight for the last time did the race unfold properly, and the pace pick up.

Pharmacist still seemed to be going quite well and even jumped to the front over the second last. Ian began to breathe a little more easily, but then the horse appeared to fade rapidly, jumping the final fence in a very tired manner and almost coming to a halt on landing. He was easily passed by the others on the run-in up the hill, and he crossed the finishing line in last place, almost walking.

I didn't know what to say.

'Oh God,' said Ian. 'He can't run at the Festival, not now.'

Pharmacist certainly did not look like a horse that could win a Gold Cup in six weeks' time.

Ian stood rigidly behind the sofa, his white-knuckled hands gripping the corduroy fabric to hold himself upright.

'Bastards,' he whimpered. 'I'll kill the bastards who did this.'

I was not the only angry young man in Lambourn.

2

To say my homecoming was not a happy event would not have been an exaggeration.

No 'Hello, darling', no kiss on the cheek, no fatted calf, nothing. But no surprise, either.

My mother walked straight past me as if I had been invisible, her face taut and her lips pursed. I knew that look. She was about to cry but would not do so in public. To my knowledge, my mother had never cried in public.

'Oh, hello,' my stepfather said by way of greeting, reluctantly shaking my offered hand.

Lovely to see you too, I thought, but decided not to say so. No doubt, as usual, we would fight and argue over the coming days, but not tonight. It was cold outside and beginning to rain. Tonight, I needed a roof over my head.

My stepfather and I had never really got on.

In the mixed-up mind of an unhappy child, I had tried to make my mother feel guilty for driving away my father and had ended up alienating not only her but everyone else.

My father had packed his bags and left when I was just eight, finally fed up with being well behind the horses in my mother's affection. Her horses had always come first, then her dogs, then her stable staff, and finally, if there was time, which there invariably wasn't, her family.

How my mother ever had the time to have three children had always been a mystery to me. Both my siblings were older than I, and had been fathered by my mother's first husband, whom she had married when she was seventeen. Richard Kauri had been rich and thirty, a New Zealand playboy who had toyed at being a racehorse trainer. My mother had used his money to further her own ambition in racing, taking over the house and stables as part of their divorce settlement after ten years of turbulent marriage. Their young son and daughter had both sided with their father, a situation I now believed she had encouraged as it gave her more chance of acquiring the training business if her ex-husband had the children.

Almost immediately she had married my father, a local seed merchant, and had produced me like a present on her twenty-ninth birthday. But I had never been a much-wanted, much-loved child. I think my mother looked upon me as just another of her charges to be fed and watered twice a day, mucked out and exercised as required, and expected to stay quietly in my stable for the rest of the time.

I suppose it had been a lonely childhood but I hadn't known anything different and, mostly, I'd been happy enough. What I missed in human contact at home I made up for with dogs and horses, both of which had plenty of time for me. I would make up games with them. They were my friends. I could remember thinking the world had ended when Susie, my beloved beagle, had been killed by a car. What had made it much worse was that my mother, far from comforting me, had instead told me to pull myself together, it was only a dog.

When my parents divorced there had been a long and protracted argument over custody of me. It was not until many years later that I realized that they had argued because neither of them had wanted the responsibility of bringing up an eight-year-old misfit. My mother had lost the argument, so I had lived with her, and my father had disappeared from my life for good. I hadn't thought it a great loss at the time, and I still didn't. He had written to me a few times, and had sent an occasional Christmas or birthday card, but he clearly thought he was better off without me, and I was sure I was without him.

'So, darling, how was Afghanistan? You know, to start with, before you were injured?' my mother asked rather tactlessly. 'Were you able to enjoy yourself at all?'

My mother had always managed to call me 'darling' without any of the emotion the word was designed to imply. In her case there was perhaps even a degree of sarcasm in the way she pronounced it with a long 'r' in the middle.

'I wasn't sent there to enjoy myself,' I said slightly irritated. 'I was there to fight the Taliban.'

'Yes, darling. I know that,' she said. 'But did you have any good times?'

We were sitting round the kitchen table having dinner and my mother and stepfather both looked at me expectantly.

It was a bit like asking President Lincoln's wife if she had been enjoying the play before her husband was shot. What should I say?

In truth, I had enjoyed myself immensely before I was blown up, but I wondered if I should actually say so.

Recording my first confirmed 'kill' of a Taliban had been exhilarating; and calling in the helicopter gunships to pound an enemy position with body-bursting 50mm shells had been spine-chillingly exciting. It had sent my adrenalin levels to maximum in preparation for the charge through to finish them off at close quarters.

One wasn't meant to enjoy killing other human beings, but I had.

'I suppose it was OK,' I said. 'Lots of sitting around doing nothing, really. That, and playing cards.'

'Did you see anything of the Taliban?' my stepfather asked.

'A little,' I said matter-of-factly. 'But mostly at a distance.'

A distance of about two feet, impaled on my bayonet.

'But didn't you get to do any shooting?' he asked. He made it sound like a day's sport of driven pheasant.

'Some,' I said.

I thought back to the day my platoon had been ambushed and outnumbered by the enemy. I had sat atop an armoured car laying down covering fire with a GPMG, a general purpose machine gun, known to us all as 'the gimpy'. I had done so much shooting that day that the gimpy's barrel had glowed red-hot.

I could have told them all of it.

I could have told them of the fear. Not so much the fear of being wounded or killed, more the fear of failing to act. The fear of fear itself.

Throughout history, every soldier has asked themselves the same questions: What will I do when the time comes to fight? How will I perform in the face of the enemy? Shall I kill, or be killed? Shall I be courageous, or will I let down my fellow men?

In the modern British army, much of the officer training is designed to make young men, and young women, behave in a rational and determined manner in extreme conditions and when under huge stress. Command is what they are taught, the ability to 'command' when all hell is breaking loose around them. The 'command moment' it is called, that moment in time when something dramatic occurs like an ambush, or a roadside-bomb explosion, the moment when all the men turn and look to their officer – that's you – waiting to be told what to do, and how to react. There's no one else to ask. You have to make the decisions, and men's lives will depend on them.

The training also teaches teamwork and, in particular, reliance. Not reliance on others, but the belief that others are reliant on you. When push comes to shove, a soldier doesn't stick his head up and shoot back at the enemy for his Queen and Country. Instead, he does it for his mates, his fellow soldiers all around him who will die if he doesn't.

My biological family might have considered me a loner, but I was not. Members of my platoon were my chosen family and I had regularly placed myself in extreme danger to protect them from harm.

Eventually my luck had been bound to run out.

Killing the enemy with joy and gusto might lead an onlooker to believe that the soldier places a low value on human life. But this would be misleading, and untrue. The death of a comrade, a friend, a brother has the most profound effect on the fighting man. Such moments are revisited time and again with the same question always uppermost: could I have done anything to save him?

Why him and not me? The guilt of the survivor is ever present and is expunged only by continuation of the job in hand – the killing of the enemy.

'You're not very talkative,' my mother said. 'I thought that soldiers liked nothing better than to recount stories of past battles.'

'There's not much to tell you, really,' I said.

Not much to tell, I thought, that wouldn't put her off her dinner.

'I saw you both on the television today,' I said, changing the subject, 'at Cheltenham. Good win in the novice chase. Shame about Pharmacist, though. At one point I thought he was going to win as well.' I knew that it was not a tactful comment, but I was curious to see their reaction.

My mother kept her eyes down as she absent-mindedly pushed a potato round and round her plate.

'Your mother doesn't want to talk about it,' my stepfather said in an attempt to terminate conversation on the topic.

He was unsuccessful.

'Your head lad seems to think the horse was nobbled,' I said.

My mother's head came up quickly. 'Ian doesn't know what he's talking about,' she said angrily. 'And he shouldn't have been talking to *you*.'

I hoped that I hadn't dropped Ian into too much hot water. But I wasn't finished yet.

'Shouldn't have been talking to me about what?' I asked.

No reply. My mother went back to studying her plate of food and my stepfather sat stony-faced across the table from her.

'So are the horses being nobbled?' I asked into the silence.

'No, of course not,' my mother said. 'Pharmacist simply had a bad day. He'll be fine next time out.'

I wondered if she was trying to convince me, or herself.

I stoked the fire a little more. 'Ian Norland said it wasn't the first time that your horses haven't run as well as expected.'

'Ian knows nothing.' She was almost shouting. 'We've just had some bad luck of late. Perhaps there's a bit of a bug going round the stable. That's all. It'll pass.'

She was getting distressed and I thought it would be better to lay off, just for a bit.

'And Mrs Kauri doesn't need you spreading any rumours,' my stepfather interjected, somewhat clumsily. My mother gave him a look that was close to contempt.

I also looked at my stepfather and I wondered what he really thought of his wife still using the name of another man.

Only when the other children at my primary school had asked me why I was Thomas Forsyth, and not Thomas Kauri, had I ever questioned the matter. 'My father is Mr Forsyth,' I'd told them. 'Then why isn't your mother Mrs Forsyth?' It had been a good question and one I hadn't been able to answer.

Mrs Josephine Kauri had been born Miss Jane Brown and

was now, by rights, Mrs Derek Philips, although woe betide anyone who called her that in her hearing. Since first becoming a bride at seventeen, Josephine Kauri had worn the trousers in each of her three marriages and it was no coincidence that she had retained the marital home in both of her divorces. From the look she had just delivered across the kitchen table, I thought it might not be too long before her divorce lawyer would again be picking up his telephone. Mr Derek Philips may soon be outstaying his welcome at Kauri House Stables.

We ate in silence for a while, finishing off the chicken casserole that my mother's cleaner-cum-housekeeper had prepared that morning and which had been slow-cooking in the Aga all afternoon. Thankfully there had been more than enough for an uninvited guest.

But I couldn't resist having one more go.

'So will Pharmacist still run in the Gold Cup?'

I thought my stepfather might kick me under the table, such was the fury in his eyes. My mother, however, was more controlled.

'We'll see,' she said, echoing the major from the MOD. 'It all depends on how he is in the morning. Until then I can't say another word.'

'Is he not back here yet, then?' I asked, not taking the hint to keep quiet.

'Yes,' she said without further explanation.

'And have you been out to see him?' I persisted.

'In the morning,' my mother replied brusquely. 'I said I'd see how he was in the morning.' She swallowed noisily. 'Now, please, can we drop the subject?'

Even I didn't have the heart to go on. There were limits to the pleasure one could obtain from other people's distress, and distressed she clearly was. It was not a condition I was used to observing in my mother, who had always seemed to be in complete control of any and every situation. It was more usually a state she created in others rather than suffered from herself.

As Ian Norland had said, something very strange was going on.

I went for a walk outside before going to bed. I had done something similar all my life and the loss of a foot wasn't going to be allowed to change my lifestyle more than I could help it.

I wandered round the garden and along the concrete path to the stables. A few security lights came on as I moved under the sensors but no one seemed to care and there was no halting shout. There was no one on stag here, no sentries posted.

Not much had changed since I had run away all those years before. The trees had grown up a bit and the border of bushes down the far side of the house was less of a jungle than I had remembered. Perhaps it was just the effects of the winter months.

I had loved that border as a child and had made no end of dens amongst the thick undergrowth, fantasizing great adventures, and forever lying in wait for an unseen 'enemy', my toy rifle at the ready.

Not much may have changed in the place, but plenty had changed within me.

I stood in the cold and dark and drew deeply on a cigarette, cupping the glowing end in my hand so that it wasn't visible. Not that anyone would be looking, it was just force of habit.

I didn't really consider myself a smoker, and I'd never had a cigarette until I first went on 'ops' to Iraq. Then that had changed. Somehow the threat of possibly developing lung cancer in the future was a minor one compared with the risk of having one's head blown off in the morning.

It had seemed that almost everyone smoked in Afghanistan. It had helped to control the fear, to steady the hand, and to relieve the pressure when a cold beer, or any other alcohol for that matter, was strictly against standing orders. At least I hadn't smoked opium like the locals. That was also against standing orders.

I leaned against the corner of the house and drew a deep breath of smoke into my lungs, feeling the familiar rush as the nicotine flooded into my bloodstream and was transported to my brain. Finding the opportunity for a crafty fag in hospital had been rare but here, now, I was my own master again and I revelled in the freedom.

A light went on in the first-floor room above my head.

'Why the bloody hell did he have to turn up? That's all we bloody need at the moment.'

I could clearly hear my mother in full flow.

'Keep your voice down, he'll hear you.'

That was my stepfather.

'No, he won't,' she said, again at full volume. 'He's gone outside.'

'Josephine,' my stepfather said angrily, 'half the bloody village will hear you if you're not careful.'

I was quite surprised that he would talk to her like that. Perhaps there was more to him than I thought. My mother even took notice of him and they continued their conversation much more quietly. Annoyingly, I couldn't hear anything other than a faint murmur, although I stood there silently for quite a while longer, just in case they reverted to fortissimo.

But sadly, they didn't and, presently, the lights in the room went out.

I lifted the leather flap that covered the face of my watch. The luminous hands showed me it was only ten thirty. Clearly, racehorse trainers went to bed as early as hospital patients, even on Saturday nights. I was neither, and I enjoyed being outside in the dark, listening and watching.

I had always been completely at home in darkness and I couldn't understand those who were frightened of it. I suppose it was one thing I should thank my mother for. When I was a child, she had always insisted I sleep with my bedroom lights off and my door firmly closed. Since then the dark had always been my friend.

I stood silently and listened to the night.

In the distance there was music, dance music, the thump, thump, thump of the rhythm clearly audible in the still air. Perhaps someone was having a party. A car drove along the road at the bottom of the driveway and I watched its red lights as it travelled beyond the village, up the hill and out of sight.

I thought I heard a fox nearby with its high-pitched scream but I wasn't sure. It might have been a badger. I would have needed a pair of army-issue night-vision goggles to be sure, or better still a US military set, which were far superior.

I lit another cigarette, the flare of the match instantly rendering me blind in the night. Out in Afghanistan I'd had a fancy lighter that could light a cigarette in complete darkness. Needless to say, it hadn't accompanied me on my evacuation. In fact, nothing I had owned in Afghanistan had so far made it back to me.

An infantry soldier's life at war was carried round with him in his back-pack, his bergen. Either that or on his body in the form of helmet, radio, body armour, spare ammunition, boots, and camouflage uniform. Then there was his rifle and bayonet to carry in his hands. It all went everywhere with him. Leave a bergen unattended for even a second and it was gone, spirited away like magic by some innocent-looking Afghan teenager. Leaving a rifle unattended could be a court-martial offence. Everything and anything would 'walk' if not tied down or guarded.

The Taliban have described the British soldier as a ferocious fighter but one who moves very slowly. Well, Mr Taliban, you try running around with seven stone of equipment on your back. It was like carrying your grandmother into battle, but without the benefits.

I wondered where my bergen had gone. For that matter, I wondered where my uniform had gone, and everything else too. Thanks largely to the dedicated and magnificent volunteers of the CCAST, the Critical Care Air Support Teams, I had arrived back in England not only alive, but less than thirty hours after the explosion. But I'd woken up in the Birmingham hospital, naked and without a foot, with not even a toothbrush, just a pair of metal dog-tags round my neck, embossed with my name and army service number, an age-old and trusted method of identifying the living, and the dead.

There had been a letter to my mother in the breast pocket of my uniform, to be posted in the event of my death. I wondered where that was, too. My mother obviously hadn't received it. But there again, I hadn't died. Not quite.

Eventually it was the cold that drove me inside.

I went slowly and quietly through the house so as not to disturb the human residents sleeping upstairs or the canine ones asleep in the kitchen. In the past I would have removed my shoes and padded around silently in bare feet, but now, as I could have only one bare foot, I kept my shoes on.

Good as it was, my new right leg had an annoying habit of making a metallic clinking noise every time I put it down, even when I moved slowly. I didn't sound quite like a clanking old truck engine, but an enemy sentry would still have heard me coming from more than a hundred paces on a still night. I would have to do something about that, on top of everything else, if I was ever to convince the MOD major.

I went up the stairs to my old bedroom. My childhood things were long gone, packed up by my mother and either sent to the charity shop or to the council tip just as soon as I had announced I wasn't coming back.

However, the bed looked the same and the chest of drawers in the corner definitely was, the end now repainted where I had once stuck up bubble-gum cards of army regimental crests.

This wasn't the first night I had been back in this bed. There had been other occasional visits, all started with good intentions but invariably ending in argument and recrimination. To be fair, I was as much, if not more, to blame than my mother and stepfather. There was just something about the three of us together that caused the ire in us to rise inexorably to the point of mutual explosion. And none of us were very good firemen. Rather, we would fan the flames and pour petrol on them in gay abandon. And not one of us was ever prepared to back down or apologize. Nearly always I would end up leaving in anger, vowing never to return.

My most recent visit, five years previously, had been optimistically expected to last five days. I had arrived on Christmas Eve all smiles, with bags of presents and good intent, and I'd left before lunch on Christmas morning, sent on my way by a tirade of abuse. And the silly thing was, I couldn't now remember why we had argued. We didn't seem to need a reason, not a big one anyway.

Perhaps tomorrow would be better. I hoped so, but I doubted it. The lesson of experience over expectation was one I had finally begun to learn.

Maybe I shouldn't have come, but somehow I had needed to. This place was where I'd grown up and in some odd way it still represented safety and security. And, in spite of the shouting, the arguments, and the fights, it was the only home I'd ever had.

I lay on the bed and looked up at the familiar ceiling with its decorative moulding round the light fitting. It reminded me so much of the hours I had spent lying in exactly the same way as a spotty seventeen-year-old longing to be free, longing to join the army and escape from my adolescent prison. And yet here I was again, back in the same place, imprisoned again, this time by my disability, but still longing to be in the army, determined to rejoin my regiment, hungry to be back in command of my troops, and eager to be, once more, fighting and killing the enemy.

I sighed, stood up, and looked at myself in the mirror on the wardrobe door. I looked normal, but looks could be deceptive.

I sat down on the edge of the bed and removed my prosthesis, rolling down the flesh-coloured rubber sleeve that gripped over my real knee, keeping the false lower leg and foot from falling off. I slowly eased my stump out of the tight-fitting cup and removed the foam-plastic liner. It was all very clever. Moulded to fit me exactly by the boys at Dorset Orthopaedic, they had constructed a limb that I could walk on all day without causing so much as a pressure sore, let alone a blister.

But it still wasn't *me*.

I looked again at the mirror on the wardrobe door. Now my reflection didn't appear so normal.

Over the past few months, I suppose I had become familiar with the sight of my right leg finishing so abruptly some seven inches below my knee. Familiar, it might have been, but I was far from comfortable with the state of affairs and, every time I caught a glimpse of myself in a mirror without my prosthesis, I was still shocked and repulsed by the image.

Why me? I thought for the millionth time.

Why me?

I shook my head.

Feeling sorry for myself wasn't going to help me get back to combat-ready fitness.

3

'HAS JOSEPHINE LOST HER MAGIC?'

The front-page headline of Sunday's *Racing Post* couldn't have been more blunt. The paper lay on the kitchen table when I went downstairs at eight o'clock to make myself some coffee after a disturbed night.

I wondered if my mother or stepfather had been down to the kitchen yet and, if so, had they seen the headline? Perhaps I should hide it. I looked around for something to casually place over the paper as I could hear my mother coming down the stairs, but it was too late anyway.

'That bastard Rambler,' she was shouting. 'He knows sod all.'

She swept into the kitchen in a light-blue quilted dressing gown and white slippers. She snatched up the newspaper from the table and studied the front-page article intently.

'It says here that Pharmacist was distressed after the race.' My mother was shouting over her shoulder, obviously for the benefit of my stepfather who had sensibly stayed upstairs. 'That's not bloody true. How would Rambler know anyway? He'd have been propping up a bar somewhere. Everyone knows he's a drunk.'

I shifted on my feet, my false leg making its familiar metallic clink.

'Oh, hello,' said my mother, apparently seeing me for the first time. 'Have you read this rubbish?' she demanded.

'No,' I said.

'Well, don't,' she said, throwing the paper back down on the table. 'It's a load of crap.'

She turned on her heel and disappeared back upstairs as

quickly as she had arrived, shouting obscenities and telling all the world how she would 'have Rambler's head on a platter for this'.

I leaned down and turned the paper round so I could read it.

FROM OUR SENIOR CORRESPONDENT GORDON RAMBLER AT CHELTENHAM was printed under the headline. I read on:

Josephine Kauri was at a loss for words after her eight-year-old Gold Cup prospect, Pharmacist, finished last in the Janes Bank Trophy yesterday at Cheltenham. The horse clearly did not stay the three-mile trip and finished at a walk and in some distress. The Cheltenham stewards ordered that the horse be routine tested.

This is not the first time in recent weeks that the Kauri's horses have seemingly run out of puff in big races. Her promising novice chaser, Scientific, suffered the same fate at Kempton in December, and questions were asked about another Kauri horse, Oregon, at Newbury last week when it failed to finish in the first half dozen when a heavily backed favourite.

Is Josephine losing her magic touch that has won her such respect as well as numerous big prizes? With the Cheltenham Festival now only five weeks away can we expect a repeat of last year's fantastic feats or have the Kauri horses simply flattered to deceive?

Gordon Rambler had pulled no punches. He went on to speculate that Mrs Kauri might be over-training the horses at home so that they had passed their peak by the time they reached the racecourse. It would not have been the first time a trainer had inadvertently 'lost the race on the gallops', as it was known, although I would be surprised if my mother had, not after so many years of experience. Not unless, as the paper said, she had lost her magic touch.

But she hadn't lost her touch for shouting. I could hear her upstairs in full flow although I couldn't quite make out the words. No doubt my stepfather was suffering the wrath of her tongue. I almost felt sorry for him. But only almost.

I decided it might be prudent for me to get out of the house for a while so I went for a wander around the stables.

The block nearest the house, the one over which Ian Norland lived, was just one side of three quadrangles of stables, each containing twenty-four boxes, that stretched away from the house.

When my mother had acquired the place from her first husband there had been far fewer stables laid out in two lines of wooden huts. But by the time my father had packed up and left nine years later, my mother had built the first of the current red-brick rectangles. The second was added when I'd been about fifteen, and the third more recently in what had once been a lunging paddock. And there was still enough of the paddock remaining to add a fourth, if required.

Even on a Sunday morning, the stables were a hive of activity. The horses needed to be fed and watered, seven days a week, although my mother, along with most trainers, still resisted the temptation to treat Sunday as just another day and send strings of horses out on the gallops. But that was probably more to do with having to pay staff double time on Sundays rather than any wish to keep the Sabbath special.

'Good morning,' Ian Norland called to me as he came out of one of the boxes. 'Still here, then?'

'Yes,' I said. Surely, I thought, I hadn't implied anything to him the previous afternoon. 'Why wouldn't I still be here?'

'No reason,' he said, smiling. 'Just . . .'

'Just what?' I asked with some determination.

'Just that Mrs Kauri doesn't seem to like guests staying overnight. Most go home after dinner.'

'This is my home,' I said.

'Oh,' he said. 'I suppose it is.'

He seemed slightly flustered, as if he had already said too much to the son of his employer. He was right. He had.

'And how is Pharmacist this morning?' I asked, half hoping for some more indiscretion.

'Fine,' he said rather dismissively.

'How fine?' I persisted.

'He's a bit tired after yesterday,' he said. 'But, otherwise, he's OK.'

'No diarrhoea?' I asked.

He gave me a look that I took to imply that he wished he hadn't mentioned anything about diarrhoea to me yesterday.

'No,' he said.

'Does he look well in his eyes?' I asked.

'Like I said, he's just tired.' He picked up a bucket and began to fill it under a tap. 'Sorry, I have to get on.' It was my cue that the conversation was over.

'Yes, of course,' I said. I started to walk on but I stopped and turned round. 'Which box is Pharmacist in?'

'Mrs Kauri wouldn't want anyone seeing him,' Ian said. 'Not just now.'

'Why on earth not?' I said, sounding aggrieved.

'She just wouldn't,' he repeated. 'Mrs Kauri doesn't like anyone snooping round the yard. Won't even allow the owners to see their own horses without her there to escort them.'

'Nonsense,' I said in my best 'voice-of-command'. 'I'm not just anyone, you know, I'm her son.'

He wavered, and I thought he was about to tell me when he was saved by the arrival of his employer.

'Morning, Ian,' my mother called, striding round the corner

towards us. She had swapped the light-blue dressing gown and white slippers for a full-length waxed Barbour coat and green wellington boots.

'Ah, morning, ma'am,' Ian replied with some relief. 'I was just talking to your son.'

'So I see,' she said in a disapproving tone. 'Well, don't. You've talked to him too much already.'

Ian blushed bright pink, and he stole a glance of displeasure at me.

'Sorry, ma'am,' he said.

She nodded firmly at him as if to close the matter. Ian's rebuke may have been short but I had the distinct impression that his indiscretion would be remembered for much longer. But for now, she turned her attention to me. 'And what are *you* doing out here exactly?' she asked accusingly.

'I was just having a look around,' I said as innocently as I could.

I was thirty-two years old and still a serving captain in Her Majesty's Armed Forces. Until recently, I had been commanding a platoon of thirty men fighting and killing her enemies with zest and gusto, but here I was feeling like a naughty fourth-former caught having a smoke behind the bike sheds by the headmistress.

'Well, don't,' she said to me in the same tone that she had used towards Ian.

'Why not?' I said belligerently. 'Have you something to hide?'

Ian almost choked. It hadn't been the most tactful of comments and I could see the irritation level rise in my mother's eyes. However, she managed to remain in control of her emotions. There were staff about.

One didn't fight with family in front of staff.

'Of course not,' she said with a forced smile. 'I just don't want anyone upsetting the horses.'

I couldn't actually see how wandering around the stable blocks would upset the horses but I decided not to say so.

'And how is Pharmacist this morning?' I asked her.

'I was on my way to see him right now,' my mother replied, ignoring the implication in my voice. 'Come on, Ian,' she said, and set off briskly with him in tow.

'Good,' I said walking behind them. 'I'll come with you.'

My mother said nothing but simply increased her already breakneck pace with Ian almost running behind her to keep up. Perhaps she thought that, with my false foot, I wouldn't be able to. Maybe she was right.

I followed as quickly as I could along the line of boxes and through the corridor into the next stable rectangle. If my mother thought she could go fast enough so that I wouldn't see where she had gone, she was mistaken. I watched as she slid the bolts and went into a box on the far side, almost pushing Ian through the gap and pulling the door shut behind them. As if that would make them unreachable. Even I knew that stable doors are bolted only from the outside. Perhaps I should lock them in and wait. Now, that would be fun.

Instead, I opened the top half of the door, leaned on the lower portion, and looked in.

My mother was bent over, away from me, with her sizeable bottom facing the door. I did not take this as any particular gesture of disapproval as she was simply running her hands down the backs of Pharmacist's legs, feeling for heat that would imply a soreness of the tendon. Ian was holding the horse's head-collar so that it couldn't move.

'Nothing,' my mother said, standing up straight. 'Not even a twinge.'

'That must be good,' I said.

'How would you know?' my mother said caustically.

'Surely it's good if there's no heat in his tendons,' I said.

'Not really,' she replied. 'It means there must be another reason for him finishing so badly yesterday.'

That's true, I thought.

'Does he look all right?' I asked.

'No, he's got two heads.' My mother's attempts at humour rarely came off. 'Of course he looks all right.'

'Has he got diarrhoea?' I asked.

Ian gave me a pained look.

'And why, pray, would he have diarrhoea?' my mother asked haughtily with strong accusation in her tone.

Ian stood quite still, looking at me. His jaw set as in stone.

'I just wondered,' I said, letting him off this particular hook. 'I know horses can't vomit so I just wondered if he had a stomach upset that might show itself as diarrhoea.'

'Nonsense,' my mother said. 'Horses only get diarrhoea with dirty or mouldy feed and we are very careful to keep our feed clean and fresh. Isn't that right, Ian?'

'Oh, yes, ma'am,' he said immediately.

I thought, perhaps unfairly, that Ian would have said 'Yes, ma'am' to any request at that precise moment, even if she'd asked him to jump off the stable roof.

The inspection of Pharmacist was over and my mother came out through the door followed by Ian, who slid home the door bolts.

Personally, if it had been my best horse that had inexplicably run so badly, I would have had a vet out here last night drawing blood and giving him the full once over, testing his heart, his lungs, and everything else for that matter. Strangely, my mother seemed satisfied with a quick look and a cursory feel of his legs.

'How long before the dope test results are out?' I said, somewhat unwisely.

'What dope test?' my mother asked sharply.

'The one that was ordered by the stewards.'

‘And how do you know they ordered a dope test?’ she demanded.

‘It says so in today’s *Racing Post*.’

‘I told you not to read that article,’ she said crossly.

‘I don’t always do what I’m told,’ I said.

‘No,’ my mother said. ‘That’s the problem. You never did.’

She turned abruptly and strode away, leaving Ian and me standing alone.

‘So what do *you* think?’ I asked him.

‘Don’t involve me,’ he said. ‘I’m in enough trouble already.’

He turned to walk away.

‘But wouldn’t you have had a vet in last night?’ I said to his retreating back.

‘I told you,’ he said over his shoulder without stopping, ‘don’t involve me. I need this job.’

I called after him. ‘You do realize there won’t be a job if someone has been nobbling the horses. There won’t be any jobs here. The yard will be closed down.’

He stopped and came back.

‘Don’t you think I know that?’ he said through clenched teeth.

‘Well, what are you going to do about it?’ I asked.

‘Nothing,’ he said.

‘Nothing?’

‘That’s right. Nothing. If I say anything I’ll lose my job and then I’ll have no job and no reference. What chance would I have then?’

‘Better than having a reputation as a doper,’ I said.

He stood silently looking up at me.

‘So far the tests have all been negative. Let’s hope they stay that way.’

‘But you think otherwise, don’t you?’ I said.

‘Something strange is going on. That’s all I know. Now let me get on with my job, while I still have it.’

He strode away purposefully, leaving me alone outside Pharmacist's box. I opened the top half of the door and took another look at the horse. As yesterday on the television, he looked all right to me.

But, then, I was no vet.

The atmosphere back in the house was frosty, to put it mildly. Positively sub-zero, and it had nothing to do with Pharmacist or any of the other horses. It had to do with money.

'Josephine, we simply can't afford it.'

I could hear my stepfather almost shouting. He and my mother were in the little office off the hallway while I was sitting very quietly out of sight in the kitchen, eavesdropping. They must have been far too involved in their discussion to have heard me come in from the yard, so I had simply sat down and listened.

Some might have accused me of being somewhat underhand in secretly listening to their conversation. They would have been right.

'We must be able to afford it,' wailed my mother. 'I've had the best year ever with the horses.'

'Yes, you have, but we've also had other things to contend with, not least the ongoing fallout from your disastrous little scheme.' My stepfather's voice was full of incrimination and displeasure.

'Please don't start all that again.' Her tone was suddenly more conciliatory and apologetic.

'But it's true,' my stepfather went on mercilessly. 'Without that we would've easily been able to buy you a new BMW. As it is . . . well, let's just hope our old Ford doesn't need too much work done on it. Things are tight at present.'

I wondered what disastrous little scheme could have resulted in things being so tight financially that one of the top trainers in the country was unable to upgrade her old Ford to a new BMW. But she had never before seemed to care about what sort of car she drove.

I would have loved to listen to them for a while longer. However, I really didn't want to get caught snooping so I carefully stood up and silently swivelled back and forth on my good foot from the kitchen table to the back door. It was a technique I had developed to get around my hospital bed at night once I had removed my prosthesis. I was getting quite good at heel-and-toeing, as the physiotherapists had called it.

I could still hear my mother at high volume. 'For God's sake, Derek, there must be something we can do.'

'What do you suggest?' my stepfather shouted back at her. 'We don't even know who it is.'

I opened the back door a few inches then closed it with a bang.

Their conversation stopped.

I walked through from the kitchen to the hall, my right foot making its familiar clink whenever I put it down. My mother came out of the open office door.

'Hello,' I said as genially as I could.

'Hello, darling,' she replied, again placing too much emphasis on the 'dar'. She took a step towards me and I thought for a fleeting second she was going to give me a kiss, but she didn't. 'Tell me,' she said, 'how much longer are you planning to stay?'

'I've only just arrived,' I said, smiling. 'I hadn't thought about leaving just yet.'

Oh, yes, I had.

'It's just that one has to make plans,' my mother said. 'It's not that I want you to go, of course, it's just I would like to have some idea of when.'

'I haven't even worked out where I would go,' I said.

'But you would go back to the army.' It was a statement, not a question.

'It's not as simple as that. They want to give me time to get over the injuries. And, even then, they're not sure they actually want me any more. They'll decide when I go back after my leave.'

'What?' She sound genuinely shocked. 'But they have to have you. You were injured while working for them so surely they must have an obligation to go on employing you.'

'Mum, it's not like any other job,' I said. 'I would have to be fit and able to fight. That's what soldiers do.'

'But there must be something else you could do,' she argued. 'They must need people to organize things; people to do the paperwork. Surely those don't have to be fit enough to run around and fight?'

My stepfather came to the office door and leaned on the frame.

'Josephine, my dear, I don't think Tom here would be prepared to be in the army simply to push paper round a desk.' He looked me in the eye and, for the first time in twenty-four years, I thought there might be some flicker of understanding between us.

'Derek is so right,' I said.

'So for how long have the army sent you home on leave?' my mother asked. 'How long before they decide if they want you back or not?'

'Six months.'

'Six months! But you can't possibly stay here six months.'

That was clearly true. I had arrived only eighteen hours previously and I had already been there too long for her liking.

'I'll look for somewhere else to go this week,' I said.

'Oh, darling, it's not that I want to throw you out, you understand,' she said, 'but I think it might be for the best.'

Best for her, I thought, ungenerously. But perhaps it would be the best for us all. A full-scale shouting match couldn't be very far away.

'I could pay you rent,' I said, purposely fishing for a reaction.

'Don't be a silly boy,' my mother said. 'This is your home. You don't pay rent here.'

My home, but I can't stay in it. My mother clearly didn't appreciate the irony of her words.

'A contribution towards your food might be welcome,' my stepfather interjected.

Things must have been tight. Very tight indeed.

I lay on my bed for a while in the middle of the morning, staring at the moulded ceiling and wondering what to do.

Life in hospital had been so structured: time to wake up; cup of tea; read the paper; breakfast; morning physiotherapy session in the rehab centre; return to the ward for lunch in the day room; afternoon physiotherapy session; return to ward; watch the evening news; read a book or watch more television; evening hot drink; lights out; sleep. Every day the same, except there was no physio on Saturday afternoons or all day Sunday. A strict routine, regular as clockwork, with no decisions having to be made by me.

At first, I had hated to have such a straitjacket to my existence, but I'd become used to it. I suppose one gets used to anything.

Abruptly, here in Lambourn, I was on my own; free to make my own choice of activity without a hospital regime to do it for me. And all of a sudden I was lost, unable to make up my mind, mostly because I was at a loss to know *what* to do.

It was a new and alien sensation. Even in the boring times between contacts in Afghanistan I'd had things to do: clean my weapon, fix my kit, train my men, make plans, even write a note home. I had *always* had something to do. In fact, most of the time I had far too much to do, and not enough time.

Yet, try as I might, I couldn't think of a single thing I had to do now.

Maybe I could have written a note of thanks to the staff at the rehab clinic, but both they and I would know I didn't mean it.

I had hated feeling that I was being treated like a child, and I hadn't been slow to say so.

Looking back, even after just one day away from it, I could see that my frustration, and my anger, hadn't helped anyone, least of all myself. But it had been the only way I'd known to express my fury at the hand that fate had dealt me. There had been times when, if I'd still had my sidearm with me, I am sure I would have used it to blow my brains out, such had been the depth of my depression.

Even in recent weeks, I had often thought about suicide. But I could have walked out and thrown myself under the wheels of the London bus right outside the hospital if I'd really wanted to, and I hadn't, so at least I must be on the way up from the nadir.

My life needed targets and objectives.

In hospital my goal had been simply to be discharged.

Now that I had achieved it, a void had opened up in front of me. A future seemingly devoid of purpose and direction. Only a tentative 'we'll see' to give me any hope. Was it enough?

I looked at my watch.

It was twenty to twelve and I had been lying on my bed doing nothing for nearly three hours, ever since I had walked away from a stormy encounter with my parent out on the driveway.

She had been inspecting her car and I hadn't been able to resist telling her that it was high time she changed her old blue Ford for a new, smarter make.

'Mind your own bloody business,' she had hissed at me, thrusting her face towards mine.

'I'm sorry,' I'd said, feigning surprise. 'I didn't realize the matter touched such a sore nerve.'

'It doesn't,' she'd replied, back in some sort of control. 'And there's nothing wrong with this one.'

'But surely a trainer of your standing should have a better car than this; how about a BMW, for example?'

I had really believed she was about to cry again and, quite suddenly, I had been angry with myself. What was I doing? I tried to see myself as she would have done and I didn't like it. I didn't like it one bit. So I had turned away and climbed the stairs to my room like a naughty boy.

How long, I wondered, should I remain in my room before I had paid sufficient penance for my misdeeds? An hour? A day? A week? A lifetime?

I sat up on the side of the bed and decided to write to the staff at the rehab centre to thank them for their care *and* to apologize for my consistent lack of good humour.

Maybe, then, they might just believe that I meant it.

4

The remainder of Sunday proved to be a quiet day at Kauri House Stables with the human residents managing to stay out of arguing distance.

In the afternoon I ventured out into Lambourn, deciding to go for a walk mostly just to get me out of the house but also because I was curious about how much the place had changed over fifteen years. I didn't intend to go very far. It had been only a week or so since I'd thrown away the crutches and my leg tended to tire easily.

There were a few more houses than I remembered, a new estate of smart little homes with postage-stamp gardens having sprung up in what once had been a field full of ponies. But, overall, the village was as familiar as it had been when I'd delivered the morning papers as a teenager.

And why wouldn't it have been? The previous fifteen years may have changed *me* a great deal but it was a mere blink of an eye compared to the long history of human habitation in Lambourn.

'Modern' documented Lambourn dates from the ninth century, when the church and village were named in the will of King Alfred, the mighty king of the Saxons, the only monarch of England to have ever been designated 'The Great'.

But Lambourn has a history that stretches back far further than medieval times. Numerous Bronze Age burial grounds exist on the hills just north of the modern village, together with The Ridgeway, the Stone Age super-highway that had once stretched from the Dorset coast to The Wash.

Nowadays, Lambourn and its surroundings are known as 'The Valley of the Racehorse', but the racing industry is a relative newcomer. First records show that racehorses were trained here in the late eighteenth century, but it was not until the arrival of the railway a hundred years later that Lambourn became established as a national centre for racing, and jump-racing in particular, to rival that at Newmarket. Trains enabled the horses to be sent to racecourses further and further from home and hence a national sport was established.

But the major factor that made Lambourn such a wonderful place for horses was simple geology, and nothing to do with man.

Whereas the rolling Berkshire Downs certainly lend themselves so ideally to the formation of the gallops and the training of the horses, it is what lies beneath the turf that makes the real difference. The Downs, together with the Chiltern Hills, were created many millions of years ago, laid down as sediment in some prehistoric organism-rich sea. Billions and billions of primitive sea creatures died and their skeletons drifted to the bottom, over time being compressed into rock, into the white chalk we see today. It is almost pure calcium carbonate and the grass that grows on such a base is rich in calcium, ideal for the formation of strong bones in grass-eating racehorses.

I wandered down to the centre of the village, past the Norman church that, sometime in the twelfth century, had replaced the earlier Saxon version. Even though I was not what is known as a 'regular' churchgoer, I had been into Lambourn church many times, mostly along with the other boys and girls from the local primary school. My memory was of somewhere cold, and that was not just because the temperature was always low. It was also due to the realization that people were actually buried beneath my feet, under the stones set in the church floor. I could recall how my over-active childhood imagination had caused me to shiver, and I did so again now.

I stopped and thought it anomalous that the bodies of those buried so long ago could still have such an effect on me, whereas the bodies of the Taliban, those I had so recently sent to their graves, seemingly had none.

I walked on.

The centre of the village was mostly unchanged although some of the shops had different names, and others had a different purpose.

I went into the general store to buy a sandwich for lunch and waited for my turn at the checkout.

'Oh, hello,' said the woman behind the till, looking at me intently. 'It's Tom, isn't it? Tom Kauri?'

I casually looked back at her. She was about my age with long fair hair tied back in a ponytail. She wore a loose-fitting dark grey sweatshirt that did a moderate job of camouflaging the fairly substantial body beneath.

'Tom Forsyth,' I said, correcting her.

'Oh, yes,' she said. 'That's right. I remember now. But your mum is Mrs Kauri, isn't she?' I nodded and she smiled. I handed her my sandwich and can of drink. 'You don't remember me, do you?' she said.

I looked at her more closely.

'Sorry,' I said. 'No.'

'I'm Virginia,' she said expectantly.

I went on looking at her, obviously with a blank expression.

'Virginia Bayley,' she went on. 'Ginny.' She paused, waiting for a response. 'From primary school.' Another pause. 'Of course, I was Ginny Worthington then.'

Ginny Worthington, from primary school? I looked at her once more. I vaguely remembered a Ginny Worthington but she'd definitely had black hair, and she'd been as thin as a rake.

'Dyed my hair since then.' She laughed nervously. 'And put on a few pounds, you know, due to having had the kids.'

Virginia Bayley, plump and blonde, née Ginny Worthington, skinny and brunette. One and the same person.

'How nice to see you again,' I said, not really meaning it.

'Staying with your mother, are you?' she asked.

'Yes,' I said.

'That's nice.' She scanned my sandwich and the can of drink. 'Such a lovely woman, your mother. That's three pounds twenty, please.' I gave her a five-pound note. 'A real star round here.' She gave me my change. 'Real proud of her, we are, winning that award.' She handed me my sandwich and drink in a plastic bag. 'Lovely to see you again.'

'Thanks,' I said taking the bag. 'You too.' I started to leave but turned back. 'What award?'

'You must know,' she said. 'The National Woman of the Year Award. Last month. In London. Presented by the Prince of Wales, on the telly.'

I looked blank. Had I really been so involved with my own life that I hadn't even noticed my mother receiving such an accolade?

'I can't believe you don't know,' Ginny said.

'I've been away,' I replied absent-mindedly.

I turned away from her again.

She spoke to my back. 'You can come and buy me a drink later, if you like.'

I was about to ask why on earth I would like to buy her a drink when she went on. 'My old man has arranged a bit of a get-together in the Wheelwright for my birthday. There'll be others there, too. Some from school. You're welcome to come.'

'Thank you,' I said. 'Where did you say?'

'The Wheelwright,' she repeated. 'The Wheelwright Arms. At seven o'clock.'

'Tonight?'

'Yeah.'

'So, is it your birthday today?'

'Yeah,' she said again, grinning.

'Then, happy birthday, Ginny,' I said with a flourish.

'Ta,' she said, smiling broadly. 'Do come tonight if you can. It'll be fun.'

I couldn't, offhand, think of a less fun-filled evening than going to the pub birthday party of someone I couldn't really remember, where there would be other people I also wouldn't be able to remember, all of whom had nothing more in common with me than having briefly attended the same school twenty years previously.

But, I supposed, anything might be preferable to sitting through another excruciating dinner with my mother and stepfather.

'OK,' I said. 'I will.'

'Great,' Ginny said.

So I did.

The evening proved to be better than I had expected, and I so nearly didn't go.

By seven o'clock the rain was falling vertically out of the dark sky with huge droplets splashing back from the flooded area between the house and the stables.

I looked at my black leather shoes, my only shoes, and wondered if staying at home in front of the television might be the wiser option. Perhaps I could watch the weekly motoring show and use it to bully my mother further over her car.

Well, perhaps not, but it was tempting.

I decided instead to find out if it would be possible to pull a wellington boot over my false leg. I suppose I could always have worn only one boot while leaving the prosthesis completely bare. I don't think the water would have done it much harm, but the sight of a man walking on such a night with one bare foot might have scared the neighbours, to say nothing of the people in the pub.

I borrowed the largest pair of wellies I could find in the boot room and had surprisingly little difficulty in getting both of them on. I also 'borrowed' my mother's long Barbour coat and my stepfather's cap. I set off for the Wheelwright Arms relatively well protected but still with the rain running down my neck.

'I thought you wouldn't come,' said Ginny as I stood in the public bar removing my mother's coat with pools of water forming on the bleached stone floor. 'Not with the weather this bad.'

'Crazy,' I agreed.

'You or me?' she said.

'Both.'

She laughed. Ginny was trying very hard to make me welcome. Too hard, in fact. She would have been better leaving me alone and enjoying herself with her other guests. Her husband didn't like it either, which I took to be a good sign for their marriage. But he had no worries with me. Ginny was nice enough but not my sort.

What was my sort? I wondered.

I'd slept with plenty of girls but they had all been casual affairs, sometimes just one-nighters. I'd never had a 'real' girlfriend.

Whereas many of my fellow junior officers had enjoyed long-term relationships, even marriages, both at Sandhurst and in the regiment, I was, in truth, married only to the military.

There was no doubt that I had been, as I remained, deeply in love with the army and I had certainly betrothed myself to 'her', *forsaking all others until death do us part*.

But it seemed it wouldn't be death that would do us part: just the small matter of a missing foot.

'So what do you do for a living?' Ginny's husband asked me.

'I'm between jobs,' I said unhelpfully.

'What *did* you do?' he persisted.

Why, I thought, didn't I simply tell them I was in the army? Was I not proud to be a soldier? I had been before I was injured. Wasn't I still?

'A banker,' I said. 'In the city.'

'Recession got you, did it?' he said with a slightly mocking laugh in his voice. 'Your trouble was too many big bonuses.' He nodded. He knew.

'You're probably right,' I said.

There were seven of us standing in a circle near the bar. As well as Ginny and her husband, there were two other couples. I didn't recognize any of them and none of the four looked old enough to have been at school with me.

One of the men stepped forward to buy a round at the bar.

'Should I know any of these?' I said quietly to Ginny, waving a hand at the others.

'No, not these,' she said. 'I think the weather has put some people off.'

I was beginning to wish it had put me off as well when the door of the pub opened and another couple came in, again dripping water into puddles on the floor.

At least, I thought they were a couple until they removed their coats. Both of them were girls – more correctly they were young women – and one of them I knew the instant she removed her hat and shook out her long blonde hair.

'Hello, Isabella,' I said.

'My God,' she replied. 'No one's called me Isabella for years.' She looked closely at my face. 'Bloody hell. It's Tom Kauri.'

'Tom Forsyth,' I corrected.

'I know, I know,' she said, laughing. 'I was just winding you up. As per usual.'

It was true. She had teased me mercilessly, ever since I had told her, aged about ten, that I was deeply in love with her, and I had asked her to marry me. She had clearly filled out a bit since then, and in all the right places.

'So what do people call you now?' I asked.

'Bella,' she said. 'Or Issy. Only my mother calls me Isabella, and then only when I've displeased her.'

'And do you displease her often?' I asked flippantly.

She looked me straight in the eyes, and smiled. 'As often as possible.'

Wow, I thought.

Both Isabella and I rather ignored Ginny's birthday celebration as we renewed our friendship and, in my case anyway, renewed my feelings of longing.

'Are you married?' I asked her almost immediately.

'Why do you want to know?' she replied.

'To know where I stand,' I said somewhat clumsily.

'And where exactly do you think you stand?' she said.

I stand on only one leg. Now, what would she say to that?

'You tell me,' I said.

But, throughout the whole evening, she never did answer my question even though, in a roundabout manner, I asked it three or four times. In the end, I took her silence on the matter to be answer enough, and I wondered who was the lucky man.

At ten o'clock, as people were beginning to drift away, I asked her if I could walk her home.

'How do you know I walked?' she asked.

'When you arrived you were too wet to have simply come in from the car park.'

'Clever clogs!' She smiled. 'OK. But just a walk home. No bonus.'

'I've never heard it called a bonus before.' I laughed. 'No wonder all those bankers are so keen to keep their bonuses.'

She also laughed, and we left the pub in congenial companionship but with her hands firmly planted in her coat pockets so there was no chance of me being able to casually take one of them in mine.

Part of me longed to be with a woman again, just for the sex.

It had been a long time. It was six months or more since I had talked a girl into my bed with stories of heroic encounters with a mysterious enemy, stories of men being men, sweating testosterone through every pore and satisfying ten maidens each before breakfast. I was good at the game but recent opportunities had been limited, almost non-existent.

Six months was a long time with only the occasional misplaced sponge by a blushing nurse to fulfil the need.

I positively ached to 'have a bonus' with Isabella, even here, in the street, in the still-pouring rain.

But there was little likelihood of that and my chances weren't exactly helped when she suddenly stopped.

'What's that noise?' she asked.

'What noise?' I said, stopping next to her and dreading the moment.

'That clicking noise?' She listened. 'That's funny. It's stopped now.'

She walked on and I followed.

'There it is,' she shouted triumphantly. 'It's you, when you walk.'

'It's nothing,' I said quietly. 'Just the boots.'

I could see she was confused. I was wearing rubber boots. They would make no noise, certainly not a clicking noise.

'No, come on,' she said. 'That's definitely a sharp metal sound and you've got wellies on. So what is it?'

'Leave it,' I said sharply, embarrassed and angry. In truth, more angry with myself for not saying than with her for asking.

But she wouldn't leave it.

'Come on,' she said again, laughing. 'What have you got down there? It's a toy, isn't it? Part of your chat-up technique?' She danced away from me, looking down, searching for the source of the noise and laughing all the while.

I had no choice.

'I've got a false leg,' I said quietly.

'What?' She hadn't really heard and was still dancing around, laughing.

'A false leg,' I said more loudly. She stopped dancing.

'I've only got one leg.'

She stood still, looking at me.

'Oh, Tom, I'm sorry.' I thought for a moment that she was crying, but it might have been the rain on her face. 'Oh God, I'm so sorry.'

'It's all right,' I said sharply.

But it wasn't.

Isabella stood in the street getting wetter, if that was possible, while I told her everything I could remember about being blown apart by an IED and my subsequent medical history.

She listened, first with horror, and then with concern.

She tried to comfort me and I despised it. I didn't want her pity.

Suddenly I knew why I had come back to Lambourn, to my 'home'. I must have subconsciously understood that my mother would not have given me the lovey-dovey consoling parental hugs I would have hated. She would not have tried to be reassuring and sympathetic. And she would not have tried to commiserate with me for my loss. I preferred the Kauri 'get on with your own life and let me get on with mine' attitude.

Grief, even the grief for a lost foot or a lost career, was easier to cope with alone.

'Please don't patronize me,' I said.

Isabella stopped talking in mid sentence.

'I wasn't,' she said.

'Well, it felt like it,' I replied.

'God, you're awkward,' she said. 'I was only trying to help.'

'Well, don't,' I said rather cruelly. 'I'm fine without it.'

'OK,' she said, obviously hurt. 'If that's the way you feel, then I'll bid you goodnight.'

She turned abruptly and walked away, leaving me standing alone in the rain, confused and bewildered, not knowing whether to be pleased or disappointed, angry or calm.

I felt as though I wanted to run, to run away, but I couldn't even do that, not without a cacophony of metallic clinking.

On Monday morning I went to Aldershot to try to collect my car and my other belongings out of storage.

Isabella came with me.

In fact, to be totally accurate, I went with her.

She drove her VW Golf in a manner akin to a world championship rally driver.

'Do you always drive like this?' I asked as we almost collided with an oncoming truck during a somewhat dodgy overtaking manoeuvre.

'Only when I'm not being patronizing,' she said, looking at me for rather longer than I was happy with.

'Watch the road,' I said.

She ignored me.

'Please, Isabella,' I implored. 'I don't want to survive an IED only to be killed on the Bracknell by-pass by a lunatic woman.'

She had phoned the house early. Too early. I had still been in bed.

'That Warren woman called for you,' my mother had said with distaste when I went down to breakfast.

'Warren woman?'

'Married to Jackson Warren.'

I'd been none the wiser.

'Who's Jackson Warren?'

'You must know,' my mother had said. 'Lives in the Hall. Family made pots of money in the colonies.' She had sounded very old fashioned. 'Married that young girl when his wife died. She must be thirty years younger than him, at least. That's the one who called. Brazen hussy.'

The last two words had been spoken under her breath, but had been clearly audible nonetheless.

'Is her name Isabella?' I'd asked.

'That's the one.'

So she was married.

'What did she want?' I'd asked.

'I don't know, do I? She wanted to speak to you, that's all I know.'

My mother had never liked being in a position where she did not know everything that was going on, and this had been no exception.

'I didn't even know that you knew that woman.' She'd said the words with a mixture of disapproval and nosiness.

I hadn't risen to the bait.

Instead I'd gone out of the kitchen into the office to return the call to Isabella.

'I'm so sorry about last night,' she'd said.

'So am I.'

'Please can we meet again today so that I can apologize in person?'

'I can't,' I'd said. 'I'm going to Aldershot.'

'Can't I take you?' she had replied rather too eagerly.

'It's all right,' I'd said. 'I'll get the train from Newbury.'

'No.' She had almost screamed down the phone. 'Please let me take you. It's the least I can do after being so crass last night.'

So here we were, dodging trucks on the Bracknell by-pass.

Everything I owned, other than my kit for war, had been locked away in a metal cage at an army barracks in Aldershot prior to the regiment's move to Afghanistan. Everything, that is, except my car, which I hoped was still sitting at one end of the huge parking lot set aside for the purpose within the military camp down the road from Aldershot, at Pirbright.

'Let's get my car first,' I said. 'Then I can load it up with my stuff.'

'OK,' she said. 'But are you sure you'll be able to drive it?'

'No, I'm not at all sure,' I said. 'But I'll find out soon enough.' It was something that had been worrying me. My Jaguar was an automatic, so at least there were only two pedals to cope with, but both of them were designed to be operated by the driver's right foot. I planned to use my false right for the accelerator, and my real left for the brake; two pedals, two feet, just like driving a Formula One racing car.

'But are you insured, you know, to drive with only one leg?'

'To be honest, I'm not really sure about that either, so I'm not asking. I had intended cancelling my insurance and taking the car off the road before I was deployed but, somehow, I never found the time. It's been taxed and insured for the past five months without anyone driving it so they must owe me something. And I haven't told the insurance company about being wounded.'

She drove in silence for a while.

'Why didn't you just tell me you were married?' I asked.

'Does it matter?' she replied.

'It might.'

'What exactly might matter; the fact that I'm married or that my husband is more than twice my age?'

'Both.'

'I'm actually amazed you didn't know already. Everyone else seems to. Quite the scandal, it was, when Jackson and I got married.'

'How long ago?' I asked.

'Seven years now,' she said. 'And before you ask, no, it wasn't for his money. I love the old bugger.'

'But the money helped?' I said with some irony.

She glanced at me. It was not a glance of approval.

'You're just like everyone else,' she said. 'Why does everyone assume that it's all about his money?'

'Isn't it?'

'No,' she said defiantly, 'it's not. In fact, I won't get anything when he dies. I said I didn't want it. It all goes to his children.'

'Are any of them your children too?' I asked.

'No.' I could detect a slight disappointment in her voice. 'Sadly not.'

'You tried?' I asked.

'At the beginning, but not now. It's too late.'

'But you're still young enough.'

'I'm all right. It's Jackson that's the problem.' She paused as if wondering whether she should go on. She decided to. 'Bloody prostate.'

'Cancer?' I asked.

'Yeah,' she sighed. 'It's a bugger. The doctors say they've caught it early and that it's completely controllable with drugs. But there are some, shall we say, unfortunate side effects.'

She drove on in silence, swerving round a slow-moving truck just in time to avoid an oncoming car.

'Has he tried Viagra?' I asked.

'Tried it?' She laughed. 'He's swallowed them like bloody Smarties but still not a flicker. It's the fault of the Zolodex – that's one of the drugs. It seems to switch off his sex drive completely. That's the physical side; mentally, he's as rampant as ever.'

'I can see that would be a tad frustrating,' I said.

'A tad? I'll tell you it's extremely frustrating. And for both of us.' She looked at me as if in embarrassment. 'Sorry, I shouldn't have said anything. Far too much information.'

'It's fine,' I said. 'I'm really quite discreet. I'll only tell the Sunday papers if they pay me well.'

She laughed.

'From what the Sunday papers said after our wedding, you'd believe that I only married him for the money and that sex between a twenty-three-year-old woman and a man nearing sixty was all in the imagination – his imagination, that is. What rubbish. It was the sex that attracted me to him in the first place.'

I sat in silence, just listening. What could I say?

'I was eighteen when I first met him. He was fifty-four, but he didn't look it. He used to play golf with my dad every Sunday morning. Then one Sunday when Mum and Dad were away he came round to make sure everything was OK. It seems Dad hadn't told Jackson he wouldn't be playing golf that week, at least that's what Jackson told me at the time, but I've since often wondered if it was true.' She smiled. 'Anyway, to cut a long story short, we ended up in bed together.' She laughed. 'And the rest is history, or in the papers, at least.'

'Was Jackson married at the time?'

'Oh, yes,' she said. 'With two children. They're both older than me. But his wife was already ill by then. She had breast cancer. I helped look after her for nearly three years until she died.'

'Were you sleeping with him all the time?' I asked.

She smiled again. 'Of course.'

'But did you live in their house?'

'Not to start with, but I did for the last six months or so of Barbara's life. His son and daughter treated me as their kid sister.'

'But did they know you were sleeping with their father?'

'They didn't exactly say so,' she said, 'but I think they knew. Their mother certainly did.'

'What? Jackson's wife knew that he was sleeping with you?'

'Absolutely. We discussed it. She even gave me advice about what he liked. She used to say it took the pressure off her.'

Annoyingly, at this point we arrived at Pirbright Camp so I heard no more juicy Warren revelations.

Isabella remained in her car while I went into the guardroom to sign in.

'Sorry, sir,' said the corporal behind the desk, 'I can't let a civilian onto the camp without suitable ID.'

'What sort of suitable ID does she need?' I asked him.

'A driving licence or passport,' he said.

She had neither with her. I'd already asked.

'Can't I vouch for her?' I asked.

'Not without proper authority.'

'Well get the proper authority,' I said in my most commanding-officer voice.

'I can't, sir,' he said. 'You would have to apply to the adjutant, and he's away.'

I sighed. 'So what do you expect me to do?' I asked him.

'You can go in, sir, but you'll have to walk to get your car.'

'But it's miles away.' The park was at the other end of the camp.

'Sorry, sir,' he said adamantly. 'That's the security rules we've been told. No ID, no entrance.'

I suppose it was fair. In the army one learned very early on that rules were rules. Security was security, after all.

'Can you please get me some transport, then,' I said.

'Sorry, sir,' he said again. 'There's nothing available.'

I stepped back and lifted my right trouser leg up six inches. 'How am I going to walk to my car with this damn thing?' I lifted my foot up and down with its familiar metallic clink.

'Afghanistan?' the corporal asked.

I nodded. 'IED. In Helmand,' I said. 'Four months ago.'

'No problem, then, sir,' he said, suddenly making a decision. 'Just get the lady to hand this in when she leaves.' He handed me a temporary vehicle pass. 'Just don't tell anyone.'

'Thanks,' I said. 'I won't.'

False legs clearly brought some small benefit after all.

Funny how rules can be so easily ignored with the application of a modicum of common sense. Security? What security?

I found it was surprisingly easy to drive with a false foot. A few practice circuits of the car park and I was ready for the public highway. And I was much more confident about arriving safely at my destination with me driving with only one real leg than I had been in Isabella's VW with her driving with two.

She insisted on following me the nine miles from Pirbright to Aldershot.

'You might need help carrying your things,' she said. 'And you won't get much of it into that.'

True, my XK Jaguar coupé was pretty small, but Isabella obviously had no idea how little I had acquired in the way of 'stuff' during fifteen years in the army. I could probably have fitted it into my car twice over. But, who was I to turn down the help of a pretty girl, even if she was married?

We negotiated the busy Surrey and Hampshire roads without any mishaps and, surprisingly, without my Jag being overtaken by Isabella's dark blue Golf, although I was sure she was going to on a couple of occasions before she obviously remembered she didn't know the way.

'Is that *all*?' Isabella was amazed. 'I'd take more than that on a dirty weekend to Paris.'

I was standing next to two navy-blue holdalls and a four-foot by four-inch black heavy-duty cardboard tube. Between them they contained all my meagre worldly possessions.

'I've moved a lot,' I said as an explanation.

'At least you don't have to engage Pickfords to shift that lot.' She laughed. 'What's in the tube?'

'My sword.'

'What, a real sword?' She was surprised.

'Absolutely,' I said. 'Every officer has a sword, but it's for ceremonial use only these days.'

'But don't you have any furniture?'

'No.'

'Not any?'

'No. I've always used the army stuff. I've lived in barrack blocks all my adult life. I've never even known the luxury of an en-suite bathroom, except on holiday.'

'I can't believe it,' she said. 'What century is it?'

'In the army? Twenty-first for weaponry, other than the sword, of course, but still mostly in the nineteenth for home comforts. You have to understand that it's the weapons that matter more than the accommodation. No soldier wants a cheap rifle that won't fire when his life depends on it, or body armour that won't stop a bullet, all because some civil-service jerk spent the available money on a flush toilet.'

'You men,' Isabella said. 'Girls wouldn't put up with it.'

'The girls don't fight,' I said. 'At least, not in the infantry. Not yet.'

'Will it happen?' she asked.

'Oh, I expect so,' I said.

'Do you mind?'

'Not really, as long as they fight as well as the men. But they will have to be strong to carry all their kit. The Israeli army scrapped their mixed infantry battalions when they suspected the men were carrying the girls' kit in return for sex. They were also worried that the men would stop and look after a wounded female colleague rather than carry on fighting.'

'Human nature is human nature,' Isabella said.

'Certainly is,' I replied. 'Any chance of a bonus?'

5

Back at Kauri House Stables there was still tension in the air between my mother and her husband. I suspected that I'd interrupted an argument as I went through the back door into the kitchen with my bags at three o'clock on Monday afternoon.

'Where has all that stuff come from?' my mother asked with a degree of accusation.

'It's just my things that were in storage,' I said, 'while I was away.'

'Well, I don't know why you've brought it all here,' she said rather crossly.

'Where else would I take it?'

'Oh, I don't know,' she said with almost a sob. 'I don't know bloody anything.' She stormed out clutching her face. I thought she was crying.

'What's all that about?' I asked my stepfather, who had sat silently through the whole exchange.

'Nothing,' he said unhelpfully.

'It must be something.'

'Nothing for you to worry about,' he said.

'Let me be the judge of that,' I said. 'It's to do with money, isn't it?'

He looked up at me. 'I told you, it's nothing.'

'Then why can't you afford to buy her a new car?'

He was angry. Bloody furious, in fact. He stood up quickly.

'Who told you that?' He almost shouted at me.

'You did,' I said.

'No, I bloody didn't,' he said, thrusting his face towards mine and bunching his fists.

'Yes, you did. I overheard you talking to my mother.'

I thought for a moment he was going to hit me.

'How dare you listen in to a private conversation.'

I thought of saying that I couldn't have helped it, so loud had been their voices, but that wasn't completely accurate. I could have chosen not to stay sitting in the kitchen, listening.

'So why can't you afford a new car?' I asked him bluntly.

'That's none of your business,' he replied sharply.

'I think you'll find it is,' I said. 'Anything to do with my mother is my business.'

'No, it bloody isn't!' He now, in turn, stormed out of the kitchen leaving me alone.

And I thought I was meant to be the angry one.

I could hear my mother and stepfather arguing upstairs so I casually walked into their office off the hall.

My stepfather had said that they would have been able to afford a new car if it hadn't been for the 'ongoing fallout' from my mother's 'disastrous little scheme'. What sort of scheme? And why was the fallout ongoing?

I looked down at the desk. There were two stacks of papers on each side of a standard keyboard and a computer monitor that had a moving screen-saver message, 'KAURI HOUSE STABLES', ran across it, over and over.

I tried to make a mental picture of the desk so that I could ensure that I left it as I found it. I suppose I had taken the decision to find out what the hell was going on as soon as I had walked into the office, but that didn't mean I wanted my mother to know I knew.

The stacks of papers had some order to them.

The one on the far left contained bills and receipts to do with the house: electricity, bottled gas, council tax, etc. All paid by bank direct debit. I scanned through them but there was nothing out of the ordinary, although I was amazed to see how expensive it was to heat this grand old house with its ill-fitting windows. Of course, I'd never had to pay a heating bill in my life, and I hadn't been concerned by the cost of leaving a window wide open for ventilation, not even if the outside temperature was below freezing. Perhaps the army should start installing meters in every soldier's room and charge them for the energy used. That would teach them to keep the heat in.

The next stack was bills and receipts for the stables: power, heat, feed, maintenance, together with the salary and PAYE tax papers for the stable staff. There were also some training-fee accounts, one or two with cheques still attached and waiting to be banked. Nothing appeared out of place, certainly nothing to indicate the existence of any 'scheme'.

The third pile was simply magazines and other publications including the blue-printed booklets of the racing calendar. Nothing unusual there.

But it was in the fourth pile that I found the smoking gun. In fact, there were two smoking guns that, together, gave the story.

The first was in a pile of bank statements. Clearly, my mother had two separate accounts, one for her training business and one for private use. The statements showed that, amongst other things, my mother was withdrawing two thousand pounds in cash every week from her private account. This, in itself, would not have been suspicious – many people in racing dealt in cash, especially if they like to gamble in ready money. But it was a second piece of paper that completed the story. It was a simple handwritten note in capital letters scribbled on a sheet torn from a wire-bound notebook. I found it folded inside a plain white envelope addressed to my mother. The message on it was bold and very much to the point:

THE PAYMENT WAS LATE. IF IT IS LATE ONE MORE TIME THEN IT WILL INCREASE TO THREE THOUSAND. IF YOU FAIL TO PAY, A CERTAIN PACKAGE WILL BE DELIVERED TO THE AUTHORITIES.

Plain and simple, it was a blackmail note.

The 'ongoing fallout' my stepfather had spoken about was having to pay two thousand pounds a week to a blackmailer. That worked out at over a hundred thousand pounds a year out of their post-tax income. No wonder they couldn't afford a new BMW.

'What the bloody hell do you think you're doing?'

I jumped.

My mother was standing in the office doorway. I hadn't heard her come downstairs. My mind must have been so engaged by what I'd been reading that I hadn't registered that the shouting match above my head had ceased. And there was no way to hide the fact that I was holding the blackmail note.

I looked at her. She looked down at my hand and the paper it held.

'Oh, my God!' Her voice was little more than a whisper and her legs began to buckle.

I stepped quickly towards her but she went down so fast that I wouldn't have been able to catch her if we had been standing right next to each other.

Fortunately she went down vertically on her collapsing legs, rather than falling straight forward or back, her head making a relatively soft landing on the carpeted floor. But she was still out cold in a dead faint.

I decided to leave her where she had fallen although I did straighten out her legs a bit. I would have been unable to lift her anyway. As it was I had a struggle to get down to my knees to place a small pillow under her head.

She started to come round, opening her eyes with a confused expression.

Then she remembered.

'It's all right,' I said, trying to give her some comfort.

For the first time I could remember, my mother looked frightened. In fact, she looked scared out of her wits with wide staring eyes, and I wasn't sure if the wetness on her brow was the result of fear or the fainting.

'Stay there,' I said to her. 'I'll get you something to drink.'

I went out into the kitchen to fetch a glass of water. As I did so, I carefully folded the blackmail note back into its envelope and placed it in my pocket along with her private-account bank statement. When I went back, I found my stepfather kneeling down beside his wife, cradling her head in his hands.

'What did you do to her?' he shouted at me in accusation.

'Nothing,' I said calmly. 'She just fainted.'

'Why?' he asked, concerned.

I thought about saying something flippant about lack of blood to the brain but decided against it.

'Derek, he knows,' my mother said from her prone position.

'Knows what?' he demanded, sounding alarmed.

'Everything,' she said.

'He can't!'

'I don't know everything,' I said to him. 'But I do know you're being blackmailed.'

It was brandy, not water, that was needed to revive them both, and I had some too.

We were sitting in the drawing room, in deep chintz-covered armchairs with high sides. My mother's face was as pale as the cream-painted walls behind her and her hands shook as she tried to drink from her glass without it chattering against her teeth.

Derek, my stepfather, sat tight-lipped on the edge of his chair knocking back Rémy Martin VSOP like it was going out of fashion.

'So tell me,' I said for the umpteenth time.

Again there was no reply from either of them.

'If you won't tell me,' I said, 'then I will have no choice but to report a case of blackmail to the police.'

I thought for a moment that my mother was going to faint again.

'No,' she did little more than mouth the word. 'Please, no.'

'Then tell me why not,' I said. My voice had seemed loud and strong compared to my mother's.

I remembered back to what my platoon colour sergeant had said at Sandhurst: 'Command needs to be expressed in the correct tone. Half the struggle is won if your men believe you know what you're doing, even if you don't, and a strong decisive tone will give them that belief.'

I was now *in command* of the present situation whether my mother or stepfather believed it or not.

'Because your mother would go to prison,' Derek said slowly.

The brandy must be going to his head, I thought.

'Don't be ridiculous,' I said.

'I'm not,' he said. 'She would. And me too, probably, as an accessory.'

'An accessory to what?' I said. 'Have you murdered someone?'

'No.' He almost smiled. 'Not quite that bad.'

'Then what is it?'

'Tax,' he said. 'Evading tax.'

I looked at my mother.

The shaking had spread from her hands to much of her body, and she was crying as openly as I had never seen her. She certainly didn't look like the woman the entire village was proud of. And she was a shadow of the person who must have collected the National Woman of the Year Award on television just a month before. She suddenly looked much older than her sixty-one years.

'So what are we going to do about it?' I said in my voice-of-command.

'What do you mean?' Derek asked.

'Well, you can't go on paying two thousand pounds a week, now can you?'

He looked up at me in surprise.

'I saw the bank statements,' I said.

He sighed. 'It's not just the money. We might cope if it was just the money.'

'What else?' I asked him.

His shoulders slumped. 'The horses.'

'What about the horses?'

'No,' my mother said but it was barely a whisper.

'What about the horses?' I asked again forcefully.

He said nothing.

'Have the horses had to lose to order?' I asked into the silence.

He gulped and looked down, but his head nodded.

'Is that what happened to Pharmacist?' I asked.

He nodded again. My mother, meanwhile, now had her eyes firmly closed as if no one could see her if she couldn't see them. The shaking had abated but she rocked gently back and forth in the chair.

'How do you get the orders?' I asked Derek.

'On the telephone,' he said.

There were so many questions: how, what, when and, in particular, who?

My mother and stepfather knew the answers to most of them but, sadly, not the last, of that they were absolutely certain.

I refilled their brandy glasses and started the inquisition.

'How did you get into this mess?' I asked.

Neither of them said anything. My mother had shrunk down into her chair as if trying to make herself even more invisible while Derek just drank heavily from his glass, hiding behind the cut crystal.

'Look,' I said, 'if you want me to help you then you will have to tell me what's been going on.'

There was a long pause.

'I don't want your help,' my mother said quietly. 'I want you to go away and leave us alone.'

'But I'm sure we can sort out the problem,' I said in a more comforting manner.

'I can sort it out myself,' she said.

'How?' I asked.

There was another long pause.

'I've decided to retire,' she said.

My stepfather and I sat there looking at her.

'But you can't retire,' he said.

'Why not?' she asked with more determination. She almost sounded like her old self.

'How would we pay?' he said in exasperation. I thought he was now about to cry.

My mother shrank back into her chair.

'The only solution is to find out who is doing this and stop them,' I said. 'And for that I need you to answer my questions.'

'No police,' my mother said.

It was my turn to pause.

'But we might need the police to find the blackmailer.'

'No,' she almost shouted. 'No police.'

'So tell me about this tax business,' I said, trying to make light of it.

'No,' she shouted again. 'No one must know.'

She was desperate.

'I can't help you if I don't know,' I said with a degree of frustration.

'I don't want your help,' my mother said again.

'Josephine, my dear,' Derek said. 'We do need help from someone.'

Another long pause.

'I don't want to go to prison.' She was crying again.

I suddenly felt sorry for her.

It wasn't an emotion with which I was very familiar. I had, in fact, spent most of my life wanting to get even with her; getting my own back for hurts done to me, whether real or imagined; resenting her lack of motherly love and comfort. Perhaps I was now older and more mature. Blood, they say, is always thicker than water. They must be right.

I went over to her chair and sat on the arm, stroking her shoulder and speaking kindly to her for almost the first time in my life.

'Mum,' I said, 'they won't send you to prison.'

'Yes, they will,' she said.

'How do you know?' I asked.

'He says so.'

'The blackmailer?'

'Yes.'

'Well, I wouldn't take his word for it,' I said.

'But . . .' she tailed off.

'Why don't you allow me to give you a second opinion?' I said to her calmly.

'Because you'll tell the police.'

'No, I won't,' I said. But not doing so might make me an accessory as well.

'Do you promise?' she asked.

What could I say? 'Of course, I promise.'

I hoped so much that it was a promise I would be able to keep.

Gradually, with plenty of cajoling and the rest of the bottle of Rémy Martin, I managed to piece together most of the sorry story. And it wasn't good. My mother might indeed go to prison if the police found out. She would almost certainly be convicted of tax evasion. And she would undoubtedly lose her reputation, her home and her business, even if she did manage to retain her liberty.

My mother's 'disastrous little scheme' had, it seemed, been the brainchild of a dodgy young accountant she had met at a party about five years previously. He had convinced her that she should register her training business offshore, in particular, in Gibraltar. Then she would enjoy the tax-free status that such a registration would bring.

Somehow he had managed to assure her that, even though she could go on adding the Value Added Tax amount to the owners' accounts, she was no longer under any obligation to pass on the money to the taxman.

Now, racehorse training fees are not cheap, about the same as sending a teenage child to boarding school, and my mother had seventy-two boxes that were always filled to overflowing. She was in demand, and those in demand could charge premium prices. The tax, between fifteen and twenty per cent of the fees, must have run into several hundred thousand pounds a year.

'But didn't you think it was a bit suspicious?' I asked her in disbelief.

'Of course not,' she said. 'Roderick told me it was all above board and legal. He even showed me documents that proved it was all right.'

Roderick, it transpired, had been the young accountant.

'Do you still have these documents?'

'No. Roderick kept them.'

I bet he did.

'And Roderick said that the owners wouldn't be out of pocket because all racehorse owners can claim back the VAT from the government.'

So it was the government she was stealing from. She wasn't paying the tax in as she should, yet, at the same time, the owners were claiming it back. What a mess.

'But didn't you think it was too good to be true?' I asked.

'Not really,' she said. 'Roderick said that everyone would soon be doing it and I would lose out if I didn't get started quickly.'

Roderick sounded like quite a smooth operator.

'Which firm does Roderick work for?' I asked.

'He didn't work for a firm, he was self-employed,' my mother said. 'He'd only recently qualified at university and hadn't joined a firm. We were lucky to find someone who was so cheap.'

I could hardly believe my ears.

'What happened to John Milton?' I asked her. John Milton had been my mother's accountant for as long as I could remember.

'He retired,' she said. 'And I didn't like the young woman who took over at his office. Far too brusque. That's why I was so pleased to have met Roderick.'

I could imagine that any accountant who didn't do exactly as my mother demanded would be thought of by her as brusque at the very least.

'And what is Roderick's surname?'

'His name was Ward,' she said.

'Was?'

'He's dead,' my mother said with a sigh. 'He was in a car accident. About six months ago.'

'Are you sure?' I asked.

'What do you mean, am I sure?'

'Are you sure that he's dead and hasn't just run away?' I said. 'Are you certain he's not the blackmailer?'

'Thomas,' she said, 'don't be ridiculous. The car crash was reported in the local paper. Of course I'm sure he's dead.'

I felt like asking her if she had actually seen Roderick Ward's lifeless body. In Afghanistan there were no confirmed Taliban 'kills' without the corpse, or at least a human head, to prove it.

'So how long did the little scheme of yours run? When did you stop paying the taxman?'

'Nearly four years ago,' my mother said in a whimper.

'And when did you start paying again?'

'What do you mean?' she asked.

'Are you paying the VAT now?' I asked, dreading the answer.

'No, of course not,' she said. 'How could I start paying again without them asking questions?'

How, I wondered, had she stopped paying without them asking? Surely it could only be a matter of time before she was investigated. Four years of non-payment of VAT must add up to nearly a million pounds in unpaid tax. She should indeed be worried about going to prison.

'Who is doing your accounts now?' I asked. 'Since this Roderick Ward was killed.'

'No one,' she said. 'I was frightened of getting anyone.'

With good reason, I thought.

'Can't you pay the tax now?' I said. 'If you pay everything you owe and explain that you were misled by your accountant, I'm sure that it would prevent you being sent to prison.'

My mother began to cry again.

'We haven't got the money to pay the taxman,' Derek said gloomily.

'But what happened to all of the extra you collected?' I asked.

'It's all gone,' he said.

'It can't have all gone,' I said. 'It must be close to a million pounds.'

'More,' he said.

'So where did it all go?'

'We spent a lot of it,' he said. 'In the beginning, mostly on holidays. And Roderick had some of it, of course.'

Of course.

'And the rest?'

'Some has gone to the blackmailer.' He sounded tired, and resigned. 'I don't honestly know where it went. We've only got about fifty thousand left in the bank.'

That was a start.

'So how much are the house and stables worth?' I asked.

My mother looked horrified.

'Mother, dear,' I said, trying to be kind but firm. 'If I'm going to keep you out of prison then we have to find a way to pay the tax.'

'But you promised me you wouldn't tell the police,' she whined.

'I won't,' I replied. 'But if you really think the taxman won't find out eventually, then you're wrong. The tax office is bound to do a check sometime. And it will be much better for you if we go and tell them before they uncover it for themselves.'

'Oh, God.'

I said nothing, allowing the awful truth to sink in. She must have known, as I did, that the tax inspectors at Her Majesty's Revenue and Customs had little compassion for those they discovered were defrauding the system. The only way to win any friends amongst them was to make a clean breast of things and pay back the money, and before they demanded it.

'Not if I retire,' she said suddenly. 'The taxman won't ever know if I simply retire.'

'But Josephine,' my stepfather said, 'we've already discussed that. How would we pay *him* if you retired?'

I, meanwhile, wasn't so sure that her retirement wouldn't in fact be the best course of action. At least, then she wouldn't be perpetuating the fraud, as she was now, and selling the property might raise the necessary sum. I certainly didn't share my mother's confidence that her retirement would guarantee the taxman wouldn't find out. It might even attract the very attention she was trying to avoid.

Overall, it was quite a mess, and I couldn't readily see a way out of it.

My mother and stepfather went off to bed at nine o'clock, tired and emotional from too much brandy and with the awful realization that their secret was out, and their way of life was in for radical change – and probably for the worse.

I, too, went up to my bedroom, but I didn't go to sleep.

I carefully eased my stump out of the prosthetic leg. It was not a very easy task as I had been overdoing the walking and my leg was sore, the flesh below my knee being swollen by excess fluid. If I wasn't more careful I wouldn't be able to get the damn thing back on again in the morning.

I raised the stump by placing it on a pillow to allow gravity to assist in bringing down the fluid build-up, and then I lay back flat to think.

There was little doubt that my mother and stepfather were up to their necks in real trouble, and they were sinking deeper into the mire with every day that passed.

The solution for them was simple, at least in theory: raise the money, pay it to the taxman, submit a retrospective tax return, report the blackmail to the police, and then pray for forgiveness.

The blackmailer would no longer have a hold over them and maybe the police might even find him and recover some of their money, but I wouldn't bet my shirt on it.

So the first thing to be done was to raise more than a million pounds to hand over to the Revenue.

It was easier said than done. Perhaps I could rob a bank.

Reluctantly, my mother and stepfather had agreed that the house and stables, even in the recent depressed property market, could fetch about two and a half million pounds, if they were lucky. But there was a catch. The house was heavily mortgaged, and the stables had been used as collateral for a bank loan to the training business.

I thought back to the brief conversation I'd had with my stepfather after my mother had gone upstairs.

'So how much free capital is there altogether?' I'd asked him.

'About five hundred thousand.'

I was surprised that it was so little. 'But surely the training business has been earning good money for years.'

'It's not as lucrative as you might think, and your mother has always used any profits to build more stables.'

'So why is there so little free capital value in the property?'

'Roderick advised us to increase our borrowing,' he'd said. 'He believed that capital tied up in property wasn't doing anything useful. He told us that, as it was, our capital wasn't working properly for us.'

'So what did Roderick want you to do with it instead?'

'Buy into an investment fund he was very keen on.'

I again hadn't really wanted to believe my ears.

'And did you?' I'd asked him.

'Oh, yes,' he'd said. 'We took out another mortgage and invested it in the fund.'

'So that money is still safe?' I had asked with renewed hope.

'Unfortunately, that particular investment fund didn't do too well in the recession.'

Why was I not surprised?

'How not too well?' I'd asked him.

'Not well at all, I'm afraid,' he said. 'In fact the fund went into bankruptcy last year.'

'But surely you were covered by some kind of government bailout protection insurance?'

'Sadly not,' he'd said. 'It was some sort of offshore fund.'

'A hedge fund?'

'Yes, that's it. I knew it sounded like something to do with gardens.'

I simply couldn't believe it. I'd been stunned by his naïvety. And it was of no comfort to know that hedge funds had been so named because they had initially been designed to 'hedge' against fluctuations in overall stock prices. The original intention of reducing risks had transformed, over time, into high-risk strategies, capable of returning huge profits when things went well, but also huge losses if they didn't. Recent unexpected declines in the world's equity markets, coupled with banks suddenly calling in their loans, had left offshore tax shelters awash with hedge-fund managers in search of new jobs.

'But didn't you take any advice? From an independent financial adviser or something?'

'Roderick said it wasn't necessary.'

Roderick would. Mr Roderick Ward had obviously spotted my complacent mother and her careless husband coming from a long way off.

'But didn't you ever think that Roderick might have been wrong?'

'No,' he'd said, almost surprised by the question. 'Roderick showed us a brochure about how well the fund had done. It was all very exciting.'

'And is there any money left?'

'I had a letter that said they were trying to recover some of the funds and they would let investors know if they succeeded.'

I took that to mean 'no', there was nothing left.

'How much did you invest in this hedge fund?' I'd asked him, dreading his reply.

'There was a minimum amount we had to invest to be able to join.' He had sounded almost proud of the fact that they had been allowed into the club. Like being pleased to have won tickets for the maiden voyage of the *Titanic*.

I had stood silently in front of him, blocking his route away, waiting for the answer. He hadn't wanted to tell me but he could see that I wasn't going to move until he did.

'It was a million US dollars.'

More than six hundred thousand pounds at the prevailing rate. I suppose it could have been worse, but not much. At least there was some capital left in the real estate, although not enough.

'What about other investments?'

'I've got a few ISAs,' he'd said.

Individual Savings Accounts. Ironically, they were designed for tax-free saving but there was a limit on investment and they could amount to only a few thousand pounds per year. They would help, but alone they were not the solution.

I wondered if the training business itself had any value. It would have if my mother was still the trainer but I doubted that anyone buying the stables would pay much for 'the business'. I had spent my childhood, at my mother's knee, being amazed how contrary racehorse owners could be.

Some of them behaved just like the owners of football clubs, firing the team manager because their team of no-hopers wasn't winning, when the solution would have been to buy better, and more expensive, players in the first place. A cheap, slow horse is just like a cheap two-left-footed footballer – neither will be any good however well they're trained.

There is no telling if the owners would stay or take their horses elsewhere. The latter would be the more likely, unless the person who took over the training was of the same standing as Josephine Kauri, and who could that be who didn't already have a stable full of their own charges?

I had to assume that the business had no intrinsic value other than the real estate in which it operated, plus a bit extra for the tack and the rest of the stable kit.

I lay on my bed and did some mental adding-up: the house and stables might raise half a million; the business might just fetch fifty thousand; and there was another fifty thousand in the bank. Add the ISAs and a few pieces of antique furniture and we were probably still short by more than four hundred thousand.

And my mother and Derek had to live somewhere. Where would they go and what could they earn if Kauri House Stables was sold? My mother was hardly going to find work as a cleaner, especially in Lambourn. She would have rather gone to prison.

But going to prison wasn't an 'either/or' solution anyway. If she was sent down she would still have to pay the tax, and the penalties.

Over the years I had saved regularly from my army pay and had accumulated quite a reasonable nest egg that I had planned to use sometime as a down-payment on a house. And I had invested it in a far more secure manner than my parent so I could be pretty sure of still having about sixty thousand to my name.

I wondered if the Revenue would take instalments on the never-never.

The only other solution I came up with was to approach the circumstances as if I had been in command of my platoon in the middle of Afghanistan, planning a Combat Estimate for an operation against the Taliban:

Problem:	*Enemy in control of objective (tax papers and money).*
Mission:	*Neutralize enemy and retake objective.*
Situation:	*Enemy forces – number, identity and location all unknown.* *Own forces – self only, no reinforcements available.*
Weapons:	*As required and/or as available.*
Execution:	*Initially find and interrogate Roderick Ward or, if really dead, his known associates. Follow up on blackmail notes and telephone messages to determine source.*
Tactics:	*Absolute stealth, no local authorities to be alerted, enemy to be kept unaware of operation until final strike*
Timings:	*Task to be completed asap, and before exposure by local authorities – their timescale unknown.*
H-hour:	*Operation start time:* **right now.**

6

All I could see of him were his eyes, his cold, black eyes that stared at me from beneath his turban. He showed no emotion but simply raised a rusty Kalashnikov to his shoulder. I fired at him but he continued to lift the gun. I fired at him again, over and over, but without any visible effects. I was desperate. I emptied my complete magazine into him but still he swung the barrel of the AK-47 round towards me, lining up the sights with my head. A smile showed in his eyes and I began to scream.

I woke with a start, my heart pumping madly and with sweat all over my body.

'Thomas! Thomas!' someone was shouting, and there was banging on my bedroom door.

'Yes,' I called back into the darkness. 'I'm fine.'

'You were screaming.' It was my mother. She was outside my room on the landing.

'I'm sorry,' I said. 'It was just a bad dream.'

'Goodnight, then,' she called suddenly, and I could hear her footfalls as she moved away.

'Goodnight,' I called back, too quietly and too late.

I suppose it was too much to expect my mother to change the habits of a lifetime but it would have been nice if she had asked me how I was, or if I needed anything, or at least if she could come in to my room to cool my sweating brow, or anything.

I laid my head back onto the pillow.

I could still remember the dream so clearly. In the last couple of months, I had started to have them fairly regularly about the war. They were always a jumble of memories of real incidents coupled with the imagination of my subconscious brain, unalike in so far as they were of different events but all with a common thread – they all ended with me in panic and utter terror. I was always more terrified by the dreams than I remember ever having been in reality.

Except, of course, at the roadside after the IED.

I could remember all too vividly the terrible fear and the awful dread of dying I had experienced as Sergeant O'Leary and I had waited for the casevac helicopter. If I closed my eyes and concentrated I could, even now, see the faces of my platoon as we had passed those ten or fifteen minutes – minutes that had felt like endless hours. I could still remember the look of shock in the face of the platoon's newest arrival, a young eighteen-year-old replacement for a previously wounded comrade. It had been his first sight of real war, and the horror it can do to the frail human body. And I could also recall the mixture of anxiety and relief in the faces of those with more experience: their anxiety for me, and their almost overwhelming relief that it wasn't them lying there with no right foot, their lifeblood draining away into the sand.

I reached over and turned on the light. My bedside clock showed me that it was two thirty in the morning.

I must have been making quite a lot of noise for it to have woken my mother at the other end of the house. That was assuming that she had actually been sleeping and not lying awake contemplating her own troubles.

I sat up on the side of the bed. I needed to pee, but it was not as simple as it sounded. The bathroom was three doors away and that was too far to 'heel-and-toe', or to hop.

I now wished I'd accepted the hospital's offer of crutches.

Instead, I went through the whole wretched rigmarole of attaching my false foot and ankle just in order to go to the loo. How I longed for the days of springing out of bed ready and able to complete a five-mile run before breakfast, or to fight off a Taliban early-morning attack.

Once or twice I had done just that, half asleep and forgetting that I was 'sans foot'. But I had soon been reminded when I'd crashed to the floor. On one occasion I'd done myself a real mischief, opening up the surgical wound on my stump as well as splitting the back of my head on a hospital bedside locker. My surgeon had not been amused.

I made it without upset to the bathroom along the landing and gratefully relieved myself. I caught a glimpse of my face in the shaving mirror as I clumsily turned round in the enclosed space.

'What do you want from life?' I asked my image.

'I don't know,' it answered.

What I really wanted I knew, in my heart, I couldn't have. Flying an aeroplane with tin legs, even a Spitfire, was a completely different ball game to commanding an infantry platoon. The very word 'infantry' implied a foot soldier. I suppose I could ask for a transfer to a tank regiment but, even then, the 'tankies' became foot soldiers if and when their carriage lost a track. I could hardly say, 'Sorry, chaps, you'll have to carry on fighting without me,' as I sat there with my false leg waiting for a lift, now could I?

So what were the reasons I had so enjoyed being an infantry platoon commander? And could I find the same things elsewhere?

I went back to my room, and back to bed, leaving my prosthesis standing alone by the bedroom wall as if on sentry duty.

But sleep didn't come easily.

For the first time since my injury I had faced the true reality of my future, and I didn't like it.

Why me? I asked, yet again. Why had it been me who'd been injured?

Yes, I was angry with the Taliban, and also with life in general and the destiny it had dealt me, but, almost more so, I was frustrated and fed up with myself.

Why had I allowed this to happen? Why? Why?

And what could I do now?

Why me?

I lay awake for a long while trying to find solutions to the unanswerable puzzles of my mind.

In the morning, I set to the more immediate task in hand: identifying the blackmailer, recovering the papers and my mother's money, and making things good with the taxman. It sounded deceptively simple. But where did I start?

With Roderick Ward, the con-man accountant. He had been the architect of this misery, so discovering his whereabouts, alive or dead, must be the first goal. Where had he come from? Was he actually qualified, or was that a lie too? Were there co-conspirators or did he work alone? There were so many questions. Now it was time for answers.

I called Isabella Warren from the phone in the drawing room.

'Oh, hello,' she said. 'We're still speaking, then?'

'Why shouldn't we be?' I asked.

'No reason,' she said. 'Just thought you were disappointed.'

I had been but, if I didn't speak to people who disappoint me, then I'd hardly speak to anyone.

'What are you up to today?' I asked her.

'Nothing,' she said, 'as usual.'

Did I detect a touch of irritation?

'Do you fancy helping me with something?'

'No bonus payments involved?'

'No,' I said. 'I promise. And none will even be requested.'

'I don't mind you asking,' she said with a laugh. 'As long as you don't mind being refused.'

I wouldn't ask, though, I thought, because I *did* mind being refused.

'Can you pick me up at ten?' I asked.

'I thought you said you'd never let me drive you again.' She was still laughing.

'I'll chance it,' I said. 'I need to go into Newbury and the parking is dreadful.'

'Can't you park anywhere,' she said, 'with that leg?'

'I haven't applied for a disabled permit,' I said. 'And I don't intend being qualified to.'

'What do you mean?'

'I want to be able to walk as well as the next man,' I said. 'I don't want to be identified as "disabled".'

'But parking is so much easier with a blue badge. You can park almost anywhere, even on double yellow lines in most places.'

'No matter,' I said. 'I don't have one today and I need a driver. Are you on?'

'Definitely,' she said. 'I'll be there at ten.'

I went out into the kitchen to find my mother coming in from the stables.

'Good morning,' I said to her, still employing my friendlier tone from the previous evening.

'What's good about it?' she said.

'We're both alive,' I said.

She gave me a look that made me wonder if she had thought about not being alive this morning. Was suicide really on her mind?

'We will sort out this problem,' I said in reassurance. 'You've done the hard bit by admitting it to me.'

'I didn't have any choice, did I?' she said angrily. 'You snooped through my office.'

'Please don't be annoyed with me,' I said in my most calming way. 'I'm here to help you.'

Her shoulders drooped and she slumped onto a chair at the kitchen table.

'I'm tired,' she said. 'I don't feel I can carry on.'

'What, with the training?'

'With life,' she said.

'Now, don't be ridiculous.'

'I'm not,' she said. 'I've spent most of the night thinking about it. If I died it would solve all the problems.'

'That's crazy,' I said. 'What would Derek do, for a start?'

She placed her arms on the table and rested her head on them. 'It would clear all the problems for him.'

'No, it wouldn't,' I said with certainty. 'It would just create more. The training business would still have to pay the tax it owes. The house and stables would then definitely have to be sold. You dying would leave Derek homeless and alone as well as broke. Is that what you want?'

She looked up at me. 'I don't know what I want.'

How strange, I thought. I had said the same thing to myself in the night. Neither of us was happy with the futures we saw staring us in the face.

'Don't you want to go on training?' I asked.

She didn't reply but placed her head back down on her arms.

'Assuming the tax problems were solved and the blackmailer was stopped, would you still want to go on training?'

'I suppose so,' she said without looking up. 'It's all I know.'

'And you are so good at it,' I said, trying my best to raise her spirits. 'But tell me, how did you stop Pharmacist winning on Saturday?'

She sat back in the chair and almost smiled. 'I gave him tummy ache.'

'But how?' I asked.

'I fed him some rotten food.'

'Mouldy oats?' I asked.

'No,' she said. 'Green sprouting potatoes.'

'Green potatoes! How on earth did you think of green potatoes?'

'It had worked before,' she said. 'When *he* called the first time and said that Scientific had to lose, I was at my wits end of what to do. If I'd over-galloped him everyone in the stable would know.' She gulped. 'I had to do something. I was desperate. But what could I give him? I had some old potatoes that had gone green and they were mouldy and sprouting. I remembered one of my dogs being ill after eating a green-skinned potato so I peeled them all and then liquidized the peel. I simply poured it down Scientific's throat and hoped it would make him ill.'

'How on earth did you get him to swallow it? It must be so bitter.'

'I simply tied his head up high using the hay-net hook and used a tube to pour it down into his stomach.'

'And it worked?' I asked.

'Seemed to, although the poor old boy was really very ill afterwards. Horses can't vomit so the stuff had to go right through him. I was really scared that he'd die. So I reduced the amount the next time.'

'And it still worked?'

'Yes. But I was so frightened about Pharmacist that I used more again that time. I was worried the potatoes weren't green and rotten enough. I'd had to buy some more.'

'Do you have any of them left?' I asked her.

'They're in the boiler room, with the light on,' she said. 'I read somewhere that high temperatures and bright light make potatoes go green quicker.'

'And how many times have you done this altogether?' I asked her.

'Only six times,' she said, almost apologetically. 'But Perfidio won even though I'd given him the potato peel. It didn't seem to affect him one bit.'

'Did you give it to Oregon at Newbury last week?' Oregon had been one of the horses that Gordon Rambler had written about in the *Racing Post*.

She nodded.

I walked through and opened the boiler room by the back door. The light was indeed on, and there were six neat rows of potatoes sitting on top of the boiler, all of them turning nicely green, some with sprouting eyes.

Would the British Horseracing Authority ever have thought of dope testing for liquidized green sprouting rotten potato peel?

I somehow doubted it.

Isabella took me first to the Newbury Public Library. I wanted to look at past editions of the local newspapers to see what they had to say about the supposed death of one Roderick Ward.

My mother was right. The story of his car crash had been prominently covered on page three of the *Newbury Weekly News* for Thursday 16 July:

ANOTHER FATAL ACCIDENT AT LOCAL BLACKSPOT

Police are investigating after yet another death at one of the most dangerous spots on Oxfordshire's roads. Roderick Ward, 33, of Oxford was discovered dead in his car around 8 a.m. on Monday morning. It is assumed by police that Mr Ward's dark blue Renault Mégane left the road in the early hours of Monday after failing to negotiate the S-bends in the A415 near Standlake. The vehicle is thought to have collided with a bridge wall before toppling into the River Windrush near where it joins the Thames at Newbridge. Mr Ward's car was found almost totally immersed in the water and he is thought to have died of drowning rather than as a result of any trauma caused by the accident. An inquest was opened and adjourned on Tuesday at Oxford Coroner's Court.

The piece discussed at length the relative merits of placing a safety barrier and/or altering the speed limits at that point in the road. It then went on to report on two other fatal accidents in the same week elsewhere within the newspaper's region. I searched the following Thursday's paper for any follow-up report on Roderick Ward but with no success.

I used the library's computerized index to check for any other references to Roderick Ward in the *Newbury Weekly News*. There was nothing else about his accident or death, but there was a brief mention from three months before it. The paper reported that a Mr Roderick Ward, of Oxford, had pleaded guilty in Newbury Magistrates' Court to a charge of causing criminal damage to a private home in Hungerford. It stated that he had been observed by a police officer throwing a brick through a window of a house in Willow Close. He was bound over to keep the peace by the magistrates and warned as to his future conduct. In addition, he was ordered to pay £250 to the home owner in compensation for the broken glass and for the distress caused.

Unfortunately, the report gave no further details, for example the name of the house owner or the identity of the policeman who witnessed the event.

I searched through the index again but there was no report of any inquest into Roderick Ward's untimely death. For that, I suspected, I would have to go to Oxford, to the archive of the *Oxford Mail* or the *Oxford Times*.

Isabella had been waiting patiently, exploring the fiction

shelves of the library as I had been scanning the newspapers using the microfiche machines.

'Finished?' she asked as I reappeared from the darkened room where the machines were kept.

'Yes,' I said. 'For the time being.'

'Where to now?' she said as we climbed back into her Golf.

'Oxford,' I said. I thought for a moment. 'Or Hungerford.'

'Which?'

'Hungerford. I think I can probably find what I want from Oxford on the internet.' If I could get onto it, I thought. My mother had to have broadband. Surely it was needed for her to do the race entries.

'So where in Hungerford?'

'Willow Close.'

'Where's that?'

'I've no idea,' I said. 'But it's in Hungerford somewhere.'

Isabella looked at me quizzically but resisted the temptation to actually ask why I wanted to go to Willow Close in Hungerford. Instead, she started the car and turned out of the library car park.

In truth, I could have easily parked my Jaguar at the library, and I was pretty sure from its name that parking in Willow Close wouldn't be a problem either. I probably hadn't needed to ask Isabella to drive me but it felt more like an adventure with someone else to share it.

Willow Close, when we finally found it, was deep in a housing estate off the Salisbury road in the south-western corner of the town. There were twenty or so houses in the close, all little detached boxes with neat open-plan front gardens, each one indistinguishable from those recently built in Lambourn. I feared for the individual character of villages and towns with so many identical little homes springing up all over the countryside.

'Which number?' Isabella said.

'I've no idea,' I said again.

'What are we looking for?' she asked patiently.

'I've no idea of that either.'

'Useful.' She was smiling. 'Then you start at one end and I'll start at the other.'

'Doing what?' I asked.

'Asking if anyone has any idea why we're here.'

'Someone threw a brick through the window of one of these houses and I would like to know why.'

'Any particular brick?' she asked sarcastically.

'OK, OK,' I said. 'I know it sounds odd but that's why we're here. I'd like to talk to the person whose window was smashed.'

'Why?' she asked, unable to contain her curiosity any longer. 'What is this all about?'

It was a good question. Coming to Hungerford had probably been a wild-goose chase anyway. I didn't particularly want to tell Isabella about Roderick Ward, mostly because I had absolutely no intention of explaining anything to her about my mother's tax situation.

'The young man who's been accused of throwing the brick is a soldier in my platoon,' I lied. 'It's an officer's job to look after his troops and I promised him I would investigate. That's all.'

She seemed satisfied, if a little uninterested. 'And do you have a name for the person whose window was broken?'

'No.'

'And no address,' she said.

'No,' I agreed, 'but it was reported in the local newspaper as having happened in Willow Close, Hungerford.'

'Right then,' she said decisively. 'Let's go and ask someone.'

We climbed out of the car.

'Let's start at number sixteen,' I said, pointing at one of the houses. 'I saw the net curtains in the front room twitch when we arrived. Perhaps they keep an eye on everything that goes on here.'

'I'm not buying,' an elderly woman's voice shouted through the door of number sixteen. 'I never buy from door-to-door salesmen.'

'We're not selling,' I shouted back through the wood. 'We'd just like to ask you some questions.'

'I don't want any religion, either,' the woman shouted again. 'Go away.'

'Do you remember someone throwing a brick through one of your neighbours' windows?' I asked her.

'What?' she said.

I repeated the question with more volume.

'That wasn't one of my neighbours,' she said with certainty. 'That was down the end of the close.'

'Which house?' I asked her, still through the closed door.

'Down the end,' she repeated.

'I know,' I said, 'but which house?'

'George Sutton's house.'

'Which number?' I asked.

'I don't know numbers,' she said. 'Now go away.'

I noted that there was a Neighbourhood Watch sticker on the frosted glass next to the door, and I didn't really want her calling the police.

'Come on, let's go,' I said to Isabella. 'Thank you,' I called loudly through the door at the woman. 'Have a nice day.'

We went back to the Golf and I could see the net curtains twitching again. I waved as we climbed back into Isabella's car and she drove away down towards the end of the close and out of the woman's sight.

'Which house do you fancy?' I asked as we stopped at the end.

'Let's try the one with the car in the drive,' Isabella said.

We walked up the driveway past a bright yellow Honda Jazz and rang the doorbell. A smart young woman answered, carrying a baby on her hip.

'Yes?' she said. 'Can I help you?'

'Hello,' said Isabella, jumping in and taking the lead. 'Hello, little one,' she said to the child, tickling its chin. 'We're trying to find Mr Sutton.'

'Old Man Sutton or his son?' the young woman asked helpfully.

'Either,' Isabella said, still fussing over the child.

'Old Man Sutton has gone into an old-folks nursing home,' the woman said. 'His son comes round sometimes to collect his post.'

'How long has Mr Sutton been in a nursing home?' I asked.

'Since just before Christmas. He'd been going downhill for quite a while. Such a shame. He seemed a nice old chap.'

'Do you know which home he's in?' I asked her.

'Sorry,' she said, shaking her head.

'And which house is his?'

'Number eight,' she said, pointing across the road.

'Do you remember an incident when someone threw a brick through his window?' I asked.

'I heard about it, but it happened before we moved in,' she said. 'We've only been here eight months or so. Since Jimbo here was born.' She smiled down at the baby.

'Do you know how I can contact Mr Sutton's son?' I asked her.

'Hold on,' she said. 'I've got his telephone number somewhere.'

She disappeared into the house but was soon back with a business card, but without little Jimbo.

'Here it is,' she said. 'Fred Sutton.' She read out his number and Isabella wrote it down.

'Thank you,' I said. 'I'll give him a call.'

'He might be at work right now,' the woman said. 'He works shifts.'

'I'll try him anyway,' I said. 'What does he do?'

She consulted the business card that was still in her hand.

'He's a policeman,' she said. 'A detective sergeant.'

'So why, all of a sudden, don't you want to call this Fred Sutton?' Isabella demanded. We were again sitting in her car, having driven out of Willow Close and into the centre of Hungerford.

'I will. But I'll call him later.'

'But I thought you wanted to know about this brick through the window,' she said.

'I do.' I dearly wanted to know why the brick was thrown, but did I now dare ask?

'Well, call him, then.'

I was beginning to be sorry that I had asked Isabella to drive me. How could I explain to her that I didn't want to discuss anything to do with Willow Close with any member of the police, let alone a detective sergeant? If he was any good at his job, his detective's antennae would be throbbing wildly as soon as I mentioned anything to do with a Roderick Ward, especially if, as I suspected, DS Fred Sutton had been the policeman who had witnessed young Mr Ward throwing the brick through his father's window in the first place.

'I can't,' I said. 'I can't involve the police.'

'Why on earth not?' she asked, rather self-righteously.

'I just can't,' I said. 'I promised my young soldier I wouldn't talk to the police.'

'But why not?' she asked again, imploring me to answer.

I looked at her. 'I'm really sorry,' I said. 'But I can't tell you why.' Even to my ears, I sounded melodramatic.

'Don't be so bloody ridiculous.' She was clearly annoyed. 'I think I'd better take you home now.'

'Maybe that would be best,' I said.

My chances of any future bonuses had obviously diminished somewhat.

I passed the afternoon using my mother's computer in her office and its internet connection. She probably wouldn't have liked it but, as she was out when Isabella had dropped me back, I hadn't asked.

I did have my own computer, a laptop. It had been in one of the blue holdalls I'd retrieved from Aldershot, but my mother hadn't moved into the wireless age yet, so it was easier to use her old desktop model and with its internet cable plugged straight into the telephone point in the wall.

I looked up reports of inquests using the online service of the *Oxford Mail*. There were masses of them, hundreds and hundreds, even thousands.

I searched for an inquest with the name Roderick Ward and there it was, reported briefly on by the paper on Wednesday 15 July. But it had been only the opening and adjournment of the inquest immediately after the accident.

It would appear that the full inquest was yet to be heard. However, the short report did contain one interesting piece of information that the *Newbury Weekly News* had omitted. According to the *Oxford Mail* website, Roderick Ward's body had been formally identified at the short hearing by his sister, a Mrs Stella Beecher, also from Oxford.

Perhaps Mr Roderick Ward really was dead, after all.

7

At nine o'clock sharp on Tuesday evening my mother received another demand from the blackmailer.

The three residents of Kauri House were suffering through another unhappy dinner round the kitchen table when the telephone rang. Both my mother and stepfather jumped, and then they looked at each other.

'Nine o'clock,' my stepfather said. '*He* always calls at exactly nine o'clock.'

The phone continued to ring. Neither of them seemed very keen to answer it so I stood up and started to move towards it.

'No,' my mother screamed, leaping to her feet. 'I'll get it.'

She pushed past me and grabbed the receiver.

'Hello,' she said tentatively into the phone. 'Yes, this is Mrs Kauri.'

I was standing right next to her and I tried to hear what the person at the other end was saying, but he or she was speaking too softly.

My mother listened for less than a minute.

'Yes. I understand,' my mother said finally. She placed the phone back in its cradle. 'Scientific at Newbury, on Saturday.'

'To lose?' I asked.

She nodded. 'In the Game Spirit Steeplechase.'

She walked like a zombie back to her chair and sat down heavily.

I picked up the phone and dialled 1471, the code to find the number of the last caller.

'Sorry,' said a computerized female voice, 'the caller withheld their number.'

I hadn't expected anything else but it had been worth a try. I wondered if the phone company might be able to give me the number but that, I was sure, would involve explaining why I needed it. I also thought it highly unlikely that the blackmailer had been using his own phone or a number that was traceable back to him.

'What chance would you expect Scientific to have anyway?' I asked.

'Fairly good,' she said. 'He's really only a novice and this race is a considerable step up in class, but I think he's ready for it.' Her shoulders slumped. 'But it's not bloody fair on the horse. If I make him ill again it may ruin him for ever. He'll always associate racing with being ill.'

'Would he really remember?' I asked.

'Oh yes,' she said. 'Lots of my good chasers over the years have been hopeless at home only to run like the wind on a racecourse because they liked it there. One I had years ago, a chestnut called Butterfield, he only ran well at Sandown.' She smiled remembering. 'Old boy loved Sandown. I thought it was to do with right-handed tracks but he wouldn't go at Kempton. It had to be Sandown. He definitely remembered.'

I could see a glimpse of why my mother was such a good trainer. She adored her horses and she spoke of Butterfield as an individual, and with real affection.

'But Scientific is not the odds-on sure thing that Pharmacist was meant to be at Cheltenham last week?'

'No,' she said. 'There's another very good chaser in the race, Sovereign Owner. He'll probably start favourite, although I really think we could beat him, especially if it rains a bit more before Saturday. And Newark Hall may run in the race as well. He's one of Ewen's and he should have a reasonable chance.'

'Ewen?' I asked.

'Ewen Yorke,' she said. 'Trains in the village. Has some really good horses this year. The "up and coming" young opposition.'

From her tone, I concluded that Ewen Yorke was more of a threat to her position as 'top dog' in Lambourn than she was happy with.

'So Scientific is far from a dead cert?' I said.

'He should win,' she stressed again. 'Unless he crossfires.'

'Crossfires?' I asked. 'What's that?'

'It's when a horse canters and leads with a different leg in front than he does at the rear,' she explained.

'OK,' I said slowly, none the wiser. 'And does Scientific do that?'

'Sometimes. Unusually, he tends to canter between his walk and gallop,' she said. 'And, if he crossfires, he can cut into himself, hitting his front leg with his hind hoof. But he hasn't done it recently. Not for ages.'

'OK,' I said again. 'So, even supposing that Scientific doesn't crossfire, no one would be vastly surprised if he didn't win.'

'No,' she agreed. 'It would be disappointing, but no surprise.'

'So,' I said, 'after that call from our friend just now, all we have to do is ensure he doesn't win on Saturday without making him so ill he gives up on the idea of racing altogether.'

She stared at me. 'But how?'

'I can think of a number of ways,' I said. 'How about if he doesn't run in the first place? You could simply not declare him and tell everyone he was lame or something.'

'*He* said the horse had to run,' she replied gloomily.

Time to move on to plan B.

'Well how about a bit of over-training on Thursday or Friday? Give him too much of a gallop so he's worn out on Saturday.'

'But everyone would know,' she said.

'Would they really?' I thought she was being overly worried.

'Oh, yes, they would,' she said. 'There are always people watching the horses work. Some of them are from the media, but most are spotters for the bookmaking firms. They know every horse in Lambourn by sight and they would see all too easily if I gave Scientific anything more than a gentle pipe-opener on Thursday or Friday.'

Was there a plan C?

'Can't you make his saddle slip or something?' I asked.

'The girths will be tightened by the assistant starter just before the race starts.'

'But can't you go down to the start and do it yourself and just leave them loose?' Was I clutching at straws?

'But the jockey would fall off,' she said.

'At least that would stop him winning,' I said with a smile.

'But he might be injured.' She shook her head. 'I can't do that.'

Plan D?

'How about if you cut through the reins just enough so that they break during the race? If the jockey can't steer then he surely can't win.'

'Tell that to Fred Winter,' she said.

'What?'

'Fred Winter,' she repeated. 'He won the Grand Steeple-Chase de Paris on Mandarin with no steering, way back in the early sixties. The bit broke, which meant he had no brakes either. He used his legs, pressing on the sides of the horse to keep it on the figure-of-eight course. It was an absolutely amazing piece of riding.'

'And will this Fred Winter be the jockey on Scientific on Saturday?' I asked.

'No, of course not,' she said. 'He died years ago.'

'Well, in that case, don't you think it's a good idea?'

'What?'

'To make the reins break.' God, this was hard work.

'But . . .'

'But, what?' I asked.

'I'd be the laughing stock,' she said miserably. 'Horses from Kauri House Stables don't go to the races with substandard tack.'

'Would you rather be laughed at or arrested for tax evasion?'

It was a cruel thing to say but it did bring the problems she faced into relative order.

'Thomas is right, dear,' my stepfather said, somewhat belatedly entering the conversation.

'So, it's agreed, then,' I said. 'We won't subject Scientific to the green-potato-peel treatment but we will try to arrange for his reins to break during the race. And we take our chances.'

'I suppose so,' my mother said reluctantly.

'Right,' I said positively. 'That's the first decision made.'

My mother looked up at me. 'And what other decisions do you have in mind?'

'Nothing specific as yet,' I said. 'But I do have some questions.'

She looked back at me with doleful eyes. Why did I think she knew the questions wouldn't be welcome?

'Firstly,' I said, 'when is your next Value Added Tax return due?'

'I told you, I don't pay VAT,' my mother said.

'But the stables must have a VAT registration for the other bills like the horses' feed, the purchase of tack, and all sorts of other stuff. Don't the race entries attract VAT?'

'Roderick cancelled our registration,' she said.

If Roderick hadn't already been dead, I'd have wrung his bloody neck.

'How about the other tax returns?' I said. 'Your personal one and the training business return. When are they due?'

'Roderick dealt with all that.'

'But who has been doing it since Roderick died?' I asked in desperation.

'No one,' she said. 'But I did manage to do the PAYE return last month on my own.'

At least that was something. PAYE, or pay as you earn, was the way most UK workers paid their income tax. The tax amount was deducted from their salaries by their employer and paid directly to the Treasury. The non-arrival of the PAYE money was usually the first indication to the taxman that a company was in deep financial trouble. It would have rung serious alarm bells at the tax office, and representatives of HM Revenue and Customs would have been hammering on the kitchen door long before now.

'Where do you keep your tax papers?' I asked.

'Roderick had them.'

'But you must have copies of your tax returns,' I implored.

'I expect so,' she said. 'They might be in one of the filing cabinets in the office.'

I was amazed that anyone who was so brilliant at the organization and training of seventy-two racehorses, with all the decisions and red tape that must be involved to satisfy the Rules of Racing, could be so completely hopeless when it came to anything financial.

'Don't you have a secretary?' I asked.

'No,' she said. 'Derek and I do all the paperwork between us.'

Or not, I thought, as the case may be.

I was pretty certain that my mother's individual self-assessment tax return, as for every other self-employed person in the United Kingdom, should have been filed with the tax office by midnight on 31 January at the very latest, along with the payment of any income tax due.

I looked up at the calendar on the wall above her desk. It was already 9 February. There were no exceptions to the deadline so she would have already incurred a penalty for late filing, to say nothing of the interest for late payment.

I'd checked the HMRC website on the internet. It confirmed that she would have notched up an automatic £100 late-filing penalty plus interest on the overdue tax. It also said that she had until the end of February before a five per cent surcharge of the tax due was added, on top of the interest.

Very soon now, the Revenue was probably going to start asking difficult questions about my mother's accounts. The time left to sort out the mess was unknown, but it had to be short. Maybe it was already too late and the Revenue would be at her door in the morning.

I wondered about my own tax affairs.

As an employee, I paid my tax as I earned it, which meant I didn't need to complete an annual tax return. The army deducted my tax and National Insurance before it paid the remainder of my salary into my bank account. Mostly they took off my board and lodging costs too, but there hadn't been any of those for a while. Even the army couldn't charge me to stay in a National Health hospital.

Sometime soon I should be receiving a tax-free lump sum of nearly a hundred thousand pounds from the Armed Forces Compensation Scheme, although how they could put a value on the loss of a lower leg and foot is anyone's guess. The major from the MOD had taken away my completed AFCS form with a promise that it would be dealt with promptly. That had been nearly three weeks ago now but I had long ago learned that anything less than six months was 'promptly' as far as army finances were concerned.

Perhaps it might help to keep the taxman's handcuffs from my mother's wrists. But would it be enough? And would it arrive in time?

*

I searched through my mother's filing cabinets and, eventually, I found her previous year's tax return filed under R, for Roderick. Where else?

The tax return was a piece of art. It clearly showed that my mother had only minimal personal income, well below that which would have incurred any tax to be paid. It stated that her monthly income was just two hundred pounds from her business, mere pocket money.

Perhaps the Revenue might not be knocking at her door in the morning after all, even if they could find it.

Possibly designed to confuse them, the return was not in the name of Mrs Josephine Kauri and her address was not recorded as Kauri House Stables. It wasn't even in Lambourn but at 26 Banbury Drive, Oxford. However, I did recognize the signature as being that of my mother, in her familiar curly handwriting.

Only the name was unfamiliar. She had signed the form Jane Philips, her real, legal, married name.

In the same filing cabinet, I also found a Kauri House Stables corporate tax return for the previous year. It was dated May, so at least we had some breathing space before the next one was due.

I looked through it. Roderick had worked his magic here as well.

How, I wondered, did my mother afford to pay two thousand pounds a week in blackmail demands if, as according to the tax returns, her personal income was less than two and a half thousand a year, and her business made such a small profit that it paid tax only in three figures, in spite of all the extras paid by the horse owners in non-existent VAT.

But, of course, I could find no records of the profits made by the company called Kauri House Stables (Gibraltar). In fact, there was no reference to any such entity anywhere in the R for Roderick drawer of the filing cabinet, or anywhere else for that matter. However, I did find one interesting sheet of paper nestling amongst the tax returns. It was a letter from an investment fund manager welcoming my mother and stepfather into the select group of individuals invited to invest in his fund. The letter was dated three years previously and had been signed by a Mr Anthony Cigar of Rock Bank (Gibraltar) Ltd.

Mr Cigar hadn't actually used the term 'hedge fund' but it was quite clear from his letter, and from the attached fee schedule, that a hedge fund was what he'd managed.

I sat at my mother's desk and looked up Rock Bank (Gibraltar) Ltd on the internet. I typed the name into Google and then clicked on the bank's own web address. The computer came back with the answer that the website was under construction and was unavailable to be displayed.

I went back to the Google page and clicked on the site for the *Gibraltar Chronicle*, one of the references that had mentioned the Rock Bank. It reported that, back in September, Parkin & Cleeve Ltd, a UK-based firm of liquidators, had unsuccessfully filed a suit in the High Court in London against the individual directors of Rock Bank (Gibraltar) Ltd in an attempt to recover money on behalf of several of their clients. The directors were not named by the report and the *Chronicle* had been unable to obtain a response from any representative of the bank.

It didn't bode well for the recovery of my mother's million dollars.

I yawned and looked at my watch. It was ten to midnight and my mother and Derek had long before gone up to bed, and it was also well past my bedtime.

I flicked off the light in the office and went up the stairs.

My first day as 'sleuth-in-residence' at Kauri House Stables hadn't gone all my own way. I hoped for better news in the morning.

*

When I came down to breakfast at eight o'clock I found my stepfather sitting silently staring at a single brown envelope, which was lying on the bleached-pine kitchen table with ON HER MAJESTY'S SERVICE in bold type along the top.

'Have you opened it?' I asked him.

'Of course not,' he said. 'It's addressed to your mother.'

'Where is she?' I asked.

'Still out with the first lot,' he said.

I picked up the envelope and looked at the back. 'IN CASE OF NON-DELIVERY PLEASE RETURN TO HMRC was printed across the flap, so there was no mistake – it was definitely from the taxman.

I slid my finger under the flap and ripped open the envelope.

'You can't do that,' my stepfather said indignantly.

'I just did,' I said, taking out the contents. I unfolded the letter. It was simply a routine monthly reminder for her PAYE payments for the stable staff.

'It's OK,' I said. 'This is just a reminder notice. It was generated by a computer. No one is going to come here. Not yet, anyway.'

'Are you sure?' he asked, still looking worried.

'Yes,' I said. 'But they will come in the end if we don't do something about this mess.'

'But what can we do?' he said.

It was a good question.

'I don't know yet,' I said, 'but I do know that we will be in even more trouble if we do nothing and then the taxman comes calling. We simply have to go to them with answers before they come to us with questions.'

My mother swept into the kitchen and placed her hands on the Aga.

'God, it's cold out there,' she said. Neither my stepfather nor I said anything. She turned round. 'What's wrong with you two? Quiet all of a sudden?'

'A letter has arrived from the tax office,' my stepfather said.

In spite of her cold-induced rosy cheeks, my mother went a shade paler.

'It's all right,' I said in a more reassuring tone than her husband's. 'It's just an automatic PAYE reminder. Nothing to worry about.' I tossed the letter onto the kitchen table.

'Are you certain?' she asked, moving forward and picking it up.

'Yes,' I said. 'But I was saying to Derek here, we will have to tell the taxman soon about what's happened, and before he starts asking us difficult questions we can't answer.'

'Why would he?'

'Because you should have sent them a tax return by January the thirty-first.'

'Oh,' she said. 'But why does that mean we have to tell them everything? Why can't I just send them a tax return now?'

Why not indeed? I thought. As things stood, I could just about argue that I was not an accessory to tax evasion, but I certainly wouldn't be able to if I helped her send in a fraudulent tax return.

Junior officers have to learn, from cover to cover, the contents of a booklet entitled *Values and Standards of the British Army*. Paragraph twenty-seven states:

Those entrusted with public and non-public funds must adhere unswervingly to the appropriate financial regulations. Dishonesty or deception in the control and management of these funds is not a 'victimless crime' but shows a lack of integrity and moral courage which has a corrosive effect on operational effectiveness through the breakdown in trust.

'Let's leave it for a few days,' I said. 'The tax website says you won't get any more penalties until the end of the month.' Other than the interest, of course.

*

I left my mother and Derek to reflect on things in the kitchen while I went out to the stable yard in search of Ian Norland.

'You're still here, then?' he said as I found him in the feed store.

'Seems so,' I said.

I stood in silence and watched him measure out some oats from a hopper into some metal bowls.

'I'm not going to talk to you,' he said. 'It nearly cost me my job last time.'

'We've moved on since then.'

'Who has?'

'My mother and me,' I said. 'We're now on the same side.'

'I'll wait for her to tell me that, if you don't mind.'

'She's in the kitchen right now,' I said. 'Go and ask her.'

'I think I'll wait for her to come out.'

'No,' I insisted. 'Please go and ask her now. I need to talk to you.'

He went off reluctantly in the direction of the house, looking back once or twice as if I might call him back and say it was all a joke. I hoped my mother wouldn't actually bite his head off.

In his absence I went from the feed store into the tack room next door. It was all very neat and smelled strongly of leather, like those handbag counters in Oxford Street department stores. On the left-hand wall there were about twenty metal saddle racks, about half of which were occupied by saddles with their girths wrapped round them. On the opposite wall there were rows of coat hooks holdings bridles and, at the end between the saddles and bridles, there were shelves of folded horse rugs and other paraphernalia including a box of assorted bits and a couple of riding helmets.

It was the bridles I was most interested in.

As I looked at them one of the stable staff came in and collected a saddle from one of the racks and a bridle from a hook.

'Are these bridles specific to each horse?' I asked him.

'No, mate,' he said. 'Not usually. The lads have one each and there are a few spare. This is mine.' He held up the one he had just removed from a hook. 'My saddle, too.'

'Did you have to buy it?' I asked him.

'Naah, of course not,' he said with a grin. 'This is the one the guv'nor gives me to use, while I'm 'ere, like.'

'And are these saddles also used in the races?'

'Naah,' he said again. 'The jocks have their own saddles.'

'And their own bridles?'

'Naah,' he said once more. 'But we 'ave special racing ones of those. Jack keeps them in the racing tack room with the other stuff.'

'Who's Jack?' I said.

'Travelling 'ead lad.' He paused. 'Who are you, anyway?'

'I'm Mrs Kauri's son,' I said.

'Oh, yeah,' he said, glancing down at my right leg. 'I 'eard you were 'ere.'

'Where is the racing tack room?' I asked him.

'Round the other side,' he said, pointing through the far wall, the one with the shelves.

'Thank you, Declan,' my mother said domineeringly, coming into the tack room. 'Now, get on.'

Declan went bright pink and scurried away with his saddle and bridle under his arm.

'I'll thank you not to interrogate my staff,' she said.

I walked round her and pulled the tack-room door shut.

'Mother,' I said formally. 'If you want me to go now, I will.' I paused briefly. 'I'll also try to visit you in Holloway Prison.' She opened her mouth to speak but I cut her off. 'Or you can let me help you and I might just keep you out of jail.'

Actually, secretly, I was beginning to think that the chances of managing that were very slight.

She stood tight-lipped in front of me. I thought she might cry again but at that moment Ian Norland opened the tack-room door behind her and joined us.

'Ian,' my mother said without turning round, her voice full of emotion. 'You may say what you like to my son. Please answer any questions he might ask you. Show him whatever he wants to see. Give him whatever help he needs.'

With that, she turned abruptly and marched out of the tack room, closing the door behind her.

'I told you last week that something bloody strange was going on round here,' Ian said. 'And it sure is.' He paused. 'I'll answer your questions and I'll show you what you want to see, but don't ask me to help you if it's illegal.'

'I won't,' I said.

'Or against the Rules of Racing,' he said.

'I won't do that either,' I said. 'I promise.'

I hoped it was another promise I'd be able to keep.

To my eye, the racing bridles looked identical to those in the general tack room. However, Ian assured me they were newer and of better quality.

'The reins are all double stitched to the bit rings,' he said, showing me, 'so that there's less chance of them breaking during the race.'

Both the bridles and the reins were predominantly made of leather, although there was a fair amount of metal and rubber as well.

'Does each horse have its own bridle?' I asked.

'They do on any given race day,' Ian said. 'But we have fifteen racing bridles in here and they do for all our runners.'

We were in the racing tack room. Apart from the bridles hanging on hooks there was a mountain of other equipment, the most colourful being the mass of jockeys' silks hanging on a rail. There were also two boxes of special bits, and others of blinkers, visors, cheek-pieces, and sheepskin nosebands. Up against the far wall, on top of a sort of sideboard, there were neat stacks of horse blankets, weight cloths, and under-saddle pads, and there was even a collection of padded jackets for the stable staff to wear in the parade ring.

'So, say on Saturday, when Scientific runs at Newbury,' I said. 'Can you tell which bridle he'll use?'

Ian looked at me strangely. 'No,' he said. 'Jack will take any one of these.' He waved a hand at the fifteen bridles on their hooks.

To be honest, that wasn't the most helpful of answers.

'Don't any of the horses have their own bridle?' I asked, trying not to sound desperate.

'One or two,' he said. 'Old Perfidio has his own. That's because he has a special bit to try and stop him biting his tongue during the race.'

'But doesn't sharing tack result in cross-contamination?' I said.

'Not that we've noticed. We always dip bridles in disinfectant after every use, even the regular exercise ones.'

I could see that making Scientific's bridle or reins break on Saturday in the Game Spirit Steeplechase was not going to be as easy as I had imagined, at least not without Ian or Jack knowing about it.

'How about special nosebands?' I asked. 'Why, for example, do some horses run in sheepskin nosebands?'

'Some trainers run all their horses in sheepskin nosebands,' Ian said. 'It helps them to see which horse is theirs. The colours aren't very easy to see when the horses are coming straight at you, especially if it's muddy.'

'Do my mother's horses all wear them?'

'No,' he said. 'Not as a general rule. But we do use them occasionally if a horse tends to run with his head held up.'

'Why's that?'

'If a horse runs with his head too high he isn't looking at the bottom of the fences, and also when the jockey pulls the reins the horse will lift it higher, not put it down like he should. So we put a nice thick sheepskin on him and he has to lower his head a little to see where he's going.'

'Amazing,' I said. 'Does it really work?'

'Of course it works,' he said, almost affronted. 'We wouldn't do it if it didn't work. We also sometimes put cross nosebands on them to keep their mouths shut, especially if they're a puller. Keeping their mouths closed often stops them pulling too hard. Or an Australian noseband will lift the bit higher in the mouth to stop a horse putting his tongue over it.'

'Is that important?' I asked.

'It can be,' Ian said. 'If a horse puts his tongue over the bit it can push on the back of the mouth and put pressure on the airway so the horse can't breathe properly.'

There was clearly so much I didn't know about racehorse training.

'I think you might have to revert to the liquidized green-potato-peel,' I said to my mother when I went back into the kitchen.

'Why?' she said.

'Because I can't see how we are going to arrange for Scientific's reins to break during the race on Saturday if we can't even be sure which bridle he'll be wearing.'

'I'll ask Jack,' she said.

'That might be a bit suspicious,' I said. 'Especially after the race. Much better if we can be sure ahead of time which bridle he'll be wearing. Can't you run him in a sheepskin noseband?'

'That won't help,' she said. 'We simply fit the sheepskin to a regular bridle using Velcro.'

'Can't you think of anything?' I asked, not quite in desperation. 'How about a cross or an Australian noseband?'

'He could run in an Australian, I suppose. That would mean he would have to have the one bridle we have fitted with it.'

'Good,' I said. 'But you'll have to show me.'

'What, now?'

'No, later, when Ian and Jack have gone,' I said. 'And make sure Scientific is the only horse this week that runs in it.'

The phone rang. My mother walked across the kitchen and picked it up.

'Hello,' she said. 'Kauri House.'

She listened for a moment.

'It's for you,' she said, holding the telephone out towards me. I thought I detected a touch of irritation in her voice.

'Hello?' I said.

'Hi, Tom. It's Issy Warren. Would you like to come to supper tomorrow night?'

'I thought you were cross with me,' I said.

'I am,' she replied bluntly. 'But I always invite people I'm cross with to supper. Have you tasted my cooking?'

I laughed. 'OK, I'll chance it. Thanks.'

'Great. Seven thirty or thereabouts, at the Hall.'

'Black tie?' I asked.

'Absolutely,' she said, laughing. 'No, of course not. Very casual. I'll be in jeans. It's just a kitchen supper with friends.'

'I'll bring a bottle.'

'That would be great,' she said. 'See you tomorrow.'

She disconnected and I handed the phone back to my mother, smiling.

'I don't know why you want to associate with that woman,' she said in her most haughty voice. She made it sound as though I was fraternizing with the enemy.

I wasn't in the mood to have yet another argument with her

over whom I should and should not be friends with. We had done enough of that throughout my teenage years, and she had usually won by refusing entry to the house for my friends of whom she hadn't approved, which, if I remembered correctly, had been most of them.

'Are you going to the races today?' I asked her instead.

'No,' she replied. 'I've no runners today.'

'Do you only go to the races if you have a runner?' I asked.

She looked at me as if I was a fool. 'Of course.'

'I thought you might go just for the enjoyment of it.' I said.

'Going to the races is my job,' she said. 'Would you do your job on days you didn't have to just for the enjoyment?'

Actually, I would have but, there again, I enjoyed doing the things others might have found squeamish.

'I might,' I said.

'Not to Ludlow or Carlisle on a cold winter Wednesday, you wouldn't.' She had a point. 'It's not like Royal Ascot in June.'

'No,' I agreed. 'So you can show me which bridle Scientific will use after lunch when the stable staff are off.'

'Do you really think you can make the reins break during the race?' she asked.

'I had a good look at them,' I said. 'I think it might be possible.'

'But how?'

'The reins are made of leather but they have a non-slip rubber covering sewn round them, like the rubber on a table-tennis bat but with smaller pimples.' She nodded. 'The rubber is thin and not very strong. If I was able to break the leather inside the rubber then it wouldn't be visible and the reins would part during the race when the jockey pulls on them.'

'It seems very risky,' she said.

'Would you rather use your green-potato-peel soup?' I asked.

'No,' she said adamantly. 'That would ruin the horse for ever.'

'OK,' I said. 'You show me which bridle Scientific will wear and I'll do the rest.'

Was I getting myself in too deep here?

Was I about to become an accessory to a fraud on the betting public as well as to tax evasion?

Yes. Guilty on both counts.

8

I spent much of Thursday morning on a reasonably fruitful journey to Oxford.

Banbury Drive was in Summertown, a northern suburb of the city, and number 26 was one of a row of 1950s built semi-detached houses with bay windows and pebble-dash walls. This was the supposed address of Mrs Jane Philips, my mother, which Roderick Ward had included on her tax return.

I parked my Jaguar a little way down the road, so it wouldn't be so visible, and walked to the front door of number 26. I rang the bell.

I didn't really know what to expect but, nevertheless, I was a little surprised when the door was opened a fraction by an elderly white-haired gentleman wearing maroon carpet slippers, no socks, and brown trousers that had been pulled up a good six inches too far.

'What do you want?' he snapped at me through the narrow gap.

'Does someone called Mr Roderick Ward live here?' I asked.

'Who?' he said, cupping a hand to his ear.

'Roderick Ward,' I repeated.

'Never heard of him,' said the man. 'Now go away.'

The door began to close.

'He was killed in a car crash last July,' I said quickly, but the door continued to close. I placed my false foot into the diminishing space between the door and the frame. At least it wouldn't hurt if he tried to slam the door shut.

'He had a sister called Stella,' I said loudly. 'Stella Beecher.'

The door stopped moving and reopened just a fraction. I removed my foot.

'Do you know Stella?' I asked him.

'Someone called Stella brings my meals-on-wheels,' the man said.

'Every day?' I asked.

'Yes,' he said.

'What time?' I asked. It was already nearly twelve o'clock.

'Around one,' he said.

'Thank you, sir,' I said formally. 'And what is your name, please?'

'Are you from the council?' he asked.

'Of course,' I said.

'Then you should know my bloody name,' he said, and he slammed the door shut.

Damn it, I thought. That was stupid.

I stood on the pavement for a while but it was cold and my real toes became chilled inside my inappropriately thin leather loafers.

Of course, I had no toes on my right side but that didn't mean that I had no feeling there. The nerves that had once stretched all the way to my toes now ended seven inches below my knee. However, they often sent signals as if they had come from my foot.

In particular, when my real left foot was cold, the nerves in my right leg tended to confuse the situation by sometimes sending cold signals to my brain or worse, as now, hot ones. It felt like I had one foot inside a block of ice while the other was resting on a red-hot griddle plate. The sensation from the truncated nerves may only have been from a phantom limb but they were real enough in my head, and they hurt.

I took shelter from the cold in my car. I started the engine and switched on the heater.

Consequently, I almost missed the arrival of the old man's meal.

A dark blue Nissan came towards me and pulled up in front of the house and a middle-aged woman leapt out and almost ran to the old man's door carrying a foil-covered tray. She had a key and let herself in. Only a few seconds later she emerged again, slammed the door shut and was back in her car almost before I had a chance to get out of mine.

I walked in the road so she couldn't leave without reversing or running me over. She sounded the horn and waved me out of the way. I put up a hand in a police-style stop signal.

'I'm in a hurry,' she shouted.

'I just need to ask you a question,' I shouted back.

The driver's window slid down a few inches.

'Are you Stella Beecher?' I asked, coming alongside the car.

'No,' she said.

'The old man said Stella delivered his meals.'

She smiled. 'He calls all of us Stella,' she said. 'Someone called Stella used to do it for him but she hasn't been here for months.'

'Is her name Stella Beecher?' I asked.

'I don't really know,' the woman said. 'We're volunteers. I'd only just started when she stopped coming.' She looked at her watch. 'Sorry, I've got to go. The old people don't like me being late with their food.'

'How can I contact Stella?' I asked.

'Sorry,' she said. 'I've no idea where she is now.'

'What's his name?' I asked, nodding at the house.

'Mr Horner,' she said. 'He's a cantankerous old git. And he never even bothered to wash up his plate from yesterday.' I could see his dirty plate lying on the front seat beside her. 'Must dash.'

She revved the engine and was gone.

I stood there wishing I'd asked her name, or for her contact details, or at least for the name of the organization for whom she acted as a volunteer. Perhaps the council would know, I thought. I'd ask them.

I walked back up the driveway of number 26 and rang the bell.

There was no reply.

I leaned down and called through the letterbox. 'Mr Horner,' I shouted. 'I need to ask you some questions.'

'Go away.' I could hear him in the distance. 'I'm having my lunch.'

'I only want a minute,' I shouted, again through the letterbox. 'I need to ask you about your post.'

'What about my post?' he said from much closer.

I stood up straight and he opened the door a crack on a security chain.

'Do you ever receive post for other people?' I asked him.

'How do you mean?' he said.

'Do letters arrive here for other people with your house address on them?'

'Sometimes,' he said.

'What do you do with them?' I asked.

'Stella takes them,' he said.

'And did Stella take them today?' I asked, knowing that the lady he called Stella hadn't taken anything away from here except the dirty plate.

'No,' he said.

'Have you got any post for other people at the moment?' I asked.

'Lots of it,' he said.

'Shall I take it away for you?' I asked him.

He closed the door and I thought I had missed my chance, but he was only undoing the security chain. The door opened wide.

'It's in there,' he said, pointing at a rectangular cardboard box standing next to his feet.

I looked down. There must have been at least thirty items of various shapes and sizes lying in a heap in the box.

'I've been wondering about it,' he said. 'Most of it's been there for months. Stella doesn't seem to take it any more.'

Without asking again I reached down, picked up the box, and walked off with it towards my car.

'Hey,' old Mr Horner shouted after me. 'You can't do that. I need that box to put the next lot into.'

I poured the contents out onto the front seat of the Jaguar and took the empty box back to him.

'That's better,' he said, dropping the box back onto the floor and kicking it into position next to the door.

'Don't forget your lunch,' I said, turning back towards my car. 'Don't let it get cold.'

'Oh,' he said. 'Right. Bye.' He closed the door and I was back in my car and speeding off before he had time to rethink the last few minutes.

I spent the afternoon in my bedroom, first impersonating a government official and then knowingly opening other people's mail. I was pretty sure that both actions were illegal and, even if they weren't against the letter of the law, they would certainly be in breach of the *Values and Standards of the British Army*.

First, using the local Yellow Pages directory, I started calling nursing homes, claiming to be an official from the Pensions Office enquiring after the well-being of a Mr George Sutton. I told them that I was checking that Mr Sutton was still alive and entitled to his state pension.

I had never before realized there were so many nursing homes. After about fifty fruitless calls, I was on the point of giving up when someone at the Silver Pines Nursing Home in Newbury Road, Andover, informed me in no uncertain terms that Mr George Sutton was indeed very much alive and kicking, and that his pension was an essential part of the payment for his care and I'd better leave it alone, or else.

I had to assure them profusely that I would take no action to stop it.

Next, I turned to the mail sent to 26 Banbury Drive, Oxford.

In all, there had been forty-two different items in Mr Horner's cardboard box but most of them were junk circulars and free papers with no name or address. Six of them, however, were of particular interest to me. Three were addressed to Mr R. Ward, a fourth to Mrs Jane Philips, my mother, and the two others to a Mrs Stella Beecher, all three persons supposedly resident at 26 Banbury Drive, Oxford.

Two of the letters to Roderick Ward had not been that informative, simply being tax circulars giving general notes of new tax bands. The third, however, was from Mr Anthony Cigar of Rock Bank (Gibraltar) Ltd, formally confirming the immediate closure of the bank's investment fund and the imminent proceedings in the Gibraltar bankruptcy court. The letter was, in fact, a copy of one addressed to my mother and stepfather at Kauri House. It was dated 7 July 2009 and almost certainly did not arrive in Banbury Drive until after Roderick's fatal car accident of the night of 12 July.

On the other hand, the letter to my mother was much more recent. It was a computer-generated notice of an automatic penalty of £100 for the late filing of her tax return which had been due just ten days ago.

But it was the two letters to Mrs Stella Beecher that were the real find.

One was from the Oxford coroner's office informing her that the adjourned inquest into the death of her brother, Roderick

Ward, was due to be reconvened on 15 February, the following Monday.

And the other was a handwritten note on lined paper that simply read, in capital letters:

I DON'T KNOW WHETHER THIS WILL GET THERE IN TIME BUT TELL HIM I HAVE THE STUFF HE WANTS.

I picked up the envelope in which it had arrived. It was a standard white envelope available from any high-street stationer's. The address had also been handwritten in the same manner as the note. The postmark was slightly blurred and it was difficult to tell where it had been posted. However, the date was clear to see. The letter had been mailed on Monday 13 July, the day after Roderick Ward supposedly died, the very day his body had been discovered.

I sat on my bed for quite a while looking at the note and wondering if 'in time' meant before the 'accident' occurred and if 'THE STUFF' had anything to do with my mother's tax papers.

I looked carefully at it once again. Now, I was no handwriting expert, but this message to Stella Beecher looked, to my eyes, to have been written in the same style, and to be on the same type of paper, as the blackmail note that I had found on my mother's desk.

On Thursday evening, at seven forty-five, I carried a bottle of fairly reasonable red wine round from Kauri House to the Hall in Lambourn for a kitchen supper with Isabella and her guests. I was looking forward to a change in both venue and company.

As I had expected, the supper was not quite as casual as Isabella had made out. Far from being in jeans, she herself was wearing a tight black dress that showed off her alluring curves to their best advantage. I was pleased with myself for having decided to put on a jacket and tie but, there again, I'd worn a jacket and tie for dinner in officers' messes for years, especially on a weekday. Dressing for dinner, even for a kitchen supper, was like a comfort blanket. For all its preoccupation with killing the enemy, the British Army was still very formal in its manners.

'Tom,' she squealed, opening the front door and taking my offered bottle. 'How lovely. Come and meet the others.'

I followed her from the hallway towards the kitchen, and the noise. The room was already pretty full of guests. Isabella grabbed my arm and pulled me into the throng where everyone seemed to be talking at once.

'Ewen,' she shouted to a fair-haired man about forty years old. 'Ewen,' she shouted again, grabbing hold of his sleeve. 'I want you to meet Tom. Tom, this is Ewen Yorke. Ewen, Tom.'

We shook hands.

'Tom Forsyth,' I said.

'Ah,' he said in a dramatic manner, throwing an arm wide and nearly knocking over someone's glass behind him. 'Jackson, we have a spy in our midst.'

'A spy?' Isabella said.

'Yes,' Ewen said. 'A damn spy from Kauri Stables. Come to steal our secrets about Saturday.'

'Ah,' I said. 'You must mean about Newark Hall in the Game Spirit.' His mouth opened. 'You've got no chance with Scientific running.'

'There you are,' he boomed. 'What did I tell you? He's a bloody spy. Fetch the firing squad.' He laughed heartily at his own joke and we all joined in. Little did he know.

'Where is this spy?' said a tall man pushing his way past people towards me.

'Tom,' said Isabella. 'This is my husband, Jackson Warren.'

'Good to meet you,' I said, shaking his offered hand and hoping he couldn't see the envy in my eyes, envy that he had managed to snare my beautiful Isabella.

Jackson Warren certainly didn't give the impression of someone suffering from prostate cancer. I knew that he was sixty-one years old because I'd looked him up on the internet, but his lack of any grey hair seemed to belie the fact. Rather unkindly, I wondered if he dyed it, or perhaps just being married to a much younger woman had helped keep him youthful.

'So, are you spying on us, or on Ewen?' he asked jovially with an infectious booming laugh.

'Both,' I said jokily, but I had partially misjudged the moment.

'Not for the Sunday papers, I hope,' he said, changing his mood instantly from amusement to disdain. 'Though, I suppose, one more bastard won't make any difference.' He laughed once more, but, this time, the amusement didn't reach his eyes and there was an unsettling seriousness about his face.

'Come on, darling,' said Isabella, sensing his unease. 'Relax. Tom's not a spy. In fact he's a hero.'

I gave her a stern look as if to say, 'No, please don't,' but the message didn't get through.

'A hero?' said Ewen.

Isabella was about to reply when I cut her off sharply.

'Isabella exaggerates,' I said quickly. 'I'm in the army, that's all. And I've been in Afghanistan.'

'Really,' said an attractive woman in a low-cut dress who was standing next to Ewen. 'Was it very hot?'

'No, not really,' I said. 'It's very hot in the summer but it's damn cold in the winter, especially at night.' Trust a Brit, I thought, to talk about the weather.

'Did you see any action?' Ewen asked.

'A fair bit,' I said. 'But I was only there for a couple of months this last time.'

'So you've been before?' Ewen said.

'I've been in the army since I was seventeen,' I said. 'I've been most places.'

'Were you in Iraq?' the woman asked with intensity.

'Yes. In Basra. And also in Bosnia and Kosovo. The modern army keeps you busy.' I laughed.

'How exciting,' she said.

'It can be,' I agreed. 'But only in short bursts. Mostly it's very boring.' Time, I thought, to change the subject. 'So, Ewen,' I said, 'how many horses do you train?'

'There you are,' he said expansively. 'I told you he was a spy.'

We all laughed.

The attractive woman next to Ewen turned out to be his wife, Julie, and I found myself sitting next to her at supper at one of two large round tables set up in the extensive Lambourn Hall kitchen.

On the other side, on my left, was a Mrs Toleron, a rather dull grey-haired woman who didn't stop telling me about how successful her 'wonderful' husband had been in business. She had even introduced herself as Mrs Martin Toleron, as if I would recognize her spouse's name.

'You must have heard of him,' she exclaimed, amazed that I hadn't. 'He was head of Toleron Plastics until we sold out a few months ago. It was all in the papers at the time, and on the television.'

I didn't tell her that a few months ago I had been fighting for my life in a Birmingham hospital and, at the time, the business news hadn't been very high on my agenda.

'We were the biggest plastic drainpipe manufacturer in Europe.'

'Really,' I said, trying to keep myself from yawning.

'Yes,' she said, incorrectly sensing some interest on my part. 'We made white, grey or black drainpipe in continuous lengths. Mile after mile of it.'

'Thank goodness for rain,' I said, but she didn't get the joke.

As soon as I was able, and without appearing too rude, I managed to stem the tide of plastic drainpipe from my left, turning more eagerly towards Julie on my right.

'So, how many horses does Ewen train?' I asked her as we tucked in to lasagne and garlic bread. 'He never did tell me.'

'About sixty,' she said. 'But it's getting more all the time. We're no longer really big enough at home so we are looking to buy the Webster place.'

'Webster place?' I asked.

'You must know, on the hill off the Wantage road. Old Larry Webster used to train there but he dropped down dead a couple of years ago now. It's been on the market for months and months. Price is too high, I reckon, and it needs a lot doing to it. Ewen's dead keen to open another yard but I'd rather stay the size we are.' She sighed. 'Ewen says we're too small but, the truth is, he's not very good at saying no to new owners.' She smiled wearily.

'He's lucky in the current economic climate to have the option,' I said.

'I know,' she agreed. 'Lots of trainers are having troubles. I hear it all the time from their wives at the races.'

'Do you go racing a lot?' I asked.

'Not as much as I once did,' she said. 'Ewen is always so busy these days that I never see him like I used to, either at the races or at home.'

She sighed again. Clearly, success had not brought happiness, at least not for Mrs Yorke.

'But, enough about me. Tell me about you.' She turned in her chair to give me her full attention, and a much better view of her ample cleavage. Ewen should spend more time with her, I thought, both at home and at the races, or he might soon find her straying.

'Not much to tell,' I said.

'Now, come on. You must have lots of stories.'

'None that I'd be happy to repeat,' I said.

'Go on,' she said, putting her hand on my arm. 'You can tell me.' She fluttered her eyelashes at me. It made me think that it was probably already too late for Ewen, far too late.

Isabella insisted that everyone moved around after the lasagne and so, in spite of Julie Yorke's best efforts, I escaped her advances before they became too obvious, but not before she'd had the shock of her life trying to play footsie under the table with my prosthesis.

'My God! What's that?' she had exclaimed, but quietly, almost under her breath.

And so I'd been forced to explain about the IED and all the other things I would have preferred to keep confidential.

Far from turning her off, the idea of a man with only one leg had seemed to excite her yet further. She had become even more determined to invade my privacy with intimate questions that I was seriously not prepared to answer.

As soon as Isabella suggested it, I was quick and happy to move seats, opting to sit between Jackson Warren and another man at the second table.

I'd had my fill of the female of the species for one night.

'So how long have you been back?' Jackson asked me as I sat down.

'In Lambourn?' I asked.

'From Afghanistan.'

'Four months,' I said.

'In hospital?' he asked.

I nodded. Isabella must have told him.

'In hospital?' the man on my other side asked.

'Yes,' I said. 'I was wounded.'

He looked at me and was clearly waiting for me to expand on my answer. As far as I was concerned, he was waiting in vain.

'Tom, here, lost a foot,' Jackson said, filling the silence.

It felt as though I'd jumped out of one frying pan into another.

'Really,' said the man with astonishment. 'Which one?'

'Does it matter?' I asked with obvious displeasure.

'Er . . . er . . .' He was suddenly uncomfortable, and I sat silently, doing nothing to relieve his embarrassment. 'No,' he said finally, 'I suppose not.'

It mattered to me.

'I'm sorry,' he said, looking down and intently studying his dessert plate of chocolate mousse with brandy snaps and cream.

I nearly asked him if he was sorry for my losing a foot, or sorry for asking me which one I'd lost, but it was Jackson I should have been really cross with for mentioning it in the first place.

'Thank you,' I said. I paused. 'It was my right foot.'

'It's amazing,' he said, looking up at my face. 'I watched you walk over here just now and I had no idea.'

'Prosthetic limbs have come a long way since the days of Long John Silver,' I said. 'There were some people at the rehab centre who could run up stairs two at a time.'

'Amazing,' he said again.

'I'm Tom Forsyth,' I said.

'Oh, I'm sorry,' he replied. 'Alex Reece. Good to meet you.'

We shook hands in the awkward manner of people sitting alongside each other. He was a small man in his thirties with thinning ginger hair and horn-rimmed spectacles of the same colour. He was wearing a navy cardigan over a white shirt, and brown flannel trousers.

'Are you a trainer too?' I asked.

'Oh no,' he said with a nervous laugh. 'I haven't a clue about horses. In fact, to tell you the truth, I'm rather frightened of them. I'm an accountant.'

'Alex, here,' Jackson interjected, 'keeps my hard-earned income out of the grasping hands of the taxman.'

'I try,' Alex said with a smile.

'Legally?' I asked, smiling back.

'Of course legally,' said Jackson, feigning annoyance.

'The line between avoidance, which is legal, and evasion, which isn't, can sometimes be somewhat blurred,' Alex said, ignoring him.

'And what exactly is that meant to mean?' demanded Jackson, the simulated irritation having been replaced by the real thing.

'Nothing,' Alex said, back-pedalling furiously, and again embarrassed. 'Just that sometimes what we believe is avoidance may be seen as evasion by the Revenue.' Alex Reece was digging himself deeper into the hole.

'And who is right?' I asked, enjoying his discomfort.

'We are,' Jackson stated firmly. 'Aren't we, Alex?' he insisted.

'It is the courts who ultimately decide who's right,' Alex said, clearly oblivious to the thinness of the thread by which his employment was dangling.

'In what way?' I asked.

'We put in a return based on our understanding of the tax law,' he said, seemingly unaware of Jackson's staring eyes to my left. 'If the Revenue challenge that understanding, they might demand that we pay more tax. If we then challenge their challenge and refuse to pay, they have to take us to court and then a jury will decide whose interpretation of the law is correct.'

'Sounds simple,' I said.

'But it can be very expensive,' Alex said. 'If you lose in court, you will end up paying far more than the tax you should have paid in the first place because they will fine you on top. And, of course, the court has the power to do more than take just away your money. They can also send you to prison if they think you were knowingly trying to evade paying tax. To say nothing of what else the Revenue might turn up with their digging. It's a risk we shouldn't take.'

'Are you trying to tell me something, Alex?' Jackson asked angrily, leaning over me and pointing his right forefinger at his accountant's face. 'Because, I'm warning you, if I end up in court I will tell them it was all my accountant's idea.'

'What was his idea?' I asked tactlessly.

'Nothing,' said Jackson, suddenly realizing he'd said too much.

There was an uncomfortable few moments of silence. The others at the table, who had been listening to the exchange, suddenly decided it was best to start talking amongst themselves again, and turned away.

Jackson stood up, scraping his chair on the stone floor, and stomped out of the room.

'So, how long have you been Jackson's accountant?' I asked Alex.

He didn't answer but simply watched the door through which Jackson had disappeared.

'Sorry. What did you say?' he said eventually.

'I asked you how long you'd been Jackson's accountant.'

He stared at me. 'Too long,' he said.

The kitchen supper soon broke up and most of the guests departed, Alex Reece being the first out of the door, almost at the run. Eventually there were only a handful remaining and I found myself amongst them. I had tried, politely, to depart but Isabella had insisted on my staying for a nightcap and I had been easily persuaded. I had nothing much to get up early for in the morning.

In all, five of us moved through from the kitchen into the equally spacious drawing room, including a couple I had seen only at a distance across the room earlier. He was wearing a dark suit and blue striped tie while she was in a long charcoal-coloured jersey over a brown skirt. I placed them both in their early sixties.

'Hello,' I said to them. 'I'm Tom Forsyth.' I held out my hand.

'Yes,' said the man rather sneeringly, not shaking it. 'We know. Bella spoke of little else over dinner.'

'Oh, really,' I said with a laugh. 'All good, I hope. And you are?'

The man said nothing.

'Peter and Rebecca Garraway,' the woman said softly. 'Please excuse my husband. He's just jealous because Bella doesn't speak about him all the time.'

I wasn't sure if she was joking or not. Peter Garraway certainly wasn't laughing. Instead he turned away, sat down on a sofa, and patted the seat beside him. His wife, obediently, went over and joined him. What a bundle of fun, I thought – not. Why didn't they just go home?

Isabella handed round drinks while her husband remained conspicuous by his continued absence. But no one mentioned it, not even me.

'I thought all you trainers went to bed early,' I said to Ewen Yorke as he sank into the armchair next to me and buried his nose in a brandy snifter.

'You must be joking,' he said. 'And turn down our Bella's best VSOP? Not bloody likely.' He tilted his head right back and poured the golden-brown liquid down his throat. I couldn't help but think of my mother pouring her green-potato-peel concoction down her horses' throats in the same manner.

Ewen's wife, Julie, had departed with the other guests saying that she was tired and was going home to bed. Her husband seemed to be in no hurry to join her. Isabella refilled his glass.

'So, Tom,' he said, taking another sizable mouthful. 'Where does the army send you next? Back to Afghanistan? Back to the fight?'

Isabella was looking at me intently.

'I think my fighting days are over,' I said. 'I'm getting too old for that.'

'Nonsense,' Isabella said. 'You're the same age as me.'

'But front-line fighting is for younger men. More than half of those in the army that have been killed in Afghanistan were under twenty-four, and more of them were teenagers than were older than me. In the modern infantry, you're past it by the age of thirty.'

'I can't believe that,' Ewen said. 'I was still wet behind the ears until I was at least thirty.'

'But it's true,' I said. 'In a ten-year period, Alexander the Great, the Greek King of Macedonia, conquered Turkey and Egypt, much of the rest of the Middle East, as well as all of Persia and parts of India as far away as the Himalayas, and he managed it all by the time he was thirty. He is still revered by soldiers the world over as one of the greatest military commanders of all time, yet he was only thirty-two when he died. Sadly, the truth of the matter is that I'm over the hill already.'

Was I trying to convince them, or myself?

'So what will you do instead?' Ewen asked.

'I'm not really sure,' I said. 'Perhaps I'll take up racehorse training.'

'It's not always as exciting as it appears,' he said. 'Particularly not at seven thirty on cold wet winter mornings.'

'Especially after a late night out, drinking,' said Isabella with a laugh.

'Oh, God,' said Ewen, looking at his watch. 'Quick. Give me another brandy.'

Isabella and I laughed. Peter Garraway sat stony-faced on the sofa.

'At least it would be a bit safer than you're used to,' Rebecca Garraway said.

'I don't really think I'll be joining the ranks of racehorse trainers,' I said with a smile. 'It was only a joke.'

However, neither Rebecca nor her husband seemed amused by it.

'I think it's time I was off,' I said, standing up. 'Isabella, thank you for a lovely evening. Goodnight all.'

'Goodnight,' Ewen and Rebecca called back as Isabella showed me out into the hallway. Peter Garraway said nothing.

'Thank you for tonight,' I said, as Isabella opened the front door. 'It's been great fun.'

'I'm sorry about the Garraways,' she said, lowering her voice. 'They can be a bit strange at times, especially him. I think he fancies me.' She laughed. 'But I think he's creepy.'

'And rather rude,' I whispered back, pulling a face. 'Who are they?'

'Old friends of Jackson's.' She rolled her eyes. 'Unfortunately, they're our house guests. The Garraways always come over for the end of the pheasant-shooting season – Peter is a great shot – and they're staying on for the races on Saturday.'

'At Newbury?'

She nodded. 'Are you going?'

'Probably,' I said.

'Great. Maybe see you there.' She laughed. 'Unless, of course, you see the Garraways first.'

'What exactly does Peter Garraway do?' I asked.

'He makes pots and pots of money,' she said. 'And he owns racehorses. Ewen trains some of them.'

I thought that explained a lot.

'I don't think Mr Garraway is over impressed by his trainer drinking your brandy until all hours of the night.'

'Oh, that's not the problem,' she said. 'I think it's because Peter and Jackson had a bit of a stand-up row earlier. Over some business project they're working on together. I didn't really listen.'

'What sort of business?' I asked.

'Financial services or something,' she said. 'I don't really know. Business is not my thing.' She laughed. 'But Peter must do very well out of it. We go and stay with them occasionally and their house makes this place look like a weekend cottage. It's absolutely huge.'

'Where is it?' I asked.

'In Gibraltar.'

9

The Silver Pines Nursing Home was a modern red-brick monstrosity built onto the side of what had once been an attractive Victorian residence on the northern edge of the town of Andover, in Hampshire.

'Certainly, sir,' said one of the pink-uniformed lady carers when I asked if I might visit Mr Sutton. 'Are you a relative?'

'No,' I said. 'I live in the same road as Mr Sutton. In Hungerford.'

'I see,' said the carer. She wasn't really interested. 'I think he's in the day room. He sits there most mornings after breakfast.'

I followed her along the corridor into what had once been the house. The day room was the large bay-windowed front parlour and there were about fifteen high-backed upright armchairs arranged around the walls. About half of the chairs were occupied, and most of the occupants were asleep.

'Mr Sutton,' called the pink lady, walking towards one elderly gentleman. 'Wake up, Mr Sutton. You've got a visitor.' She shook the old boy and he slowly raised his head and opened his eyes. 'That's better.' She spoke to him as if he were a child, then she leaned forward and wiped a drop of dribble from the corner of his mouth. I began to think that I shouldn't have come.

'Hello, Mr Sutton.' I spoke in the same loud manner that the lady had used. 'Do you remember me?' I asked. 'It's John, John from Willow Close.' Unsurprisingly, he stared at me without recognition. 'Jimbo and his mum send their love. Has your son, Fred, been in yet today?'

The pink lady seemed satisfied. 'Can I leave you two together, then?' she asked. 'The tea trolley will be round soon if you want anything.'

'Thank you,' I said.

She walked away, back towards the entrance, and I sat down on an empty chair next to Old Man Sutton. All the while, he went on staring at me.

'I don't know you,' he said.

I watched with distaste as he used his right hand to remove a set of false teeth from his mouth. He studied them closely, took a wooden toothpick from his shirt pocket, and used it to remove a piece of his breakfast that had become stuck in a crevice. Satisfied, he returned the dentures to his mouth with an audible snap.

'I don't know you,' he said again, the teeth now safely back in position.

I looked around me. There were six other residents in the room and all but one had now drifted off to sleep. The one whose eyes were open was staring out through window at the garden and ignoring us.

'Mr Sutton,' I said straight to his face, 'I want to ask you about a man called Roderick Ward.'

I hadn't been sure what reaction to expect. I'd thought that, maybe, Old Man Sutton wouldn't be able to remember what he'd had for dinner last night, let alone something that happened nearly a year previously.

I was wrong.

He remembered all right. I could see it in his eyes.

'Roderick Ward is a thieving little bastard.' He said it softly, but very clearly. 'I'd like to wring his bloody neck.' He held out his hands towards me as if he might wring my neck instead.

'Roderick Ward is already dead,' I said.

Old Man Sutton dropped his hands into his lap. 'Good,' he said. 'Who killed him?'

'He died in a road accident,' I said.

'That was too good for him,' the old man said with venom. 'I'd have killed him slowly.'

I was slightly taken aback. 'What did he do to you?' I asked. It had to be more than throwing a brick through his window.

'He stole my life savings,' he said.

'How?' I asked.

'Some hare-brained scheme of his that went bust,' he said. He shook his head. 'I should never have listened to him.'

'So he didn't exactly steal your savings?'

'As good as,' Mr Sutton replied. 'My son was furious with me. Kept saying I'd gambled away his inheritance.'

I didn't think it had been the most tactful of comments.

'And what exactly was Roderick Ward's hare-brained scheme?' I asked.

He sat silently for a while looking at me, as if deciding what to tell. Or perhaps he was trying to remember.

He again removed his false teeth and studied them closely. I wasn't at all sure that he had understood my question but, after a while, he replaced his teeth in his mouth and began. 'I borrowed some money against my house to invest in some fancy investment fund that Roderick Bastard Ward guaranteed would make me rich.' He sighed. 'All that happened was the fund went bust and I now have a bloody great mortgage, and I can't afford the interest.'

I could understand why Detective Sergeant Fred had been so furious.

'What sort of investment fund was it?' I asked.

'I don't remember,' he said. Perhaps he just didn't want to.

'So how come Ward threw a brick through your window?' I asked.

He smiled. 'I poured tea in his lap.'

'What?' I said, astonished. 'How?'

'He came to tell me that I'd lost all my money. I said to him that there must be something we could do, but he just sat there arrogantly telling me that I should have realized that investments could go down as well as up.' He smiled again. 'So I simply poured the hot tea from the teapot I was holding straight into his lap.' He laughed and his false teeth almost popped out of his mouth. He pushed them back in with his thumb. 'You should have seen him jump. Almost ripped his trousers off. Accused me of scalding his wedding tackle. Wish now I'd cut them off completely.'

'So he went out and threw the brick through your window?'

'Yeah, as he was leaving, but my son saw him do it and arrested him.' He stopped laughing. 'But then I had to tell Fred the whole story about losing the money.'

So he had lost his money about a year ago. Before the same fate had befallen my mother.

'Mr Sutton,' I said. 'Can you remember anything at all about the investment fund that went bust?'

He shook his head.

'Was it an offshore fund?' I asked.

He looked quizzically at me. The term 'offshore' clearly hadn't rung any bells in his memory.

'I don't know about that,' he said. 'I don't think so.'

'Did it have anything to do with Gibraltar?' I asked.

He shook his head once more. 'I can't remember.' He began to dribble again from the corner of his mouth and there were tears in his eyes.

It was time for me to go.

Saturday morning dawned crisp and bright with the winter sun doing its best to thaw the frosty ground. The radio in the kitchen reported that there was to be a second inspection of the course at Newbury at nine o'clock to decide whether racing could go ahead. Apparently, the take-off and landing areas of every jump had been covered overnight, and the stewards were hopeful the meeting could take place.

I, meanwhile, was crossing my fingers that it would be abandoned.

I had spent more than an hour in the racing tack room on Friday afternoon doing my best to try to ensure that Scientific's reins would part during his race. My mother had shown me which one of the bridles had the Australian noseband fitted and I had been dismayed to see its pristine condition. As my mother had said, horses from Kauri House Stables didn't go to the races with sub-standard tack.

I had thought that it would be an easy task to bend the leather back and forth a few times inside the non-slip rubber sleeve until it broke, leaving only the rubber holding the reins together. The rubber should then part in the hustle and bustle of the race when the jockey pulled on the reins.

Sadly, I found that it was not as simple as I had thought. The leather was far too new.

I'd looked at where the reins were attached to the metal rings on either side of the bit. The leather was sewn back on itself with multiple stitches of strong thread. I had tested it with all my strength without even an iota of separation. How about if I cut through most of the stitches? But with what? And wouldn't it show? Wouldn't Jack be sure to see it when he gathered the tack together?

There were four green first-aid boxes stacked on a shelf in the racing tack room and I'd opened one, looking for a pair of scissors. I'd found something better. Carefully protected by a transparent plastic sheath had been a surgical scalpel.

With great care I had started to cut through the stitches on the right side of the bridle, the side that would be furthest from the stable lad when he led the horse around the parade ring. I'd been careful to cut only the stitches in the middle, leaving both ends intact so the sabotage was less obvious. In the end I had severed all but a very few stitches at either end. I had no idea if it was enough, but it would have to do.

I hovered nervously round the racing tack-room door as Jack gathered together all the equipment for the day, loading it into a huge wicker basket. I saw as he lifted the bridle with the Australian noseband and placed it in the basket.

There was no shout of discovery, no tut-tutting over the state of the reins.

So far, so good. But the real test would come when he placed the bridle on to Scientific later in the afternoon in the racecourse stables.

I had done my best to disguise the effects of the scalpel. The stiffness of the leather had helped to keep the sides together and I had been careful not to leave any frayed ends of thread visible. It had been a matter of trying to make the reins appear to be normal and intact while, at the same time, ensuring they were sufficiently weakened to separate during the race. And I had absolutely no idea if I had managed to get the balance right.

Unfortunately, the covers had done their job in saving the meeting from the frost and so my mother drove the three of us to Newbury in her battered old blue Ford, my stepfather sitting next to her in the front while I was in the back behind her, as I had been so often before on the way to and from the races.

Going racing had been such a huge part of my young life that, at one time, my knowledge of British geography had been based solely on the locations of the country's racecourses. By the time I learned to drive when I was seventeen, I had no idea where the big cities might be but I could unerringly find my way to such places as Market Rasen, Plumpton or Fakenham, and I also knew the best short-cuts to beat the race-day traffic.

Newbury is the most local course to Lambourn, being just fifteen miles away, and is thought of as 'home' for most of the village's trainers, who all have as many runners here as possible, not least because of the low transport costs.

By the time my mother pulled into the trainers' car park it was nearly full and I noticed with dismay how far I was going to have to walk to get into the racecourse. I was still suffering from excess fluid in the tissues of my leg and I had promised myself to take things a little easier for a while. So much for my good intentions.

'Hello, Josephine,' called a voice as we stepped out of the car. Ewen Yorke was standing just in front of us, struggling into his sheepskin overcoat.

'Oh, hello, Ewen,' replied my mother without warmth.

'Hiya, Tom.' Julie Yorke called as she climbed out of their top-of-the-range, brand-new, white BMW, a fact not lost on my mother, who positively fumed. Now I realized why she had suddenly become so keen on upgrading her old Ford.

For once, Julie was accompanying Ewen to the races, and she was dressed in a thin figure-hugging silk dress with a matching, but equally thin, print-patterned topcoat. Rather inappropriate, I thought, for a cold and dank February afternoon, but it clearly warmed the hearts of several male admirers who walked by with smiles on their faces and sparkles in their eyes.

'Hi, Julie,' I replied with a small wave that brought the same response of recognition from Ewen.

My mother looked across the car at me disapprovingly. I was sure that she would be desperate to discover how it was that I knew them, and be eager for me to enlighten her. But I decided not to. I'd not mentioned to her where I had gone to dinner on Thursday night. I had simply let her assume, incorrectly, that I had gone down to one of the village pubs. She obviously hadn't suffered under my Sandhurst colour sergeant or she would have known never to assume anything but always to check.

We hung back, putting on our own coats and hats, as the Yorkes made their way across the grass to the entrance. We watched them go.

'If Scientific is not able to win today,' my mother said icily, 'I just hope it's not bloody Newark Hall. I can't stand that man.'

I looked round quickly to see if anyone had heard her comment.

'If I were you,' I said forcefully, but quietly, 'I'd keep my voice down. This car park is also used by the stewards.'

We made it unchallenged into the racecourse, my mother obtaining a member's club ticket for me at the gate, just as she always had. But now I was no longer the little boy in a cap that the gateman had let through with a smile, although I felt the same excitement.

However, my excitement today was combined with acute nervousness.

Had I done enough to make Scientific's reins part? Would the horse and rider be all right? Would I be found out by Jack?

The Game Spirit Steeplechase was the second race on the card and, so anxious was I that I didn't take the slightest notice of the first. Instead I stood nervously at the entrance to the pre-parade ring, waiting for the horses to be led in by the stable lads.

To say that I was relieved when Scientific came into the ring was an understatement. I started breathing again. As the horse was walked round and round I looked closely at his bridle and it certainly appeared to be the same one that I had tampered with on the previous afternoon.

So far, so good.

I wandered over to the saddling boxes and leaned on a white

wooden rail, waiting for Scientific to be brought over by the stable lad who, I noticed, was Declan, the young man I had spoken to in the Kauri Stables tack room.

Presently my mother and stepfather arrived and then Jack appeared, trotting into the saddling box with the jockey's minuscule saddle under his arm.

Declan stood in front of the horse restraining its head, using the reins on both sides of the bit. I was again holding my breath. Would he notice the sabotage?

My mother and Jack busied themselves, one on each side of the animal, applying under-saddle pad, weight cloth, number cloth, and then the saddle to its back, pulling the girths tight round its belly. Next Jack threw a heavy red, black, and gold horse rug over the whole lot to keep the horse warm against the February chill. With a slap on his neck from Jack, Scientific was sent to the parade ring for inspection by the betting public.

Why, I wondered, did the blackmailer want Scientific to lose?

Was it because he wanted another specific horse to win?

Probably not, I thought.

Before the onset of internet gambling, the only people who could really gain financially from knowing a horse would definitely lose a race were the bookmakers, who could then offer much better odds on it and rake in the bets, safe in the knowledge that they wouldn't have to pay out. However, nowadays, anyone could act as a bookmaker by 'laying' the horse on the internet, effectively betting that it would lose. It didn't matter which other horse won as long as it wasn't the sure-fire loser.

So anyone could gain by knowing that Scientific would not win this race. If only I had access to see who was 'laying' the horse on the net. But there would be no chance of that, even if I had been prepared to tell the authorities why I needed it.

I watched absent-mindedly as the twelve horses in the race were walked round and round. I had never been a gambler myself and had never really understood the passion and concentration with which some punters would study the runners in the parade ring before making their bets. I had been told over and over again by my mother that how well a horse looks in the paddock can be such a good indicator of how fast it will run on the course, but I personally couldn't see it.

A racecourse official rang a hand-bell and I watched with interest as Declan turned Scientific inwards, waiting for my mother and stepfather to walk over with the horse's owner and jockey. My mother made great play in removing the rug and checking the girths but without going near the bridle or the reins. Declan stood impassively, holding the horse's head as my mother helped the lightweight rider up onto his equally slight saddle.

The jockey placed his feet in the stirrup irons and then gathered the reins, making a knot with the ends to ensure they didn't separate. After another brief circuit of the ring the horses moved down the horse-walk towards the racecourse and the crowd moved as if one, towards the grandstand, in search of a good viewing position. I was amongst them.

'Hello, Tom,' said a voice from behind my shoulder.

I turned round. 'Oh, hello.' I kissed Isabella on the cheek. Jackson was with her, and they had the Garraways in tow.

'Fancy a drink?' Jackson said, clapping me on the shoulder.

A drink sounded just the thing to calm my nerves.

'Later,' I said. 'I want to watch this race.'

'So do we,' said Jackson with his booming laugh. 'Come on up to our box and we can do both.'

I had been trying to spot my mother in the throng of people so I could watch the race with her. I had one last look around but I couldn't see her or my stepfather anywhere. It was probably just as well, I thought, as together we would have been a pair of nervous wrecks.

'Thank you, I'd love to,' I said to Jackson, smiling at Isabella.

'Good,' she said, smiling back.

'And thank you both for such a lovely evening on Thursday,' I said. 'I meant to bring you round a note.'

'That's all right, don't bother,' said Jackson. 'It was a pleasure to have you. We all really enjoyed it.' Unsurprisingly, he made no mention of his early departure from supper, nor his untimely row with Alex Reece.

'How's Alex?' I asked, perhaps unwisely.

'Alex?' he said, looking at me.

'Alex Reece,' I said. 'Your accountant.'

'Oh, him,' Jackson said with a forced smile. 'Bloody little weasel needs a good kick up the arse.' He guffawed loudly.

'Really?' I said with mock sincerity. 'I'll be needing an accountant soon myself. I thought I might go and see him. Are you saying I shouldn't?'

I was playing with him, and he suddenly didn't like it. The amusement evaporated from his eyes.

'Ask whoever you bloody like,' he said dismissively.

As we climbed the few steps to the entrance to the Berkshire Stand we were joined by the Yorkes.

'Ah, the spy again,' said Ewen, smiling.

I smiled back at him.

I found myself crammed into the lift with my back against the wall and with Julie Yorke standing far too close in front. Ewen would almost certainly have had a fit if he had realized that, without any discernible sign to the others, she managed to slide her silk-sheathed firm and rounded buttocks back and forth across my groin in a manner guaranteed to excite.

By the time we arrived at the fourth floor I was glad to be able to pull my overcoat tight around me to save myself from major embarrassment. Julie smiled as I held the door of the box open for her, a seductive inviting smile with an open mouth and her tongue visible between her teeth.

'Come and see me sometime,' she whispered in my ear as she went past.

I reckoned she must be crazy if she thought it was an invitation I was going to accept. Avoidance and evasion were definitely the names of the game here too. Jackson offered me a glass of champagne and I took it out onto the balcony to watch the horses, and to escape from Julie Yorke.

'Do you think he'll win?' It was a moment before I realized that Rebecca Garraway was talking to me.

'Sorry?' I said.

'Do you think he'll win,' she repeated.

'Who?' I asked.

'Newark Hall, of course,' she said. 'Our horse.'

I hadn't realized that the Garraways were Newark Hall's owners. I looked down at my racecard but it stated that the horse was owned by a company called Budsam Ltd.

'He has a good chance,' I said back to her.

In truth, he had a better chance than she appreciated.

Ewen Yorke was standing to my left looking through his large racing binoculars towards the two-and-a-half-mile start.

'Oh, hello,' he said without lowering his binoculars. 'Seems we have a problem.'

'What problem?' Rebecca Garraway demanded with concern in her voice.

'It's OK,' Ewen said while still looking. 'It's not Newark Hall, it's Scientific. Seems his reins have snapped. He's running away.'

I looked down the course in horror but, without the benefit of Ewen's multi-magnification, I was unable to see exactly what was going on. I took a large gulp of my champagne. I should have asked Jackson for a whisky.

'Good. They've caught him,' Ewen said, putting down his glasses. 'No real harm done.'

'So what will happen now?' I asked, trying hard to keep my voice as normal as possible. 'Will Scientific be withdrawn?'

'Oh no, he'll run all right, no problem. They'll just fit a new bridle on him down at the start,' Ewen said. 'The starter always has a spare, just in case something breaks. Indeed, just for situations like this. Most unlike your mother to have a tack malfunction.' He almost laughed.

I felt sick. All that hard work with the scalpel, to say nothing about the expenditure of so much nervous energy since, and for what? Nothing. The horse would now run with perfect, uncut, unbreakable reins.

'That's good,' I said, not actually thinking it was good for a second.

What, I wondered, would the blackmailer do if Scientific won?

I was doubly glad that I wasn't standing next to my mother on the owners' and trainers' stand. By now she would have become more of a head-case than was usual. I just hoped she wasn't planning an Emily Davison suffragette-style dash out in front of her horse during the race to prevent it winning. But in her present state of mind, I'd not put anything past her.

'They're off!' announced the public-address system and all twelve runners moved away slowly, not one of the jockeys eager to set the early pace. They jumped the first fence without breaking into a gallop and, only then, did the horses gather pace and the race was on.

Even though I wanted to, I couldn't take my eyes off Scientific.

I suppose I was hoping he might have crossfired and cut into himself, but the horse appeared to gallop along easily, without any problems. Perhaps he would make an error, I thought, peck badly on landing, and unseat his rider.

But he didn't.

My mother had said that Scientific was a good novice but that the Game Spirit Steeplechase was a considerable step up in class. It didn't show. The horse jumped all the way round without putting a hoof wrong and he was well placed in the leading trio as they turned into the finishing straight for the second and final time. The other two contenders were, as my mother had predicted they would be, Newark Hall and Sovereign Owner.

The three horses jumped the last fence abreast and battled together all the way to the finish line with the crowd cheering them on. Even the quiet, reserved Rebecca Garraway was jumping up and down, screaming encouragement, urging Newark Hall to summon up one last ounce of energy.

'Photograph, photograph!' announced the judge as the horses flashed past the winning post, each of them striving to get his nose in front.

No one in the box was sure which of the three had won.

Ewen Yorke and the Garraways rushed out to get to the winner's enclosure, confident that their horse had done enough, and Jackson went with them, leaving me in the box alone with Isabella and Julie.

'Do you think we won?' Julie asked without much enthusiasm.

I was about to say that I had no idea when the public address announced: 'Here is the result of the photograph. First number ten, second number six, third number eleven.'

Number ten, the winner, was Scientific. He'd won by a short-head from Newark Hall. Sovereign Owner had been third, another nose behind.

Oh shit, I thought.

'Oh, well,' said Julie, shrugging her shoulders. 'There's always next time. But Ewen will be like a caged tiger tonight, he hates so much to lose.' She smiled at me again and raised her eyebrows in a seductive and questioning manner.

It wasn't Ewen, I thought, who was the caged tiger, it was his wife. And I had no desire to release her.

I watched on the television in the corner of the box as my

mother greeted her winner, a genuine smile of triumph on her face. In the euphoria of victory, in the moment of ecstasy of beating Ewen Yorke, she had clearly forgotten that she had disobeyed the instructions of the man who might hold the keys to her prison cell.

It was too late to change anything now, I thought, so she might as well enjoy it while she could. Perhaps the stewards would find that Scientific had bumped into or somehow impeded one of the other horses.

But, of course, they didn't. And there were no objections, other than mine, and that wouldn't carry much authority.

Scientific had won against the orders.

Only time would tell what the blackmailer thought.

10

'What the bloody hell is going on?' Ian Norland stood full square in the middle of the Kauri House kitchen shouting at my mother and me. He had thrown the bridle with the broken reins onto the bleached pine table.

'Ian, please don't shout at me,' my mother said. 'And what's the problem, anyway? Scientific won, didn't he?'

'More by luck than judgement,' Ian almost shouted at her. 'It was just fortunate that the reins parted on the way to the start rather than in the race itself.'

Or unfortunate, I thought.

'Why?' Ian said in exasperation. 'Just tell me why.'

'Why what?' I asked.

'Why did you made the reins break?'

'Are you accusing us of deliberately sabotaging the reins?' my mother asked in her most pompous manner.

'Yes,' he said flatly. 'I am. There's no other explanation. This bridle was brand new. I put the Australian noseband on it myself just a few days ago.'

'Perhaps there was a fault in its manufacture,' I said.

He looked at me with contempt. 'Do you take me for an idiot or something?'

I assumed it was a rhetorical question and so I kept quiet.

'If I don't get some answers,' he said, 'then I'm leaving here tonight for good and I will take this to the racing authorities on Monday morning.' He picked up the bridle in his hand.

I wondered if it was worth pointing out to him that the bridle was not actually his to take away.

'But why?' my mother said. 'Nothing happened. Scientific won the race.'

'But you tried to make him lose it,' Ian said, his voice again rising in volume towards a shout.

'What on earth makes you think we had anything to do with the reins breaking?' I asked him, all innocently.

He again gave me his contemptuous look. 'Because you've been so bloody interested in the racing tack all week, asking questions and all. What else am I going to think?'

'Don't be ridiculous,' said my mother.

'And how about the others?' he said.

'What others?' my mother asked rather carelessly.

'Pharmacist last week and Oregon the week before. Did you stop them winning, too?'

'No, of course not.' My mother sounded affronted.

'Why should I believe you?' Ian said.

'Because, Ian,' I said in my best voice-of-command, 'you must.' He turned to look at me with fire in his eyes. I ignored him. 'Of course you can go to the authorities if that is what you want. But what would you tell them? That you suspect your employer of stopping her horses. But why? And how? By cutting the reins? But it would not have been the first time that reins have broken on a racecourse, now would it?'

'But—' Ian started.

'But nothing,' I replied, cutting him off. 'If you choose to leave here now, then I will have to insist that you do not take any of my mother's property with you and that includes that bridle.' I held out my hand towards him with the palm uppermost and curled my fingers back and forth. Reluctantly, he passed the bridle over to me.

'Good,' I said. 'Now let us understand each other. My mother's horses are always doing their best to win and the stable is committed to winning on every occasion the horses run. My mother will not tolerate any of her employees who might suggest otherwise. She expects complete loyalty from her staff and if you are not able to guarantee such loyalty then, indeed, you had better leave here this evening. Do I make myself clear?'

He looked at me in mild surprise.

'I suppose so,' he said. 'But you have to promise me that the horses will always be doing their best to win, and that there will be no more of this.' He pointed at the bridle.

'I do promise,' I said. There was no way I would be trying this cutting-the-reins malarkey again, I thought, and the horses would be doing their best even if they might be somewhat hampered by feeling ill. 'Does that mean you're staying?'

'Maybe,' he said slowly. 'I'll decide in the morning.'

'OK,' I said. 'We'll see you in the morning, then.' I said it by way of dismissal and he reluctantly turned away.

'I'll put the bridle back in the tack room for repair,' he said, turning back and reaching out for it.

'No,' I said, keeping a tight hold of the leather. 'Leave it here.'

He looked at me with displeasure, but there was absolutely no way I was going to let Ian leave the kitchen with the sabotaged bridle. Without it, he had nothing to show the authorities, even though, to my eyes, the ends of the stitches that I had cut with the scalpel looked identical to the few I had left intact, and which had then broken on the way to the start.

Ian must have seen the determination with which I was holding on to the bridle and, short of fighting me for it, he had to realize he wasn't going anywhere with it. But still he didn't leave.

'Thank you, Ian,' my mother said firmly. 'That will be all.'

'Right, then,' he said. 'I'll see you both in the morning.'

He slammed the door in frustration on his way out. I went over to the kitchen window and watched as he crunched across the gravel in the direction of his flat.

'How good a head lad is he?' I asked without turning round.

'What do you mean?' my mother said.

'Can you afford to lose him?'

'No one is indispensable,' she said rather arrogantly.

I turned to face her. 'Not even you?'

'Don't be ridiculous,' she said again.

'I'm not,' I said.

Dinner on Saturday night was a grim affair. Had it really been only one week since my arrival at Kauri House? It felt more like a month.

As before, the three of us sat at the kitchen table eating a casserole that had been slow cooking in the Aga while we had been at the races. I think that, on this occasion, it was beef but I didn't really care, and the conversation was equally unappetizing.

'So what do we do now?' I asked into the silence.

'What do you mean?' my stepfather said.

'Do we just sit and wait for the blackmailer to come a-calling?'

'What else do you suggest?' my mother asked.

'Oh, I don't know,' I said in frustration. 'I just feel it's time for us to start controlling him, not the other way round.'

We sat there in silence for a while.

'Have you paid him this week?' I asked.

'Yes, of course,' my stepfather replied.

'So how did you pay?'

'In cash,' he said.

'Yes, but how did you give him the cash?'

'The same way as always.'

'And that is?' I asked. Why was extracting answers from him always such hard work?

'By post.'

'But to what address?' I asked patiently.

'Somewhere in Newbury,' he said.

'And how did you get the address in the first place?'

'It was included with the first blackmail note.'

'And when did that arrive?'

'In July last year.'

When Roderick Ward had his accident.

'And the address has been the same since the beginning?' I asked him.

'Yes,' he said. 'I have to place two thousand pounds in fifty-pound notes in a padded envelope and post it by first-class mail each Thursday.'

I thought back to the blackmail note that I had found on my mother's desk. 'What happened that time to make you late with the payment?'

'I got stuck in traffic and I didn't get to the bank in time to draw out the money before they shut.'

'Couldn't you use a debit card in a cash machine?'

'It would only give me two hundred and fifty.'

'Can you get me the address?' I asked.

As he stood up to fetch it, the telephone rang. As one, we all looked at the kitchen clock. It was exactly nine o'clock.

'Oh God,' my mother said.

'Let me answer it,' I said, standing up and striding across the kitchen.

'No,' my mother shouted, jumping up. But I ignored her.

'Hello,' I said into the phone.

There was silence from the other end.

'Hello,' I said again. 'Who is this?'

Again, nothing.

'Who is this?' I repeated.

There was a click on the line and then a single tone. The person at the other end had hung up.

I replaced the receiver back on its cradle.

'Talkative, isn't he?' I said, smiling at my mother.

She was cross. 'Why did you do that?' she demanded.

'Because he has to learn that we aren't going to just roll over and do everything he says.'

'But it's not you that would go to prison,' my stepfather said angrily.

'No,' I said. 'But I thought we'd agreed that we can't go on paying the blackmailer for ever. Something has to be done to resolve the VAT situation, and the first thing I need to know is who the blackmailer is. I need to force him into a mistake. I want him to put his head up above the parapet, just for a second, so I can see him.'

Or better still, I thought, so I can shoot him.

The phone rang again.

My mother stepped forward but I beat her to it.

'Hello,' I said. 'Kauri House Stables.'

There was silence again.

'Kauri House Stables,' I repeated. 'Can I help you?'

'Mrs Kauri please,' said a whispered voice.

'Sorry?' I said. 'Can you please speak up? I can't hear you.'

'Mrs Kauri,' the voice repeated still in the same quiet whisper.

'I'm sorry,' I said extra loudly. 'She can't speak to you just now. Can I give her a message?'

'Give me Mrs Kauri,' the person whispered again.

'No,' I said. 'You will have to talk to me.'

The line went click again as he hung up.

My mother was crosser than ever. 'Thomas,' she said, 'please do not do that again.' She was almost crying. 'We must do as he says.'

'Why?' I asked.

'Why!' she almost screamed. 'Because he'll send the stuff to the taxman if we don't.'

'No he won't,' I said confidently.

'How can you know?' she shouted. 'He might.'

'I think it most unlikely that he'll do anything,' I said.

'I hope you're right,' my stepfather said gloomily.

'What has he to gain?' I said. 'In fact, he has everything to lose.'

'I'm the one with everything to lose,' my mother said.

'Yes,' I agreed. 'But you are paying the blackmailer two thousand a week and he won't get that if he tips off the taxman. He's not going to give up that lucrative arrangement just because I won't let him speak to you on the telephone.'

'But why are you antagonizing him?' my stepfather said.

More than two thousand years ago Sun Tzu, a mysterious Chinese soldier and philosopher, wrote what has since become the 'text book' of war, a volume that is still studied in military academies today. In *The Art of War* he stated that one should 'Beat the grass to startle the snake'. What he meant was to do something unexpected to make the enemy give away their position.

'Because I need to see who it is,' I said. 'If I knew the identity of the enemy, I could then start to fight him.'

'I don't want you to fight him,' my mother said forlornly.

'Well, we have to do something. Tax returns are overdue and it is only a matter of time before the VAT fraud is discovered. I need to identify the enemy, neutralize him, recover your money and tax papers, and then pay the tax. And we need to do it all quickly.'

The phone rang again. I picked it up.

'Kauri House Stables,' I said.

Silence.

'Now, listen here you little creep,' I said, beating the grass still further. 'You can't speak to Mrs Kauri. You'll have to speak to me. I'm her son, Thomas Forsyth.'

More silence.

'And another thing,' I said, 'all the horses from these stables will, in future, be trying their best to win. And if you don't like it, hard bloody luck. You can come and speak to me about it any time you like, face to face. Do you understand?'

I listened. There was another few seconds of silence followed by the now-familiar click as he disconnected.

I had just committed a huge tactical gamble. I had put *my* head way up over the parapet, exposing myself to the enemy, beating the grass in the hope that this particular snake would be startled enough to give away his position, so I could shoot him.

But would he shoot me first?

Sunday had been an uneventful day with apparently no further telephone calls from the whispering blackmailer. However, I couldn't be certain that he hadn't called during the time I'd been out in the middle of the day.

My mother had responded to my initiative of Saturday evening by withdrawing into her shell and not appearing at all from her bedroom until six in the evening, and only then briefly to raid the drinks cabinet before returning upstairs to bed. Derek had been despatched downstairs later to make her a sandwich for her dinner.

I was certain that, if the whisperer had called while I was out, my mother wouldn't have told me. Perhaps she felt like most of the civilians I had encountered in Afghanistan. Even though we firmly believed that we were fighting the Taliban on behalf of the Afghan people, they didn't seem to share the same view. The old adage 'my enemy's enemy is therefore my friend' simply didn't apply. It was true that most of the population loathed the Taliban but, deep down, they also hated the foreigners in their midst who were fighting them.

In the same way, I wondered if my mother considered that I was as much her enemy as her blackmailer.

Ian Norland had not made another appearance in the house on Sunday morning, and I had watched through the kitchen window as he had directed the stable staff in the mucking out, feeding, and watering of the horses. I had taken it to mean that he had decided to stay, at least for the time being. Meanwhile, the broken reins in question were sitting safely in the locked boot of my car.

At noon on Sunday I had driven into Newbury, using the Jaguar's satellite-navigation system to find the address that Derek had finally given me, the address to which he sent the weekly cash payments.

'But it's so close,' I'd said to my stepfather. 'Surely you've been to see where it is you send all this money.'

'He said not to,' he'd replied.

'And you obeyed him?' I'd asked incredulously. 'Didn't you just drive past to see? Even in the middle of the night?'

'We mustn't. We have to do exactly what he says.' He had been close to tears. 'We're so frightened.'

I could see. 'And how specifically did he tell you not to go and see where the money was going?'

'In a note.'

'And where's the note now?' I'd asked him.

'I threw it away,' he'd said. 'I know I shouldn't have, but they made me feel sick. I threw all the notes away.'

All of them except the one I'd found on my mother's desk.

'So when did the telephone calls start?'

'When he started telling us the horses must lose.'

'And when was that?' I'd asked.

'Just before Christmas.' Two months ago.

I hadn't really expected the address to provide any great revelation into the identity of the blackmailer, and I'd been right.

Number 46B Cheap Street, Newbury, turned out to be a shop with rentable mailboxes, a whole wall of them, and Suite 116 was not a suite of offices as one might have thought, but a single, six- by four-inch grey mailbox at shoulder level. The shop had been closed on a Sunday, but I had no great expectation that, had the staff been there, they would have told me who had rented box number 116. In due course, when I was ready, the police might be able to find out.

I had returned to Kauri House from Newbury via the Wheelwright Arms in the village for a leisurely lunch of roast beef with all the trimmings. I'd been in no particular hurry to get back to the depressing atmosphere at home. I decided it was time to start looking for more agreeable accommodation – past time, in fact.

Early the next morning, I drove to Oxford and parked in the multi-storey car park near the Westgate shopping centre. The city centre was quiet, even for a Monday in February. The persistent cold snap had deepened with a bitter wind from the north that cut through my overcoat as effortlessly as a well-honed bayonet through a Taliban's kurta. Most sensible people had obviously decided to stay at home, in the warm.

Oxford Coroner's Court was housed next door to the Oxfordshire County Council building in New Road, near the old prison. According to the court proceedings notice, the case in which I was interested was the second on the coroner's list for the day, the case of Roderick Ward, deceased.

It was too cold to hang around outside so I sat in the public gallery for the first case of the day, the suicide of a troubled young man in his early twenties who had hanged himself in a house he'd shared with other students. The two girls who had been his housemates cried almost continuously throughout the short proceedings. They had discovered the swinging body when they had returned from a nightclub at two o'clock in the morning, having literally stumbled into it in the dark.

A pathologist described the mechanics of death by strangulation due to hanging, and a policeman reported the recovery of a suicide note from the house.

Then the young man's father spoke briefly about his son and his expectations for the future that would now not be fulfilled. It was a moving eulogy, delivered with great dignity, but with huge sadness.

The coroner, having listened to the evidence, thanked the witnesses for attending, then officially recorded that the young man had taken his own life.

We all stood up, the coroner bowed to us, we bowed back, and he departed through a door behind his chair. In all, the formal proceedings had taken just twenty minutes. It seemed to me to be a very swift finale to a life that had lasted some twenty-two years.

Next up was the inquest into the death of Roderick Ward.

There was an exchange of personnel in the courtroom. The young suicide's father and his weeping ex-housemates trooped out, along with the policeman and the pathologist who had given evidence. In came different men in suits plus one in a navy-blue jumper and jeans who joined me in the public gallery.

I glanced at him and, just for a moment, I thought he looked familiar but, when he turned full-face towards me, I didn't know him, and he showed no sign of having recognized me.

There was no young woman in the court who might have been Stella Beecher. But, there again, she had never received the letter sent to her at 26 Banbury Drive, Summertown, by the coroner's office, to inform her that the inquest was going to reconvene today. I was absolutely sure of that because the said letter was currently in my pocket.

The inquest began with the coroner giving the details of the deceased, Mr Roderick Ward. His address was given as 26 Banbury Drive, Oxford but even I knew that was false. So why didn't the court? I wanted to stand up and tell them they were wrong but how could I do it without explaining how I knew? Once I started there would be no stopping and the whole sorry saga of the tax evasion would be laid bare for all to see, and especially for the Revenue to see. My mother would be up on a charge quicker than a guardsman found sleeping on sentry duty.

The coroner went on to say that the body of the deceased had been identified by his sister, Mrs Stella Beecher, of the same address. Another lie. Had the whole identification been a lie? Was the body found in the car actually that of Roderick Ward or of someone else? And where was Stella Beecher now? Why wasn't she here? The whole business seemed fishy to me but only because I knew that Roderick Ward himself had been busily working outside the law. To everyone else it was a simple, but tragic, road accident.

The first witness was a policeman from the Thames Valley Road Traffic Accident Investigation Team who described the circumstances, as he had determined them, surrounding the death of Roderick Ward on the night of Sunday 12 July.

'Mr Ward's dark blue Renault Mégane had been proceeding along the A415 in a southerly direction,' he said formally. 'The tyre marks on the grass verge indicate that the driver failed to negotiate the bend, veered over to the wrong side of the road and struck the concrete parapet of the bridge where the A415 crosses over the River Windrush. The vehicle appeared to have then gone into the river, where it was found by a fisherman at 8 a.m. on the morning of Monday 13 July. The vehicle was lying on its side with just six inches or so of it visible above the water level.'

The coroner stopped him there as he made some handwritten notes. 'Go on,' he said eventually, looking up at the policeman.

'The vehicle was removed from the river by crane later that morning at approximately ten thirty. The deceased's body was discovered inside the vehicle when it was lifted. He was still strapped into the driver's seat by his seat belt. The coroner's office was immediately informed and a pathologist attended the scene arriving at,' he consulted his notebook, 'eleven twenty-eight, by which time I had also arrived at the scene to begin my investigation.'

The policeman paused again as the coroner wrote furiously in his own notebook. When the writing paused, the policeman went on.

'I examined the vehicle both at the scene and also at our vehicle testing facility in Kidlington. It had been slightly damaged by the collision with the bridge but, other than that, was found to be in full working order with no deficiencies observed in either the braking or the steering. The seat belts were also noted to be in perfect condition, locking and unlocking with ease. At the scene I examined the concrete parapet of the bridge and the tyre skid marks on the grass verge. There were no marks visible on the road surface. It appeared to me from my examinations that, while the vehicle had struck the bridge wall, this collision in itself was unlikely to have been of sufficient force to prove fatal. While it was noted that the air bag in the vehicle had deployed, the damage to both vehicle and bridge indicated that the collision was minor and had occurred at a relatively low speed.'

He paused and drank some water from a glass.

'From the position and directions of the marks on the grass and the lack of skid marks on the road, I conclude that the driver might have fallen asleep at the wheel, been awakened when the vehicle rose up onto the grass verge, had then braked hard, slowing the vehicle to between ten and fifteen miles per hour before it struck the bridge parapet. The force of the collision, although fairly minor, had been sufficient to bounce the vehicle sideways into the river, the damage to the car and the bridge being consistent with that conclusion.'

The policeman stopped and waited while the coroner continued to make notes.

'Has anyone any questions for this officer,' said the coroner, raising his head from his notebook.

'Yes, sir,' said a tall gentleman in a pin-striped suit, standing up.

The coroner nodded at him, clearly in recognition.

'Officer,' the tall man said, turning to the policeman in the witness box. 'In your opinion, would this life have been saved if a crash barrier had been fitted at the point where the car went off the road into the water?'

'Most probably, yes,' said the policeman.

'And would you agree with me,' the pin-stripe suit went on, 'in your capacity as a senior police accident investigator, that the failure of the Oxfordshire County Council to erect a crash barrier at that known accident black spot was tantamount to negligence on their behalf, negligence that resulted in the death of Roderick Ward?'

'Objection,' said another suit, also standing up. 'Counsel is leading the witness.'

'Thank you, Mr Sims,' said the coroner. 'I know the procedures of this court.' He turned towards the first suit. 'Now, Mr Hoogland, I agreed that you could ask questions of the witnesses in this case but you know as well as I do that the purpose of this court is to determine the circumstances of death and not to apportion blame.'

'Yes, sir,' replied Mr Hoogland, 'but it can be within the remit of this court to determine if there has been some failure in the system. It is my client's position that a systematic failure by

Oxfordshire County Council to address the safety of the public at this point on the highway network has contributed to the death of Mr Ward.'

'Thank you, Mr Hoogland. I am also well aware of the remits and responsibilities of this court.' The coroner was clearly not amused at being lectured in his own courtroom. 'However, your question of the officer was whether, in his opinion, there had been negligence in the matter of this death. This question is not answerable by this court and would be better asked in any civil case that may be brought at a county court.' He turned to the witness. 'I uphold Mr Sims' objection. Officer, you need not answer Mr Hoogland's question.'

The policeman looked relieved.

'Are there any further questions of this witness?'

There was no fresh movement from Mr Hoogland other than to sit down. He had made his point.

However, I now wanted to stand up and ask the officer if, in his opinion as a senior police accident investigator, the circumstances of this death could have been staged such that it only appeared that the deceased had fallen asleep, hit the bridge, and ended up in the river when, in fact, he had been murdered?

But, of course, I didn't. Instead, I sat quietly in the public gallery in frustration, wondering why I was suddenly becoming obsessed with the idea that Roderick Ward had been murdered. What evidence did I have? None. And, indeed, was the deceased actually Roderick Ward in the first place?

'Thank you, officer,' said the coroner. 'You may step down, but please remain within the vicinity of the court in case you are needed again.'

The policeman left the witness box and was replaced by a balding, white-haired man with half-moon spectacles wearing a tweed suit. He stated his name as Dr Geoffrey Vegas, resident pathologist at the John Radcliffe Hospital in Oxford.

'Now, Dr Vegas,' said the coroner, 'can you please tell the court what knowledge you have concerning the deceased, Mr Roderick Ward?'

'Certainly,' replied the doctor, removing some papers from the inside pocket of his jacket. 'On the morning of July the thirteenth I was asked to attend the scene of an RTA – a road traffic accident – near Newbridge where a body had been discovered in a submerged vehicle. When I arrived at the scene the body was still in the car but the car had been lifted from the river and was on the road. I examined the body in situ and confirmed that it was of a male adult and that life was extinct. I gave instructions that the body be removed to my laboratory at the John Radcliffe.'

'Did you notice any external injuries?' asked the coroner.

'Not at that time,' replied the doctor. 'The surface of the skin had suffered from immersion in the water and the extremities and the face were somewhat bloated. The cramped conditions in the car did not lend themselves to more than a limited examination.'

And I bet they weren't very pleasant conditions, either, I thought. I'd once had to deal with some dead Taliban whose bodies had been submerged in water and it was not a task I chose to dwell on.

'And did you perform a post-mortem examination at the hospital?'

'Yes,' replied Dr Vegas. 'I completed a standard autopsy examination of the deceased that afternoon in my laboratory. My full report has been laid before the court. I concluded that death was due to asphyxia, that's suffocation, resulting in cerebral hypoxia – a reduced supply of oxygen to the brain – and then cardiac arrest. The asphyxia appeared to be due to prolonged immersion in water. Put simply, he drowned.'

'Are you certain of that?' the coroner asked.

'As certain as any pathologist could be. There was water present in the lungs, and in the stomach, both of which indicate that the deceased was alive when he entered the water.'

'Are there any other findings that you would like to bring specifically to the court's attention?' asked the coroner, who, I thought, must have surely read the pathologist's full report prior to the hearing.

'A blood test indicated that the deceased had been more than three times over the legal alcohol limit for driving a vehicle on the public highway.' He said it in a manner that clearly indicated that the accident, and the death, had been the deceased's own fault, and nothing else mattered.

'Thank you, Doctor,' said the coroner. 'Does anyone else have any questions for this witness?'

I wanted to jump up and ask him if he had carried out a DNA test to be certain that the body was actually that of Roderick Ward. The police must have had his DNA on record after his arrest for throwing the brick in Hungerford. And I also wanted to ask the doctor why he was so certain that the deceased had died in the way he had described. Had he done a test to confirm that the water in the lungs had actually come from the river? Could the man not have been forced to drink heavily, then been drowned elsewhere and just tipped into the river in his car when he was already dead? Could the pathologist be certain it wasn't murder? Had he, in fact, even considered murder as an option?

But, of course, again I didn't. Once more I remained sitting silently in the public gallery wondering if I was looking for something sinister in this death that didn't actually exist. Something that might begin to lead me to a resolution of my mother's problems.

Mr Hoogland, however, did stand up again to ask some questions of the doctor, but even he would have had to admit that, in the light of the blood-alcohol evidence, he was on a hiding to nothing.

'Dr Vegas,' he began anyway, 'can you tell the court if, in your opinion, Mr Ward would be alive today if a crash barrier had been installed at that location, preventing his vehicle from entering the water? Were there, for example, any injuries you found that he had sustained in the accident that would, by themselves, have proved fatal without his drowning?'

'I can state that there were no injuries that Mr Ward had suffered in the collision which would normally have resulted in loss of life,' the doctor replied. 'In fact, there were almost no injuries of note, just a minor contusion to the right side of the head that would be consistent with it banging against the driver's-side window during the collision with the bridge.' He turned to the coroner. 'This may have been sufficient to render the deceased briefly unconscious or unaware, especially in his inebriated condition, but it would have been insufficient, on its own, to cause death. On examination of the deceased's brain, I found no evidence of injury as a result of the collision.'

It was obviously not the specific unequivocal answer that Mr Hoogland had been hoping for. He tried again. 'So let me get this clear, Dr Vegas. Are you saying that Mr Ward would now be alive if a safety barrier had been present at the spot?'

'That I cannot say,' replied the doctor. He pulled himself up to his full height and delivered the killer blow to Mr Hoogland's argument. 'In the state that Mr Ward must have been in that night from drink there is no saying that, if he had been able to drive on from that point, he wouldn't have killed himself, and possibly others, in another road traffic accident somewhere else.'

The coroner, using his notes, summed up the evidence and then recorded a verdict of accidental death with Mr Ward's excessive alcohol consumption as a contributory factor.

No one objected, no one cried foul, no one believed that a

whitewash had occurred. No one other than me, that was. And maybe I was just being paranoid.

I stood up and followed the man in the navy-blue jumper and jeans out of the courtroom.

'Are you family?' I asked his back.

He turned towards me and I thought again that I recognized him.

'No,' he said. 'Are you?'

'No,' I said.

He smiled and turned away. In profile, I was struck once more by his familiarity. I was about to say something more to him when I realized who he must be.

It was true that I'd never met the man before, but I was certain I'd spoken to his father only the previous Friday. They had exactly the same shape of head.

The other man in the public gallery had been Fred Sutton, the detective sergeant son of Old Man Sutton, he of the broken window and the false teeth.

I hung back as Fred Sutton made his way out of the court building. I didn't really want to talk to him, but I did want to speak to the unfortunate Mr Hoogland.

I caught up with him in the lobby. Close up he was even taller than he had appeared in court. I was almost six foot but he towered over me.

'Excuse me, Mr Hoogland,' I said, touching him on the arm. 'I was in the court just now and I wondered who you were acting for.'

He turned and looked down at me. 'And who are you?' he demanded.

'Just a friend of Roderick Ward,' I said. 'I wondered if you were acting for his family. None of them seem to be here.'

He looked at me for a second or two as if deciding whether to tell me or not. 'I am acting for a life-insurance company,' he said.

'Really,' I said. 'So was Roderick's life insured?'

'I couldn't say,' said the lawyer, but it was pretty obvious it had been, otherwise why was he here asking questions and trying to imply negligence by the county council? Insurance companies would try anything to save themselves from having to pay out.

And who, I wondered, was the potential beneficiary of the insurance?

'So were you satisfied with the verdict?' I asked.

'It's what we expected,' Mr Hoogland said dismissively, looking past my right shoulder.

Time to dive in, I thought. 'Are you absolutely sure that the dead man in the car was Roderick Ward?'

'What?' he said, suddenly giving me his full attention.

'Are you sure that it was Roderick Ward in that car?' I asked again.

'Yes, of course. The body was identified by his sister.'

'Yes, but where is the sister today?' I said. 'And is she the beneficiary of your client's insurance policy?'

He stared at me. 'What are you implying?'

'Nothing,' I lied. 'I'm just curious. If my brother had died, and I'd been the one to identify him, then I'd be at the inquest.' Mr Hoogland wasn't to know that the coroner's letter to Stella Beecher was in my pocket.

'Why didn't you say this in court?' he asked.

'I'm not what they call "an officially interested party",' I said, 'so why would I be allowed to speak? And it's not compulsory for members of the deceased's family to be present at an inquest. Anyway, I don't have access to the full pathologist's report. For all I know, he might have already done a DNA test and double checked it against the national DNA database.'

'Why would Roderick Ward's DNA be on the database?' he asked.

'Because he was arrested two years ago for breaking windows,' I replied. 'It should be there.'

Mr Hoogland opened a notebook and made some notes.

'And what is your name?' he asked.

'Is that important?' I said.

'You can't go round making accusations anonymously.'

'I'm not accusing anyone,' I said. 'I just asked you if you were sure it was Roderick Ward in that car.'

'That in itself is an accusation of fraud.'

'Or murder,' I said.

He stared at me again. 'Are you serious?'

'Very,' I said.

'But why?'

'It just seems too easy,' I said. 'Late at night on a country road with little or no traffic, low-speed collision, contusion on the side of the head, alcohol, car tips into convenient deep stretch of river, no attempt to get out of the car, life insurance. Need I go on?'

'So what are you going to do about your theory?'

'Nothing,' I said. 'It's not me that has the client who's about to pay out a large sum in life assurance.'

I could see by his expression that he was having doubts. He must be asking himself if I was a complete nutter.

'You've nothing to lose,' I said. 'At least find out for sure if the deceased really was Roderick Ward by getting a DNA test done. Maybe the pathologist already has. Look in his report.'

He said nothing but stared at a point somewhere over the top of my head.

'And ask the pathologist if he tested to determine if the water in the lungs actually came from the river.'

'You *do* have a suspicious mind,' he said, again looking down at my face.

'Did Little Bo Peep actually lose her sheep or were they stolen?'

He laughed. 'Did Humpty Dumpty fall or was he pushed?'

'Exactly,' I said. 'Do you have a card?'

He fished one out of his jacket pocket and gave it to me.

'I'll call you,' I said, turning away.

'Right,' he shouted to my departing back. 'You do that.'

11

I woke in agony. And in the dark, pitch-black dark.

Where was I?

My arms hurt badly and my head was spinning, and there was some sort of cloth on my face, rough cloth like a sack.

What had happened?

It felt as if I was hanging by my arms and my shoulders didn't like it, not one bit. My whole back ached and my head pounded as if there were jackhammers trying to break out of my skull behind my eyes. I felt sick, very sick, and I could smell the rancid odour of vomit on the cloth over my face.

How had I got here?

I tried to remember but the pain in my arms clouded every thought. Being blown up by an IED had nothing on this. My upper body screamed in agony and I could hear myself screaming with it. Whoever thought too much pain brought on unconsciousness was an idiot. My brain, now awake, clearly had no intension of switching off again. How much pain does it take to kill? I wondered. Surely it was time for me to die?

Was this just another bad dream?

No, I decided, this was no dream. This agony, sadly, was reality.

I wondered if my arms were actually being pulled from their sockets. I couldn't feel my hands, and I was suddenly very afraid.

Had I been captured by the Taliban? The very thought struck terror into my heart. I could feel myself coming close to panic, so I put such thoughts back in their box and tried to concentrate solely on the locations of my pain and its causes.

Apart from the ongoing fire in my back and arms, my left leg also hurt, in particular my heel. 'Concentrate,' I shouted out loud at myself. 'Concentrate.' Why does my heel hurt? Because it's pressing on the floor. Now I realized for the first time that I wasn't hanging straight down. My left foot was stretched out in front of me. I bent my knee, pulled my foot back, and stood up. The searing agony in my shoulders instantly abated. The change was dramatic. I no longer wanted to die. Instead, I became determined to live.

Where was I? Who had brought me here? And why?

The same questions kept rotating over and over in my head.

I knew that I couldn't have been captured by the Taliban. I remembered that I was in England, not in Afghanistan. At least, I assumed I was still in England. But could I assume anything? The world had suddenly gone mad.

I felt dizzy. Why couldn't I stand up properly?

Then I remembered that too.

I reached down to the floor with my right leg. Nothing. My prosthesis was missing. I could feel the empty right trouser-leg flapping against my left calf as I moved my leg back and forth.

Standing up, even on one leg, had vastly improved the pain in my back and shoulders, and feeling was beginning to return to my hands with the onset of horrendous pins and needles. But that was a pain I could bear. It was a good sign. In fact, it was the only good sign I could think of at the moment.

My head went on throbbing and I continued to feel sick.

I turned my head from side to side, which did nothing to improve my nausea. Not a chink of light was visible at any point through the hood. I heel-and-toed myself through half a revolution and looked again. Still nothing.

I was at home in darkness but, even so, I closed my eyes tight. I had discovered many years ago that with my eyes firmly held shut I could somehow switch off that part of my brain that dealt with visual images and increase the concentration on my other senses.

I listened but could hear nothing, save my own breathing inside the hood.

I smelled the air but the overpowering stench of vomit clouded out almost everything. There was, however, a faint sweet smell alongside it. Glue, perhaps, I thought, or something like an alcoholic solvent.

With my now recovered and responsive fingers, I searched the space above my head. My wrists were tightly bound together by some sort of thin plastic, which was in turn attached to a chain. I followed the chain along its short length until I came to a ring fixed into the solid wall. The ring was set just over my head height and was about two inches across. I could feel that the chain was secured to it by a padlock.

I leaned forward against the wall. There was something running horizontally that was sticking into my elbows. I couldn't quite get my hands low enough to feel it, so I used my face through the cloth. The horizontal bar ran in both directions as far as I could feel with a small ledge above it. I banged on the wall with my arms and suddenly I knew where I was.

I was in a stable. The horizontal bar and ledge that I could feel was the top of the wooden boarding that runs round a box to protect a horse from kicking out at the unforgiving brick or stone. And the ring in the wall was there to tie up the horse, or to hang a hay-net.

But which stable was I in? Was it in my mother's stable yard? Was Ian Norland asleep upstairs?

I shouted. 'Can anyone hear me? Help! Help!'

I went on shouting for ages but no one came running. I don't think the hood helped. My voice sounded very loud to me inside it but I wondered if the noise had even penetrated beyond the stable.

I was pretty sure I wasn't at Kauri House Stables. When I stopped shouting to listen, it was too quiet. Even if there had been an empty box in my mother's yard there would be horses nearby, and horses make noises – even at night – and especially if someone is shouting their head off next door.

I was beginning to be particularly irritated by the hood, not least by having to breathe vomit fumes, even if it was my own vomit. I tried to hold the material and pull it off but it was tied too tightly round my neck and I couldn't reach down with my hands far enough to untie it. I would just have to stand the irritation. It was nothing compared to the previous pain in my shoulders.

I stood on my one leg for a long time. Occasionally I would lean back against the wall, but mostly I just stood.

I wondered how long I had been here before I woke, and how much longer I was to remain. But that decision wasn't mine.

Night turned into day. I found that I could distinguish between them because a very small amount of light did penetrate the dark cloth of the hood and, if I turned my head, I could tell that there was a window to my left as I stood with the wall behind me.

The day brought nothing new.

I went on standing for hours.

I was hungry and thirsty, and my leg began to ache. And to make matters worse, I desperately needed to pee.

I tried to remember how I had come to be here. I could recall the inquest and speaking to Mr Hoogland. What had happened after that?

I had walked back to my car in the multi-storey car park. I could remember being annoyed that someone had parked so close to my Jaguar on the driver's side. I had purposely parked it on a high level well away from any other cars and it was not just because I didn't want to get my paintwork scratched. The attaching system for my prosthetic leg meant I couldn't bend my right knee through more than about seventy degrees, so getting into my low sports car was not as easy now as it had once been.

My annoyance had stemmed from the fact that the particular level of the car park was still almost empty but, nevertheless, someone had parked within a foot of the offside of my car. I remembered wondering how on earth I was going to open the driver's door wide enough to get my arm in, let alone my whole body.

But I had never reached the door to try.

Something had knocked me down and I remembered having a towel wrapped around my face. The towel had been soaked in ether. I had known immediately what it was. The boys from the transport pool had used ether in Norway when the battalion had been there on winter exercise. They'd injected it straight into the engine cylinders to get the army trucks started when the diesel fuel was too cold to ignite. All the troops, including me, had tried sniffing the stuff to get high. But ether was also an anaesthetic.

And the next thing I'd known had been waking up in this predicament.

Who could have done such a thing?

And why had I been so careless as to let it happen? I'd been off my guard, thinking about the inquest and my conversation with the lawyer Hoogland. I had stuck my head up over the parapet but I hadn't been shot, I'd been kidnapped.

I wasn't sure which was worse.

As time passed, I became hungrier and the pain in my bladder grew to the extent that, in the end, I had to let go, the urine briefly warming my leg as it ran down to the floor.

But it was the thirst and the fatigue that were becoming my greatest problems.

In the army, soldiers were used to standing for long periods, especially in the Guards regiments. Lengthy stints of ceremonial duty outside the royal palaces in London taught all guardsmen to stand completely still for hours, unmoved and unamused by the antics of camera-wielding tourists or little boys with water pistols.

I had done my time there as a young guardsman, but nothing had prepared me for half a day standing on only one leg, unable to go for a march to alleviate the pain, and especially the cramp that was now starting to affect my calf. I tried rocking back and forth from heel to toe but my heel was still sore and it didn't do much good. I tried resting my elbows on the ledge at the top of the wooden panelling to relieve the pressure. But nothing helped for long.

I bent my knee and allowed some of my weight to hang once more from my hands, but soon the pain in my shoulders returned and my hands started to go numb once more.

I spent some more time shouting, but no one came and it just made me even thirstier.

What did the people who did this want from me?

I would gladly give them everything I owned just to sit down with a glass of water.

Values and Standards of the British Army states that prisoners must be treated with respect and in accordance with both British and international law. International law is based on the four Geneva Convention treaties and the three additional protocols that set the standards for the humanitarian treatment of victims of war.

I knew; I'd been taught as much at Sandhurst.

In particular the conventions prohibit the use of torture. Hooding, sleep deprivation, and continuous standing had all been designated as torture by case law in the European Court of Human Rights. To say nothing of the withholding of food and water.

Surely someone had to come soon.

But they didn't, and the light from the window went away as day turned into my second night in the stable.

I passed some of the time counting seconds.

Mississippi one, Mississippi two, Mississippi three, and so on . . . and on . . . and on. Mississippi sixty to one minute, Mississippi sixty times sixty to one hour. Anything to keep my mind off the pain in my leg.

Eventually, sometime after midnight by my Missippippi calculations, it dawned on me that my kidnapper simply wasn't going to arrive with food and water for his hostage. If he had been going to, he'd have come during the daylight hours or in the early evening.

I faced the shocking reality that I wasn't here to be ransomed, I was here to die.

In spite of the pain in my leg, I went to sleep.

I only realized when I lost my balance and was woken by the jerk of the chain attached to my wrists. I twisted round so I was facing the wall and stood up again.

I was cold.

I was only in my shirtsleeves. I'd been wearing an overcoat when I walked back to the car from the coroner's court but it had obviously been removed.

I shivered, but the cold was the least of my worries.

I was desperately thirsty and I knew that my body must be dehydrating. My kidneys had gone on making urine and I had peed three times during the day, losing liquid down my leg that I could ill afford. I knew from my training that, in these cool conditions, human beings could live for several weeks without food but only a matter of a few days without water.

The knowledge was not comforting.

I thought back to the survival-skills instructor at Sandhurst who had told me that. The whole platoon had sat up and taken special notice of the attractive female captain from the Royal Army Medical Corps who had taught us about the physiological effects of the various situations in which we might find ourselves.

Sadly, there hadn't been a lecture on how to stand for ever on one leg.

But the captain had turned out to be more than just an army medico who knew the theory, she was a get-up-and-go girl who had put it into practice. She was the female equivalent of Bear Grylls, spending all her army leave on expeditions to remote parts, and she could count both Poles as well as the top of Everest in her CV.

'If you're in a bit of a spot,' she had said, grossly understating some of the 'spots' she had described from her own experiences, 'never just sit and wait to be rescued. Your best bet for survival is always to evacuate under your own steam if that is humanly possible. There are well-documented occasions when people with broken legs or worse, left for dead high up on Everest, have subsequently turned up alive at Base Camp. They crawled off the mountain. No one else was going to save them, so they saved themselves.'

I was definitely in a bit of a spot.

Time, I thought, to save myself.

First things first. I had to get myself disconnected from the ring in the wall. It sounded deceptively easy.

I reached up with my hands to where the chain was attached

by the padlock. The ring stuck straight out from the wall as if it had been screwed in as a single piece. I grabbed hold of it with my right hand and tried to twist it anticlockwise. It didn't budge an iota.

I went on trying for a long time. I wrapped the chain round the ring and put all my weight on it. I then tried to twist the chain, rotating my body round and round, back and forth, hoping that I would find a weak link to snap. Nothing.

Next I tried turning the ring clockwise in case it had a left-hand thread. Still nothing, other than sore fingers.

I jerked it with the chain, on one occasion throwing myself off balance and back into the hanging-by-shoulders position. But still the damn ring didn't shift. If I couldn't detach myself from the ring then I would simply hang here until I died of dehydration, and the exertions of trying to escape would reduce the time that would take.

'Always evacuate under your own steam if that is humanly possible.' That's what the lady captain had said. Maybe freeing myself from the ring wasn't humanly possible.

I felt like crying, but I knew that would be another loss of precious fluid.

And I desperately needed an evacuation of a different kind.

How degrading bodily functions could be when they occurred in the wrong place at the wrong time. At least in hospital, when I'd been bedridden and incapable, there had been bedpans and nurses close by to assist. Here I was standing on my one very sore leg, imprisoned in a stable, unable to even to remove my trousers, let alone to squat or sit on a toilet.

Who was the bastard who would force me to shit in my pants?

I was angry. Bloody angry.

I tried to channel my anger into a resurgence of energy and strength as I once more gripped the ring and tried to turn it. Again it resisted.

'Come on you bugger, move!' I shouted at the ring. But it didn't.

I rested my head in frustration on the ledge at the top of the wooden panelling. So fed up was I that I bit through the cloth of the hood into the wood.

It moved.

I thought I must be imagining it so I bit the wood again. It definitely moved.

I felt around with my face. The ledge on the top of the panelling was about four centimetres wide with its front edge curved, and it was the curved edge that had moved. It was obviously a facing strip that had been glued or nailed on to the front of the ledge.

I bit into the wood again. Even through the hood, I found I could get my front teeth behind the curved beading. I bit hard and pulled backwards, using my arms to press on the wall. The curved beading strip came away from the ledge far enough for me to get my mouth round it properly. I pulled back again and it came away some more.

I was pulling so hard with my mouth that, when one end of the strip pulled completely free, I again lost my balance and ended up hanging from the chain.

But I didn't care.

I pulled my knee back under me and stood up. The beading was flapping with one end free and the other still attached. There had obviously been a join in the wood just a little way to my left.

I held the wood in my mouth and twisted my neck to the right, making the free end bend upwards. I could feel the free end on my arms and finally, after nearly twisting myself again off my foot, I was able to grasp the strip in my hands.

I now bent myself to the right, folding the strip back on itself.

It snapped with a splintering crack, leaving me holding a free length of the beading. I couldn't see how long it was but I carefully fed it through my fingers until I reached the end. This I put through the ring and then I used it like a crowbar.

Still the ring resisted and I again lost my balance and ended hanging by the chain as the end of the wood broke off. But I didn't let go of the rest of it.

I stood up once more and passed the broken end back through the ring.

This time I turned the wood through ninety degrees so that it was edge on, and hoped it would be more difficult to break. Then I leaned on it with as much weight as I dared.

The ring moved. I felt it. I leaned again. It moved some more.

I was so excited that I was laughing.

The ring had almost moved half a revolution. I put the wooden strip into my mouth to hold it, almost gagging on the vomit-tasting cloth. I then reached up and tried to turn the ring with my fingers. It was stiff but it turned, slowly at first, then over and over until I could feel it part company with the wall.

I could lower my arms. I was free of my shackle. What bliss!

I quickly hauled down my trousers and pants, and then crouched against the wall to defecate. I could remember from my boyhood that my father had often described his morning constitutional on the lavatory as his golden moment of the day. Now, at long last, I knew what he meant. The relief was incredible. So much so that I hardly cared that disengaging myself from the wall was only the first step in my escape.

I pulled my things up and heel-and-toed my way along the wall until I found a corner. With difficulty, I sat down on the floor. I still had my wrists tied and I was still wearing the hood but the joy of not having to stand up any longer was immense.

Stage one was complete. Now I had to remove the hood and free my wrists. No problem, I thought. If I could get away from that wall everything else must be a piece of cake.

I lifted my hands to my neck and found the drawstring of the hood. With my hands still bound together at the wrists, it was not easy to untie the knot, and I'd probably tightened it with all my earlier tugging. However, I finally managed to get the string free and I gratefully pulled the oppressive, fetid cloth over my head. I breathed deeply. The atmosphere may not have been that fresh, for obvious reasons, but it was a whole lot better than the rancid, vomit-smelling air I'd been breathing for the past thirty-six hours.

I shook my head and pushed my fingers through my hair.

Stage two complete. Now for my hands.

It was too dark to see exactly how they were tied but, by feeling with my tongue, I worked out that my kidnapper had used the sort of ties that gardeners use to secure bags of garden waste, or saplings to poles. The loose end went through a collar on the other end, and was then pulled tight, very tight, one tie on each wrist looped through both each other and the chain.

I tried biting my way through the plastic but it was too tough and my efforts ended with me still tied up, but now with a sore mouth where the free ends of the ties kept sticking into my gums.

I looked around. It may have been dark but there was just enough light entering for me to see the position of the window. I thought that, if I could get outside, I might be able to find something to cut the plastic. But how was I going to get outside with only one leg, and with my wrists tied up?

How about the glass in the window? Could I use that to cut the plastic?

If getting down to the floor had been difficult, it was nothing compared to getting up again. Finally, I was upright, but cramp in my calf had me hopping around to try to ease it. I leaned on the wall and stretched forward and the cramp thankfully subsided.

I hopped along the wall to the window.

It wasn't glass, it was perspex. It would be. I suppose the horses would break glass. The window was actually made of two panes of perspex in wooden frames, one above the other, like a sash window. I slid the bottom pane up. The real outdoor fresh air tasted so sweet.

But now I discovered there was another problem.

The window was covered on the outside by metal bars set about four inches apart. I'd had no food for two days but even I wasn't yet slim enough to fit through that gap. I rested my head on my arms. I could feel the panic beginning to rise in me again. I was so thirsty and I could hear the rain. I held my arms out through the window as far as they would go but they didn't reach the falling water. There was just enough light for me to see that the roof had an overhang. I would have needed arms six feet long to reach the rain. And, to add insult to injury, it began to fall more heavily, beating like a drum against the stable roof.

Water, water everywhere, Nor any drop to drink.

More in hope than expectation, I hopped further along the wall to the stable doors. As I'd expected, they were bolted. I pushed at them but they didn't shift. I would have stood and kicked them down if only I'd had a second leg to stand on while I did so.

Instead I slithered down in the corner by the door until I was again sitting on the floor. Wiggling myself into position on my back, I tried to use my left leg to kick the lower section of the door. I kicked as hard as I could but the door didn't budge. All I managed to do was to slide myself in the other direction across the stone floor.

I gave up and went to sleep.

It was light when I woke and I could see my prison cell properly for the first time. It was nothing extraordinary, just a regular stable stall with black-painted wooden boarding round the walls, and timber roof beams visible above.

I worked myself back into the corner by the door and sat up, leaning against the wall, to inspect the bindings on my wrists.

The black plastic ties looked so thin and flimsy but, try as I might, I couldn't break them. I twisted my wrists first one way then the other but all that happened was that the plastic dug painfully into my flesh, causing it to bleed. The damned plastic ties seemed totally unaffected.

The length of chain was still attached to the ties. It was grey and looked to me like galvanized steel. There were fifteen links in all, I counted them, each link a little under one inch long with a shiny brass padlock still attaching the end link to the now-unscrewed ring. The chain looked brand new. No wonder I hadn't been able to break it.

I tried to use the point of the ring to cut through one of the ties but I couldn't get a proper grip on it and only managed instead to cut through the skin at the base of my thumb as the point slipped off the surface of the plastic.

I looked around the stable for something sharp, or for a rough brick corner, anything I could use to saw my way through my bonds. Up on the wall opposite the window was a salt-lick housing, a metal slot about four inches wide, seven high and one inch deep, into which a block of salt or minerals could be dropped so that, as the name suggested, the horse could lick it. The housing was empty, old and rusting.

I struggled up from the floor and hopped over to it. As I had hoped, the top of the metal slot had been roughened by the rust. I hooked the plastic ties over one of the edges, with a wrist on either side, and sawed back and forth. The plastic was no match for the metal edge and the tie on my left wrist parted quite easily. Wonderful!

I massaged the flesh, then set about ridding myself completely of the remaining tie round my right wrist, and the chain that still hung from it. That task proved a little more difficult but, after a few minutes, I was finally free of the damn things.

Stage three was complete. Now to get out of this stable.

*

Stable doors are always locked from the outside, whether or not the horse has bolted first, and this one was no exception.

I could just see the locks from the window. The metal bars were bowed away slightly from the frame and, by turning sideways I could use my left eye to see the bolts, top and bottom in the lower door and a single bolt in the upper. All three had been slid fully away from me, and then folded flat.

I took the window bars in my hands and tried to shake them. Not even a quiver. It was as if they were set in concrete.

So there was no easy way out, but I'd hardly expected there to be. No one was going to go to the trouble of shackling me to the wall with a chain and padlock only then to leave the door wide open.

The way out, as I saw it, was to go up.

I could see from the window that the stable where I was imprisoned was just one in a whole line of them that stretched away in both directions. The walls between the individual stalls did not go all the way to the pitched roof; they were the same height as the walls at the front and rear of the building, about nine feet high. So there was a triangular space between the top of the wall and the roof. A wooden roof truss sat on top of the wall but there was still plenty of room for someone to get through the gap from one stall to the next. All I had to do was climb the wall.

Easy, I thought. There had been walls much higher than this on the assault course at Sandhurst, walls I had been forced to cross time and time again. However, there were some big differences. Either there had been a rope hanging from the top or there'd been a team of us working together. And I had been much fitter and stronger when at Sandhurst, and, of course, I'd had two feet to work with.

I looked at either side of the stable. Which way should I go?

In the end, the decision was simple. In the corner opposite the door was a metal manger set across the angle. It was about four feet from the floor. I may have had only one foot, but I had two knees and I was soon using them to kneel on the edge of the manger while reaching up with my fingers for the top of the wall.

All those hours of trying to break the battalion record for pull-ups finally paid off. Fuelled by a massive determination to free myself, together with the all-consuming craving for a drink, I pulled myself up onto the top of the wall and swung my legs through the gap in the truss and into the next stall.

Dropping down was less easy and I ended up sprawled on my back. But I didn't care, I was laughing again. I turned over and crawled on my hands and knees to the door.

It was locked.

My cries of joy turned to tears of frustration.

OK, I thought, getting a grip on things, how about the window?

More bars. Squeezing myself up against them, I could see that there were bars on all the stable windows.

OK, I just have to keep going. One of these damn stables must have a door that's open.

Having done it once, the manoeuvre was easier the second time. I even managed not to end up horizontal on the floor. But the next door was also locked.

What if they were all bolted shut? Was I wasting my energy and, worse still, breathing out precious water vapour in a fruitless attempt?

I clambered onto the manger in the corner and went over the next wall. The door to that box was also locked. I sat in the corner and wept. I realized that I must be dehydrated as I wept without tears.

What would happen, I wondered, when the lack of water became critical? I'd been thirsty now for so long that every part of my mouth and throat was sore, but I didn't feel that I was dying yet. How would my body react over the next day or so?

What would be the first sign that it was shutting down? Would I even realize?

I thrust such thoughts from my mind. Come on, I told myself. Maybe the door will be open in the next stable.

It wasn't.

My fingers hurt from pulling myself up and, on that occasion, I had twisted my ankle when I dropped down. Thankfully, it wasn't a bad injury, but it was enough to send me into another bout of despair. Was this how it would happen? Would I become an emotional, gibbering wreck? Would I eventually just curl up in a ball in a corner and die?

'No!' I shouted out loud. 'I will not die here.'

Willpower alone pulled me up over the next wall. Beyond it I found not another stable but an empty and disused tack room at the end of the row. I used the saddle racks to ease my way to the floor and save my ankle from further punishment.

The tack-room door was locked, of course. It would be.

And I could see there was nowhere else to go. The far wall of the tack room went all the way to the roof. It was the end of the building, the end of the line.

The door had a mortice deadlock, I could see through the keyhole. Why, I wondered, had someone bothered to lock an empty room?

I leaned against the locked door in renewed frustration. For the very first time I really began to believe that I would die in this stable block.

My stomach hurt from lack of food and my throat felt as though it was on fire from lack of water. I had expended so much of my reserves just getting to the tack room that the thought of going all the way back to where I'd started, and then beyond, filled me with horror. And there was no saying that I would be able to. The mangers would now all be on the wrong side of the walls.

I looked through the small window alongside the door. The light was beginning to fade as fresh, delicious, glorious rain fell again into puddles that were tantalizingly out of my reach. It would soon be dark. This would be my third night of captivity. Without water to drink, would I still be alive for a fourth?

Suddenly, as I looked through at the gloom and rain, I realized there were no bars on this window. The bars had been placed over the stable windows to keep the horses' heads in, not to keep burglars out. There were no horses in the tack room, so no bars.

And the single pane of this window was glass, not plastic like the others.

I looked around for something with which I could break it. There was absolutely nothing, so I sat on one of the saddle racks and removed my shoe.

The glass was no match for a thirsty man in a frenzy. I used the shoe to knock all the glass from the frame, careful to leave no jagged shards behind.

The window was small, but it was big enough. I clambered through head first, using the end of my stump to stand on the frame while I pulled my complete leg through. Soon I was standing outside the building.

What a magnificent feeling. Stage four was complete.

I hopped out from under the overhanging roof to stand in the rain with my head held back, and my mouth wide open.

Never had anything tasted so sweet.

12

Escaping from the stable building was only the first of the hurdles.

I didn't know where I was and I could hardly hop very far. I was hungry, with no food, and, perhaps most important of all, I had no idea who had tried to kill me.

Would they try again when they discovered that I was still alive?

And would they come back here to check? To dispose of the body?

Why had they not made sure by bashing my head in rather than leaving me alive to die slowly?

I knew from my own experience that killing another person wasn't easy. It was fine if you could do it at a distance. Firing a rocket-propelled grenade into an enemy position was easy. Taking out an enemy commander from half a mile away using a sniper rifle and a telescopic sight was a piece of cake. But sticking a bayonet into the chest of a squirming, screaming human being at arm's length was quite another matter.

Whoever had done this had left me alive in the stable for their own benefit, not for mine. They had intended to kill me but had wanted time and dehydration to do their dirty work for them.

In that respect, I had an advantage over them. If, and when, we met again they might hesitate before killing me outright and that hesitation would be enough for me, and an end for them. Another Sandhurst instructor floated into my memory. 'Never hesitate,' he'd said. 'Hesitate, and you're dead.'

*

The falling rain did not give me anywhere near enough water to quench my roaring thirst so I tried one of the taps that were positioned outside each stable. I turned the handle but no water came out. Not surprisingly, the water was off.

In the end, I lay down on the concrete and lapped water from a puddle like a dog. It was easier and more fulfilling than using my cupped hands to try to lift it to my mouth.

Hunger and mobility were now my highest priorities.

What I needed was a crutch, something like a broom to put under my arm. I crawled on hands and knees back along the line of stables until I came to the one I had been held in. I pulled myself upright, slid the bolts on both parts of the door, and opened them wide. I had become used to the fresh outside air and the rank, disgusting smell in the stable caught me unawares. I retched but there was nothing in my stomach to throw up. Had I really lived in there for two days? How bad would the smell have been if I'd died there?

There was no broom in the stable, I knew that, but I had decided to take the ring, the chain and the padlock away with me. If I did go to the police, I would have them as evidence. I also collected the bits of the plastic ties. One never knew, perhaps they were distinctive enough to point to whoever had bought them.

I looked around my prison cell one last time before closing the door. I slid home the bolts as if wanting to lock the place out of my memory.

I hopped along the line and opened the next stable. I was looking for a broom, but I discovered something a whole lot better.

Suddenly things were looking up. Lying on the floor was my artificial leg, together with my overcoat.

Hanging me up to die had been a calculated evil. But removing my leg had been nothing more than pure malice. I resolved, there and then, that I would make the person who did this to me pay a heavy price.

I leaned against the door frame and put the leg on, rolling the securing rubber sleeve up over my knee.

I had always rather hated it, this *thing* that wasn't a real part of me. But now I gladly accepted it back as more than just a necessary evil – it was a chum, an ally, and a brother. If nothing else, the last two days had taught me that, without my metal-and-plastic companion, I would be a helpless and incapable warrior in battle. But, together, my prosthesis and I would be a force to be reckoned with.

The joy of walking again on two legs was immense. The familiar clink-clink was like music to my soul.

I picked up my coat and put it on against the cold. My shirt was still wet from standing in the rain and I was grateful for the coat's thick, warm, fleecy lining. I put my hands into the pockets and found, to my surprise, my mobile telephone, my wallet, my car keys, and the business card from Mr Hoogland.

The phone was off. I'd switched it off for the inquest. I turned it on and the familiar screen appeared. I wondered who I should call.

Who did I trust?

I explored the stable block to try to find out where I was.

I could have probably used my mobile to call the police and they would have been able to trace where the signal came from, but I really wanted to find out for myself.

I had visions of lying in wait for my would-be murderer to come back to check that I was dead. What chance would I have of getting my pay-back if the boys in blue arrived with flashing lights and sirens, clomping round the place in their size-ten boots, letting the world know I'd been found and frightening away my quarry?

But, before all that, I desperately needed some food. And a shower.

There were no horses in any of the stalls. And there were no people in the big house alongside them. The place was like a ghost town. And all the doors were locked. So I walked across the gravel turning area, past the house, and down the driveway.

For the umpteenth time I went to look at my watch, but it wasn't on my wrist. It was the one thing I'd had with me in Oxford that was still missing, other than my Jaguar. My would-be murderer must have removed it to tie me up. I had looked all around to try to find it without success.

However, I judged from the light that it must be after five p.m. There was just enough brightness for me to see where I was going, but full darkness would not be far away.

The driveway was long but downhill, which helped, and, at the end, there were some imposing, seven-feet-high wrought-iron gates between equally impressive stone pillars. The gates were closed and firmly locked together by a length of chain and a padlock that both looked suspiciously similar to those in my coat pocket.

I looked up at the top of the gates. Did I really have to start climbing again?

No, I didn't. A quick excursion ten yards to the left allowed me to step through a post-and-rail fence. The imposing gates were more for show than for security. But the chain and padlock would have been enough to prevent some passing nosey parker from driving up to the house to have a look round, someone who might then have found me in the stables.

There was a plastic sign attached to the outside of one of the gateposts.

FOR SALE, it said in bold capital letters, then gave the telephone number of an estate agent. I recognized the dialling code: 01635 was Newbury.

The estate agent's sign was nailed over another wooden notice. I pulled the for-sale sign away to reveal the notice beneath and I could just see the painted words in the gathering gloom. GREYSTONE STABLES, it read. And in smaller letters underneath, LARRY WEBSTER – RACEHORSE TRAINER.

I could remember someone had told me about this place. 'The Webster place,' they'd said. 'On the hill off the Wantage road.' So I was back in Lambourn, or just outside. And I could see the village lights about half a mile or so down the road.

What do I do now, I thought.

Do I phone my mother and ask her to collect me, or do I call the police and report a kidnapping and an attempted murder? I knew I should. It was the right and sensible thing to do. I should have done it as soon as I found my phone. It was easy – just push 999 and wait. And then my mother would simply have to take her chances with the taxman, and the courts.

Yet something was stopping me from calling the police, and it wasn't only the belief that my mother would then end up losing everything: her house, her stables, her business, her freedom, and, perhaps worst of all for her to bear, her reputation.

It was something more than that. Maybe it was the need to fight my own battles, to prove to myself that I still could. Possibly it was to show the major from the MOD that I wasn't ready for retirement and the military scrap-heap.

But, above all, I think it was the desire to inflict personal revenge on the individual who had done this to me.

Perhaps it was some sort of madness, but I put the phone in my pocket and called no one. I simply started walking towards the lights, and home.

I was alive and free and, for as long as someone believed that I was tied up and dying, I had the element of surprise on my side.

In strategic terms, surprise was everything. The air attack on Pearl Harbor just before eight o'clock on a sleepy Sunday morning in December 1941 was testament to that. Eleven ships had been either sunk or seriously damaged and nearly two hundred aircraft destroyed on the ground for fewer than thirty of the attackers shot down. More than three and a half thousand Americans had been killed or wounded for the loss of just sixty-five Japanese. I knew because, at Sandhurst, each officer cadet had to give a presentation to their fellow trainees about a Second World War engagement, and I had been allocated Pearl Harbor.

Surprise had been crucial.

I had already shown myself to the enemy once and I had barely survived the consequences. Now I would remain hidden and, better still, my enemy must surely believe that I'd already been neutralized and was no longer a threat. Just when he thought I was dead I would rise up and bite him. I wanted my Glenn-Close-in-the-bath moment from *Fatal Attraction*, but I wasn't going to then get shot and killed, as her character had been.

I walked through the village, keeping to the shadows and avoiding the busy centre where someone might have spotted me near the brightly lit shop windows. Only the damn clink-clink of my right leg could have given me away. I resolved to find a way to make my walking silent once more.

When I arrived at the driveway of Kauri House I paused.

Did I really want my mother and stepfather to know what had happened to me? How could I explain my dirty and dishevelled condition to them without explaining how I came to be in such a state? And could I then trust them not to pass on the knowledge to others, even accidentally? Absolute secrecy might be vital. 'Loose talk costs lives' had been a wartime slogan. I certainly didn't want it costing mine.

But I urgently needed to eat, and I also wanted to wash and put on some clean clothes.

As I approached I could see that the lights were on in the stables and the staff were busily mucking out and feeding their charges.

I skirted around the house and approached down the outside of the nearest stable rectangle, trying to keep my leg as quiet as possible. Only at the very last instant did I briefly step into the light, and only then when I was sure no one was looking.

I went quickly up the stairs and let myself in to Ian Norland's unlocked flat above the stables.

I'd taken a chance that Ian would not have locked the door while he was downstairs with the horses, and I'd been right. Now I had to decide what to tell him. It had to be enough to engage his help but, amongst other things, I thought it best not to inform him that his employer was effectively trading while insolvent, something that was strictly against the law. And I didn't want to scare him into instantly calling the police. I decided that I wouldn't tell him the whole truth, but I would try not to tell him any outright lies.

While I waited for him to finish with the horses, I raided his refrigerator. Amongst the cans of beer there were precious few food items so I helped myself to a two-litre plastic bottle of milk. It had been as much as I could do not go into the Rice Bowl Chinese takeaway in the village on my way through. But I had every intention of convincing Ian that he needed to go there for me the minute he came up from the stables.

I'd completely finished his two litres of milk by the time I heard him climbing the stairs.

I stood tight behind the door as he came in, but he saw me as soon as he closed it. After the cut-bridle altercation of the previous Saturday, I wasn't exactly expecting a warm welcome, and I didn't get it.

'What the bloody hell are you doing here?' he demanded loudly.

'Ian, I need your help,' I said quickly.

He looked at me closely, at my filthy and torn clothes and the stubble on my chin. 'Why are you in such a mess?' he asked accusingly. 'What have you been up to?'

'Nothing,' I said. 'I'm just a bit dirty and hungry, that's all.'

'Why?' he said.

'Why what?' I said.

'Why everything?' he said. 'Why are you lurking in my flat like a burglar? Why didn't you go to the house? And why are you hungry and dirty?'

'I'll explain everything,' I said. 'But I need your help and I don't really want my mother to know I'm here.'

'Why not?' he demanded. 'Are you in trouble with the law?'

'No, of course not,' I said, trying to sound affronted.

'Then why don't you want your mother to know you're here?'

What could I say that would convince him?

'My mother and I have had an argument,' I said. I'd clearly failed dismally in my aim of not telling him any lies.

'What over?' he said.

'Does it matter?' I said. 'You know my mother. She can argue over the smallest of things.'

'Yeah, I know,' he said. 'But what was this particular argument about?'

I could see that he was going to be persistent. He needed an answer.

'Over the running of the horses,' I said.

Now he was interested.

'Tell me.'

'Can I use your bathroom first?' I asked. 'I'm desperate for a shower. I don't suppose you have any spare clothes my size?'

'Where are yours?'

'In the house.'

'Do you want me to fetch them?' he asked.

'How could you?' I said. 'My mother would surely see.'

'She's out,' he said. 'She and Mr Philips have gone to some big event in London. Saw them go myself around five o'clock. All dressed up to the nines, they were. She told me she'd be back for first lot in the morning.'

'But there are lights on in the house.'

'For the dogs,' he said. 'I'll go over and let them out before I go to bed. I'll turn off the lights and lock up then.'

So I could have probably gone into the house all along and never bothered Ian. I remonstrated with myself for insufficient reconnaissance of the place before I'd come up to Ian's flat. I'd assumed my mother was at home, but I should have checked.

'But my mother's car is in the driveway,' I said. I remember having seen it as I rounded the house.

'They were collected by a big flash car with a driver,' he said. 'Seems like Mrs Kauri was the guest of honour or something.'

'Will they be back tonight?'

'I don't know,' he said. 'All she said was she'd see me at seven thirty in the morning.'

Maybe I hadn't needed to involve Ian at all, but now that I had, could he still help me?

'Right, then,' I said decisively, using my voice-of-command. 'I'll go over to the house to have a shower and change while you go to the Chinese takeaway and get us both dinner. I'll have beef in black-bean sauce with fried rice.' I held out some money from my wallet. 'And buy some milk as well. I'm afraid I've drunk yours.'

He stood silently looking at me, but he took the money.

I glanced at the clock on his wall. 'I'll be back here in forty-five minutes to eat and talk.'

*

It was nearer to fifty minutes by the time I climbed back up the stairs to Ian's flat, having enjoyed a long soak in a hot bath to ease my still-aching shoulders. And I'd brought some of my stuff with me.

'What's in the tube?' Ian asked.

'My sword,' I said. 'I thought it might be useful.'

'For what?' he said in alarm. 'I'm not doing anything illegal.'

'It's OK,' I said. 'Calm down. I promise I won't ask you to do anything illegal.'

'How about you?' he asked, still disturbed.

'I won't do anything illegal either,' I assured him. 'I promise.'

Another of those promises that I wondered whether I could keep. In this case, I was rather hopeful that I wouldn't be able to, but I decided not to tell that to Ian.

He relaxed somewhat.

'So, can I stay here?' I asked, placing my bag, and the tube, on the floor.

'What? Sleep here?' he said.

'Yes.'

'But I've only got the one bed.' From his tone I gathered that he had no desire to share.

'That's OK,' I said. 'I only want the floor.'

'You can have the sofa.'

'Even better,' I said 'Now, how about that food? I'm starving.'

He served it out onto two fairly clean plates on his tiny kitchen table and I tucked into mine with gusto. I suspect a doctor would have told me that a bellyful of Chinese was not really the best medicine for a starved stomach, but I didn't care. It tasted pretty good to me.

Finally, I sat back and pushed the plate away with a sigh. I was full.

'Blimey,' said Ian, who had only just started his sweet-and-sour pork. 'Anyone would think you hadn't eaten for a week.'

'What day is it?' I asked.

He looked at me strangely. 'Wednesday.'

Had it really only been on Monday that I'd gone to Oxford for the inquest? Just two and a half days ago? It seemed like longer. In fact, it felt like half a lifetime.

Did I want to tell Ian why I was so hungry? Did he need to know why I hadn't eaten since Monday morning? Perhaps not. It would take too much explaining, and he might not be very happy that I hadn't called the cops.

'Not too many restaurants about when you're living rough,' I said.

'Living rough?'

'Yeah,' I said. 'I've been up on the Downs for a couple of nights in a shelter I made.'

'But it's so cold, and it's done nothing but rain all week.'

'Yeah, and don't I know it. I couldn't light my fire,' I said. 'But it's all good training. Nothing like a bit of discomfort to harden you up.'

'You army blokes are barmy,' Ian said. 'You wouldn't catch me outside all night in this weather.' He poured more bright pink sweet-and-sour sauce over his dinner.

So much for not telling him outright lies; I'd hardly uttered a word that was true.

'So tell me,' he said. 'What was it about the running of the horses that you argued with your mother about?'

'Oh, nothing, really,' I said, back-pedalling madly. 'And I am sure she wouldn't want me talking to you about it.'

'You might be right there,' he said, smiling. 'But tell me anyway.'

'I told you, it was nothing,' I said. 'I just told her that, in my opinion, and based on his last run at Cheltenham, Pharmacist wasn't ready for the Gold Cup.'

'And what did she say?' Ian asked, pointing his fork at me.

'She told me to stick my opinion up my you-know-where.'

He laughed. 'For once, I agree with her.'

'You do?' I said, sounding surprised. 'When I was here, you know, when we watched the race on the television, you said that he couldn't now run at the Festival.'

'Well,' he said defensively, 'I may have done at the time, in the heat of the moment like, but I didn't really mean it. One bad performance doesn't make him a bad horse, now, does it?'

'But I only said it to my mother because I thought that's what you thought.'

'You should have bloody asked me, then.' He speared a pork ball on his fork and popped it into his mouth.

'Looks like I'll have to beg forgiveness and ask to be allowed home.'

'Did she throw you out just for saying that?' He spoke with his mouth full, giving me a fine view of his sweet-and-sour pork-ball rotating like the contents of a cement mixer.

'Well, there were a few other things too,' I said. 'You know, personal family things.'

He nodded knowingly. 'In a good row, one thing just leads to another and then another, don't it.' He sounded experienced in the matter, and I wondered whether there had once been a Mrs Norland.

'You are so right.'

'So, do you still want to stay here?' he asked.

'Absolutely,' I said. 'I'm not going home to my mother with my tail between my legs, I can tell you. I'd never hear the end of it.'

He laughed again and took another mouthful of his pork. 'Fine by me, but I warn you, I get up early.'

'I want to be gone before first light.'

'The sun comes up at seven these days,' he said. 'It's light for a good half an hour or so before then.'

'Then I'll be well gone by six,' I said.

'To avoid your mother?'

'Perhaps,' I said. 'But you can ask her where she thinks I am. I'd love to know what she says, but don't tell her I've been here.'

'OK, I'll ask her, and I won't tell her you're here, or what we talked about,' he said, 'but where are you going?'

'Back to where I've been for these past few days,' I said. 'I've some unfinished business there.'

I took my sword, still safely stowed in its tube, when I slipped out of Ian's flat at just after five thirty on Thursday morning. I also took the remains of our Chinese takeaway, and half the milk that Ian had bought the night before.

In addition, I took my freshly charged mobile telephone and the card from Mr Hoogland. I might need something to pass the time.

I retraced my path from Kauri House, through the still-sleeping village, and down the Wantage road to Greystone Stables. One of the major successes of the night was that I had managed to stop my leg clinking every time I put it down. The problem, I discovered, had been where the leg post met the ankle. The joint was tight enough, but the clink was made by two metal parts coming together when I put my weight on it. I'd eventually silenced it using an adjustable spanner and a square of rubber that Ian had cut from an old leaking wellington boot. Now I relished being able to move silently once more.

The gates at the bottom of the driveway were still locked together with the chain and padlock, and they didn't appear to have been touched since I'd left them the previous evening. However, I wasn't going to assume that no one had been up to the stables in the intervening twelve hours; I would check.

I stepped back through the post-and-rail fence and climbed

carefully and clink-free up the hill, keeping off the tarmac surface to reduce noise, listening and watching for anything unusual. Halfway up the drive I checked the spot where, the previous evening, I had placed a stick leaning on a small stone. A car's tyre would have had to disturb it to pass by, but the stick was still in place. No one had driven up this hill overnight, not unless they had come by motorbike.

I wasn't sure whether I should be pleased or disappointed.

Even so, I was still watchful as I approached the house, keeping within the line of vegetation to one side of a small overgrown front lawn. The sky was lightening in the east with a lovely display of blues, purples, and reds. In spite of being completely at home in the dark, I had always loved the coming of the dawn, the start of a new day.

The arrival of the sun, bringing light and warmth and driving away the cold and darkness of the night, was like a piece of daily magic, revered and worshipped by man and beast alike. How does it happen? And why? Let us just be thankful that it does. If the sun went out we would all be in the poop, and no mistake.

The rim of the fiery ball popped up over the horizon and flooded the hillside with an orange glow, banishing the gloom from beneath the bushes.

I silently tried the doors of the house. They were still locked.

I went right round the house, across the gravel turning area and back into the familiar stable yard beyond. In the bright morning light it looked very different from the rain-soaked space of the evening before. The stables had been built as a rectangular quadrangle with boxes along three sides and the open end facing the house.

First I went down to the far end of the left-hand block, knelt down, and carefully picked up all the shards of glass that still lay on the concrete below the window I'd broken. I placed them all carefully back through the window and out of sight. I had no way of replacing the glass pane but one had to look closely to see that it was missing.

I walked down the row of boxes to my prison cell and opened both leaves of the stable door, hooking them open so that no one could quickly shut me in again before I could react.

I searched the stall once more, mostly for my watch, but also in case I had missed anything else in the murk of the previous evening. I found nothing other than the small pile of my own excrement drying nicely next to the wall beneath where the ring had been secured. I knew that Special Forces teams such as the British SAS or the American Delta Force, when dropped in behind enemy lines, were trained not to leave any trace of their presence, and that included collecting their own faeces in sealable plastic bags and keeping them in their packs.

In the absence of a suitable plastic bag, I decided to leave mine exactly where they were.

I quickly searched the stall next door, the one where I had found my prosthetic leg and my coat. My watch wasn't there either. Damn it, I thought, I really liked that watch.

I closed and re-bolted the stable doors and spent a moment or two checking that the positions of the bolts were precisely as I had found them. Now all I needed was a place to hide, and wait.

I thought of using one of the other stalls further along but I quickly rejected the idea. For one thing, I would have had no obvious route of retreat if things started going badly. And secondly, I really did not want my enemy to spot that the bolts were not properly shut and simply lock me in as he passed, maybe even unaware that I was waiting inside. I'd had my fill of being locked in stables for this week.

In the end I found the perfect location.

In the middle of the row opposite the block of boxes in which

I'd been imprisoned was a passageway that ran right through the building from front to rear. The passage had a door in it, on the stable-yard end, but the latch was a simple lever, not a bolt. The door was made from slats of wood screwed to a simple frame with inch-wide gaps between the slats to allow the wind to blow through. The door had a spring near the hinge to keep it closed, but that would not have been there as a security measure, merely to keep the door shut so as to prevent any loose horses getting through and escaping.

I lifted the latch, pulled open the door, and went through the passageway. Behind the stables was a muck heap, the pile of soiled straw and woodchip bedding where the stable staff would dump the horse dung ready for the manure man to collect periodically and sell to eager gardeners. Except that this muck heap hadn't been cleared for a long while and there were clumps of bright green grass growing through the straw on its surface.

The passageway had obviously been placed there to provide access to the muck heap from the stable yard. And it made an ideal hiding place.

Behind the block I found an empty blue plastic drum that would do well as a seat, and I was soon sitting behind the door in the passageway, watching and waiting for my enemy to arrive.

I longed to have my trusty SA80 assault rifle beside me, with fixed bayonet. Or, better still, a gimpy with a full belt of ammunition.

Instead, all I had was my sword, but it was drawn from its scabbard and ready for action.

13

I waited a long time.

I couldn't see the sun from my hiding place but I could tell from the movement of the shadows that many hours had passed, a fact borne out by the clock read-out on the screen of my mobile phone when I turned it on briefly to check.

I drank some of the milk, and went on waiting.

No one came.

Every so often I would stand up and walk back and forth a few times along the short passageway to get the blood moving in my legs. But I didn't want to go out into the stable yard in case my quarry arrived while I was there.

I began to wish that I had chosen a spot where I could see the gate at the bottom of the drive. From my hiding place in the passageway, I wouldn't have any warning of an arrival before they were upon me.

I went over and over the scenario, rehearsing it in my mind.

I fully expected that my would-be murderer would arrive by car, drive across the gravel turning area, through the open gateway into the stable yard, and park close to the box where he would expect me still to be. My plan was to leave my hiding place just as he entered the stable, to move silently and quickly across the yard, and simply to lock him into my erstwhile prison cell almost before he had a chance to realize that I wasn't still hanging there, dead.

What would happen next remained a little hazy in my mind. Much might depend on who it was. A young fit man would be able to escape over the walls and through the tack room, as I had done. An elderly or overweight adversary would prove less of a problem. I would simply be able to leave them in the stable for a bit of their own medicine. But would I leave them there to die?

And what would I do if my enemy turned out to be more than one person?

It was a question I had pondered all morning. An unconscious man, even a one-legged unconscious man, was heavy and cumbersome to move. Could one person have had enough strength to carry me into the stable and also hold me up while padlocking me to the ring? If so, it must have been a very strong individual and escape through the tack-room window would be a real possibility.

The more I thought about it, the more convinced I became that there must have been at least two of them. And that put a completely different slant on things. Would I consider taking on an enemy that outnumbered my own forces – just me – by two to one, or even more?

Sun Tzu, the father of battle tactics, stated, *If you are in equal number to your enemy, then fight if you are able to surprise. If you are fewer, then keep away*.

I decided that if two or more turned up then I would just watch from my hiding place, and I'd keep away.

At three in the afternoon, while still maintaining a close watch of the stable yard, I called Mr Hoogland. I was careful to withhold my phone number as I didn't want him inadvertently passing it on to the wrong person.

'Ah, hello,' he said. 'I've been waiting for you to call.'

'Why?' I asked.

'I got some answers to your questions.'

'And?' I prompted.

'The deceased definitely was Roderick Ward,' he said.

'Oh.'

'You sound disappointed.'

'No, not really,' I said. 'Just a bit surprised. I'd convinced myself that Roderick Ward had staged his own apparent death while he was actually still alive.'

'So who did you think was found in the car?' he asked.

'I don't know. I was just doubtful that it was Ward. How come you're so sure it was him?'

'I asked the pathologist.'

'So he had done the DNA test, then?'

'Well, no, he hadn't. Not until after I asked him.' He laughed. 'I think I gave the poor man a bit of a fright. He went pale and rushed off to his lab. But he called me this morning to confirm that he has now tested some of the samples he kept, and the profile matches the one for Ward in the database. There's absolutely no doubt that the body in the river was who we thought it was.'

Well, at least that ruled out Roderick as the blackmailer.

'Did the pathologist confirm if the water in Ward's lungs matched that from the river?'

'Oh, sorry. I forgot to ask him.'

'And how about Ward's sister?' I asked. 'Did you find out anything about her?'

'Yes, as a matter of fact I did. It seems her car broke down on the morning of the inquest and she couldn't get to the court in time. The coroner's office told her they would have to proceed without her and she agreed.'

'But she only lives in Oxford,' I said. 'Couldn't she have taken a bus? Or walked?'

'Apparently, she's moved,' he said. 'They did give me her address but I can't remember it exactly. But it was somewhere in Andover.'

'Oh,' I said. 'Well, thanks for asking. Seems I may have been barking up the wrong tree.'

'Yeah,' he said wistfully. 'It's a shame. It would have made for a good story.'

'Yeah,' I echoed.

'For your paper?' he said, fishing.

'I'm not a journalist,' I replied with a laugh. 'I'm just a born sceptic. Bye, now.'

I hung up, smiling, and turned off my phone.

And still no one came.

I ate the cold remains of the previous evening's Chinese food and drank some more of the milk.

Why would anyone want me dead? And there was now no doubt that my death was what they had intended. I couldn't imagine what state I would have been in if I'd had to stand on one leg for four whole days and three nights. I would surely have been close to death by then, if not already gone.

So who wanted me dead? And why?

It seemed a massive over-reaction to being told on the telephone that Mrs Kauri's horses would, henceforth, be running on their merits and not to the order of a blackmailer.

Deliberate cold-blooded murder was a pretty drastic course of action, and there was no doubt that my abduction and imprisonment had been premeditated as well as cold-blooded. No one carries an ether-soaked towel around on the off-chance that it might be useful to render someone unconscious; or have some plastic ties, a handy length of galvanized chain, and a padlock lying about just in case someone needs to be hung on a wall. My kidnap had been well planned and executed, and I didn't expect there would be much forensic evidence available that would point to the perpetrators, if any.

So would they even bother to come back and check on their handiwork? Returning here would greatly increase their chances of leaving something incriminating, or of being seen. Wouldn't they just assume that I was dead?

But didn't they know? Never assume anything – always check.

The sun went down soon after five o'clock, and the temperature went down with it.

Still I waited, and still no one came.

Was I wasting my time?

Probably, I thought, but what else did I have to do with it? At least being out in the fresh air was better for me than lying on my bed, staring at the moulded ceiling of my room.

I stamped around a bit to get some warmth into my left toes. Meanwhile my phantom right toes were baking hot again. It was all very boring.

When my telephone told me it was nine p.m. I decided that enough was enough, and it was time to go back to Ian's flat before he went to bed and locked me out. I had never intended to stay at Greystone Stables all night. Twenty-four-hour stag duty was too much for one person. I had already found myself nodding off during the evening, and a sleeping sentry was worse than no sentry at all.

I put my sword back in its scabbard, and then I put that back in the cardboard tube, which I swung over my shoulder.

Halfway down the driveway I checked that the stick was still resting on the stone. It was. I set up another on the other side of the drive a few yards further down, just in case the strengthening breeze blew one of them over.

Apart from the slight chill of the wind, it was a beautiful evening with a full canopy of bright stars in the jet-black sky. But it was going to be a cold night. The warm blanket of cloud of the previous few days had been blown away and there was already a frost in the air that caused my breath to form a white mist in front of my face as I walked down towards the gates.

I was climbing through the post-and-rail fence when I saw the headlights of a car coming along the Wantage road from the direction of Lambourn village. I thought nothing of it. The road could hardly be described as busy, but three or four cars had passed by the gates in the time it had taken for me to walk down the driveway.

I decided, however, that it would not be such a clever idea to be spotted actually climbing through the fence, so I lay down in the long grass and waited for the car to pass by.

But it didn't pass by.

It pulled off the road and stopped close to the gates. The headlights went out and I heard rather than saw the driver get out of the car and close the door.

I lay silently face-down in the grass about ten yards away. I had the tube with my sword in it close to my side but there would be no chance of extracting it here without giving away my position.

I lifted my head just a fraction but I couldn't see anything. The glare of the headlights had destroyed my night vision and, in any case, the person would have been out of my sight behind the stone gatepost.

I closed my eyes tight shut and listened.

I could hear the chain jingling as it was pulled through the metal posts of the gates. Whoever had just arrived in the car had brought with them the key to the padlock. This was indeed my enemy.

I heard the gates squeak a little as they were opened wide.

I again lifted my head a fraction and stole a look as the driver returned to the car but my view was obstructed by the open car door. I was lying in a shallow ditch beneath the post-and-rail fence and my eye-line was consequently below the level of the driveway. From that angle it had been impossible to see who it was.

I heard the engine start and the headlights came back on.

I was sure the car would go up the driveway, but I was wrong.

It reversed out onto the road and drove away, back towards the village. I rose quickly to my knees. If I'd only had my SA80 to hand I could easily have put a few rounds through the back window and taken out the driver, as I had once done when a Toyota truck had crashed through a vehicle checkpoint in Helmand. As it was, I simply knelt in the grass with my heart thumping loudly in my chest.

I hadn't identified my enemy but, even in the dark, I thought I'd recognized the make of the car, even if I couldn't see the colour.

'So what did my mother say?' I asked Ian when I returned to his flat at Kauri House Stables.

'About what?' he said.

'About where I was.'

'Oh, that. She was rather vague. Just said you'd gone away.'

'So what did you say?' I pressed.

'Well, like you told me to, I asked her where you'd gone.' He paused.

'And?'

'She told me it was none of my business.'

I laughed. 'So what did you say to that?'

'I told her, like you said, that you'd left a pen here when you watched the races and I wanted to give it back.' He infuriatingly paused once more.

'And?'

'She said to give the pen to her and she'd get it returned to you. She said that you had unexpectedly been called to London by the army and she didn't know when you would be back. Your note hadn't said that.'

'My note?' I said in surprise.

'Yeah. Mrs Kauri said you sent her a note.'

'From London?' I asked.

'Oh, I don't know that,' Ian said. 'She didn't say, but there was no note, right?'

'No,' I said truthfully. 'I definitely didn't send her any note.'

But someone else may have.

I woke at five after another restless night on Ian's couch. My mind was too full of questions to relax, and I lay awake in the dark, thinking.

Why had my enemy not gone up to the stables to make sure I was dead? Was it because they were convinced that by now I would be? Perhaps they didn't want to chance leaving any new evidence, like fresh tyre tracks in the stable yard. Maybe it was because it didn't matter any more. Or was it just because they didn't want to have to see the gruesome results of their handiwork? I didn't blame them on that count. Human bodies – dead ones, that is – are mostly the stuff of nightmares, especially those that die from unnatural or violent causes. I knew, because I'd seen too many of them over the years.

If my enemy hadn't bothered to go up to the hill the previous evening after unlocking the gates, I didn't expect them ever to go back there again. So I decided not to spend any more of my time waiting for them in the Greystone Stable passageway. Anyway, I had different plans for today.

'Andover,' the lawyer Hoogland had said.

Now, why did that ring a bell?

Old Man Sutton, I thought. He now lived in a care home in Andover. I'd been to see him. And Old Man Sutton's son, Detective

Sergeant Fred, had been at Roderick Ward's inquest. And Roderick Ward's sister had moved to live in Andover. Was that just a coincidence?

I heard Ian get up and have a shower at six.

I sat on the sofa and attached my leg. Funny how quickly one's love for something can sway back and forth like a sail in the wind. On Wednesday afternoon I had embraced my prosthesis like a dear long-lost brother. It had given me back my mobility. Now, just thirty-six hours later, I was reverting to viewing it as an alien being, almost a foe rather than a friend, a necessary evil.

Perhaps the major from the MOD had been right. Maybe it really was time to look for a different direction in my life. If I survived my present difficulties, that was.

'Can I borrow your car?' I asked Ian over breakfast.

'How long for?' he said.

'I don't know,' I said. 'I've got to go to a cashpoint to get some money, for a start. And I might be out all morning, or even all day.'

'I need to go to the supermarket,' he said. 'I've run out of food.'

'I'll buy you some,' I said. 'After all, I'm the one who's eaten all your cereal.'

'All right, then,' he said, smiling. 'I'd much rather stay here and watch the racing from Sandown on the telly.'

'Do we have any runners?' I asked, surprising myself by the use of the word 'we'.

'Three,' Ian said. 'Including one in the Artillery Gold Cup.'

'Who's riding it?' I asked. The Royal Artillery Gold Cup was restricted to amateur riders who were serving, or who had served, in the armed forces of the United Kingdom.

'Some chap with a peculiar name,' he said, somewhat unhelpfully.

'Which peculiar name in particular?'

'Something to do with football,' he said. 'Hold on.' He dug into a pile of papers on a table by the television. 'I know it's here somewhere.' He went on looking. 'Here.' He triumphantly held up a sheet of paper. 'Everton.'

'Everton who?' I asked.

'Major Jeremy Everton.'

'Never heard of him,' I said. It was not that surprising. There were more than fourteen thousand serving officers in the regular army, and more still in the Territorials, to say nothing of those who had already left the service.

Ian laughed. 'And he's never heard of you, either.'

'How do you know?' I asked.

He laughed again. 'I don't.'

I laughed back. 'So can I borrow your car?'

'Where's yours?'

'In Oxford,' I said truthfully. 'The head gasket has blown,' I lied. 'It's in a garage.'

I thought that my Jaguar was probably still in the multi-storey car park in Oxford city centre, and I had decided to leave it there. To move it would be to advertise, to those who might care, that I wasn't hung-up dead in a deserted stable.

'OK. You can borrow it,' he said, 'provided you're insured.'

I should be, I thought, through the policy on my own car, provided they didn't object to my driving with an artificial foot.

'I am,' I said confidently. 'And I'll fill it with fuel for you.'

'That would be great,' Ian said. He tossed me the keys. 'The handbrake doesn't work too well. Leave it in gear if you park on a hill.'

I caught the keys. 'Thanks.'

'Will you be back here tonight?' he asked.

'If you'll have me,' I said. 'Do you fancy an Indian?'

'Yeah,' he said. 'Good idea. Get me a chicken balti and a

couple of onion bhajis. And some naan.' He spoke with the assurance of a man who dined often from the village takeaway menus. 'And I'll have some raita on the side.'

It was only fair, I thought, that I bought our dinner.

'OK,' I said. 'About seven thirty?'

'Make it seven,' he said. 'I go down the Wheelwright on a Friday.'

'Seven it is, then. See you later.'

I slipped out of Ian's flat while it was still dark and, as quietly as possible, I drove his wreck of a Vauxhall Corsa down the drive and out into the village.

Newbury was quiet at seven o'clock on a Friday morning, although Sainsbury's car park was already bustling with early-morning shoppers eager to beat the weekend rush for groceries.

I parked in a free space between two other cars, but I didn't go into the supermarket. Instead, I walked in the opposite direction, out of the car park, across the A339 dual-carriageway, and into the town centre.

Number 46B Cheap Street was just one amongst the long rows of shops that lined both sides of the road, most of them with flats or offices above. The mailbox shop that occupied the address opened at eight thirty and closed at six, Monday to Friday, and from nine until one on Saturdays. It said so on the door.

If, as usual, my stepfather had posted the weekly package to the blackmailer, the one containing the two thousand pounds, on Thursday afternoon, then the package he sent yesterday should arrive at 46B Cheap Street sometime today and be placed in mailbox 116, ready for collection.

Mailbox 116 was visible through the front window of the shop and I intended watching it all day to see if anyone arrived to make a collection. However, I could hardly stand outside on the pavement scrutinizing every customer who came along. For a start, they would then be able to see me, and I certainly didn't want that to happen.

That was why I had come to Newbury so early, so that I could make a full reconnaissance of the area and determine my tactics to fit in with the local conditions and pattern of life.

At first glance there seemed to be two promising locations from which to observe the comings and goings at number 46B without revealing my presence. The first was an American-style coffee shop about thirty yards away, and the second was the Taj Mahal Indian restaurant that was directly opposite.

I decided that the restaurant was the better of the two, not only because it was in such a good position, but because there was a curtain hanging from a brass bar halfway down the window, behind which I could easily hide while keeping watch through the gap in the middle. All I needed was to secure the correct table. A notice hanging on the restaurant door told me that it opened for lunch at noon. Until then I would have to make do with the coffee shop, which began serving in half an hour, at eight o'clock.

I wanted to be well in place before the mailbox shop opened. I had no idea at what time the post was delivered but, if I'd been the blackmailer, I wouldn't have left the package lying about for long, not with that much money in it.

I went round the corner into Market Street and found a bank with a cashpoint. I drew out two hundred pounds and used some of it to buy a newspaper at the newsagent's on the corner. It wasn't that I needed something to read, doing that might cause me to miss seeing the collector, but I did need something to hide behind while sitting in the large windows of the coffee shop.

*

At eight thirty sharp I watched from behind my newspaper as a man and a woman arrived, unlocked the front door of the mailbox shop, and went in. From my vantage point I could just about see box number 116, but the reflection from the window didn't make it very easy. As far as I could tell, neither of the two arrivals opened that box, or any other for that matter, but, as they were the shop staff, they wouldn't have had to. They would have had access to all the boxes from behind.

I drank cups of coffee and glasses of orange juice and hoped that I looked to all the world like a man idling away the morning reading his newspaper. On two occasions one of the coffee-shop staff came over and asked me if I needed refills, and both times I accepted. I didn't want them asking me to move on, but I was becoming worried about my level of liquid intake, and the inevitable consequences. I could hardly ask one of the staff to watch the mailbox for me while I nipped to the loo.

By ten o'clock I had drunk nearly three large cups of coffee, as well as three orange juices, and I was becoming desperate. It reminded me of the agony I'd suffered in the stable, but on this occasion I wasn't chained to a wall. I left my newspaper and coffee cup on the table by the window to save my place, and rushed to the gents.

Nothing outside appeared to have changed in the short time I was away. The street had become gradually busier as the morning wore on but, so far, I'd not recognized anyone. I quickly rescanned the faces in front of me so as not to miss a familiar one, but there were none.

At ten to eleven I did spot someone coming slowly down the street who I recognized. I didn't know the man himself, but I did know his business. It was the postman. He was pushing a small four-wheeled bright-red trolley and he was stopping at each shop and doorway to make his deliveries. He went into the mailbox shop with a huge armful of mail held together by rubber bands. From that distance I couldn't tell whether my stepfather's package had been amongst it or not, but I suspected it had. And the blackmailer would surely assume so.

'Are you staying all day?' A young waitress was standing at my elbow.

'Sorry?' I asked.

'Are you staying all day?' she asked again.

'Is there a law against it?' I asked. 'I've ordered lots of coffee, three orange juices, and a Danish pastry.'

'But my friend and I think you're up to something,' she said. I turned in my chair and looked at her friend, who was watching me from behind the relative safety of the chest-high counter. I turned back and checked the street outside.

'Now, why is that?' I asked.

'You're not reading that newspaper,' she said accusingly.

'And why do you think that?'

'You've been on the same page for at least the past hour,' she said. 'We've been watching. No one reads a paper that slowly.'

'So what do you think I'm doing?' I asked her, still keeping my eyes on the mailbox shop.

'We think you're keeping watch for bank robbers.' She smiled. 'You're a cop, aren't you?'

I put a finger to my lips. 'Shhh,' I said with a wink.

The girl scuttled back to her friend and, when I looked at them a minute or two later, they both put fingers to their lips and collapsed in fits of giggles.

I had half an hour to go before the Taj Mahal opened but I reckoned I couldn't stay here any longer. I wasn't keen on the attention I was now receiving from just about all the coffee-shop staff as well as from some of the customers.

I beckoned the girl back over to me.

'I've got to go now,' I said quietly, paying my bill. 'My shift is over. But remember,' I put my finger to my lips again, 'shhh. No telling.'

'No, of course not,' she said seriously.

I stood up, collected my unread newspaper, and walked out. I thought that, by lunchtime, she would have told all her friends of the encounter, and half of their friends' friends would probably know by this evening.

I walked away down the street, certain that my every move was being watched by the girl, her friend, and most of the other coffee-shop staff. I couldn't just hang around outside, so I went into the shop right next door to the Indian restaurant. It sold computers and all things electronic.

'Can I help you, sir?' asked a young man, approaching me.

'No thanks,' I said. 'I'm just looking.'

Looking through the window.

'Just call if you want anything,' he said, and he returned to where he was fiddling with the insides of a stripped-down computer.

'I will,' I assured him.

I stood by a display case in the window and went on watching the shop across the road through the glass. I glanced at the display case. It was full of cameras.

'I'd like to buy a camera,' I said without turning round.

'Certainly, sir,' said the young man. 'Any particular one?'

'I want one I can use straight away,' I said. 'And one with a good zoom.'

'How about the new Panasonic?' he said. 'That has an eighteen times optical zoom and a Leica lens.'

'Is that good?' I asked, still not turning round to him.

'The best,' he said.

'OK, I'll have one,' I said. 'But will it work straight away?'

'It should do,' he said. 'You'll have to charge the battery pretty soon but they usually come with a little bit of charge in them.'

'Can you make sure?' I asked.

'Of course.'

'And can you set it up so it's ready to shoot immediately?'

'Certainly, sir,' said the young man. 'This one records direct to a memory card. Would you like me to include one?'

'Yes, please.' I said, keeping my eyes on the mailbox shop.

'Two gigabyte?' he asked.

'Fine.'

I went on watching the street as the young man fiddled with the camera, checking the battery and installing the memory card.

'Shall I put it back in the box?' he asked.

'No,' I said. 'Leave it out.'

I handed him my credit card and looked down briefly to enter my PIN, and also to check that I wasn't spending a fortune.

'And please leave the camera switched on.'

'The battery won't last if I do that,' he said. 'But it's simple to turn on when you need it. You just push this here.' He pointed. 'Then you just aim and shoot with this.' He pointed to another button 'The camera does the rest.'

'And the zoom?'

'Here,' he said. He showed me how to zoom in and out.

'Great, thanks.'

He held out a plastic bag. 'The charger, the instructions, and the warranty are in the box.'

'Thanks,' I said again, taking the bag.

I went swiftly out of the camera shop and into the adjacent Taj Mahal Indian restaurant just as a waiter turned the CLOSED sign to OPEN on the door.

'I'd like that table there, please,' I said, pointing.

'But, sir,' said the waiter, 'that is for four people.'

'I'm expecting three others,' I said, moving over to the table and sitting down before he had a chance to stop me.

I ordered a sparkling mineral water and, when the waiter

departed to fetch it, I opened the curtains in the window a few inches so I could clearly see mailbox 116.

The package was collected at twenty past one, by which time the Indian waiter no longer really believed that another three people were coming to join me for lunch.

I had almost eaten the restaurant out of poppadoms and mango chutney, and I was again getting desperate to have a pee, when I suddenly recognized a face across the road. And I would have surely missed the person completely if I'd gone to the loo.

It took only a few seconds for the collector to go into the mailbox shop, open box 116 with a key, remove the contents, close the box again, and leave.

But not before I had snapped away vigorously with my new purchase.

I sat at the table and looked through the photos that I'd taken.

Quite a few were of the back of the person's head, and a few more had missed the mark altogether, but there were three perfect shots, in full zoom close-up. Two of them showed the collector in profile as the package was being removed from the box, and one was full face as the person left through the shop door.

In truth, I hadn't really known who to expect, but the person who looked out at me from the camera screen hadn't even been on my list of possible candidates.

The face in the photograph, the face of my mother's blackmailer, was that of Julie Yorke, the caged tigress.

14

On Saturday morning at nine o'clock, I was sitting in Ian's car parked in a gateway halfway up the Baydon road. I had chosen the position so I could easily see the traffic that came up the hill towards me out of Lambourn village. I was waiting for one particular vehicle, and I'd been here for half an hour already.

I had woken early again after another troubled night's sleep.

The same questions had been revolving round and round in my head since the early hours. How could Julie Yorke be the blackmailer? How had she obtained my mother's tax papers – or, at least, the information in them?

And, in particular, who was she working with?

There had to be someone else involved. My mother had always referred to the blackmailer as 'him', and I had heard the whisperer myself, on the telephone, and was pretty certain that it had been a man.

A horsebox came up the hill towards me. I sank down in the seat so that the driver wouldn't see me. I was not waiting for a horsebox.

I yawned. I was tired due to lack of sleep but I knew I could exist indefinitely on just a few hours a night. Sometimes I'd survived for weeks on far less than that. And my overriding memory of my time at Sandhurst was that I was always completely exhausted, sometimes to the point of collapse, but I somehow kept going, as had all my fellow officer cadets.

I had again left Kauri House in Ian's car well before dawn, and before the lights had gone on in my mother's bedroom. I'd driven out of the village along the Wantage road and had chanced driving in through the open gates of Greystone Stables and up the tarmac driveway. I'd crept forward slowly, scanning the surface in front of me in the glow of the headlights. My two sticks remained exactly where I'd left them, leaning on the small stones. Still no cars had been driven up here since the gates had been unlocked.

It had been a calculated risk to drive up to the sticks, but no more so than leaving the car down by the gate and walking. As it was, I'd been there no more than a minute in total.

I had then driven into Wantage and parked in the market square under the imposing statue of King Alfred the Great with his battle-axe in one hand and roll of parchment in the other, designed to depict the Saxon warrior who became the lawgiver.

I'd bought the *Racing Post* from a newsagent's in the town, not having wanted to buy one at the shop in Lambourn village in case I was spotted by someone who thought I was dead.

According to the paper, Ewen Yorke had seven horses running that afternoon at two different racecourses: three at Haydock Park and four at Ascot, including two in their big race of the day, the Group 1 Make-a-Wager Gold Cup.

Haydock was about midway between Manchester and Liverpool and a good three hours' drive away. Ascot, meanwhile, was much closer, in the same county as Lambourn, and just a fifty-minute trip down the M4 motorway, with maybe a bit extra to allow for race-day traffic.

Ewen had a runner in the first race at both courses and, if he was going to be at Haydock Park in time for the first, he would be expected to drive his distinctive top-of-the-range white BMW up the hill on the Baydon road sometime around ten o'clock, and by ten thirty at the very latest.

So I sat and waited some more.

I turned on the car radio but, like the handbrake, it didn't work too well. In fact, it made an annoying buzzing noise even when the engine wasn't running. It was worse than having no radio at all, so I turned it off again.

I looked at the new watch I'd bought in Newbury the previous afternoon. It told me it was nine thirty.

At nine forty-five I recognized a car coming up the hill towards me. It wasn't a white BMW but an ageing and battered blue Ford – my mother's car.

I sank down as far as I could in the seat as she drove by, hoping that she wouldn't identify the vehicle in the gateway as that of her head lad. Even if she'd done so, I knew she wouldn't have stopped to enquire after 'staff', and I gratefully watched as her car disappeared round the next corner. As I had expected, my mother was off to Haydock Park races, where she had Oregon running in the novice hurdle, his last outing before the Triumph Hurdle at the Cheltenham Festival. Ian had told me that he was looking forward to watching the race on Channel 4.

I went back to watching and waiting, but there was no sign of a white BMW.

At ten to eleven I decided it was time to move. I hadn't seen Ewen's car go past but that didn't mean he hadn't gone to Haydock, it just meant he hadn't gone there via the Baydon road. It was the most likely route from the Yorkes' house but certainly not the only one.

I moved Ian's car from the gateway on the Baydon road to another similarly positioned on Hungerford Hill, another of the roads out of Lambourn. If Ewen Yorke was going to Ascot this afternoon he would almost certainly pass this way, and would do so by twelve thirty at the absolute latest if he was going to be in time to saddle his runner in the first race.

The distinctive white top-of-the-range BMW swept up the hill at five minutes to twelve and I pulled out of the gateway behind it.

I had planned to follow him at a safe distance to avoid detection, and to make sure that he actually did drive to the motorway and join it going east towards Ascot. As it was, I had no need to worry about keeping far enough back so that the driver couldn't see that it was me behind him. Ian Norland's little Corsa struggled up Hungerford Hill as fast as it could, but Ewen Yorke's powerful BMW was already long gone, and was well out of sight by the time I reached the top road by the Hare pub.

I didn't like doing it, but I'd have to assume that he had, in fact, gone to Ascot and wouldn't be back in Lambourn for at least the next five hours. Once upon a time I would have been able to check by watching the racing from Ascot on BBC television. That was sadly no longer the case as, except for the Grand National, the BBC had cut back its jump-race coverage to almost nothing. Someone in that organization seemed to believe that if a sport didn't involve wheels, balls or skis, it was hardly worth reporting.

Instead, I pulled into the car park of the Hare and waited, watching the road, to see if the white BMW came back. Maybe he had forgotten something and would return to get it.

He didn't.

I waited a full thirty minutes before I was sure enough that Ewen and his BMW were away for the afternoon. He wouldn't now have had enough time to return home and then make it to Ascot for the first race.

I drove the Corsa out of the pub car park, down the hill to Lambourn village, and pulled up on the gravel driveway next to the Yorkes' front door.

Julie seemed surprised to see me, but maybe not so surprised as if she had believed me dead.

'What are you doing here?' she asked from behind the door through a six-inch gap.

'I thought you said at Newbury races to come and see you sometime,' I said. 'So here I am.'

She blushed slightly across her neck.

'What's in the bag?' she asked, looking at the plastic bag I was holding.

'Champagne,' I said.

She blushed again and, this time, it reached her cheeks.

'You had better come in, then,' she said, opening the door wide for me to pass. She looked out beyond me as if concened that someone had seen my arrival. It was not just her who hoped they hadn't.

'How lovely,' I said, admiring the white curved staircase in the hallway. 'Which way's the bedroom?'

'My,' she said with a giggle. 'You are an eager boy.'

'No time like the present,' I said. 'Is your husband in?'

'No,' she said, giggling again. 'He's gone to the races.'

'I know,' I said. 'I watched him go.'

'You are such a naughty boy,' she said, wagging a finger at me.

'So what are you going to do about it, then?' I asked her.

She breathed deeply with excitement, her breasts rising and falling under her flimsy jumper.

'Get some glasses,' I said, starting to climb the stairs. 'Go on,' I said, seeing her still standing in the hallway.

She skipped away while I continued up.

'In the guest room,' she shouted. 'On the left.'

I went into the guest room, on the left, and pulled back the duvet on the king-size bed.

A couple of life's little questions crossed my mind.

Was I really going to have sex with this woman?

I suppose it depended if she wanted it and, so far, the signs had been pretty positive. But did I want it too?

And there was one other pressing question.

Did I leave my leg on, or did I take it off?

On this occasion I decided that 'on' was definitely better, especially as a quick getaway would be a likely necessity.

I went into the en-suite bathroom. I thought briefly about having a shower but it would mean taking off my leg and then putting it on again. The foot may have been waterproof but the join between the real me and the false was not.

I stripped off, left my clothes on the bathroom floor, and climbed into the bed, pulling the duvet up to my waist.

I had never paid for sex, although I'd bought quite a few expensive dinners in my time, which was tantamount to the same thing. On this occasion, however, my mother had been paying two thousand pounds a week for the past seven months. I hoped it was going to be worth it.

Julie appeared in the doorway carrying two champagne flutes in her left hand and wearing a flimsy housecoat that she let fall open to reveal her nakedness beneath.

'Now, just how naughty have you been?' she asked, swinging a leather riding whip into view.

'Very,' I said, opening the champagne with a loud pop.

'Oh, goody,' she replied.

It wasn't quite what I had in mind but I went along with her little game for a while as she became more and more excited.

'Just a minute,' I said, getting off the bed.

'What?' she gasped. 'Get back here now!'

'Just a minute,' I repeated. 'I need the bathroom.'

She was lying on her back, half sitting up, resting on her elbows with the whip in her right hand, her knees drawn up, and her legs spread wide. She threw her head back. 'I just don't believe it,' she cried. 'You get back here right now or you'll really be in trouble.'

I ignored her, went into the bathroom and put on my boxer shorts. I then took my new camera from the cupboard under the sink, where I had placed it when I arrived, and checked that it was switched on. The champagne hadn't been the only thing in the plastic bag.

'Hurry up, you naughty boy,' she shouted.

'Coming,' I shouted back.

I came out of the bathroom taking shot after shot of her naked body as she lay on the bed, still in the same compromising position. She'd had her eyes closed and it was a few seconds before she realized what was I was doing.

'What the fuck's going on?' she screamed, throwing the whip at me and grabbing the duvet to cover herself.

'Just taking some photos,' I said calmly.

'What the fuck for?' she shouted angrily.

'Blackmail,' I replied.

'Blackmail!' she shrieked.

'Yes,' I said. 'Do you want to see?'

I held the camera towards her so she could see the screen on the back of it. But the photograph I showed her wasn't one of those I'd just taken; it was the one with her face in profile from yesterday, the one with her hand reaching into mailbox number 116 to collect the package of my mother's money.

She cried a lot.

We were still in her guest bedroom. I had thrown her the housecoat when I'd gone into the bathroom to put on my shirt and trousers and, when I'd re-emerged, she had been sitting up in bed wearing the coat with the duvet pulled right up. Somehow she didn't look like someone up to their neck in a criminal conspiracy. She had even straightened her hair.

'It was only a game,' she said.

'Murder is never a game,' I said, standing at the end of the bed.

'Murder?' She went very pale. 'What murder?'

My murder, I thought. Hanging on a wall in Greystone Stables.

'Who was murdered?' she demanded.

'Someone called Roderick Ward,' I said, even though I had no evidence that it was true.

'No,' she wailed. 'Roderick wasn't murdered; he died in a car crash.'

So she knew of Roderick Ward.

'That's what it was meant to look like,' I said. 'Who killed him?'

'I didn't kill anybody,' she shouted.

'Someone did,' I said. 'Was it Ewen?'

'Ewen?' She almost laughed. 'The only thing Ewen is interested in is bloody horses. That and whisky. Horses all day and whisky all night.'

Perhaps that explained her sexually flirtatious nature – she couldn't get any satisfaction in the marital bed, so she had looked elsewhere.

'So who killed Roderick Ward?' I asked her again.

'No one,' she said. 'I told you. He died in a car crash.'

'Who says so?' I asked. She didn't respond. I looked down at her. 'Do you know what the sentence is for being an accessory to murder?' There was still no response. 'Life in prison,' I said. 'That's a very long time for someone as young as you.'

'I told you, I didn't murder anyone.' She was crying again.

'But do you think a jury will believe you once they've convicted you for blackmail?' She went on crying, the tears smudging her mascara and dripping black marks onto the white bed linen. 'So tell me, who did kill Roderick Ward?' I asked.

She didn't say anything; she just buried her face in a pillow and sobbed.

'You will tell me,' I said. 'Eventually. Are you aware that the maximum sentence for blackmail is fourteen years?'

That brought her head back up. 'No.' It was almost a plea.

'Oh, yes,' I said. 'And the same for conspiracy to blackmail.'

I knew. I'd looked it up on the internet.

'Where's the money?' I asked, changing direction.

'What money?' she said.

'The money you collected yesterday from Newbury.'

'In my handbag,' she whimpered.

'And how about the rest of it?'

'The rest?' she said.

'Yes, all the packages you've been collecting each week for the past seven months. Where's all that money?'

'I don't have it,' she said.

'So who has?'

She still didn't want to tell me.

'Julie,' I said, 'you are leaving me no alternative but to give the picture of you in Newbury yesterday to the police.'

'No,' she wailed again.

'But I can help you if you will help me,' I said softly. 'Otherwise I will also have to send the other photos to Ewen.' Both of us knew what the other photos showed. *Set a thief to catch a thief*, or, as in this case, set a blackmailer to catch a blackmailer.

'No, please.' She was begging.

'Then tell me who has the money.'

'Can't I pay you back in a different way?' she asked, pulling down the duvet and opening her housecoat to reveal her left breast.

'No,' I said emphatically, 'you cannot.'

She covered herself up again.

'Julie,' I said in my voice-of-command, 'this is your last chance. Either you tell me now who's got the money or I will call the police.' She wasn't to know that I had absolutely no intention of doing that.

'I can't tell you,' she said forlornly.

'What are you frightened of?' I asked.

'Nothing.'

'But you claimed it was only a game,' I said. 'Was it him who told you that?' I paused. She gave no answer. 'Did he just ask you to collect something for him from a mailbox each week?' I paused again. Again there was no answer, but she began to cry once more. 'Did he tell you that you wouldn't get caught?' She nodded slightly. 'Only now you have been.' She nodded again, tears flowing freely down her cheeks. 'And you're not going to tell me who it was. That's not very clever, you know. You'll end up taking all the blame.'

'I don't want to go to prison,' she sobbed, echoing my mother.

'You don't have to,' I said. 'If you tell me who you give the money to, I am sure the courts won't send you to prison.' Not for long, anyway, I thought. Certainly not for the maximum fourteen years.

I could see that she still didn't want to say. Was it fear, I wondered, or some misguided sense of loyalty.

'Do you love him?' I asked her.

She looked up at me, still sobbing. But she nodded.

'Then why are you doing *this*?' I waved my arm at her, at the bed, and at the riding whip that still lay on the floor where she had thrown it. She had hardly acted as if she was deeply in love with someone.

'Habit, I suppose,' she said quietly.

Some habit, I thought.

'Does he love you?' I asked.

'He says so,' she said, but I detected some hesitancy in her voice.

'But you're not so sure?' I asked.

'No.'

'Then why on earth are you protecting him?' She gave me no answer. 'OK,' I said at length. 'Don't say that I haven't warned you.' I took my mobile phone from my pocket. 'And I'm sure

Ewen is going to find the photographs of you most interesting. Does he know about your secret blackmailing lover? Because he will soon.'

I unfolded my phone and showed her as I pushed the number nine key three times in a row, the emergency number. The phone obligingly emitted a beep each time I pressed it. I then held the phone to my ear. She wasn't to know that I hadn't also pressed the connect button.

'Hello,' I said into the dead phone. 'Police, please.' I smiled down at Julie. 'This is your last chance,' I said.

'All right,' she shouted. 'All right. I'll tell you.'

'Sorry,' I said again into the dead phone. 'There's been a mistake. All is well now. Thank you.' I folded my phone together.

'So who is it?' I asked.

She said nothing.

'Come on,' I said, unfolding the phone again. 'Tell me. Who do you give the blackmail money to?'

'Alex Reece,' she said slowly.

'What?' I said, astounded. 'The weasel accountant?'

'Alex is not a weasel,' she said defensively. 'He's lovely.'

I thought back to the hours I had spent chained to a wall, and I couldn't agree with her. 'So was it you and Alex Reece who chained me to a wall to die?' I was suddenly very angry, and it showed.

'No,' she said. 'Of course not. What are you talking about?'

'I'm talking about you leaving me to die of dehydration.'

She was shocked. 'I have absolutely no idea what you're talking about.'

'Told you that he'd come back and let me go, did he?' I asked, my anger still very close to the surface.

'He didn't tell me anything of the sort,' she said.

'But you did help him to kidnap me?' I shouted at her.

'Tom, stop it,' she pleaded. 'You're frightening me. And I

really don't know what you are talking about. I have never kidnapped anyone in my life, and I've certainly never chained anyone to anything. I promise.'

'Why should I believe you?' I asked. But I had seen the fear in her eyes, and I did believe her. But if she hadn't helped kidnap and chain me to a wall, who had?

Or could Alex Reece, my mother's blackmailer, really not be the same person as my would-be murderer?

There was very little else that Julie had to tell me. She collected the package from the mailbox shop in Newbury only when Alex Reece was unable to do so, and she didn't even know how much money was in it. When we finally went downstairs to her kitchen and she took the package from her handbag, she could hardly believe her eyes when I removed the two thousand pounds.

'It's no game,' I told her. 'Two thousand every week is no game.'

'But she can afford it,' Julie said defiantly.

'No she can't. And why would that make any difference, even if she could?'

'Alex says it's just redistributing the wealth,' she said.

'And that makes it all right, does it?'

She said nothing.

'Suppose I just steal your brand-new BMW to "redistribute the wealth",' I continued. 'Is that then OK with you? Or do you call the cops?'

'Alex says—' she started.

'I don't care what Alex says,' I shouted, cutting her off. 'Alex is nothing more than a common thief, and he clearly saw you coming. And the sooner you realize it, the better it will be for you. Or else you'll be in the dock with him, and then in prison.'

And now, I thought, it was time for me to meet again with

Mr Alex Reece, and I had absolutely no intention of letting him see *me* coming.

'When and where are you meant to give this package to Reece?' I asked.

'He gets back tomorrow.'

'From where?' I asked.

'Gibraltar,' she said. 'He went there with the Garraways on Tuesday.'

So it couldn't have been him who unlocked the gates of Greystone Stables on Thursday evening.

'So when are you meant to give him the package?' I demanded.

She clearly didn't want to tell me but I stood next to her drumming my fingers noisily on the kitchen worktop. 'He said to bring it to Newbury on Monday,' she said eventually.

'Where in Newbury?'

'There's a coffee shop in Cheap Street,' she said. 'That's where we always meet on Friday mornings. Except this week, of course, when he was away.'

Thank goodness for that, I thought.

'So are you meeting him at the coffee shop on Monday?' I asked.

'Yes,' she replied. 'At ten thirty.'

It was far too public a place for what I wanted to do to him.

'Change it,' I said. 'Get him to collect it from here.'

'Oh, no. He won't ever come here. He refuses to.'

'So where else do you two get together?' I didn't think a cup of coffee or two in Newbury would be quite sufficient to satisfy her other cravings.

'At his place,' she said, blushing slightly.

'Which is where?' I asked impatiently.

'Greenham,' she said.

Greenham was a village that had almost been consumed by the ever-expanding sprawl of Newbury town. It was most famous for its common, and the US cruise missiles that had been based there at the height of the Cold War. Everyone in these parts knew of Greenham Common, and remembered the peace camps erected by anti-nuclear protestors.

'Where in Greenham?' I demanded.

'What are you going to do to him?'

'Nothing,' I said. 'As long as he cooperates.'

'Cooperates how?' she asked.

'If he gives me my mother's money back, then I'll let him go.'

I'd also take her tax papers.

'And if he doesn't?' she asked.

'Then I'll persuade him,' I said, smiling.

'How?' she said. 'Will you take photos of him naked, too?'

'I doubt that,' I said. 'But I'll think of something.'

'Blitzkrieg' is a German word that means 'lightning war'. It was used to describe the attacks on Poland, France, and the Low Countries by the Nazis. Unlike the war of attrition that had existed for mile after hundred-mile of trenches in Flanders during the First World War, blitzkrieg was the surprise and overwhelming attack on just a few points in the enemy's line. An attack that drove straight through to the heart of political power almost before any of the defenders had had a chance to react.

The blitzkrieg unleashed by the German forces on Poland had started on the first day of September 1939 and, within a week, Wehrmacht tanks and troops were in the suburbs of Warsaw, nearly two hundred miles from their starting point. The whole of Poland had capitulated within five weeks at a cost of only ten thousand Germans killed. Compare that to the advance of only six miles gained in four and a half months by British and French troops at the Battle of the Somme, and at a cost of more than six hundred thousand dead and wounded on each side.

So if the past had taught the modern soldier anything, then it was that blitzkrieg-like 'shock and awe' was the key to victory in battle, and I had every intention of creating some shock and awe in the life of one Alex Reece.

15

Bush Close in Greenham was full of those ubiquitous modern little box houses and number 16, Alex Reece's home, was at the far end of the cul-de-sac.

It was late Saturday afternoon and I had left Julie Yorke in a state of near collapse. I had merely suggested to her that to have any contact whatsoever with Alex Reece in the next thirty-six hours, in person, by e-mail or by phone, would be reason enough for me to send the explicit photographs to her husband, in addition to posting them on my new Facebook page on the internet.

She had begged me to delete the pictures from my camera but, as I had pointed out, it was she and Alex who had started this blackmail business, and they really couldn't now complain if they were receiving a bit of their own medicine.

I had parked Ian Norland's car out on Water Lane in Greenham and had walked round the corner into Bush Close. I was carrying a pile of free newspapers that I had picked up at a petrol station, and I walked down the road pushing one of them through every letterbox. The houses were not identical but they were similar, and number 16 had the same style of plastic-framed front door as all the others.

'What time does Alex get back?' I had asked Julie.

'His plane lands at Heathrow at six twenty tomorrow evening.'

'And how does he get home to Greenham?'

'I've no idea.'

I lingered for a moment outside the front door of number 16 and adjusted the pile of remaining newspapers. I glanced around, looking for suitable hiding places, but the short driveway was bordered by nothing but grass. I looked to see which of the other houses had a direct line-of-sight to the front door of number 16, set back as it was beside the single garage.

Only number 15, opposite, had an unobstructed view.

I walked away from number 16 and pushed newspapers through the front doors of a few more houses, including the one opposite, before moving off down the road, back towards Ian's car. However, instead of immediately driving away, I walked through a gateway and into the adjacent field. Alex Reece's house, together with all the other even-numbered houses in Bush Close, backed onto farmland and I spent some time carefully reconnoitring the whole area.

I looked at my watch. It was just after five thirty and the light was beginning to fade rapidly.

Alex Reece couldn't possibly be back here the following evening until eight o'clock at the earliest, and it would probably be nearer to nine if he had to collect luggage at the airport. And that was assuming his flight landed on time. By eight o'clock, of course, it would have been fully dark for hours.

Keeping in the shadows of some trees, I skirted round the backs of the gardens in Bush Close until I arrived at number 16. There were lights on in the kitchen of number 14 next door and I could see a man and a woman in there talking. That was good, I thought. No one can see outside at dusk when they have the lights on inside, due to the reflection in the window glass, and especially when they are busy talking. There was little or no chance that they could see me watching them.

I quickly rolled my body over the low back fence and into Alex Reece's garden. It was mostly simply laid to grass with no tangly flower beds or thorny rose bushes to worry about.

I moved silently to the back of the garage and looked in. Even in the fast-disappearing light I could see the shiny shape of a car in there. So Mr Reece would probably arrive home by taxi, either direct from the airport, or from the railway station in Newbury.

And I'd be waiting for him.

'Did we win?' I asked Ian as I walked in through his door at seven o'clock.

'Win what?' he said without taking his eyes off the television screen.

'Oregon,' I said, 'in the race at Haydock.'

'Trotted up,' he said, still not turning round. 'Won by six lengths. Reckon he'll be hard to beat in the Triumph.'

'Good,' I said to the back of his head. 'What are you watching?'

'Just some TV talent show.'

'Have you eaten?' I asked.

'Had a pizza for lunch,' he said. 'From the freezer. One of them you bought yesterday. But I didn't have that until after the race. I was too nervous to eat before.'

'So are you hungry?'

'Not really. Not yet. Maybe I'll have a Chinese later.'

'Great idea,' I said. 'I'll buy. Again.'

He turned round and smiled, and I guessed that was what he was hoping I'd say.

'How long are you staying?' he asked, turning back to the screen.

'I'll find somewhere else if you want,' I said. 'You know the house guests and the three-day-smell rule, and my time is up tonight.'

'Stay as long as you like,' he said. 'I'm enjoying the company.'

And the free food, I thought, perhaps ungraciously.

'I'll stay another day or two, if that's all right.'

'As I said, stay as long as you want, if you don't mind the couch.'

I didn't. It was a lot more comfortable than some of the places I'd slept, and warmer too.

'Can I borrow your car again tomorrow?' I asked.

'Sorry, mate. I need it,' he said. 'I'm going to Sunday lunch with my folks.'

'Where do they live?'

'Near Banbury,' he said.

'So what time will you be back?' I asked.

'It'll be before five,' he said. 'Evening stables are at five on Sundays.'

'Can I borrow the car after that?'

'Sure,' he said. 'But it might need more petrol by then.'

'OK,' I said. 'I'll fill it up.'

I could tell he was smiling, even though he didn't turn round. Why didn't he just ask me to pay for the use of his car? I suppose it was a little game.

I could have gone to fetch my Jaguar, but it was a very distinctive car, and I wasn't particularly keen to advertise my whereabouts to anyone. Ian's little Corsa was far more anonymous. I just hoped my Jaguar was still sitting in the car park in Oxford, awaiting my return.

I spent Sunday morning making my plans and sorting my kit. I had been back into Kauri House on Saturday afternoon after leaving Julie Yorke, and before my excursion to Greenham.

The house had been empty, save for the dogs who had watched me idly and unconcerned as I'd passed through the kitchen, stepping over their beds in front of the Aga. My mother and stepfather had been safely away at Haydock races but, nevertheless, I had remained in the house for only fifteen or twenty minutes, just time enough to have a quick shower and collect a few things from my room.

I did not really want my mother coming back unexpectedly and finding me there. It was not because I didn't trust her not to give away my presence, even unwittingly – it was more that I didn't want to have to explain to her what I was going to do. She probably wouldn't have approved, so it was much better that she didn't know beforehand, if ever.

Ian left for his Sunday-lunch trip at eleven, promising that he would be back in time to start work at five.

After I was sure Ian wasn't going to come back, I sorted the equipment I would need for my mission. Bits of it I had owned previously, but some things I'd driven into Newbury to buy specifically the previous afternoon on my way to Greenham.

I laid out my black roll-neck pullover, a pair of old, dark blue jeans, some dark socks, a black knitted ski hat, and some matching gloves that I'd bought from the sports shop in Market Street, where I'd also obtained a pair of all-black Converse basketball boots.

Next to the clothes I placed the rest of my kit: a small dark blue rucksack, some black heavy-duty garden ties similar to those that had been used to bind my wrists in the stables, a small red first-aid kit, three six- by four-inch prints of the mailbox-shop photos, a certain metal ring with a piece of galvanized steel chain attached to it by a padlock, my camera and, finally, a roll of grey duct tape.

There is a saying in every organization of the world, either military or civilian, that if something doesn't move when it should, use WD-40, and if it moves when it shouldn't, use duct tape. Originally designed during the Second World War to keep gun magazines and ammunition boxes watertight in jungle conditions, duct tape has since become the 'must-have' kit for each and every mission. It was even used to fix a fender on the

Apollo 17 Lunar Rover when it was broken on the moon, as well as making the circular CO_2 scrubbers 'fit' square holes to save the lives of the crew of the stricken *Apollo 13*.

I had decided against taking my sword. I would have loved to have had a weapon of some kind, if only for the shock value, but the sword was impractical and cumbersome. A regulation-issue Browning nine-millimetre sidearm would have been my weapon of choice, but I could hardly run around the English countryside brandishing an unlicensed gun, even if I'd had one. In the end, I also elected not to borrow one of Ian's kitchen knives.

It was not as if I intended to kill anyone. Not yet, anyway.

At ten minutes to eight I was in position alongside Alex Reece's house, on the dark side, away from the glow from the solitary street lamp outside number 12, two houses down.

I had already made a thorough reconnaissance of the area, including a special look at number 15, the house opposite, the one with a direct view of Alex Reece's front door. As far as I could tell, the house was unoccupied, but that might be temporary. Maybe the residents were just out for the afternoon.

Most of the other houses, including number 14 next door, had people going about their usual Sunday-evening activities. I was actually amazed at how few of the residents of Bush Close pulled their curtains, especially at the back. Not that they would usually expect anyone to be lurking in a field, spying on them as they watched their televisions or read their books.

Eight o'clock came and went, and I continued to wait. A fine drizzle began to fall, but that didn't worry me. Rain was likely to keep the other residents inside. I had been unable to tell if any of them had a dog to walk.

At eight eighteen a car pulled into Bush Close and drove

down to the end. I was all ready for action with the adrenalin rushing through my system, but the car pulled into the driveway of number 15 and a couple and two young children climbed out. I breathed heavily, calming myself down, and put the surprise 'jack' back in its box.

I stood silently in the shadows. I was pretty sure that no one would be able to see *me*, although I could see *them* clearly, the more so when the man turned on an outside light next to their front door. I was close to the wall and I remained completely still.

It was movement more than anything that gave people away, caught in peripheral vision and attracting immediate attention. My dark clothes would blend into the blackness of the background; only my face might be visible, and that was streaked with home-made mud-based camouflage cream to break up the familiar shape.

There were no shouts of discovery and, presently, the family gathered their things from the car and went inside. The outside light went out again, plunging me back into darkness. I eased myself back and forth, relieving the tension in my muscles, and went on waiting.

Alex Reece arrived home just before nine o'clock, but he didn't come by taxi.

Isabella Warren's dark blue Volkswagen Golf pulled into the driveway at high speed and stopped abruptly with a slight squeal of its brakes. I couldn't exactly see who was at the wheel but, from past experience of her driving on the Bracknell bypass, I was pretty sure it was Isabella herself.

I pressed myself close to the wall and peeked round the corner so I could see.

Alex Reece opened the rear door and stood up next to the car with a flight bag in his hand.

'Thanks for the lift,' he called before closing the door and removing a small suitcase from the boot.

He stood and waved as the Golf was backed out onto the road, and then rapidly driven away again. I thought the fact that Alex had been sitting in the back of the car implied that there was at least one other passenger. Maybe it was Jackson Warren.

I watched as Alex fumbled in his flight bag for the key to his front door. In those few seconds I also scanned the road and the windows of the house opposite. No one was about.

It was time for action.

In the instant after he opened the front door, and before he had time to reach down for his suitcase, I struck him hard midway between his shoulder blades, forcing him through the open doorway and onto the floor in the still-dark hallway. I crashed down on top of him, his flight bag sliding across the polished wood and into the kitchen.

'Scream and I'll kill you,' I said loudly into his ear.

He didn't scream, but it wasn't only because he was frightened of being killed. I had purposely chosen that type of blow because it would have driven the air from his chest and, without air, he couldn't scream. In fact, he didn't react in any way. Just as I had hoped, my blitzkrieg attack had rendered him shocked and awestruck.

I pulled both his arms round to the small of his back and used the garden ties from my pocket to secure his wrists. Next I used another pair of the ties to bind his ankles together.

The whole process had taken no more than a few seconds.

I stood up and went outside. I picked up Alex's suitcase from the step, glanced casually all around to check that nothing had stirred, then stepped back inside again, closing the front door. Alex hadn't moved a muscle.

Albert Pierrepoint, the renowned English hangman of the nineteen forties and fifties, always maintained that a successful execution was one when the prisoner hardly had time to realize what was happening to him before he was dangling dead at the end of the rope. He had once famously despatched a man named James Inglis within just seven and a half seconds of his leaving the condemned cell.

Pierrepoint would have been proud of me tonight. Alex wasn't actually dead, but he had been trussed up like a chicken ready for the oven in not much longer than Albert had taken to hang a man.

And now Mr Reece was ready for a spot of roasting.

'I have no idea what you're talking about.' It was only to be expected that he would deny any knowledge of blackmail.

He was still lying on the hall floor but I had rolled him over onto his back so he could see me. I'd patted down his pockets, removed his mobile telephone and turned it off. All the while he had stared at me with wide eyes, the whites showing all round the irises. But he had known immediately who I was, in spite of my dark clothes, hat, and mud-streaked face.

'So you deny you have been blackmailing my mother?' I asked him.

'I do,' he said emphatically. 'I've never heard such nonsense. Now let me go or I'll call the police.'

'You are in no position to call anyone,' I said. 'And if anyone will be calling the police, it will be me.'

'Go on, then,' he said. 'It's not me who would be in the most trouble.'

'And what is that meant to imply?'

'Work it out,' he said, becoming more sure of himself.

'Are you aware of what the maximum sentence is for blackmail?' I asked.

He said nothing.

'Fourteen years.'

His eyes didn't even flicker. He clearly thought he was onto a good thing. He was assuming that I would just threaten him a bit, then let him go and do nothing more.

But one should never assume anything.

I had told Ian that I would be out all night. No one was expecting me back for hours and hours. So I was in no hurry.

I left him lying on the hard hall floor and went into the kitchen to see if I could find myself a drink. Waiting all that time outside had made me thirsty.

'Let me go,' he shouted from the hallway.

'No,' I shouted back, putting his phone down on the worktop.

'Help,' he shouted, this time much louder.

I went quickly through into the hall.

'I wouldn't do that if I were you.'

'Why not?' he said belligerently.

I shrugged myself free of the small rucksack on my back and removed the roll of duct tape. I held it towards him and pulled the end of the tape free. 'Because I would be forced to wrap your head in this. Is that what you want?'

He didn't shout again as I went back into the kitchen and fetched a can of Heineken from his fridge. I took a drink, allowing a little of the beer to pour out of the corner of my mouth and drip onto the floor near his legs.

'Do you have any idea how long a human being can go on living without taking in any fluid?' He went on staring at me. 'How long it would be before chronic dehydration causes irreversible kidney failure, and death?'

He obviously didn't like the question but he still wasn't particularly worried.

I bent down to my rucksack and dug around for the short piece of chain attached to the ring by the padlock. I held it up for him to see, but it was clear from his lack of expression that he didn't know where it had come from, or its significance. He probably wasn't fully aware that his lack of reaction may have saved his life. Maybe I didn't now want to kill the little weasel, but that didn't mean I didn't want to use him.

'Are you a diabetic?' I asked.

'No,' he said.

'Lucky you.'

I removed the red-coloured first-aid kit from my rucksack. It was what was known in the expedition business as an 'anti-AIDS kit'. It was a small zipped-up pouch containing two each of sterile syringes, hypodermic needles, intravenous drip cannulas, ready-threaded suture needles, and scalpels, plus three small sterile pouches of saline solution for emergency rehydration. I had bought it some years previously to take on a regimental jolly, a trip to climb Mount Kilimanjaro. It was designed to allow access to sterile equipment in the event of one of the team having to have an emergency medical procedure, something that was not always readily available, especially in some of the more remote hospitals of HIV-ridden sub-Saharan Africa.

Thankfully, no one on the expedition had needed it, and the kit had returned with me to the UK intact. But, now, it might just prove to have been a worthwhile purchase.

I removed one of the syringes and attached it to one of the hypodermic needles. Alex watched me.

'What are you doing?' He sounded worried for the first time.

'Time for my insulin,' I said. 'You wouldn't want me collapsing in a diabetic coma, now, would you? Not with you in that state.'

Alex watched carefully as I unpacked one of the pouches of saline solution from its sterile packaging and hung it up on the stair banister. The packaging had an official-looking label stuck on the side with INSULIN printed on it in large bold capital letters that he couldn't have failed to see. I had asked him if he was a diabetic, and he'd said no. I hoped that he wouldn't know that insulin is nearly always provided either in ready-loaded injecting devices or in little glass bottles. I had produced the official-looking INSULIN label that afternoon using Ian Norland's printer.

I drew a very little amount of the clear liquid into the smaller of the two syringes, pulled up the front of my black roll-neck sweater, pinched the flesh of my abdomen together, and inserted the needle. I depressed the plunger and injected the fluid under my skin. I smiled down at Alex.

'How often do you have to do that?' he asked.

'Two or three times a day,' I said.

'And what exactly is insulin?'

'It's a hormone,' I said, 'that allows the muscles to use the energy from glucose carried in the blood. In most people it is created naturally in the pancreas.'

'So what happens if you don't take it?'

'The glucose level in my blood would become so high that my organs would stop working properly, and I would eventually go into a coma, and then die.'

I smiled down at him again. 'We wouldn't want that, now, would we?'

He didn't answer. Perhaps me in a coma or dead was exactly what he wanted. But it wasn't going to happen. I wasn't really diabetic, but my best friend at secondary school had been and I'd watched him inject himself with insulin hundreds of times, although he'd always used a special syringe with a finer and less painful needle. Injecting small amounts of sterile saline solution under my skin might be slightly uncomfortable, but it was harmless.

I went back into the kitchen and picked up his flight bag from where it had come to rest. It was heavy. Inside, amongst other things, were a laptop computer and a large bottle of duty-free vodka that had somehow survived the impact with the hall floor. I put the bag down on the kitchen table, removed the computer and turned it on. While it booted up I took an upright chair out into the hallway, placed it near Alex's feet, and sat down.

'Now,' I said, leaning forward. 'I have some questions I need you to answer.'

'I'm not answering anything unless you let me go.'

'Oh, I think you will,' I said. 'It's a long night.'

I stood up and went back into the kitchen. I pulled down the blind over the window, turned on a television set, and sat down at the kitchen table with Alex's computer.

'Hey,' he called after about five minutes.

'Yes,' I shouted back. 'What do you want?'

'Are you just going to leave me here?'

'Yes,' I said, turning up the volume on the television.

'How long for?' he shouted louder.

'How long do you need?'

'Need?' he shouted. 'What do mean, need?'

'How long do you need before you will answer my questions?'

'What questions?'

I went back into the hall and sat down on the chair by his feet.

'How long have you been having an affair with Julie Yorke?' I said.

It wasn't a question he had been expecting, but he recovered quickly.

'I've no idea what you're talking about.'

It seemed we hadn't come too far in the past half hour.

'Please yourself,' I said, standing up and walking back to the kitchen table, and his computer.

There was a football highlights programme on the television and I turned the volume up even higher so that Alex wouldn't hear me tapping away on his laptop keyboard.

The computer automatically connected to his wireless internet router so I clicked on his e-mail, and opened the inbox.

Careless of him, I thought, to not have it password protected. I highlighted all his messages received during the past two weeks and forwarded them, en masse, to my own e-mail account. Next I did the same to his Sent Items folder. One never knew how useful the information might prove to be, and it was no coincidence that the first thing the police searched when arresting someone was their computer hard drive.

I glanced up at the football on the television and ignored the whining from the hallway.

'Let me go,' Alex bleated. 'My hands hurt.'

I went back to studying the computer screen.

'I need to sit up,' he whinged. 'My back aches.'

I continued to ignore him.

I opened a computer folder called Rock Accounts. There were twenty or so files in the folder and I highlighted them all, attached them to an e-mail, and again sent them to my computer.

The football highlights programme finished and the evening news had started. Fortunately, there were no reports about an ongoing case of forced imprisonment in the village of Greenham.

I clicked on the search button in the computer's start menu and asked it to probe the main drive for files containing the terms 'password' or 'user name'. Obligingly, it came up with eight references, so I attached those files to another e-mail and off they went as well.

'OK, OK!' he shouted finally. 'I'll answer your question.'

The messages from one further e-mail folder, one simply named Gibraltar, were also despatched through cyberspace. I then checked that everything had gone before erasing the 'sent' records for my forwarded files so Alex would have no knowledge that I had copied them. I closed the lid of the laptop and returned it to the flight bag, which I placed back on the floor.

I then went out into the hall, sat down once again on the upright chair, and leaned over him menacingly.

But I didn't ask him the same question as before. Using my best voice-of-command, I asked him something completely different.

'Why did you murder Roderick Ward?'

He was shocked.

'I–I didn't,' he stammered.

'So who did?' I asked.

'I don't know.'

'So he *was* murdered?' I said.

'No,' he whined. 'It was an accident.'

'No, it wasn't. That car crash was far too contrived. It had to be a set-up.'

'The car crash wasn't the accident,' he said flatly. 'It was the fact that he died that was the accident. I tried to warn them but I was too late.'

'Them?' I asked, intrigued.

He clammed up.

I removed a folded piece of paper from my pocket and held it out to him.

He looked at it in disbelief.

I knew the words written there by heart, so often had I looked at them during the past few days. It was the handwritten note that had been addressed to Mrs Stella Beecher at 26 Banbury Drive in Oxford, the note I had found in the pile of mail I had taken from the cardboard box that meals-on-wheels Mr Horner kept by his front door:

I DON'T KNOW WHETHER THIS WILL GET THERE IN TIME BUT TELL HIM I HAVE THE STUFF HE WANTS.

'What stuff?' I demanded.

He said nothing.

'And tell who?'

Again there was no response.

'And in time for what?'

He just stared at me.

'You will have to answer my questions, or you will leave me with no alternative but . . .' I tailed off.

'No alternative but what?' he asked in a panic.

'To kill you,' I said calmly.

I quickly grabbed his bound feet and swiftly removed his left shoe and sock. I used the duct tape to bind his left foot upright against one of the spindles on the stairway so that it was completely immobile.

'What are you doing?' he screamed, trying to wriggle away from me but without success.

'Preparations,' I said. 'I always have to make the right preparations before I kill someone.'

'Help,' he yelled. But I had left the television on with the volume turned up and his shout was drowned out by an advertising jingle.

However, to be sure that he wouldn't be heard, I took a piece of the duct tape and fixed it firmly over his mouth to stop him yelling again. Instead, he began breathing heavily through his nose, hyperventilating, his nostrils alternately flaring and contracting below a pair of big frightened eyes.

'Now then, Alex,' I said, in as calm a manner as I could manage. 'You seem not to fully appreciate the rather dangerous predicament in which you have found yourself.' He stared at me unblinkingly. 'So let me explain it to you. You have been blackmailing my mother to the tune of two thousand pounds per week for the past seven months, to say nothing about the demands on her to fix races. Some weeks you collect the money yourself from the mailbox in Cheap Street and sometimes you get Julie Yorke to collect it for you.'

I removed the three prints of the photos I had taken of Julie through the window of the Taj Mahal Indian restaurant and held them up to him. With the tape on his mouth, it was difficult to fully gauge his reaction, but he went pale and looked from the photos to my face with doleful, pleading eyes.

'And,' I went on, 'you are blackmailing my mother over the knowledge you have that she has not been paying the tax that she should have been. Which means you either have her tax papers in your possession or have had access to them.'

I reached down into my rucksack and again brought out the red 'anti-AIDS' kit. If anything, Alex went paler.

'Now my problem is this,' I said. 'If I let you go, you will still have my mother's tax papers. And even if you give me back the papers, you would still have the knowledge.'

I took the large syringe out of the kit, attached a new needle, and then drew up a large quantity of the saline solution from the bag that was still hanging on the stair banister, the bag with the INSULIN label.

'So you see,' I said. 'If you won't help me then I will have no alternative but to prevent you speaking to the tax authorities.'

I held the syringe up to the light and squirted a little of the fluid out in a fine jet.

'Did you know that insulin is essential for proper body functions?' I asked. 'But that too much of it causes the glucose level in the blood to drop far too low, which in turn triggers a condition called hypoglycaemia? That usually results in a seizure, followed by coma and death. Do you remember the case of that nurse, Beverley Allitt, who killed those children in Grantham hospital? The media called her the Angel of Death. She murdered some of her victims by injecting them with large overdoses of insulin.'

I knew because I'd looked that up on the internet as well.

I touched his foot.

'And do you know, Alex, if you inject insulin between someone's toes it is very difficult, if not impossible, to find the puncture mark on the skin, and the insulin would be undetectable because you create it naturally in your body? It would appear you died of a seizure followed by a heart attack.'

The statement wasn't entirely accurate. The insulin used nowadays to treat diabetics is almost exclusively synthetic insulin, and it can be detected as being different from the natural human product.

But Alex wasn't to know that.

'Now, then,' I said, smiling and holding up the syringe to him again. 'Between which two toes would you like it?'

16

I was worried that he was going to pass out. His eyes started to roll back in their sockets and his breathing suddenly became shallower. I didn't want him to have a heart attack simply from fear. That might take some explaining.

'Alex,' I shouted at him, bringing his eyes back into focus on my face. 'You can prevent this, you know. All you have to do is cooperate and answer all my questions. But you have to be completely candid and tell me everything. Do you understand?'

He nodded eagerly.

'And do you agree to answer everything?'

He nodded again.

'Nothing held back?'

He shook his head from side to side, so I stepped forward and tore off the tape from across his mouth.

'Now, for a start,' I said. 'Who killed Roderick Ward?'

He still wouldn't answer.

'I won't give you another chance,' I said seriously.

'How do I know you won't kill me anyway, after I've told you?'

'You don't,' I said. 'But do you have any choice? And if I gather enough incriminating information about you, so that you would also be in big trouble if you told the taxman about my mother, then we would both have a weapon of mass destruction, as it were. Either of us telling the authorities would result in the very thing we were trying so hard to prevent. We would both have the safety of mutually assured annihilation, a bit like nuclear deterrence. Neither of us would use the information for fear of retaliation.'

'But you could still kill me,' he said.

'Yes,' I agreed, 'I suppose I could, but why would I? There would be no need, and even I don't kill people without a reason.'

He didn't look terribly reassured so I untaped his foot from the spindle and then pulled him across the floor so he was sitting up with his back against the wall by the kitchen door.

'Now,' I said, sitting down once more on the upright chair. 'If you didn't kill Roderick Ward, who did?'

I still wasn't sure he would tell me, so, seemingly absent-mindedly, I picked up the syringe and made another fine spray of fluid shoot from the needle.

'His sister,' Alex said.

I looked at him. 'Stella Beecher?'

He seemed surprised I knew her name, but I'd already shown him the note he had sent to her. He nodded.

'Now why would she kill her own brother?'

'She didn't mean to,' he said. 'It was an accident.'

'You mean the car crash?'

'No,' he said. 'He was already dead when he went into the river. He drowned in a bath.'

'What on earth was Stella Beecher doing giving him a bath?'

'She wasn't exactly giving him a bath. They were trying to get him to tell them where the money had gone.'

'What money?' I asked.

'Fred's father's money.'

I was confused. 'Fred?'

'Fred Sutton,' he said.

Old Man Sutton's son. The man I had seen in the public gallery at Roderick Ward's inquest.

'So Fred Sutton and Stella Beecher know each other?' I asked.

'Know each other!' He laughed. 'They live together. They're almost married.'

In Andover, I thought, close to Old Man Sutton and his nursing home. So it had been no coincidence at all that Stella Beecher had moved to Andover.

It took more than an hour but, in the end, Alex told me how, and why, Roderick Ward was found dead in his car, submerged in the River Windrush.

Ward had been introduced to Old Man Sutton by Stella Beecher, who had been in a relationship with Detective Sergeant Fred for some time. Unbeknown to either Fred or Stella, Roderick had somehow conned the old man into borrowing against his house and investing the cash in a non-existent hedge fund in Gibraltar. Fred found out about it only after he'd seen the brick being thrown through his father's window. It was like a soap opera.

'How do you know all this?' I asked Alex. 'What's your connection?'

'I worked with Roderick Ward.'

'So you are implicated in this sham hedge-fund business?'

He didn't really want to admit it. He must have known that my mother had been conned in the same way. He looked away from my face, but he nodded.

'So who's the brains behind it?' I asked.

He turned his eyes back to mine. 'Do you think I'm stupid, or something?' he said. 'If I told you who it was then *you* wouldn't need to kill me because they'd do it for you.'

Actually, I did think him stupid. But not as stupid as Roderick Ward. Fancy stealing from the father of your sister's boyfriend, especially when the boyfriend just happened to be a police detective – now, that was really stupid!

'Let's go back to Roderick Ward,' I said. 'Why did you send a note to Stella Beecher saying you had the stuff? What stuff? And how did you know Stella, anyway?'

'I didn't,' he said. 'But I knew her address because Roderick had said it was the same address he used, the one in Oxford.'

'So what was all this about having the stuff? And hoping it was in time?'

'Fred Sutton had been harassing Roderick and me at an office we'd rented in Wantage, threatening us and so on.'

I didn't blame him, I thought.

'He told me that he'd get a warrant for my arrest, and he'd use his police contacts to fit me up good and proper. He said I'd get ten years unless I gave him some papers he wanted about where his dad's money had gone.'

'So why the note?' I asked.

'I made the copies of the papers, but he didn't come to collect them on the Monday morning as he'd said he would. He told me he'd definitely be at the office by eight, and I was waiting. But he didn't come all day, and Roderick didn't show up either. I thought the two of them must have done a deal, and I would end up carrying the can. I was shit scared, I can tell you. And I had no other way of contacting him, so I sent the note.'

So I had been wrong about 'the stuff' being something to do with my mother's tax papers, and also 'in time' had not been about before Roderick Ward's 'accident', but about before getting an arrest warrant issued.

Never assume anything, I reminded myself.

But I'd been right about one thing: Alex Reece was indeed stupid.

'So how do you know that Fred Sutton and Stella killed Roderick Ward?' I asked him.

'Fred pitches up first thing the next day and demands the papers, but I told him to get stuffed. If he thought I was going to take the blame for what Roderick had been doing, he had another think coming. But he says Roderick's dead and I'll go the same way if I didn't give him the papers.'

He paused only to draw breath.

'So I says to him that I didn't believe Roderick was dead. I told him he was only saying it to frighten me. He tells me that I should be frightened because they murdered him in the bath, but then he thinks better of it, and claims it was an accident, that they'd only meant to scare him into telling them where the money had gone. Fred says that Stella pulled his feet and his head went under and he just . . . died. Killed her own brother, just like that, Fred said. One minute they were asking him questions, the next he was dead.'

'So did you give Fred the papers he wanted?' I asked.

'Yeah,' he said. 'But they wouldn't have done him much good. It's been ages since his money went, and they change the account numbers and stuff all the time.'

'They?' I asked.

He clammed up tight, pursing his lips and shaking his head at me.

But I'd been doing a lot of thinking while I'd sat waiting in Greystone Stables and in the Newbury coffee shop, and the more I had thought about it the more convinced I had become.

'You mean Jackson Warren and Peter Garraway,' I said. It was a statement rather than a question.

He stared at me with his mouth hanging open. So I was right.

But it had to be them.

'And who is Mr Cigar?' I asked him.

He laughed. 'No one,' he said. 'That was Roderick's idea. They all thought it a great joke as they puffed on their own great big Havanas.'

'And Rock Bank Ltd?' I said. 'Is that a myth too?'

'Oh no, that exists all right,' he said. 'But it's not really a bank. It's just a Gibraltar holding company. When money comes in, it sits there for a while, and then leaves again.'

'How much money?' I asked.

'Depends on how much people invest.'

'And where does it go when it leaves Rock Bank?'

'I arrange a transfer into another Gibraltar account but it doesn't stay long there either,' he said. 'I don't know where it goes then. I'm pretty sure it ends up in a secret numbered Swiss account.'

'How long does it stay in Rock Bank?'

'About a week,' he said. 'Just long enough to allow for clearance of the transfer and for any problems to get sorted.'

So Rock 'Bank' (Gibraltar) Ltd had no assets of its own. No wonder the London-based liquidators were attempting to pursue the individual directors.

'And where does it come from?' I asked him.

'The mugs,' he said with a laugh.

'You're the mug,' I said. 'Look at you. You don't look quite so clever at the moment. And I bet you don't get to keep much of the money.'

'I get my cut,' he boasted.

'And how long in prison will your cut be worth when this all falls apart, as it surely must? Or when will Warren and Garraway decide you are no longer worth your cut? Then you might end up drowned in a bath, just like Roderick.'

'They need me,' he boasted again. 'I'm the CPA. They need me to square the audit. You're just jealous of a successful business.'

'But it's not a business,' I said. 'You are simply stealing from people.'

'They can afford it,' he said, sneering.

I wasn't going to argue with him because there was no point.

He probably agreed with the philosophy of Pol Pot and the Khmer Rouge.

'So how do Jackson Warren and Peter Garraway know each other?'

'I don't know,' he said. 'But they've done so for years. Long before I met them.'

'And how long have you known them?' I asked.

'Too long,' he said, echoing what he'd said to me at Isabella's kitchen supper.

'And how long is that?' I persisted.

'About four years.'

'Was that when the fake hedge-fund scheme started?'

'Yeah, about then.'

'Is that what you were referring to when you had that little spat with Jackson Warren, you know, that night when I first I met you?'

'No,' he said. 'That was over his and Peter's other little fiddle.'

'And what's that?' I asked.

'No way,' he said, shaking his head. 'I've already said too much as it is.'

At least he was right on that count.

'You think the Revenue will investigate their other little fiddle?' I asked him, thinking back to the supper exchange between him and Jackson. What was it he had said then? Something about 'no telling what else the Revenue might dig up'. 'And you're worried about that investigation finding out about everything else?'

It was a guess, but not a bad one.

'Bloody stupid, if you ask me,' he said.

I *was* asking him.

'Why take the risk?' I said.

'Exactly.'

'So their other little fiddle is about tax?'

'Look,' he said, changing the subject and completely ignoring my question, 'I had a few beers on the flight, and now I desperately need to take a piss.'

I thought back to my time in the stable. Should I make him wet himself, just as I had been forced to do?

'Come on,' he shouted at me. 'I'm bloody bursting.'

Reluctantly, I took a pair of scissors from my rucksack, leaned down, and cut the ties holding Alex's hands behind his back.

'I might run away,' he said, sitting up and rubbing his wrists.

'Not like that you won't.' I pointed at the plastic ties that still bound his ankles together.

'Come on,' he said. 'Cut them too.'

'No,' I said. 'You can hop.'

Grudgingly, he pulled himself upright and hopped into the cloakroom beneath the stairs.

I thought it unlikely that there would be a phone in the cloakroom but, nevertheless, I took the precaution of removing the house telephone from its cradle in the kitchen. You can't dial out on one extension if another is off the hook, and his mobile was still lying, switched off, on the kitchen counter where I'd left it.

Alex was taking his time and I was beginning to think he might be trying to escape out of the cloakroom window when I heard the flush. Presently, he reappeared, hobbling out into the hall.

'Cut these bloody things off,' he demanded angrily. He had obviously been using the time to try to break the plastic ties around his ankles, but I knew from experience that they were tougher than they looked. Much tougher indeed than his skin, which was chafed and reddening.

'No,' I said.

'What the bloody hell more do you want?' he asked angrily.

'My WMD,' I said.

'Eh?'

'My weapon of mass destruction,' I said. 'My nuclear deterrent. I need some hard evidence.'

'What sort of evidence?'

'Evidence of conspiracy to defraud my mother of one million US dollars.'

'Dream on,' he said, smiling.

'Maybe I should just ring up Jackson Warren and ask him about my mother's money, telling him that it was you who suggested I did so.'

'You wouldn't do that?' he asked, looking a little worried.

'Don't tempt me,' I said.

'He'd bloody kill me just for talking to you.'

Good, I thought. It was much to my advantage that Alex remained more frightened of Jackson Warren than he was of me. That alone would prevent him telling Jackson anything about this nocturnal encounter. Maybe that in itself was my nuclear deterrent.

'Or perhaps I should call Jackson and ask for the number of the Swiss bank account into which he and Garraway put all the money they steal.'

'You'd better bloody not,' Alex said. 'Or I'll be on to the taxman about your mother.'

I strode into the kitchen and he hobbled in behind me. I walked straight past his flight bag and out of the corner of my eye glimpsed him pushing it further out of sight beneath the table. I didn't mind one bit that Alex believed I hadn't accessed his computer.

'Sit down,' I said sharply, pointing at one of the kitchen chairs.

I don't think he really knew how to react. He didn't move.

'Sit down,' I said again in my best voice-of-command.

He wavered but, after a few seconds, he pulled the chair out from under the table and sat down while I sat on the chair opposite him.

'So whose idea was it to get my mother's horses to lose?' I asked.

'Julie's,' he said.

'So she could bet against them on the internet?'

'No, nothing like that,' he said. 'She just wanted to give her old man's horses a better chance of winning. He gives her such a hard time when they lose. It was me who bet against the horses on the internet. Not too much, like – not enough to attract attention. But it's been a nice little earner.'

Amateurs, I thought. These people were amateurs.

The doorbell rang, making both of us jump. It was followed by a persistent gentle knocking at the door. I glanced at my watch. It was ten to one in the morning.

'Stay there,' I ordered. 'And keep quiet. Neither of us wants the police involved in this, do we?'

Alex shook his head, but I thought it most improbable that the police would knock so softly. They were far more likely to break the door down.

I walked through into the dark front room and looked out through the window. Julie Yorke was standing outside the door, rapping her knuckles gently against the glass. I went back into the hall and opened the door.

'What have you done to him?' Julie asked in a breathless voice.

'Nothing,' I said.

'Where is he, then?' she demanded.

'In the kitchen,' I said, standing aside to let her pass. I glanced out at the dark and silent road and closed the door.

When I went back into the kitchen Julie was standing behind Alex, stroking his fine ginger hair. In other circumstances, it might have been a touching scene.

I could see that she was still wearing a nightdress under her raincoat.

'Couldn't sleep?' I asked sarcastically.

'I had to wait for my bloody husband to drop off,' she said. 'I've taken a bloody big chance coming here, I can tell you. I tried to call but it was permanently engaged and Alex's mobile went straight to voicemail.'

I looked across the kitchen at the house phone still lying off the hook on the worktop, and at the switched-off mobile alongside it.

'I thought I told you not to contact Alex,' I said sharply, pointing at her.

'You said not in the next thirty-six hours,' she replied in a pained tone. 'That ran out at ten forty-five this evening.'

I hadn't been counting, but she obviously had.

'So what happens now?' Alex asked into the silence.

'Well,' I said. 'For a start, you return all the blackmail money to my mother. I reckon that's about sixty thousand pounds.'

'I can't,' he said. 'We've spent it. And, anyway, why would I?'

'Because you obtained it illegally,' I pointed out.

'But your mother should have paid it to the taxman.'

'And so she will, when you give it back.'

'Dream on,' he said again with a laugh.

'OK,' I said. 'If that's your attitude, I will have to go to Jackson Warren and Peter Garraway and ask them for it.'

'You'll be lucky,' he said, still laughing. 'They're the most tight-fisted pair of bastards I've ever met.'

'I'll tell them you said that.'

The laughter died in his throat.

'Now don't you go telling them anything of the sort, or I'll be straight on the blower to the Revenue.'

Mutually assured destruction – it was what nuclear deterrence was all about.

'And what about my pictures?' Julie demanded, gaining some confidence from Alex.

'They prove nothing,' Alex said. 'All they show is that you were in the mailbox shop. That doesn't mean you were blackmailing anyone.'

'Not those pictures,' Julie said, irritated. 'The other pictures he took of me yesterday.'

'What other pictures?' Alex demanded, turning to me.

Oh dear, I thought, this could get really nasty. How might Alex react to my taking explicit images of his naked girlfriend? I sensed that Julie had also worked out that, if Alex hadn't already seen them, it might be much better for her if he didn't do so now.

'Er,' she said, backtracking fast. 'They're not that important.'

'But pictures of what?' Alex persisted, still looking at me.

Should I tell him? Should I show him just the sort of girl she was? Or could the pictures still be useful to me as a lever to apply to Julie?

'Just some photos I took outside the Yorkes' house yesterday afternoon.'

'Show me,' he said belligerently.

I thought of my camera, still safely out of sight in my little rucksack.

'I can't,' I said. 'I don't have the camera with me.'

'But why were you taking photos of Julie outside her house?' he demanded.

I thought quickly. 'To record her reaction when I showed her the prints of her in the mailbox shop. That's when I told her not to contact you for thirty-six hours.'

Julie seemed relieved and Alex appeared satisfied by the answer, even if he was a tad confused.

'So, what happens now?' he asked again.

It was a good question.

I thought about asking Julie if she knew anything of Warren and Garraway's other little fiddle, the tax one, but I decided I might get more from her without Alex being there, especially if I were to use my photo lever on her.

'Well, I don't know about you two,' I said, standing up, 'but I'm going home to bed.' And, I thought, to read Alex's e-mails.

I collected my 'insulin' bag from the stairs, slung my rucksack onto my back, and left the two lovebirds in the kitchen. I left the house by the front door, but I didn't walk off down the road. I removed the camera from my rucksack and went quickly down the side of the house to the rear garden and the kitchen window.

I had purposely left a small space at the bottom when I'd closed the blind, and I now put my eyes up close to the glass and looked in.

Alex and Julie really weren't very discreet. Making sure the flash was switched off, I took twenty or more photos through the window of them kissing, him sliding his hands inside her coat and pulling up her nightdress. Even though Julie's back was mostly towards the window, there was little doubt where Alex was placing his fingers and my eighteen-times optical zoom Leica lens captured everything.

Presently, Julie cut the plastic ties round Alex's ankles and they went hand-in-hand out of the kitchen, and, I presumed, up the stairs to bed. Short of shinning up a drainpipe, I would see nothing more and, in spite of being called Tom, my artificial leg didn't lend itself readily to climbing up to peep through bedroom windows.

Even then I didn't return to Ian's car and go home. Instead, I went back down the side of the house and out into Bush Close, to where Julie had parked the white BMW. It was some way down the road, well beyond the glow from the street light outside number 12. I tried the doors but she had locked them, so I sat down on the pavement, leaned up against the passenger door, and waited.

I was getting quite used to waiting, and thinking.

Alex Reece clearly received more than an average bonus after being away for five days in Gibraltar, and I was just beginning to think that Julie was staying for the whole night when, about an hour after I left, I saw her coming towards me through the pool of light produced by the solitary street lamp.

I pulled myself to my feet using the car door handle but I remained crouched down below the window level so Julie couldn't see me as she walked along the road. When she was about ten yards away, she pushed the remote unlock button on her key and the indicator lights flashed once in response. As she opened the driver's door to get in, I opened the passenger one to do likewise so we ended up sitting side by side with both doors slamming shut in unison.

Startled, she immediately tried to open the door again but I grabbed her arm on the steering wheel.

'Don't,' I said in my voice-of-command. 'Just drive.'

'Where to?' she said.

'Anywhere,' I said with authority. 'Now. Drive out of this road.'

Julie started the car and reversed it into one of the driveways to turn round. In truth, it was not the best-performed driving-test manoeuvre, and there would probably be BMW tyre marks on the front lawn of number 8 in the morning, but at least she didn't hit anything, and I wasn't an examiner.

She pulled out into Water Lane and turned right towards Newbury, towards home. We went a few hundred yards in silence.

'OK,' I said. 'Pull over here.'

She stopped the car at the side of the road.

'What do you want?' she said rather forlornly.

'Just a little more help,' I said.

'Can't you just leave us alone?'

'But why should I?' I exclaimed. 'My mother has paid you more than sixty thousand pounds over the past seven months and I think that entitles me to demand something from you.'

'But Alex told you,' she said. 'You can't have it back. We've spent it.'

'On what?' I asked.

She looked across at me. 'What do you mean, on what?'

'What have you spent my mother's money on?'

'You mean you don't know?'

'No. How could I?'

She laughed. 'Coke, of course. Lots of lovely coke.'

I didn't think she meant Coca-Cola.

'And bottles of bubbly. Only the best, you know. Cases and cases of lovely Dom.' She laughed again.

I realized that she must have been sampling one or the other during the past hour with Alex. It was not only fear that had caused her to drive on the grass. I couldn't smell alcohol on her breath, so it had to have been the coke.

'Does Ewen know you take cocaine?' I asked.

'Don't be fucking stupid,' she said. 'Ewen wouldn't know a line of coke if it ran up his nose. If it hasn't got four legs and a mane, Ewen couldn't care less. I think he'd much rather screw the bloody horses than me.'

'So what is Jackson Warren and Peter Garraway's little tax fiddle?'

'Eh?'

'What is Jackson and Peter's tax fiddle?' I asked again.

'You mean their VAT fiddle?' she asked.

'Yes,' I said excitedly. I waited in silence.

She paused for a bit but eventually began to explain. 'Did you know that racehorse owners can recover the VAT on training fees?'

'My mother said something about it,' I said.

'And on their other costs as well, those they attribute to their racing "business", like transport and telephone charges and vet's fees. They can even recover the VAT they have to pay when they buy the horses in the first place.'

The VAT rate was at nearly twenty per cent. That was a lot of tax to recover on expensive horseflesh.

'So what's the fiddle?' I asked.

'What makes you think I'd ever tell you?' she said, turning in the car towards me.

'So you do know, then?' I asked.

'I might,' she said arrogantly.

'I'll delete the pictures if you tell me.'

Even in her cocaine-induced state, she knew that the pictures were the key.

'How can I trust you?'

'I'm an officer in the British Army,' I said rather pompously. 'My word is my bond.'

'Do you promise?' she said.

'I promise,' I said formally, holding up my right hand. Yet another of those promises I might keep.

She paused a while longer before starting again.

'Garraway lives in Gibraltar and he's not registered for VAT in the UK. He actually could be but he's obsessive about not having anything to do with the tax people here because he's a tax exile. He only lives in Gibraltar to avoid paying tax. Hates the place really.' She paused.

'So?' I said, prompting her to continue.

'So all Peter Garraway's horses are officially owned by Jackson Warren. Jackson pays the training fees and all the other bills and then he claims back the VAT. He even buys the horses for

Garraway in the first place and gets the VAT back on that too. He uses a company called Budsam Ltd.'

'So why is that a fiddle?' I asked. 'If Jackson buys them and pays the fees then *he* is the owner, not Garraway.'

'Yes,' she said, 'but Peter Garraway pays Jackson back for all the costs.'

'Doesn't that show up in Jackson's accounts or those of the company?'

'No.' She smiled. 'That's the clever bit. Peter pays Jackson into an offshore account in Gibraltar that Jackson doesn't declare to the Revenue. Alex says it's very clever because Jackson gets his money offshore without ever having to transfer anything from a UK bank, which would be required by law to tell the tax people about it.'

'How many horses does Peter Garraway own in this way?' I asked.

'Masses. He has ten or twelve with us and loads more with other trainers.'

'But don't they pay for themselves with the prize money?'

'No, of course not,' she said. 'Most horses don't make in prize money anything like what they cost to keep, especially not jumpers. Far from it. Not unless you count the betting winnings, and Garraway gets to keep those himself.'

'So why doesn't Peter Garraway register himself as an owner in the UK for the VAT scheme?'

'I told you,' she said. 'He's paranoid about the British tax people. They've been trying for ever to get him for tax evasion. He's obsessive about the number of days he stays here, and he and his wife even travel on separate planes so they won't both be killed in a crash and his family get done here for inheritance tax. There's no way he'll register. Alex thinks it's stupid. He told them it would solve the problem of the VAT without any risk, but Garraway won't listen.'

I listened all right.

Wasn't it Archimedes who claimed that, if you gave him a lever long enough, he could lift the world?

I listened to Julie with mounting glee. Perhaps now I had a lever long enough to prise my mother's money back from under the Rock of Gibraltar.

All I had to do was to work out on whom to apply it, and when.

17

I spent much of the night downloading Alex's files and e-mails onto my laptop using the internet connection in my mother's office.

I had let myself into the kitchen silently using Ian's key. The dogs had been unperturbed by their nocturnal visitor, sniffing my hand as I'd passed them and then going back to sleep, happy that I was friend, not foe.

I worked solely by the light of the computer screen and left everything exactly as I found it. I didn't know why I still thought it was necessary for my presence to be a secret from my mother, but I wasn't yet ready to try to explain to her what had been going on.

It might also have been safer for me if she didn't know where I was.

After I had left Julie to drive herself home in the white BMW, I'd taken Ian's car slowly up the driveway of Greystone Stables. My two tell-tale sticks on their stones were broken. Someone had been up to the stable yard; someone who would now know I wasn't dead; someone who might try to kill me again. But they would have to find me first.

I slept fitfully on Ian's sofa and he left me there snoozing when he went out to morning stables at half past six on Monday morning.

By the time he returned around noon, I had read through all of Alex's downloaded information on my laptop. Most of it was boring but, amongst the dross, there were some real gems, and three stand-out sparkling diamonds.

Maybe I wouldn't need to use my lever after all.

One of the diamonds was that Alex, it transpired, was not only the accountant for Rock Bank (Gibraltar) Ltd, but also one of the signatories of the company's bank account and, best of all, I had downloaded all the passwords and usernames that he needed to access the account online.

I would try to log in to the account tonight, I thought, when I had access to the internet from my mother's office.

The other diamonds were the e-mails sent by Jackson Warren to Alex Reece concerning me, the first a message sent on the night of Isabella's kitchen supper, and the second after the races at Newbury on the day Scientific had won. The first had been sent in a fit of anger, and the second as a warning, but nevertheless, it amazed me how lax people could be with e-mail security.

In the army, all messages were encrypted before sending so that they were not readable by the enemy. Even mobile phones were not permitted to be used in Afghanistan in case the Taliban were listening to the transmissions and gaining information that could be useful either in a tactical way, or simply to undermine the morale of the troops.

No parents, having been called by their soldier offspring one evening from a mobile telephone in Helmand province, would welcome then receiving a second call, this time from an English-speaking member of the Taliban, who would inform them that their son was going to be targeted in the morning, and that he would be returning home to them in a wooden box.

It had happened.

Yet here was a supposedly sensible person, Jackson Warren, sending clear-text messages by e-mail for all to read. Well, for me to read, anyway.

What the bloody hell do you think you were doing talking so openly in front of Thomas Forsyth? Jackson had written soon after storming out of the supper. *His mother was one of those who invested heavily in our little scheme. KEEP YOUR BLOODY LIPS SEALED – DO YOU HEAR?*

Capital letters in an e-mail were equivalent to shouting and I could vividly recall the way Jackson had stormed out of the room that night. He would certainly have been shouting.

The second e-mail was calmer, but no less direct, and had been sent by Jackson to Alex at five o'clock on the afternoon of the races. He must have written it as soon as he arrived home from Newbury.

Thomas Forsyth told me this afternoon that he wants to contact you. I am making arrangements to ensure that he cannot. However, if he manages to be in contact with you before my arrangements are in position, you are hereby warned NOT to speak with him or communicate with him in any way. This is extremely important, especially in the light of the company business this coming week.

I knew only too well what arrangements Jackson had subsequently taken to stop me speaking with Alex – my shoulders still ached from them. But what, I wondered, had been the company business? Perhaps all would be revealed by access to the company bank account later.

'So how are the horses?' I asked Ian as he slumped down onto the brown sofa and switched on the television.

'They're all right,' he said with a mighty sigh.

'What's wrong, then?' I asked. 'Would you like me to leave?'

'As you like,' he said, seemingly uninterested in the conversation as he flicked through the channels with the remote control.

'Bad day at the office?' I asked.

'Yeah,' he said. 'You could say that.'

I said nothing. He'd tell me if he wanted to.

He did.

'When I took this job I thought it would be more as an assistant trainer rather than just as "head lad". That's what Mrs Kauri implied. She told me she doesn't have an assistant, as such, so I thought the role of head lad would be more important to her than to other trainers.'

He paused, perhaps remembering that I was Mrs Kauri's son.

'And?' I prompted.

'And nothing,' he said. He turned off the TV and swivelled round on the sofa to face me. 'I was wrong, that's all. It turns out she doesn't have an assistant because she can't delegate anything to anybody. She even treats me the same as one of the young boys straight out from school. She tells the staff to do things that I should be telling them to do, and often it is directly opposite to what I've already said. I feel worthless and undermined.'

Story of my life, I thought.

At least, it had been the story of my life until I'd left home to join the army. It seemed to me that Ian was already on the road to somewhere else. It was a shame. I'd seen him working with the horses and even I could see that he was good, calming the younger ones and standing no nonsense from the old hands. He also had a passion for them, and he longed for them to win. Losing Ian Norland would be a sad day for Kauri House Stables.

'Have you been looking?' I asked.

'There's a possibility of a new stable opening that's quite exciting,' he said, suddenly more alive. 'It's some way off yet but I'm going to keep my options open. But don't you go telling your mother. She'd be furious.'

He was right, she would be furious. She demanded absolute

loyalty from everyone around her but, sadly, she repaid it in short measure, and she wasn't about to change now.

'Which stables?' I asked.

'Rumour has it that one of the trainers in the village is going to open up a second yard and he'll be needing a new assistant to run it. I thought I might apply.'

'Which trainer?' I asked.

'Ewen Yorke,' he said. 'Apparently he's buying Greystone Stables.'

He'd have to fix the broken pane in the tack-room window.

The statements of the bank account of Rock Bank (Gibraltar) Ltd were most revealing.

I had spent the afternoon re-reading all the e-mails that I had downloaded from Alex Reece's computer as well as the files from the Rock Accounts folder. Quite a few of the e-mails were communications back and forth with someone called Sigurd Bellido, the senior cashier at the real Gibraltar bank that held the Rock Bank Ltd account, discussing the transfer of funds in and out. Unfortunately there were no references to account names and numbers from which, and to which, the transfers were made, although strangely they all discussed the ongoing health of Mr Bellido's mother-in-law.

When, at two in the morning, I logged on to the online banking system in my mother's office, I could see that the recent transfers discussed with Mr Bellido were reflected in the various changes to the account balance.

As Alex had said, money periodically came into the account, presumably from the 'investors' in the UK, and then left again about a week later. If Alex was right, it disappeared eventually into some secret Swiss account belonging to Garraway or Warren.

I looked particularly at the transactions for the past week to see if they showed any evidence of the 'company business' that Jackson had referred to in his e-mail.

There had been two large deposits. Both were in American dollars, one for one million and the other for two million. A couple more mugs, I thought, duped into investing in a non-existent hedge fund.

One of the deposits had no obvious reference but the other, the two million dollars, had a name attached to it – Toleron. I knew I'd heard that name before, but I couldn't place where, so I typed 'Toleron' into the Google search bar on my computer, and it instantly gave me the answer.

TOLERON PLASTICS appeared across my screen in large red letters, with THE LARGEST DRAINPIPE MANUFACTURER IN EUROPE running underneath in slightly smaller ones. Mrs Martin Toleron had been the rather boring lady I'd sat next to at Isabella's kitchen supper who would, it appeared, very soon be finding out that her 'wonderful' husband wasn't quite as good at business as she had claimed. I almost felt sorry for her.

Had that really been only eleven days ago? So much had happened in the interim.

I searched further for Mr Martin Toleron. Nearly every reference was connected with the sale of his company the previous November to a Russian conglomerate, reputedly adding more than a hundred million dollars to his personal fortune.

Suddenly I didn't feel quite so sorry for his wife over the loss of a mere two million.

As Alex would have said, they could afford it.

Early on Tuesday morning, while my mother was away on the gallops watching her horses exercise, I borrowed Ian Norland's car once more and went to see Mr Martin Toleron.

According to the internet, he lived in the village of Hermitage, a few miles to the north of Newbury, and I found the exact address easily enough by asking directions in the village shop.

'Oh, yes,' said the plump middle-aged woman behind the counter. 'We all know the Tolerons round here, especially Mrs Toleron.' Her tone implied that Mrs Toleron wasn't necessarily the most welcome of customers in the shop. I thought it might have been something to do with the never-ending praise of her 'wonderful' husband or, more likely, was just straightforward envy of the rich.

Martin Toleron's house, near the edge of the village on the Yattenden road, was a grand affair in keeping with his 'captain of industry' billing. I pulled up in front of the firmly closed six-foot-high iron gates and pushed the button on the intercom box fixed to the gatepost, but I wasn't quite sure what I was going to say if someone answered.

'Hello?' said a man's voice through the box.

'Mr Toleron?' I asked.

'Yes,' the man said.

'Mr Martin Toleron?'

'Yes.' He sounded a little impatient.

'My name is Thomas Forsyth,' I said. 'I'd like to—'

'Look, I'm sorry,' he replied, cutting me off. 'I don't take cold calls at my gate. Goodbye.' There was a click and the box went dead.

I pushed the button again. No reply, so I pushed it once more, and for much longer.

Eventually he came back on the line. 'What do you want?' he asked with increased impatience.

'Does Rock Bank Limited of Gibraltar mean anything to you?' I asked.

There was a pause before he replied. 'Who did you say you are?'

'Thomas Forsyth.'

'Stay there,' he said. 'I'm coming out.'

I waited and soon a small portly man emerged, walking down the driveway towards me. I vaguely remembered him from Isabella's supper, even though we hadn't spoken. Looks, I thought, could be deceiving. Martin Toleron didn't give the appearance of being a multi-millionaire captain of industry but, there again, Alexander the Great had hardly been an Adonis, having reputedly been very short with a twisted neck and different-coloured eyes, one blue and the other brown.

Martin Toleron stopped some ten feet from the gates.

'What do you want?' he demanded.

'Just to talk,' I said.

'Are you from the Inland Revenue?' he asked.

I thought it a strange question but perhaps he was afraid I was going to hand him a tax summons.

'No,' I said. 'I was at the same dinner party as you, at Jackson and Isabella Warren's place last week. I sat next to your wife.'

He took a couple of paces towards the gates and squinted at me.

'But what do you want?' he said again.

'I want to talk to you about Rock Bank Limited and the investment you have just made with them in Gibraltar.'

'That's none of your business,' he said.

I didn't reply but stood silently, waiting for curiosity to get the better of him.

'Anyway, how do *you* know about it?' he asked, as I knew he would.

'I think it might be better for us to go inside to discuss this rather than to shout a conversation through these gates where anyone could overhear us. Don't you agree?'

He obviously did agree because he removed a small black box from his pocket and pushed a button. The gates swung open as I returned to Ian's car.

I parked on the gravel drive in front of the mock-Georgian front door and pillared portico of his modern red-brick mansion.

'Come into my office,' Martin Toleron said, leading the way past the grand front door to a smaller one, set between the main house and an extensive garage block. I followed him into a large oak-panelled room with a built-in matching oak desk and bookcases behind.

'Sit down,' he said decisively, pointing at one of two armchairs, and I glimpsed for the first time the confidence and resolution that would have served him well in his business. I resolved to ensure that Martin Toleron became a valuable friend rather than a challenging enemy.

'What is this about?' he said, sitting in the other chair and turning towards me, jutting out his jaw.

'I believe that you have recently sent a large sum of money to Rock Bank Limited of Gibraltar as an investment in a hedge fund.'

I paused but he didn't respond. He just continued to stare at me with unfriendly eyes. It was slightly unnerving and I began to question if coming here had been a mistake. I suddenly wondered if Toleron was, in fact, part of the conspiracy. Had I just walked into the lion's den like a naïve lamb to the slaughter?

'And I have reason to believe,' I went on, 'that the investment fund in question does not actually exist, and you are being defrauded of your money.'

He continued to sit and look at me.

'Why are you telling me this?' he demanded, suddenly standing up. 'What do you want from me?'

'Nothing,' I said.

'You must want something.' He was almost shouting 'Otherwise why are you here? You didn't come here to give me bad news so you could simply gloat. Is it money you're after?'

'No, of course not,' I said defensively. 'I came here to warn you.'

'But why?' he said aggressively. 'If, as you say, I have already invested money in a fraud, your warning would then be too late. And why is it you believe I'm being defrauded anyway? Are you the one who's doing it?'

Things were not going well.

'I just thought you would like to know so you didn't send any more,' I said, again on the defensive. 'I am not involved in the fraud other than being the son of another victim. I had hoped you might have some information that would be helpful to me in trying to recover her money. That's all.'

He sat down again and remained silent for a few seconds.

'What sort of information?' he asked eventually, and more calmly.

'Well,' I said. 'With respect, my mother is no financial wizard, far from it, and I can see how she was duped, but you . . .' I left the implication hanging in the air.

He stood up from the chair again and went to the desk. He picked up a large white envelope and tossed it into my lap. It contained the glossy offering document for what it called the 'opportunity-of-a-lifetime investment'. I skimmed through the prospectus. It was very convincing and certainly gave the impression of being from a legitimate organization with photos of supposed business offices in Gibraltar, graphs of past and predicted investment performance, all of which moved in the right direction, and with wonderful glowing testimonials from other satisfied investors.

'Why do you think it a fraud?' he asked.

'I know of two separate cases when people, including my mother and stepfather, after investing through Rock Bank Limited, have lost all their money. They were both told that the hedge fund in which their money had been placed had subsequently gone bankrupt, leaving no assets. I have reason to believe that the funds never actually existed in the first place and the money was simply stolen.'

I flicked through the glossy brochure once more.

'It's a very professional job,' he said. 'It gives all the right information and assurances.'

If they were after 'investments' in million-dollar chunks, it would have to be a professional job.

'But did you check up on any of it?' I asked.

He didn't answer, but I could tell from his face that he hadn't.

'Why didn't your mother complain to the police?' he said. 'Then there might have been a warning issued.'

'She couldn't,' I said without further clarification.

I thought back to his strange question at the gate about me being from the Revenue, and his rather belligerent attitude towards me since. 'Mr Toleron,' I said, 'excuse me asking, but are you being blackmailed?'

As in my mother's case, it wasn't the loss of his money that worried Martin Toleron the most; it was the potential loss of face because he'd been conned.

If I thought he would thank me for pointing out that his investment was a fake, then I was mistaken. Indirectly, he even offered to pay me not to make that knowledge public.

'Of course I won't make it public,' I said, horrified by his insinuation.

'Everyone else I know would have,' he said with something of a sigh. 'They would gleefully sell it to the highest bidder from the gutter press.' He may have been a highly successful businessman, and he had clearly made pots of money, but he'd obviously been accompanied by precious few real friends on the journey.

He was not being blackmailed – at least, he denied he was to me – but he did admit that someone had recently tried to extort money from him, accusing him of falsifying a tax return that stated he was not a tax resident in the UK when, in fact, he was.

'I told him to bugger off,' he said. 'But it took me a lot of time and money to get things straightened out. The last bloody thing I want is an audit by the Revenue.'

'So you are fiddling something, then?' I asked.

'No, of course not,' he said. 'I'm just sailing close to the wind, you know, trying it on with a few things.'

'VAT?' I asked.

'As a matter of fact, yes,' he said. 'Is that why your mother didn't go to the authorities and complain?'

'Is what why?' I asked.

'Because she was being blackmailed.'

I simply nodded, echoing my mother's belief that, in not saying anything out loud, it somehow diminished the admission.

'Did you know someone called Roderick Ward?'

'Don't you mention that name here,' he said explosively. 'Called himself an accountant, but he was nothing more than a damn bookkeeper. It was thanks to him that I nearly copped it with the Revenue.'

I wondered how on earth a captain of industry had become tangled up with such a dodgy accountant.

'How did you come to know him?' I asked.

'He was my elder daughter's boyfriend for a while. Kept coming round here and telling me how I could save more tax. I should never have listened to the little bastard.'

Oh! What a tangled web he weaved, when first he practised to deceive!

'Do you know what happened to him?' I asked.

'I heard somewhere that he died in a car crash.'

'Actually, he was murdered,' I said.

He was surprised, but not shocked. 'Not by me, he wasn't. Although I would've happily done it. Good riddance, I say!'

'He was murdered by someone else he stole money from.'

'Well done, them.' He smiled for the first time since I'd been there. But then the smile vanished as quickly as it had arrived. 'Hold on a minute,' he said. 'Didn't Ward die last summer?'

'Yes,' I said. 'In July.'

'So who is robbing me now?'

'Who gave you the offering document? Who was it who recommended the investment to you?'

'How do you know someone did?' he asked.

'No one invests in something from a cold call, or from a prospectus that just drops through their letterbox. Certainly not to the tune of two million dollars. You had to be told about it by someone.'

He seemed slightly surprised I knew the exact size of his investment.

'Did Jackson tell you the amount?' he asked.

'So it *was* Jackson Warren who recommended it,' I said. 'You asked me who was robbing you and that's your answer – Jackson Warren, together with Peter Garraway.'

He didn't believe it. I could read the doubt in his face.

'Surely not?' he said. 'Why would he? Jackson Warren's got lots of money of his own.'

'Maybe that's because he steals it from other people.'

'Don't be ridiculous,' he said.

'I'm not. I'll show you. Do you have an internet connection?'

'But how did you get access?' Martin Toleron was astounded as I brought up the recent transactions of Rock Bank (Gibraltar) Ltd on my laptop computer screen. 'You must be involved somehow.'

'I'm not,' I said.

'Then how did you get the passwords?'

'Don't ask,' I said. 'You don't want to know.'

He looked at me strangely, but he didn't ask, simply turning his attention back to the screen.

'Whose is the other investment?' he asked.

'I was hoping you could tell me,' I said.

'I've no idea. I've only spoken about the fund with Jackson Warren.'

'Did he raise it or did you?'

'He did. He told me at that supper that he had a great investment tip for me.'

'Did he indicate that he was going to invest in the fund himself?'

'He told me he had made his investment sometime in the past, and he claimed that it had performed very well since, very well indeed. That's why he was so keen on it.' He paused. 'I believed him and, to be fair, you haven't shown me anything substantive to contradict that belief.'

I opened one of the e-mails from Alex Reece's inbox from the previous week:

Alex
We should expect a 2-unit sum into the account this coming week from our drainpipe friend. Please ensure it takes the usual route, and issue the usual note of acceptance. Your commission will be transferred in due course.
JW

'That doesn't prove it's a fraud,' Toleron said.

'Maybe not directly,' I said. 'But did Jackson Warren tell you he was actually running the fund he was so keen to promote?'

'No. He did not.'

'But he clearly must be running it if he's ordering the issuing of acceptance notes to investors.' I paused to allow that to sink in. 'Is that enough proof for you? If not, there's plenty more.'

'Show me,' Toleron said.

I pulled up another of Alex Reece's e-mails to the screen, this time one he had sent to Sigurd Bellido, the chief cashier in Gibraltar, about a transfer:

Sigurd
Please transfer the million dollars, received into the Rock Bank Ltd account last week from the UK, *into the usual other account at your bank. I trust your mother-in-law's health problems are improving.*
AR

Martin Toleron read it over my shoulder. 'That doesn't prove anything.'

'No,' I said. 'But read this.'

I pulled up another e-mail from Alex's Gibraltar folder, this one to Jackson Warren sent on the same day as the previous one:

Jackson
I have issued the instruction to SB *(and his mother-in-law) and the funds should be available in your usual account later today for further transfer.*
AR

'What's all that mother-in-law business about?' he asked.

'I don't know,' I said. 'But it appears in all the e-mails sent to SB, that's Sigurd Bellido, the chief cashier who makes the transfers in Gibraltar. Funny thing is, he doesn't ever mention her in his replies.'

Toleron thought for a moment. 'Perhaps it's a code to prove that the transfer request really is from this AR person.'

'Alex Reece,' I said.

'Didn't I meet him at that dinner party? Ginger-haired fellow?'

'That's him,' I said. 'Slightly odd sort of person. He's Jackson Warren's accountant but he's up to his neck in the fraud.'

'But Warren must surely know that I would suspect him if the fund went bust and I lost all my money.'

'But he would simply apologize for the bad investment advice and say that he'd also lost a packet and, if the newspaper reports of your company sale are to be believed, you would have been able to afford the loss more than he would. In fact, I bet you would have ended up feeling sorry for him, rather than accusing him of stealing from you.'

'Don't ever believe what you read in the papers,' he said. 'But I get your point. The very fact that it was a relatively small investment is why I did it in the first place. I can afford to lose it. Not, of course, that I want to.'

How lovely it must be for him, I thought, to be so rich that two million dollars was a relatively small investment, and one that he could afford to lose.

'So all we need to do now is to get this Alex Reece chappy to e-mail SB in Gibraltar and get him to return the money whence it came.' Martin Toleron smiled at me. 'Then I'll have my money back. Shouldn't be too difficult to arrange, surely?'

He certainly made it sound easy, but I'm not sure that Alex Reece would play ball. He might be more afraid of Jackson Warren and Peter Garraway than he was of Martin Toleron; or even of me and my syringes.

'I have a better idea,' I said. 'We could send an e-mail to SB pretending to be Alex Reece.'

'But that's not as easy as you think,' Martin said. 'Not without his e-mail account password.'

Now it was my turn to smile at him. 'And what makes you think I don't already have it?'

18

The e-mail to Sigurd Bellido was ready to go by half past eleven:

Sigurd
There has been a mix-up at our end and I need to transfer back to the UK the last two payments that were made into the Rock Bank Ltd account on Thursday and Friday of last week. Please transfer, as soon as possible from the Rock Bank Ltd account (number 01201030866) at your bank:

(1) US$2,000,000 (two million US dollars) to Barclays Bank plc, SWIFT code BARCGB2LBGA, Belgravia branch, for further credit to Mr Martin Toleron, sort code 20-62-18, account number 81634587.

(2) US$1,000,000 (one million US dollars) to HSBC Bank plc, SWIFT code HSBCGB6174A, Hungerford Branch, for further credit to Mrs Josephine Kauri, sort code 40-28-73, account number 15638409.

Please carry out these transfers as soon as possible, preferably immediately. I trust your mother-in-law continues to make a sound recovery. Many thanks.
AR

Martin Toleron and I had looked through all the transfer requests in Alex Reece's 'Gibraltar' folder, and we had studied closely the language and layout he had used in the past.

'Are you happy with it?' Martin asked.

'As happy as I can be,' I said.

'Do you think it will work?'

'Maybe,' I said. 'But we have nothing to lose by trying.'

'I have,' he said. 'I stand to lose two million dollars.'

I decided against saying that he'd told me he could afford it. 'You've already lost it, but this might just get it back. It's worth a try, but it's a hell of a lot of money for a bank to transfer without making any other checks.'

'They'll e-mail him back, though,' Martin said.

'Oh for sure.'

They might also check that the million dollar deposit was not actually going back to where it had come from but to my mother's bank account instead. However, without a name reference, I had no idea who had sent that deposit in the first place, so I could hardly send it back to them. It may have not have been the specific one million dollars my mother had transferred to Rock Bank Ltd last year, but money was money, interchangeable and impossible to tell apart.

By looking at all the e-mail correspondence between SB and AR we had discovered a pattern. Alex would e-mail the request always around midday or five minutes either side, UK time. Sigurd would then e-mail straight back, acknowledging receipt and requesting confirmation. Alex would then instantly respond to that with a note that contained some comment, not now about Sigurd's mother-in-law, but about the weather in the UK.

The Taliban would have had a field day with this pathetic level of security. I only hoped that Alex hadn't realized that I had copied his messages and compromised his defences.

'Are you ready to intercept SB's reply?' Martin asked.

'As ready as I can be,' I said. 'I'm logged on to Alex Reece's e-mail account via the mail2web webmail service, but it will all go wrong if Alex downloads the reply straight to his computer from the server. We'll have to take the chance that he doesn't click on Send/Receive at that precise moment.'

'Do you have the reply ready?' He was hopping from foot to foot with nervousness as he stood behind me at his desk.

'Calm down, Martin,' I said. 'Let's just hope that the real Alex Reece isn't sending his own transfer e-mail to SB today.'

'Oh my God,' said Martin, 'that would really confuse things.'

'The shortest time that money has spent in the account before being moved on is six days. It is now five days since the first one arrived and four since the second. So I don't expect a real transfer request from Alex today.'

'How about if SB knows that it has to be a minimum of six days or it's a fake request?'

'We'll know that soon enough,' I said. 'It's two minutes to twelve.'

I pushed the Send button and the message disappeared from the screen. It was on its way, and we were both holding our breath.

We waited in silence as I continually refreshed the webmail page. The clock on the computer moved to 12.01. I refreshed the page once more. Nothing. I forced myself to be calm and wait for a count of ten before I clicked on the 'refresh' button again. Still nothing. I counted again, slowly, this time to fifteen, but still nothing came.

The reply arrived at nine minutes past twelve, by which time I had all but given up hope.

Alex
I acknowledge receipt of your instructions. To which party do I charge the transfer costs?
SB

I had the reply ready to send but I quickly pulled it up to make the changes. I typed in the new information.

Sigurd
I confirm receipt of your acknowledgement and I endorse the instructions. Please charge the transfer costs to the recipients. Thank goodness spring is nearly here in the UK *and the temperature has begun to rise.*
AR

I pushed the Send button and again the message disappeared from the screen. Next I used the mail2web tools to delete SB's reply from the server so that it would not appear on Alex's computer when he downloaded his mail.

'Now we wait and see,' I said. But I went on monitoring the webmail page for another forty minutes before I was happy that SB wasn't going to ask another question.

'Do you think it will work?' he said.

'Do you?' I asked in reply.

'Not really,' he said. 'It was much too easy.'

'Yes,' I said. 'Almost as easy as getting you to part with the two million dollars in the first place.'

Martin called his bank and asked them to inform him by telephone immediately if a large deposit arrived. My mother, meanwhile, might simply have to wait to see if it appeared on her bank statement.

'Call me if you hear anything,' I said, shaking his hand in the driveway.

'Don't worry, I will,' he said with a smile. 'Quite an entertaining morning, I'd say. Much more exciting than the boring existence I have now found for myself.'

'You miss running your company, then?' I asked.

'Miss it!' he said. 'I grieve for my loss.'

'But you have all that money.'

'Yes,' he said, rather forlornly. 'But what can I do every day? Count it? I started in business straight out of school aged sixteen. It wasn't plastics in those days, it was cardboard. Cardboard boxes for removal companies. They were all still using old tea chests then and I reckoned that cardboard would be better. I started by collecting old cardboard boxes from shops and passing them on to the removal men. Then I started importing boxes, both cardboard and plastic.'

He sighed.

'Where did the drainpipes come from?' I asked.

'The man who made the plastic boxes in Germany also made drainpipe and I bought the UK rights from him. And it just took off. That was years ago.'

'Why did you sell?'

'I'm sixty-eight and neither of my children are interested in running any business, let alone a drainpipe business. Far too boring for them. But I loved it. I used to get to the factory in Swindon at seven in the morning and often I'd not leave before ten at night. It was such fun.'

'Didn't your wife object?' I asked.

'Oh, I expect so,' he said laughing. 'But she does so enjoy shopping in Harrods.'

'So what will you do in the future? Will you start something else?'

'No,' he said with another sigh. 'I don't think so. I suppose I'll have to go to Harrods more often with my wife. We need to do something with all that money.'

The prospect of more shopping with his wife clearly didn't make him happy. I obviously wasn't the only person viewing his future life with anxiety and trepidation.

'Shop for some racehorses,' I said. 'I hear that's a great way to spend loads of money, and it can be lots of fun too.'

'What a great idea,' he said. 'I'll do just that.'

'And,' I said, 'I know a way to save you all the VAT.'

We both laughed out loud.

As I had hoped, Martin Toleron and I parted as friends, not foes.

Martin called my mobile at a quarter past three as I was dozing on Ian's sofa, half watching the racing from Huntingdon on the television.

'Have you heard from the bank?' I asked, instantly wide awake.

'No, nothing from them,' he said. 'But I've just had a call from Jackson Warren.'

'Wow,' I said, clapping my hands together. 'And what did he say?'

'He tried to tell me that the bank in Gibraltar had made an error and had inexplicably returned my two million dollars to my account. He asked if I would mind instructing my bank to send it again.'

'And what did you say?' I asked.

'I expressed surprise that Jackson was calling me as I had no idea that he was involved with the organization of the fund. I told him I thought he was just another satisfied investor.'

'And what did he say then?'

'He tried to tell me that he had only been called by the fund manager because he, the manager, knew that Jackson was a friend of mine.'

He paused. 'Yes?' I said. 'Go on.'

'I lost my rag a bit. I told him to get stuffed. I said that I would not be investing in anything to do with him as he had purposely misled me. I also told him I'd be reporting the incident to the Financial Services Authority.'

'I bet he didn't take kindly to that.'

'No, he didn't,' Martin said. 'In fact, he threatened me.'

'He what?'

'He told me straight-out that if I went to the FSA I'd regret it. I asked him what exactly he meant by that, but all he said was "work it out".'

That was the same phrase that Alex had said to me.

'And,' Martin went on, 'he doesn't seem to be too pleased with you either.'

'How so?' I asked.

'He point-blank accused me of conspiring with you to defraud him. I told him that was rich coming from him and he could go and boil his brains, or words to that effect.'

I wasn't altogether sure that insulting Jackson Warren was a sensible policy. Insults sometimes provoked extreme reactions and some historians now believed that Saddam Hussein's cruel invasion of Kuwait in 1990 was the direct result of a personal insult to the Iraqi people from the Emir.

'Did he ask if you knew where I was?' I asked.

'Ask me?' He laughed. 'He demanded that I tell him. I simply said that I had no idea where you were, and also that I wouldn't have told him if I did.'

'How secure are your gates?' I asked.

'Why?' He sounded slightly worried for the first time.

'I think that Jackson Warren is a very dangerous man,' I said seriously. 'Martin, this is not a game. He has already tried to kill me once, and I am sure he would do it again without hesitation. So keep your gates locked and watch your back.'

'I will,' he said, and hung up, no doubt to go outside rapidly and make sure his gates were closed and bolted.

Was it now time, I wondered, to involve the police and be damned about the tax consequences? But what could I say to them? 'Well, Officer, Mr Jackson Warren tried to kill me by hanging me up to starve to death in a disused stable when I had to stand on only one leg for days, but I escaped by unscrewing the hay-net ring, climbing over the stable walls, and breaking a window in the tack room, but I've only now decided to tell you about it, a week later, after I've been sneaking around Berkshire in camouflage cream, attacking and torturing one of Mr Warren's associates using fake insulin and a hypodermic needle, and using the information I illegally obtained from him to transfer one million American dollars from Mr Warren's company in Gibraltar into my mother's personal bank account in Hungerford.'

Somehow, I didn't think it would bring the Thames Valley Constabulary rushing to Jackson's front door to make an immediate arrest. They would be far more likely to send me to a psychiatrist, and then Jackson would know exactly where I was.

It was much safer, I thought, to lie low for a while and let things blow over.

How mistaken could I be? The answer was badly.

The first sign that things had gone dangerously wrong was a hammering on the door of Ian's flat that woke me from a deep sleep.

It was pitch black and I struggled to find my way to the light switch. The hammering continued unabated. I turned on the light and looked at the clock. It was one thirty in the morning. Who could be knocking at this ungodly hour?

I grabbed my shirt and went over to the door. I was about to unlock it when I suddenly stepped back. Could it be Jackson Warren outside? Or Alex Reece? Or Peter Garraway?

'Who is it?' I shouted.

'It's Derek Philips,' came the reply. My stepfather.

Ian appeared from his bedroom, bleary-eyed and wearing blue-striped boxer shorts.

'What the hell's going on?' he said, squinting against the brightness.

'It's my stepfather,' I said to him.

'Well, open the door, then.'

But I wasn't sure enough. 'Are you alone?' I shouted.

'What bloody difference does that make?' Ian said, striding towards me. 'Open the bloody door. Here.' He pushed past and unlocked it himself.

Derek almost fell into the room as the door opened, and he was alone.

'Thank God,' he said. Then he saw me. 'What the bloody hell are *you* doing here?'

I ignored his question. 'Derek, what's wrong?' I asked.

'It's your mother,' he said, clearly distressed.

Oh, no, I thought, she must have decided to kill herself after all.

'What about her?' I asked, dreading the answer.

'She's been kidnapped.'

'What?' I said in disbelief.

'She's been kidnapped,' he repeated.

It sounded so unlikely.

'Who by?' I asked.

'Two men,' he said. 'They came looking for you.'

Derek and Ian both looked at me accusingly.

'Who were they?' Ian asked him.

'I don't know,' Derek said. 'They were wearing those ski masks, like balaclavas, but I don't think either of them was very young.'

'Why not?'

'Something about the way they moved,' Derek said.

I, meanwhile, believed I knew exactly who they were and Derek was right, neither of them was young. Two desperate men in their sixties trying to recover the money they thought they had successfully stolen, but which I had then stolen back. But where was Alex Reece?

'Are you sure there were just two of them?' I asked. 'Not three?'

'I only saw two,' Derek said. 'Why? Do you know who they are?' He and Ian looked accusingly at me once more.

'What exactly did they say?' I asked, trying to ignore their stares.

'I don't really remember. It all happened so fast,' he said. 'They somehow got into the house and were in our bedroom. One of them poked me with the barrels of a shotgun to wake me up.' He was almost in tears and I could understand how frightened he and my mother must have been. 'They said they wanted you, but we told them we didn't know where you were. We said we thought you were in London.'

So, not telling my mother where I was had saved me a visit from the ski-masked duo. But at what cost to her?

'Why did they take her with them?' I asked, but I already knew the answer. They knew that I'd come to them if they had my mother. 'Did they tell you where they were taking her?'

'No,' Derek said. 'But they did tell me that you would know where she would be.'

'Have you called the police?' Ian asked.

'No police,' Derek said urgently. 'They told me that I mustn't call the police. "Call the police and Josephine dies", that's what they said. They told me to think about it for a while and then to call you.' He nodded at me. 'But I didn't know where you were and I don't even have your phone number.' He was crying now. 'All I could think of was asking Ian.'

I would know where she would be. That's what the kidnappers had told Derek.

I would know where she would be.

And I did.

I approached Greystone Stables, not from the road and up the driveway as my enemy might have expected, but from the opposite direction, over the undulating farmland and through the wood on the hill above.

In war, tactical surprise is essential, as it had been during the recapture of the Falkland Islands. The Argentine forces, far superior in number, had believed that it was impossible for the British to approach Stanley, the island capital, across the swampy, uncharted interior, and had dug in their defences for an attack from the sea. How wrong they were. The Royal Marines and Parachute Regiment's 'yomp' across the island, carrying eighty-pound bergens over more than fifty-six miles in three days, has since become the stuff of folklore in the army. It had been one of the major factors in that victory.

In my case, I was just glad not to have an eighty-pound bergen on my back.

I stopped just short of the limit of the trees and knelt on my left knee. I looked again at my watch with its luminous face. More than two hours had passed since Derek had arrived in such distress at the door of Ian's flat. It was now 3.42 a.m. The windless night was beautifully clear with a wonderful canopy of twinkling stars. The moon's phase was just past first quarter and it was sinking rapidly towards the western horizon to my left. In forty minutes or so the moon would be down completely and the blackness of the night would deepen for a couple of hours before the arrival of the sun, and the dawning of another day.

I liked the darkness. It was my friend.

In the last of the moonlight I studied the layout of the deserted house and stables spread out below me. I could see no lights, and no movement, but I was sure this was where the two men had meant when they'd told Derek I would know where my mother would be.

But would she actually be here, or had it been a ruse to bring me to this place on a wild-goose chase, to fall willingly into their waiting hands, while my mother was actually incarcerated somewhere else?

It had taken all my limited powers of persuasion to convince Ian not to call the police immediately. Derek, too, had begged him not to.

'But we must call them,' Ian had said with certainty.

'We will,' I'd replied. 'But give me a chance to free my mother first.'

Did I really think that Jackson Warren and Peter Garraway would harm her, or even kill her? I thought it unlikely, but I couldn't know for sure. Desperate people do desperate things, and I remembered only too well how they had left me to die horribly from starvation and dehydration.

I had left Derek and Ian in the latter's flat, Derek cuddling a bottle of brandy he had returned briefly to Kauri House to collect, and Ian with a list of detailed instructions, including one to telephone the police immediately if he hadn't heard from me by six thirty in the morning.

They had both watched with rising interest and astonishment as I had made my mission preparations. First, I'd changed into my dark clothes, together with the all-black Converse basketball boots, the right one requiring me to remove my false leg to force the shoe over the plastic foot. Next I had gathered the equipment into my little rucksack: black garden ties, scissors, duct tape, the red-coloured first-aid kit, the length of chain with the padlock still attached, a torch, and a box of matches, all of them wrapped up in a large navy-blue towel to prevent any noise when I moved.

This time, I did borrow one of Ian's kitchen knives, a large, sharp, carving knife, and I'd placed it on top of everything else in the rucksack, ready for easy access. I had then borrowed a pair of racing binoculars from my mother's office and, finally, I'd removed my sword from its protective cardboard tube and scabbard.

'Surely you're not going to use *that*,' Derek had said with his large brandy-filling eyes staring at the three-foot blade.

'Not unless I have to,' I had replied casually as I'd rubbed black boot polish onto the blade to reduce its shine. But I would use it, I thought, and without hesitation, if the need arose.

Killing the enemy had been my raison d'être for the past fifteen years, and I'd been good at it. The *Values and Standards of the British Army* demanded it. Paragraph ten states, 'All soldiers must be prepared to use lethal force to fight: to take the lives of others, and knowingly to risk their own.'

But was I still a soldier? Was this a war? And was I knowingly risking my own life or that of my mother?

I wasn't sure about the answers to any of those questions, but I knew one thing for certain. I felt alive again, whole and intact, and eager for the fray.

I scanned the buildings below me once more, using my mother's binoculars, searching for a light or a movement, any sign that would give away the enemy's position, but there was still nothing.

Was I wrong? Was this not the place they had meant?

I had skirted round the walls of Lambourn Hall on my way to this point, but it had been dark, locked and seemingly deserted.

They had to be here.

The moonlight was disappearing fast, and I would soon need to be on the move, down across the open ground between my current location and the rear of the stables. I took one last look through the binoculars and there it was, a movement, maybe only a stretching of a cramped leg or a warming rub of a freezing foot, but a tell-tale movement nevertheless. Someone was waiting for me in the line of trees just to the right of the house as I looked. From that position he would have commanded a fine view of the driveway and the road below.

But if he was looking down there, he was looking the wrong way.

I was behind him.

But where was his accomplice?

The moon finally dipped out of sight and the light rushed away with it. But I didn't move immediately, not for a minute or two, not until I was sure my eyes had fully adjusted to the change. In truth, the night had not become totally black as there was still a slight glow from the stars, but it was no longer possible for me to see Greystone Stables from this position. Likewise, it would now be impossible for anyone down there to see *me*.

I checked once more that my mobile phone was switched off, stood up, and started forward across the grass.

19

I approached the stables in such a way as to take me past the muck heap near the back end of the passageway in which I had hidden the previous week.

I was ultra-careful not to trip over any unseen debris as I eased myself silently through the fence that separated the stable buildings from the paddock behind. How I longed to have a set of night-vision goggles, the magic piece of kit that enabled soldiers to see in the dark, albeit with a green hue. My only consolation was that it was most unlikely that my enemy had them either – we would be as blind as each other.

I stood up close against the stable wall at the back of the short passageway, closed my eyes tight, and listened. Nothing. No breath, no scraping of a foot, no cough. I went on listening for well over a minute, keeping my own breathing shallow and silent. Still nothing.

Confident that there was no one hiding in the passageway, I stepped forward. Here, under the roof, it was truly pitch black. I tried to recall an image in my head of the inside of the passageway from my time here last week. I remembered that I had used an empty blue plastic drum as a seat. That would be here somewhere in the darkness. I could also recall there were some wooden staves leaning against one of the walls.

I moved along the passage very slowly, feeling ahead into the darkness with my hands and my real foot. The canvas basketball boots were thin, in truth rather too thin for such a cold night, but they allowed me to sense the underfoot conditions much better than I could have in regulation-issue, thick-soled army boots.

My foot touched the plastic drum and I eased round it to the door. I pressed my face to it, looking through the gaps between the widely spaced wooden slats.

Compared to the total blackness of the passageway, the stable yard beyond seemed quite bright, but there was still not enough light to see into the shadows of the overhanging roof. I couldn't see if any of the stable doors were open but, equally, that would mean that no one would be able to see me as I eased open the slatted door from the passageway and stepped out into the yard.

I slowly closed the spring-loaded door and then stood very still, listening again for anyone's breathing, but there was no sound, not even the slight rustling of a breeze.

Provided he hadn't changed his position, the man I had seen from the wood on the hillside, the man who had made a movement, would have been out of sight from where I was, even in bright sunshine, but I knew there had to be at least one other person around here somewhere. And, if Alex Reece had joined Warren and Garraway, there would be three of them to deal with. The quote from Sun Tzu in *The Art of War* about relative army sizes floated into my head once more.

If you are in equal number to your enemy, then fight if you are able to surprise. If you are fewer, then keep away.

I was one and they were two, maybe even three. Should I not just keep away?

Another of Sun Tzu's pearls of wisdom drifted into my consciousness.

All warfare is based on deception. When we are near, we must make the enemy believe we are far away; when far away, we must make him believe we are near. Hold out baits to entice the enemy. Feign disorder, and crush him.

I folded back the sleeve of my black roll-neck sweater and looked at the watch beneath. It was 4.47.

In eighteen minutes, at five minutes past five precisely, a car would drive through the gates at the bottom of the Greystone Stables driveway and stop. The driver would sound the car horn once, and the car would remain there with the headlights blazing and the engine running for exactly five minutes. Then it would reverse out again onto the road and drive away. At least, it would do all of those things if Ian Norland obeyed to the letter the instructions I had left him.

He hadn't been very keen on the plan, and that was putting it mildly, but I'd promised him that he was in no danger provided he kept the car doors locked. It was yet another one of those dodgy promises of mine. But I didn't actually believe that Jackson Warren and Peter Garraway would kill me there and then. Not before I'd returned the million dollars.

Warfare is based on deception. When we are near, we must make the enemy believe we are far away.

When I was in the stable yard searching for my mother, I'd make Warren and Garraway believe I was down near the gates.

Hold out baits to entice the enemy.

Make the car wait with its lights on to draw them down the hill away from the stables, and away from me.

Feign disorder, and crush him.

Only time would tell on that one.

I moved slowly and silently to my right, around the closed end of the quadrangle of stables, keeping in the darkest corners under the overhanging roof. Where would my mother be? I felt for all the bolts on the stable doors. They were all firmly closed. I decided, at this stage, not to try to open any as it would surely have made some noise.

Unsurprisingly, no one had mended the pane of glass in the tack-room window that I'd broken to get out. I leaned right in through the opening, closed my eyes tight, and listened.

I could hear someone whimpering. My mother was indeed here. The sound was slight, but unmistakable, and it came from my left. She was in one of the boxes on the same side of the stables as I had been.

I listened some more. Once or twice I heard her move but the sound was not close and, other than an occasional muffled cry, I could not hear her breathing. There were ten boxes down each of the long sides of the quadrangle and I reckoned she must be at least three away from the tack room, probably more. Maybe she was in the same box in which I had been imprisoned.

I looked again at my watch: 4.59.

Six minutes until the car arrived – I hoped.

I withdrew my head and shoulders through the broken window and moved very slowly along the line of stable boxes, counting the doors. I could remember clearly having to climb over five dividing walls to get to the tack room. I counted four stable doors then I stopped. The box I had been in was the next one along.

Would there be a sentry? Would anyone be on guard?

I stood very still and made my breathing as silent as I could. I dared not look again at my watch in case the luminosity of the face gave me away.

I waited in the dark, listening, and counting the seconds – Mississippi one, Mississippi two, Mississippi three, and so on. Just as I had done here before.

I waited and waited and I began to doubt that Ian was coming. I was well past Mississippi twenty in the third minute when I heard the car horn, a long two-second blast. Good boy.

There was immediate movement from the end of the row of stables not twenty yards from where I was standing. Someone had been sitting there in silence but now I clearly heard the person walk away, back towards the house, crunching across the gravel turning area. I heard him call out to someone else, asking what the noise was, and there was a murmured reply from further away that I couldn't catch.

I went swiftly to the door of the box and eased back the bolts. They made a slight scraping but nothing that would be heard from round near the house. The door swung outwards.

'Mum,' I whispered into the darkness.

There was no reply.

I stood and listened, trying hard to control the thump-thump of the heart in my chest.

I heard her whimper again but it still came from some way to my left. She wasn't in this box but in one a bit further along.

I recognized the need to be as fast as possible but, equally, I had to make my search undetected. I moved as quickly as I dared along the row of stables, carefully sliding back the bolt on the upper half of each door and calling into the space with a whisper.

She was in the second box from the end, close to where the man had been sitting on guard, and by the time I found her I was becoming desperate about the time it was taking.

I thought that Ian must surely be about to reverse the car to the road and depart. Five minutes would seem a very long time to someone simply sitting there afraid that something would happen, and hoping that it wouldn't. Ian must have been so nervous inside the car, willing the hands of his watch to move round faster. I wouldn't have blamed him if he'd decided to leave early.

When I'd opened the stable door and whispered, my mother had been unable to answer me properly, but she had managed to murmur loudly.

'Shhh,' I said going towards the sound and down onto my left knee. It was absolutely pitch black in the stable. I removed one of my black woollen gloves and 'saw' by feel, moving my left hand around until I found her.

She had tape stuck over her mouth and had been bound hand and foot with the same plastic garden ties as had been used to secure me. Thankfully, she hadn't been left hanging from a ring in the wall, but was sitting on the hard floor close to the door with her back up against the wooden panelling.

I laid my sword down carefully so it didn't clatter on the concrete, then I swung the rucksack off my back and opened the flap. Ian's carving knife sliced easily through the plastic ties holding my mother's ankles and wrists together.

'Be very, very quiet,' I whispered in her ear, leaning down. I decided it might be wise to leave the tape over her mouth until we were out of earshot. 'Come on, let's go.'

I helped her up to her feet and was about to bend down for the rucksack and the sword when she turned and hugged me. She held me so tightly that I could hardly breathe. And she was crying. I couldn't tell whether it was from pain, from fear, or in joy, but I could feel her tears on my face.

'Mum, let me go,' I managed to whisper in her ear. 'We have to get out of here.'

She eased the pressure but didn't let go completely, hanging on to my left arm. I prised her away from me and swung the rucksack over my right shoulder. As I reached down again for my sword, she leaned heavily against me and I stumbled slightly, kicking the sword with my unfeeling, right foot. It scraped across the floor with a metallic rattle that sounded dreadfully loud in the confines of the box, but probably wouldn't have been audible at more than ten paces outside.

But had there been anyone outside within ten paces to hear it?

I reached down, grabbed the sword, and led my mother to the door.

Ian must have completed his five-minute linger by now, and I hoped he had safely departed back to his flat to sit by the telephone, waiting for my call and ready to summon the cavalry if things went wrong. But where, I wondered, were my enemies? Were they still round at the driveway? Or had they come back?

My mother and I stepped through the stable door, out into the yard with her hanging on to my left arm as if she would never let it go again.

There were no shouts of discovery, no running feet, just the darkness, and the stillness of the night. But my enemies were out there somewhere, watching and waiting, and they outnumbered me. It was time to leave.

He who fights and runs away, lives to fight another day.

But I never did get to run away.

My mother and I were halfway across the stable yard, taking the shortest route to the muck-heap passageway, when the headlights of a car parked close to the house suddenly came on, catching us full in their beams.

Whoever was in the car couldn't help but see us.

'Run,' I shouted in my mother's ear, but running wasn't really in her repertoire, even when in mortal danger. It was only ten yards or so to the passageway door, but I wasn't at all sure we would make it. I dragged her along as all hell broke loose behind me.

There were shouts and running footsteps on the gravel near the house.

Then there was a shot, and another.

Shotgun pellets peppered my back, stinging my neck and shoulders, but the rucksack took most of them. The shooter was too far away for the shot to inflict much damage, but he would get closer, especially as my dear mother was so slow.

We reached the passageway door and I swung it open, pushing her through it ahead of me, both of us nearly falling over the blue plastic drum.

'Mum, please,' I said loudly to her. 'Go through the passage and out the back. Then hide.'

But she wouldn't let go of my arm. She was simply too frightened to move. Conditioning young men not to freeze under fire was a common problem in the army, and one that wasn't always solved, so I could hardly blame my mother for doing so now.

Another shot rang out and a piece of the wooden door splintered behind us. That was a bit closer, I thought – far too close, in fact. The shooter had now closed to within killing range and another shot tore into the wooden roof just above our heads sending splinters into our hair. Maybe I'd been wrong in thinking they'd try to keep me alive so that I could return the money.

'Come on,' I said to my mother as calmly as I could. 'Let's get out of here.'

I firmly removed her hand from my arm and then held it in mine as I almost dragged her down the passageway and out into the space behind. I could hear shouts from the stable yard as someone was directing his troops around the end of the building to find us. However, the man who was doing the shouting stayed where he was, in the yard. He obviously didn't fancy walking into the dark passageway in case I was in there waiting for him.

I pulled my mother round behind the muck heap. There was a tall, narrow space between the rear retaining wall of the heap and a hay barn beyond.

'Get in there,' I said quietly in my best voice-of-command. 'And lie face down.'

She didn't like it, I could tell by the way she kicked at the wet ground, but she couldn't protest as the tape was still over her mouth. She hesitated.

'Mum,' I said. 'Please. Otherwise we will die.'

There was just enough light from the stars for me to see the fear in her eyes. Still she clung to me, so I eased up the corner of the tape over her mouth and peeled it away.

'Mum,' I said again. 'Please do it now.' I kissed her softly on the forehead, but then I firmly pushed her away from me and into the gap.

'Oh, God,' she whispered in despair. 'Help me.'

'It's all right,' I said, trying to reassure her. 'Just lie down here for a while and it will all be fine.'

She obviously didn't really want to but she knelt down in the gap and then lay flat on her tummy, as I'd asked. I pulled some of the old straw down off the muck heap and covered her as best I could. It probably didn't smell too good, but so what? Fear didn't smell great, either.

I left her there and went back to the end of the passageway. Whoever had been shooting had still not come through but I could see that the car was being driven round the end of the stable buildings so that its lights were about to shine down the back, straight towards where I was standing.

I stepped again into the passageway.

The car headlights were both a help and a hindrance. They helped in showing me the position of at least one of my enemies but, at the same time, their brightness destroyed my night vision.

Consequently, the passageway appeared darker than ever but, from my previous visits, I could visualize the location of every obstruction on the floor and I easily stepped silently around them. I pressed my eye up against a gap between the door slats and looked out once more into the stable yard beyond.

There was plenty of light from the still-manoeuvring car for me to see clearly. Jackson Warren was standing in the centre of the yard talking with Peter Garraway. They were each holding a shotgun in a manner that suggested that they both knew how to use them. What was it that Isabella had said? 'The Garraways always come over for the end of the pheasant-shooting season – Peter is a great shot.'

I think I'd have rather not known that, not right now.

As I could see Warren and Garraway in the stable yard, it must be Alex Reece who was driving the car.

'You go round the back,' Jackson was saying to Garraway. 'Flush him out. I'll stay here in case he comes through.'

I could tell from his body language that Peter Garraway really didn't like taking orders. I also suspected that he didn't much fancy 'going round the back' either, good shot or not.

'Why don't I wait here and you go round the back?' he replied.

'Oh, for God's sake,' said Jackson, clearly annoyed. 'All right. But keep your eyes fixed on that door and, if he appears, shoot him. But try to hit him in the legs.'

That was slightly encouraging, I thought, but the notion of being captured alive was not. I had already experienced their brand of hospitality in these stables, and I had no desire to do so again.

Jackson Warren walked off towards the car leaving a nervous-looking Peter Garraway standing alone in the stable yard.

Yet another Sun Tzu quote floated into my head. *The way in war is to avoid what is strong and to strike at what is weak.*

Peter Garraway was weak. I could tell by the way he kept looking towards the car and in the direction that Jackson had gone in the hope of being relieved, rather than towards the door to the passageway as he'd been told. He obviously didn't like being left there alone. And shooting pheasants was one thing, but shooting a person would be quite another matter.

Reece had finally managed to get the car round behind the stables and I could see the glow of its lights at the back end of the passageway. That was not good, I thought, as my position was becoming outflanked and I would soon find myself liable to attack from opposite directions.

I looked at my watch. It was only 5.17. Just twelve minutes had elapsed since Ian had sounded the car horn, but it felt like so much longer, and there would still be another hour of darkness.

I took another quick glimpse through the slats at Peter Garraway in the stable yard. He was resting his double-barrelled shotgun in the crook of his right arm, as someone might do while waiting for the beaters to drive pheasants into the air from a game crop. It was not the way a soldier would hold a weapon – and it was not ready for immediate action.

I threw open the passageway door and ran right at him with my sword held straight out in front of me, the point aimed directly at his face, like a cavalry officer but without the horse.

He was quite quick in raising his gun, but nowhere near quick enough. I was on him so fast and, as he swung the barrels up, I struck his right arm, the point of my sword tearing through both his coat and the flesh beneath. In the same motion, I hit him full on the nose with the sword's nickel-plated hand guard. He immediately went sprawling straight down onto the concrete floor, dropping the gun, and clutching at his bleeding face with both hands.

I stood over him with my sword raised high, like a matador about to deliver the coup de grâce. Garraway, meanwhile, curled himself into a ball with his arms up round his head, whimpering and shaking like a scolded puppy.

I aimed at his heart and my arm began to fall.

'What are you doing?' I suddenly asked myself out loud, stopping the rapidly descending blade when it was just inches from his chest.

The *Values and Standards of the British Army*, paragraph sixteen, states that soldiers must treat all human beings with respect, especially the victims of conflict such as the dead, the wounded, prisoners, and civilians. All soldiers must act within the law. 'Soldiering,' it says, 'is about duty: so soldiers should be ready to uphold the rights of others before claiming their own.'

Killing Peter Garraway like this would certainly not be within the law, and would definitely be a breach of his rights as my unarmed and wounded prisoner. I would simply be taking revenge for the pain and suffering that he had inflicted on me.

I noticed that he had peed himself, just as I had done the previous week in the stable, although, in my case, it hadn't been from fear. Maybe that would have to be revenge enough. I leaned down, picked up his shotgun, and left him where he was, holding his face and arm and quivering like a jelly.

I went quickly across the yard and out towards the house with the gun in one hand and my sword in the other. But the sword had now outlived its usefulness. I tossed it into the shadows at the end of the stable building and put both my hands on the gun – that was better.

I had no real plan in mind, but I knew that somehow I had to draw Jackson Warren towards me and away from my mother.

I broke open the shotgun. There was a live cartridge in each of the two chambers but I cursed myself for not having looked for more in Peter Garraway's pockets. I could hear him behind me, calling out pitifully for Jackson, so I reckoned it was too late to go back and find them now.

So I had only two shots. I would need to make both of them count. I closed the gun once more and pushed the safety catch to off.

If I wanted to draw Jackson and Alex away from my mother, I would have to reveal my position, something that was utterly alien to any infantryman.

The headlights were still shining brightly down the back of the stables towards the muck heap, but I wasn't there any more. I was about forty yards away where the driveway met the turning circle near the house. I could see the car clearly from where I stood – at least, I could see the headlights, but from side-on.

How could I attract attention to myself?

I lifted the shotgun to my shoulder and fired one of my precious cartridges at the car. At this range the shot wouldn't penetrate the vehicle's skin, although it might just break a window. However, one thing was for sure, Alex Reece would certainly know all about it inside the car.

I could hear Jackson shouting. Perhaps he had been too close to the shot for comfort. But did I care? Now they would know exactly where I was, and the car was already turning my way.

I purposely lingered a moment too long, just long enough, in fact, for the headlight beams to fall on my departing back. I weaved in the light for a split second before diving once more into the darkness down the side of the house. A shot rang out but I was already safely protected around the corner.

I moved swiftly, grateful that I had made an extensive reconnaissance here the previous Thursday. I knew that the concrete path alongside the exterior walls ran completely round the rectangular building, the only obstacle being a small gate at one of the back corners.

In no time, I had completed the circuit and approached the front of the house again, but now I was behind the car, its headlamps still blazing towards where I had been just seconds before. In the glow I could see Jackson creeping forward towards the corner, his gun raised to his shoulder ready to fire.

The driver's door of the car suddenly opened and Alex stood up next to the vehicle, facing away from me, watching Jackson intently.

I moved slowly forward, being very careful to be as silent as possible in my basketball boots on the loose gravel. Alex would have certainly heard me if the engine of the car hadn't been left running. As it was, I was able to approach him undetected.

He was wearing a baggy sweatshirt and a large woollen cap.

I lifted the shotgun and placed the ends of the barrels firmly onto the bare skin visible just beneath his left ear.

'Move an inch and you will die,' I said to him in my best voice-of-command. But he immediately disobeyed me and turned round. But when I saw his face I realized I'd been so wrong, the car driver wasn't Alex Reece as I'd thought.

'Hello, Tom,' said Isabella.

I was stunned. I lowered the barrels.

'You? But why?' I asked.

'I'm so sorry,' she said in answer.

'Was it you who unlocked the gates?' I asked her.

She seemed surprised that I knew, but she nodded. 'Jackson was in Gibraltar.'

It had been a VW Golf that I had seen that night. Perhaps I had been subconsciously convincing myself ever since that it hadn't been Isabella's car, but it had.

'Why didn't you come and help me?'

All the misery of those three days in the stable floated into my mind.

She looked down at her feet. 'Because I didn't know you were there, not last week. I only found out tonight when I heard Peter talking about it, and how he couldn't believe you'd managed to escape.' She gulped. 'Jackson just phoned home on Thursday and asked me to unlock the gates.'

I wanted to believe her, but then why was she driving the car here tonight? She couldn't claim now that she didn't know what was going on, not with Warren and Garraway running round with guns.

'Why are you here?' I asked. 'Why are you doing this?'

She looked back up at my face and then towards Jackson. 'Because I love him,' she said. It was almost an apology.

I, too, looked at Jackson who was still inching carefully away from me towards the corner of the house, oblivious to the fact that I was standing behind him next to the car. I suddenly wanted nothing more than to shoot him, to kill him in revenge for what his greed had done to us all. And he was not a prisoner, but an armed enemy combatant. There were no *Value and Standards* concerns here. I lifted the gun and aimed.

'No,' Isabella screamed, grabbing the barrels.

Jackson turned towards the noise, though he would have been unable to see anything but the glare of headlights. Nevertheless, he started to move towards the car.

I threw Isabella to the ground and again raised the shotgun towards Jackson, but I hadn't bargained on Isabella's panic-driven determination. She grabbed my knees like a rugby player and pushed against the car, forcing me backwards over onto the gravel.

One of the huge disadvantages of having an artificial leg is that it seriously hampers recovery from a horizontal position, as it's impossible to bend the knee sufficiently. I rolled over so that I was lying face down and drew my good leg under me, but Isabella had been quicker.

She was already on her feet and she wrenched the shotgun from my hand, stamping on my wrist for good measure.

How embarrassing, I thought, to be disarmed by a woman. Perhaps the major from the ministry had been right all along.

But Isabella didn't turn the gun on me, she simply ran away with it while I struggled to my feet, using the car door handle to pull me up.

A shot rang out – very close – followed by a cry of despair.

I turned quickly to see Jackson running towards a figure lying very still on the ground in the light from the headlights, a figure whose hat had come off revealing long blonde hair, hair that was already soaking up an ever-increasing pool of bright red blood.

In another incident of what the military euphemistically call 'friendly fire', Jackson Warren had killed Isabella.

He sank to his knees beside her, dropping his gun onto the

gravel alongside the one that Isabella had been carrying. I walked the few yards from the car and picked up both weapons, unloading their second barrels and placing the unfired cartridges in my pocket. There had been enough shooting for one night. In fact, there had been far too much.

Jackson turned his head slightly to see me.

'I thought it was you,' he said. He made it sound like an excuse, as if shooting me would have been acceptable. He turned back and cradled his wife's lifeless head on his lap. 'I told her to stay in the car. I saw someone running with a gun.' He looked up at me again, now with tears in his eyes. 'I just assumed it was you.'

He should have checked.

Epilogue

Three weeks later, Pharmacist, this time with no green-potato-peel-induced tummy ache, romped up the finishing hill to win the Cheltenham Gold Cup by a neck. It was the second Kauri House Stables success of the afternoon after Oregon had justified his favouritism to win the Triumph Hurdle. My mother positively glowed.

In the post-Gold Cup press conference, she stunned both the massed ranks of reporters, as well as the wider public watching on television, by announcing her retirement from the sport with immediate effect.

'I'm going out on a huge high,' she told them, beaming from ear to ear. 'I'm handing over the reins to the next generation.'

I stood at the back of the room watching her answer all the journalists' questions with ease, making them laugh with her. Here was the Josephine Kauri that everyone knew and expected: confident and in control of the situation, in keeping with her status as National Woman of the Year.

I believed that she was as happy that day as I had ever seen her. It had been a somewhat different matter when I had returned to her hiding place that night at Greystone Stables to find her frightened, exhausted, bedraggled, and on the point of complete mental and physical collapse.

But much had changed since that dreadful night, not least the removal of the imminent threat of public disgrace, and the prospect of being arrested for tax evasion. Not that the senior inspector from Her Majesty's Revenue and Customs hadn't been pretty cross. He had. But nowhere near as cross as he would surely have been if we hadn't arrived to see him with a cheque for all the back tax.

Martin Toleron had worked some magic, producing a team of accountants to sift through the shambles, and to bring some order and transparency to my mother's business accounts. It had been quite an undertaking.

'It's the least I can do,' Martin had said, happily agreeing also to pay the accountant's bill.

So, the previous Monday, my mother, Derek, and I had arrived by appointment at the tax office in Newbury, not only with a cheque made out for well over a million pounds of back tax, but with a set of up-to-date business accounts and a series of signed and sworn affidavits as to how and why the tax had not been paid at the correct time.

We had sat in the senior inspector's office for over an hour as he had silently scrutinized our documents, never once putting down the cheque, which he held between the index finger and thumb of his left hand.

'Most unusual,' he'd said at some length. 'Most unusual, indeed.'

Then he had returned to his reading for another hour, still clutching the cheque.

I didn't really think the inspector knew what to say. The accountants had calculated not only the tax that was overdue, but also the amount of interest that should have been levied for its late arrival.

The amount on the cheque had taken all of the million dollars that had been returned from Gibraltar, together with every penny that the three of us had been able to muster, including Derek's ISAs, another mortgage on the house, the proceeds from some sales of my mother's favourite antique furniture, as well as all my savings, including the injury-compensation payout that had arrived from the Ministry of Defence.

'Are you sure that's wise?' Martin Toleron had asked me when I'd offered it.

'No,' I had said. 'In fact, I'm damned sure that it's not wise. But what else can I do?'

'You can come and help buy me some racehorses,' he'd replied.

'Now, are *you* sure that's wise?'

We had laughed, but he'd been entirely serious and he had already engaged the services of a bloodstock agent to find him a top young steeplechaser.

'I have to spend the money on something,' Martin had said. 'I don't want to leave it all to my bone-idle children. So I might as well enjoy spending it, and trips to the races will sure as hell beat going to Harrods every week with my wife.'

My mother, Derek, and I had sat in the tax-inspector's office for nearly three hours in total while he had read through everything twice, and then gone to consult someone at tax HQ, wherever that might be.

'Now I have to tell you, Mrs Kauri,' he'd said to my mother on his return from the consultation, 'we at the Revenue take a very dim view of people who don't pay their taxes on time.' I thought that he'd been about to wag his finger at her. 'However, in the light of these affidavits and the payment of the back tax, we have decided to take no action against you at this point.' He paused. 'But we will be carrying out our own audit of your tax affairs to ensure that you have given us a full and frank disclosure of the situation before we can close the matter entirely.'

'Of course,' my mother had replied, stony-faced.

'And finally,' the inspector had said, standing up and now with a smile, 'it is such an honour to meet you. I'm a great admirer and, over the years, I've backed lots of your winners.'

So it was official, some taxmen could be human after all.

*

The post-race press conference was still in full swing, and my mother appeared to be absolutely loving it.

'No, of course, I'm not ill,' she said, putting Gordon Rambler from the *Racing Post* in his place with a stare. 'I'm retiring, not dying.' She laughed, and the throng laughed with her.

No, I thought, my mother wasn't dying, but Isabella had, snuffed out in the prime of her life. The paramedics had tried to revive her but she had lost far too much blood, to say nothing of the gaping hole that Jackson had made in her side. There had never been any hope with a shot from such close range.

Strangely, in spite of everything, I grieved for Isabella. I hadn't been wrong when I'd told her, aged ten, that I loved her. I still did. But now there would be no bonus, nor even the prospect of one. Isabella, my sweetheart, who had unknowingly helped in her own downfall by acting as my driver the day we had been to Old Man Sutton's house in Hungerford.

Needless to say, the Thames Valley Constabulary had not been greatly impressed by all the nocturnal activity that had been going on at Greystone Stables. I had called them using my mobile phone as soon as Isabella had been hit and they had subsequently arrived in convoy with an ambulance, and had promptly arrested everyone.

'You should have called us immediately if someone had been kidnapped,' the police said later at Newbury police station, their ill-disguised anger clearly directed at me for having taken things into my own hands.

'But we couldn't,' my stepfather had said with conviction, coming to my defence. 'The kidnappers told me that they would kill Josephine if the police were involved.'

The police, of course, had considered that to be an insufficient reason for not involving them, especially, as they had pointed out, since I appeared to know exactly where the kidnappers had taken their hostage.

Alex Reece had apparently wanted nothing to do with Warren and Garraway's plan to recover the money, and had decided that flight would be a much better policy. He had consequently boarded a British Airways jumbo from Heathrow to New York just a few hours before the shoot-out at the Greystone Stables corral began.

Somewhat carelessly, however, he had failed to clean out his suitcase properly and had been apprehended by a US Customs sniffer-dog on his arrival at Kennedy Airport. He had subsequently been charged with importing cocaine into the United States, and was presently languishing in jail on Rikers Island in New York waiting to be served with extradition papers by the government of Gibraltar on fraud charges.

Garraway, meanwhile, had been singing like a canary and blaming everything on Jackson Warren, so much so that his lawyers had successfully persuaded a judge to grant him bail on the kidnapping and false-imprisonment charges. However, the judge had ordered that Garraway's passport be confiscated and, as I heard unofficially from the tax inspector, the Revenue were greatly looking forward to the day, very soon, when Peter Garraway's enforced extended stay in the United Kingdom would automatically make him resident here for tax purposes. The inspector had smiled broadly and rubbed his hands together. 'We've been trying to get him for years,' he'd said. 'And now we will.'

'So, who is taking over the training licence?' It was Gordon Rambler who asked my mother the inevitable question at the Cheltenham press conference. 'And what will happen to the horses?'

'The horses will all be staying at Kauri House Stables,' she said. 'I spoke with all my owners yesterday and they are all supportive.'

That wasn't entirely true. Some of her owners were decidedly unsupportive, but they had all been convinced, out of loyalty to her, to stay on board, at least for the immediate future. And Martin Toleron had helped here, too, vocally pledging his support, and his future horses, to the new training regime.

'So who is it?' Rambler was becoming impatient. 'Who's taking over?'

They were all expecting one of the sport's up-and-coming young trainers to be moving into the big league.

'My son,' she said with a flourish. 'My son, Thomas Forsyth, will henceforth be training the horses at Kauri Stables.'

I think it would be fair to say that there was a slight intake of breath, even amongst the most hardened of the racing journalists.

'And,' my mother went on, into the silence, 'he will be assisted by Ian Norland, my previous head lad who has been promoted to assistant trainer.'

'Can we all assume,' Gordon Rambler said, recovering his composure, 'that you will still be around to guide and advise them when necessary?'

'Of course,' she said, smiling broadly.

But one should never assume anything.